# Dying for Attention

# DYING FOR ATTENTION

JAMES T. SHANNON

**FIVE STAR**
*A part of Gale, Cengage Learning*

Detroit • New York • San Francisco • New Haven, Conn • Waterville, Maine • London

Five Star™ Publishing, a part of Gale, Cengage Learning.



**LIBRARY OF CONGRESS CATALOGING-IN-PUBLICATION DATA**

Shannon, James T.
Dying for attention / James T. Shannon. — First edition.
pages cm
ISBN-13: 978-1-4328-2751-9 (hardcover)
ISBN-10: 1-4328-2751-0 (hardcover)
1. Substitute teachers—Fiction. 2. Students—Crimes against—Fiction. 3. Serial murderers—Fiction. I. Title.
PS3619.H35545D95 2014
813'.6—dc23 2013038373

First Edition. First Printing: February 2014
Find us on Facebook– https://www.facebook.com/FiveStarCengage
Visit our website– http://www.gale.cengage.com/fivestar/
Contact Five Star™ Publishing at FiveStar@cengage.com

Printed in Mexico
1 2 3 4 5 6 7 18 17 16 15 14

To Kathy: Yesterday, Today, and all my Tomorrows

# Chapter One

The dying would begin soon. A few minutes ago he'd overheard two teachers passing through the crowded hall talking about how much they enjoyed the beginning of a school year, how the halls were so full of optimism. Kind of ironic, really. It wouldn't be long before the halls were filled with fear. And there was Chug O'Malley just down the hall.

When he first heard that Carstairs wasn't returning to teach and O'Malley would be substituting for him this year, he thought it was a disaster. The stratagem he'd been so carefully developing depended on Carstairs. All his own fault, too, for pushing Carstairs too hard psychologically, sending him finally over the edge.

But then, the more he had thought about the change, the more he realized that maybe, if he tweaked the plan a little, O'Malley would work out even better. And after some online research, he decided that the new guy would be perfect: O'Malley was nothing but a used-to-be looking for a resurrection.

Thirty feet away in the crowd, O'Malley stood out. Bigger than the students around him, he was wider at the shoulders and more confident in the way he moved through the halls. That wouldn't last long. Guaranteed.

Rumor had it that O'Malley was actually at Prescott High to do research for another book. As he watched the big man turn into the middle stairwell, he thought about those newspaper columns O'Malley used to write. He'd found some online, including the ads the newspaper used to run calling the writing *A Celebration of Life*. Well, Mr. O'Malley would soon find himself up to his neck in a celebration of death. Let's see how confidently he could handle that.

A mistake, Chug thought; this was a really big mistake. The fifth day of September, a Wednesday morning, warm already and only 7:30. He was sitting behind a teacher's desk while twenty-eight freshmen, as new to the school as he was, were sitting, standing in groups, milling nervously around the edges of the room. Waiting for him to tell them what to do next.

He dug into the bulging manila envelope he'd been given downstairs at the front office, and began pulling out official-looking sets of documents. Maybe there'd be one with a title like *Five Easy Steps to Starting the School Year.* Instead, there were stacks of insurance forms, medical forms, athletic eligibility forms, bus forms. There were schedules for the students, guidance forms for them to fill out if their schedules were screwed up, office discipline forms which, he guessed, someone had to fill out if a student objected to filling out all the other forms . . . and what the hell was this? A single sheet of paper with no heading, that began: *Could I do it? Could I show everybody how much I'd been ignored, let me finally get a little attention? I guess they'd have to pay attention now, especially . . .*

"Hey, watch it!" an angry fifteen-year-old voice quavered from the back of the room.

Chug dropped the paper, stood, and stared in the general direction of the voice. Freeze tag. No movement. No sound. All the eyes looked up at him. Obviously too old to be a rookie teacher, he had to know what was supposed to happen next. Except he didn't.

"Okay," he said, searching through the forms for the

homeroom roster. "Let's try alphabetical seating. Adams? Joshua Adams?"

A heavyset boy standing near the windows raised his hand and followed Chug's pointing finger to row one, seat one. Both the boy and the girl he replaced in that seat looked resigned but a little reassured. Everybody understood alphabetical seating. And everybody managed to get seated without much need for concentration on Chug's part. As he read out their names and waited while they moved, his thoughts kept nibbling uneasily around the edges of the idea that taking this job may have been a monumental mistake.

It had begun with Alice Bainbridge, the editor for the book he'd written after quitting Channel 23's *Action News 23 I-Squad.* Alice was responsible for developing a series dealing with a-year-in-the-life-of assorted institutions: a police station, a firehouse, a hospital emergency room. She already had the first two out and the third nearing completion and decided a high school would be a good next place to cover. And she thought that Matthew "Chug" O'Malley would be a good person to write it.

So she spoke to his agent, Jeremy, and Jeremy called Chug. And after a half hour of arguing that he didn't want to do it, that he wasn't qualified to do it, that they should find someone else to do it, Chug agreed to do it.

There was, however, one obstacle.

"To write the book Alice's suggesting," Jeremy had said cautiously, "you'll need to teach English at the high school there in Prescott. Just for a year. It's not a bad idea, since high schools are a hot topic, what with all the . . . well, the problems . . ."

"You mean the drugs, sex, and violence?"

"Well, yes, I suspect that's what Alice had in mind."

"But why a school like Prescott? With Boston so close, you'd think they'd want an inner-city school for all the, you know, problems."

Jeremy, a good negotiator, ignored the sarcasm.

"Pure synchronicity, Chug. Alice has an aunt who just happens to be on the school committee at Prescott. At some kind of family gathering, when Alice mentioned the next setting for the series she was developing, her aunt told her Prescott needed a replacement English teacher. Just for next year."

"And I live in Prescott."

"More serendipity. You're the one Alice wanted from the beginning. Chug, this is a wonderful opportunity, and she's dropping it right in your lap."

"Y'know, Jeremy, I've always figured that if somebody's gonna drop something in your lap, you'd better be wearing some kind of protection."

"Right, right, Chug." Jeremy coughed a small, forced laugh. "And you've got experience teaching that writing course of yours."

"Saint Brendan's is a college. And the course is only one night a week, for adults. These students'll all be teenagers. What the hell do I know about teaching teenagers?"

"Aren't your kids teenagers?"

"That's not the same."

In fact, Jason wouldn't be an official teenager for another month. He was entering seventh grade. Sarah, two years older, was starting high school this very day. In Bradford, the next town over, where they lived with Chug's ex, Connie, and her new husband, an orthodontist named David.

Chug resisted his agent a little longer, but it was mostly for show. Though Jeremy hadn't used it, they both knew his ace-in-the-hole argument: What did Chug have to lose? His earlier book, despite Alice's enthusiasm, hadn't gone anywhere. And the half dozen false starts he'd made on second books had all eventually wandered into dead ends that had left him frustrated and a little concerned about what the hell he was going to do with the rest of his life.

The money wasn't much of an incentive. Combine the long-term sub salary and the best possible advance Jeremy could wring out of Alice, and it wouldn't be a tenth of what he had gotten when he'd quit his newspaper column to become a talking head at Channel 23. But any money would be more than he was making now. Even Saint Brendan's, his part-time fallback source of self-respect and spare change, wasn't running his Media Writing course for the fall semester. And his savings account, fat and healthy a few years back when Connie and her orthodontist had bought out his share of the Bradford house, was now damn near terminal. Anyway, he agreed.

So Chug, his son, and his daughter had entered three different new schools on the same day. And he was supposed to send twenty-eight of Sarah's peers out on their high-school careers in forty minutes. Time to get on it.

He handed out all the forms to his alphabetically seated students and told them to be sure they all got signed. There were a few spares that he shoved back in the envelope, and . . . there was that other paper still sitting on his blotter.

*Could I do it? Could I show everybody how much I've been ignored, let me finally get a little attention? I guess they'd have to pay attention now, especially since he'd be sitting there in the moonlight by the water, in the front seat of the family Volvo station wagon, duct tape on the window, hose in from the exhaust, gone on the fumes. Maybe now they'd know how bad it feels to be like him, maybe now they'd finally give him a little attention and respect. Everyone thought he wasn't serious, but he was. I am sincere, too. It was too late for him, but so what? Sometimes it's better like that, just to find a way to end the pain. Don't you think so, Chug-Chug? Don't you think he'd be better off gone? You going to tell people about him now, Chug-Chug? You going to tell people what happened to him? You going to tell people about me?*

What the hell was this? It sounded like a suicide note, but the way it shifted between first and third person was confusing. Was it from somebody who'd seen a suicide? Or was the writer somebody who'd helped him die? Chug hadn't heard of any teens from this area dying from carbon monoxide poisoning and, with his own two kids always hovering around his thoughts, he'd have paid attention to that kind of news. Then there was that other big question: Why the hell had someone written this to him?

# Chapter Two

"Fuck me, fuck me!" she whispered throatily into his ear.

She thought it was kind of a lame thing to say since he was, in fact, already fucking her. But older guys liked to hear that kind of thing. And if it didn't make him any better at what he was doing, at least it might hurry him along. Which would be just fine with her, thank you very much.

"Agumph," he mumbled around the tip of her left breast, where his mouth was firmly fixed.

She sighed, tried to draw the sound out into a groan. Guessing what he had muttered was "again," she whispered, "Fuck me, fuck me hard," adding a thrust of her tongue into his ear. That seemed to goose him along a little.

Their whispering wasn't just to help the mood. They were in one of the school's offices. Though no one was supposed to be using the room and the door was locked, if someone came knocking, it would be a little uncomfortable. Actually, she was already uncomfortable. A glass-covered desktop was under her butt, which kept sticking to the cool surface. With every movement beneath him her butt squeaked louder than the groans of pleasure he was trying to control.

Should've finished him off in my mouth, she thought. It would've been faster. Her tongue stud sent him into meltdown every time. But that could get messy, depending on how hot he was. There might be too much come at once. And she didn't think coughing and spitting would be a good move at this time and place. And, frankly, she suspected all that goo really had to be fattening.

Couldn't be much longer now. Just couldn't. Hell, his eyes were already rolling back in his head as he huffed and puffed along.

Gonna blow my house down. She giggled, quickly shifting that sound into a gasp of what could pass as sexual pleasure.

Oh hell, he was slowing down! She considered nipping at his earlobe. That had worked once, but she'd actually drawn blood. A bleeding earlobe might be a little hard to explain first thing in the morning, first day of school.

Gotta go for the mommy thing, then. She tried to work up a little enthusiasm for the part, sort of like getting into character for a role in a play.

"You're a bad boy," she hissed into his ear and could feel him tensing in anticipation. "A nasty, really bad, bad boy."

His back muscles tightened as she took her hand from his shoulder and began slapping him on the butt hard, harder, to the beat of her hissed harangue: "A bad (whack) nasty (whack) filthy (whack) dirty (whack) nasty boy!"

It was a tricky maneuver because she had to hit him hard, make him really feel it, but she couldn't make too much noise.

With each word, each slap, he thrust deep, deeper, until, as she said, "You need to be spanked for being so . . . ," his mouth slobbering over her breast, he came colossally, fiercely bucking as they squeaked all over the glass covering the desk. Relieved, she eagerly whispered, "Yes, yes, yes, you nasty boy!" in his ear while she thought, *Gotta dress and clean up fast or, even with a pass, that bitch homeroom teacher of mine might give me a detention.*

# Chapter Three

Five minutes left in homeroom. Chug wondered if he'd have enough time before his first class came in to bring that maybe-suicide note to Paul Graves, the head of the history department. He knew Paul from a local basketball league they both used to play in. Paul might know about some kid who'd died this way. Or if there was a sick practical joker on the faculty who'd pull something like this. 'Course, as department head, Paul didn't have a homeroom, so Chug would have to go looking. The English department office was just two doors down, but he had no idea where the history office was.

"Everything all right, Mr. O'Malley?"

The principal, Dr. Prosky, was standing in the open doorway and frowning at the freshmen who had gone suddenly silent. Concern about preparations for his first class and that note had distracted Chug from the rising hum of conversations as the homeroom period neared its end. But Prosky had heard. No doubt about that.

He stood centered in the doorway, arms folded, chin up. In his mid-thirties, Dr. Prosky was average height and apparently in good shape, though it was hard to imagine him sweating his way through a workout. Or sweating at all. The couple of times Chug had seen him, Prosky looked as if he'd just stepped out of a walk-in freezer. Like now, his face pale and cool, as were the icy blue eyes that swept from the freshmen to the teacher. Every hair on his dark-blond head seemed frozen, a strand at a time, into its appropriate place. He was wearing a three-piece tan suit, yet looked twice as comfortable as Chug felt in his golf shirt and summer-weight slacks.

"Are we ready for the day?" he said from the doorway, the dissatisfaction thick enough for even the nervous freshmen to pick up on it.

Chug took a deep breath and let it out slowly as he rose and walked to the door. *Are we ready?* Jesus! He reminded himself to go carefully. He'd been told too many times that he didn't deal well with authority figures—usually told this by the authority figures. His mother used to say it came from his father's Irish side. Chug's father, before he died when Chug was ten, used to smile as he said, no, his son was clearly a stubborn Portagee, just like the mother. Chug's ex-wife referred to it as his triple-decker mentality, blaming his in-your-face reactions on his whole damned hometown of Fall River.

Whatever the source, he controlled his temper now because there were twenty-eight kids silently watching him and the principal.

"You know anything about this?" he asked quietly, ignoring Prosky's question about being prepared and handing him the paper. "It was in the envelope with the forms for my homeroom."

The principal's frown deepened as he read it.

"Anything like that happen here?" Chug whispered. "A student dead from carbon monoxide?"

Prosky shook his head, holding the paper away from him as if a whiff of exhaust fumes were drifting his way. "I don't care for the way it's written."

"Yeah, well it's not an assignment, and I'm more worried about the content than the style. I'm not sure if it's from someone who's suicidal. Or knows a potential suicide, or maybe tried to help someone else commit suicide. Or even if I'm supposed to take it seriously."

"What's that 'Chug-Chug' thing at the end?"

"Oh, that's why I know it was meant for me. It's the name I used as a reporter."

"You called yourself Chug-Chug?"

"Just Chug. Sometimes. It's a nickname I've had since I was a kid."

If he'd been paying attention, Prosky would have picked up on Chug's ambivalence with the name. But the principal only dropped the subject because, like the note, it had ceased to interest him.

"I don't think we have to worry too much about this." He handed it back. "If I were you, I'd be more concerned about preparing for my classes. Isn't one of your classes Advanced Placement English?"

"Yes."

"You do understand that the AP course is supposed to prepare the students to take an exam for college credit."

"I'm ready for the class."

But the principal had already turned his back and started down the hall. Warning delivered. End of discussion.

"Y'know," Chug said, "just to be on the safe side with this letter, I think I'll drop it off at the police station later. See if it means anything to them."

That got Prosky's attention. He was a half dozen steps down the hall when he spun around, looking as if Chug had snuck up and given him a wedgie.

"No, Mr. O'Malley," he said as he returned. "I really don't think that's necessary. I'm sure this is just some kind of prank, that's all. A practical joke, taking advantage of your reporting background. One of the students, a teacher, something like that."

He had his hand out, palm up, cupped fingers impatiently beckoning the paper.

"Could be. Still, it sounds serious to me." Chug held Prosky's look, ignoring those insistent fingers so he wouldn't be tempted to smack them away.

"I'll tell you what," the principal said, finally lowering his hand. "I think what we should do is run this past Mr. Traynor, our assistant principal. See if he knows anything about it. He's been at this school for twenty-five or thirty years and has close contacts with the students. He's the man who should see it."

"He really should share this with the police."

"Right, right. I'll tell him that, Mr. O'Malley."

"Okay. Just wait here a minute. Watch my class." Chug left the principal glowering while he walked a short way down the corridor to the English office. He'd earlier used the copier there to make handouts for one of his classes. Now, though he knew he could have simply taken a picture of the note with his cell phone, that wouldn't irritate Prosky as much. He made a copy of the note and came back into the corridor.

"Thanks for keeping an eye on my room." He handed Prosky the original.

The principal's eyes narrowed as they looked down at the copy still in Chug's hand. When his eyes came back up, Chug grinned, shrugged. He knew he didn't look particularly regretful. He also knew the same look had usually managed to piss off more important people than the man standing in front of him. He was looking forward to a reaction, but Prosky just shook his head, turned and walked away.

A couple of minutes later, as he sat at his desk watching the freshmen reluctantly leave to begin their education, Chug picked up his copy of the note and read it again.

He still couldn't quite get a handle on it, couldn't understand why, though it seemed to be begging for understanding, it left him with a vague sense of dread.

# Chapter Four

The first of the AP students, a couple of girls, came into Chug's room as tentatively as deer entering a clearing. They smiled, but cautiously, an expression reflected by the rest of the students who filtered in. They knew he wasn't Carstairs, the teacher he was replacing. Considering their cyber-connectedness, they had probably known Carstairs wouldn't be returning this year before most of the faculty had found out. But they were still curious and a little wary—about the same way Chug was feeling.

The bell sounded for the end of the passing period, but they stood around in little clusters, like strangers at a cocktail party, nobody sitting.

"This is senior AP English," Chug said. "I'm Mr. O'Malley."

A few smiled.

"Are you the AP English students?"

A disconcertingly attractive girl—long auburn hair, fair, flawless skin, deep green eyes—nodded, fixing him with what had to be a mirror-perfected, cool jade stare.

"That's us," she said in a breathy whisper.

Must've practiced that voice too.

"Well, okay, everybody take a seat. I don't really care too much where. I'm sure I'll get to know who you are soon enough."

They shuffled their feet, looked around obligingly but, except for the girl who'd spoken and now slipped into a seat up front, no one actually sat.

"Anywhere, it doesn't matter."

The girl who'd spoken, the only one with a voice apparently, and hers set at a very low volume, said, "We're not all here yet."

"Oh, sure, I was wondering. The roster has sixteen people on it. But you can all sit anyway."

Then, as if on cue, four boys came in. They seemed deliberately dressed in contrast to the current teen code, wearing short-sleeved, buttoned-down shirts and ties. They were tanned and looked healthy and wealthy. Training-machine muscles rippled through their shoulders and arms, and money shone through their confident attitudes. Four guys with life firmly gripped by the short hairs. No doubt about it.

Their obvious leader was the tallest and strongest-built, with sun-lightened dark hair, high cheekbones and a big smile setting off strong features. A good-looking kid that the other three were attending as he finished a story that seemed to be about his car. They all laughed on cue, and only then did he turn to Chug.

"Oh, hi," he said with an easy smile. "Sorry we're late. We had hall duty. Silver key."

A sandy-haired boy at his side began to point toward the small silver key that each boy had pinned near his collar, but the leader stopped him with just a sideways glance.

Chug didn't know what the hell *silver key* was, but figured he'd deal with that later. "Okay. Take a seat. Everybody take a seat, please."

There was movement toward the tablet-armed chairs, but the eleven waited while the four chose. And the three waited while the one chose first. And the beautiful girl with the auburn hair sat staring at the front board. And Chug thought it was all kind of funny but knew better than to show it.

The seat the leader chose was in the middle of the room. The three clustered around him, and the other eleven spread out over what was left. The redhead remained up front, where Chug couldn't miss her as she slowly extended her long legs from beneath a short, dark-green skirt.

He took attendance. Her name was Lacey McGovern. The head of the silver-key quartet was the last name on the list, Wainwright. Brandon Wainwright. Chug had heard that name mentioned in a faculty discussion yesterday, during teacher orientation day. Brand Wainwright. He had thought the name sounded like some upscale product. Apparently, it was.

The first thing Chug did was try to negate all their seating maneuverings by asking them to form a circle and then scrinching a chair in the circle for himself. The silver-key boys were all still together.

He began the class by talking about *Wuthering Heights,* one of the books assigned for summer reading, reminding them that there'd be a test on it the next class. For now, though, he just wanted to discuss the story-within-the-story narrative. They all listened politely, but nobody volunteered any answers to his questions. And Chug felt he was asking some fairly open-ended questions. He was patient, too, but he got the sense they were waiting for something to happen, something he hadn't been told about. A surprise fire drill, maybe, or a stunt like everyone coughing when the clock struck nine. When he asked specific people specific questions about who did what to whom in the novel, he always got the right answers. But no one volunteered a syllable extra.

As a student, Chug had disliked lectures and never used them when he taught his adult media writing class. There he followed a general outline, but let the class dynamics determine the destination. The tactic had always worked well at Saint Brendan's. After a half hour of monosyllabic responses from this class, however, he found himself out of the circle of desks and standing at the whiteboard in front, marker in hand, showing one effect of Bronte's narrative technique. He drew arrows and squared boxes around names, circled others, performing almost a parody of the kind of teaching he had always avoided. The students nodded. Many took notes, though he had told them at the beginning that notes wouldn't be necessary. But how could he tell them to stop? If they weren't supposed to take any notes, why the hell was he putting all this crap on the board? He quickly drew a couple more connecting arrows as the bell was ringing and silently vowed tomorrow's class would be better.

Wainwright and his followers had been as quiet as everyone else, although somehow that didn't feel normal. No, what the class had been expecting was something from Wainwright.

But a flow of new students was coming in just after the AP kids flowed out so Chug couldn't dwell on it. This new group was noisier, apparently more into shoulder-shoving and yapping insults back and forth. This was English 12B. Back when he was in school, the class would've been called Standard, which meant not college bound. It also probably meant most of the students were reading at least a few years below grade level. But he was relieved to see that there wasn't a tie, a buttoned-down shirt or a silver key in the whole class. Lots of pierced or tattooed body parts. Lots of hair styled and colored outrageously. The class proved to be looser than the previous one, much less predictable. But more fun.

And he was drained when the bell to end period two rang. And a senior college prep class with twenty-eight new students came in. A different class. A completely different preparation. He had expected it, but suddenly felt as if he'd just completed a marathon only to be told he still had five miles to go—three more classes and two study halls—all uphill.

By the end of the day he realized that the one thing movies and TV shows about high school never showed was the pace. One class after another, they just kept coming in and waiting for him to do something with them. He was expected to fill each unit of time, and though he only had three preparations: one AP, one 12B, and three college prep senior classes, the makeup of each class was different, with needs and demands that weren't the same as the students who had just left. And this was an upscale school, with relatively small classes. He was exhausted. And it was only the end of the first day. Jesus.

Chug's eight-year-old Chevy 4×4 pickup, that had spent the day baking in the sun, looked as tired as he felt. He used to have a Mercedes with air-conditioning that he claimed could ice your nose hairs within ten seconds of start-up. Funny, he didn't miss it much. Hell, it would've been out of place here in the faculty section anyway, since the only expensive cars in the lot—he counted two Mercedes, three BMWs, and a Land Rover—were all in the student section. Oh, and there was a red Jaguar tear-assing out the driveway, with a guy at the wheel that looked an awful lot like Mr. Silver-key Brandon Wainwright. A couple of students walking up the driveway had to bolt out of the car's path. Good thing they hadn't decided to play chicken because Chug didn't see any brake lights from the Jaguar. If anything, it sounded as if Wainwright had picked up speed as he flashed past the visibly shaken students.

# CHAPTER FIVE

"Fuck me, fuck me!" she whispered throatily and added a desperate "Please!" Unlike this morning, she now meant her plea because what he was doing down there with his tongue, between her tattooed butterfly wings had her at a point where she was ready to scream and crush his ears with her thighs. Also, unlike the guy this morning where she called all the shots, she wanted this one in her, she wanted him in and moving against her, his body taking her. With him she always surrendered, always gave in, always came out of her body, came screaming out of her mind so that, depending on where they were, he sometimes had to keep a hand over her mouth. Which just intensified the release.

This place felt private, their blanket spread on a patch of grass in a grove of trees near Lake Metacom. They'd been here a couple of times and had never seen anyone. Still, it was chancy and, though she didn't need any further stimulation, the risk was a part of the excitement.

His tongue moved up, licked at her belly button, licked hotly at her breast, and she could feel him prodding her, pushing, then entering. He knew she was just on the edge, and as she sucked in her breath and began to scream, his hand quickly clamped on her mouth. His eyes burned a warning into hers, and her muffled cry of letting go felt as if it were springing from her toes.

★ ★ ★ ★ ★

Chug sat at the small picnic table near his cabin on the lake, a bottle of Samuel Adams Boston Lager in his left hand, a pen in his right. Though Metacom was the largest lake in the area, most of the cabins along this section were small and not winterized, and the neighborhood had pretty much cleared out after the Labor Day weekend, except for those like Chug, who lived there more or less permanently. The unusual and welcome afternoon silence was interrupted only by birdsong and, a few seconds ago, one sharp, curious sound, a little like a quickly squelched call, something triumphant, exultant, maybe. Kids playing in the woods probably. Whatever it was, it sounded like the screamer was sure as hell having a good time.

Chug, on the other hand, was not. He was trying to concentrate on jotting down notes for his book on his first day at the school, but found himself missing his kids instead. Sarah and Jason had spent the Labor Day weekend with him. His daughter, a long-legged colt with dark blonde hair wagging behind in a ponytail, had inherited her mother's deep gray eyes. Sarah had always been a pretty child, but she was just about to blossom into a breathtaking beauty accompanied by trumpets and flourishes and, for Chug anyway, the inevitable alarums. Luckily, she was bright and responsible, the older child, who had become adept at sensing the changes about to happen after her parents' separation and had worked hard at cushioning those changes for her younger brother.

Jason had the same dirty-blond hair and gray eyes as his sister but was built on Chug's broader scale. Already thickening through the shoulders, Jason was an incredibly strong swimmer for his age. He'd probably develop a tackle's build, although his abiding passion seemed to be computers. He had brought along a new laptop chipful of video games, compliments of stepfather David, and Chug had tried to fake fascination. But Jason wouldn't play the games when his father was around, just nipping at the computer secretly like a closet alcoholic.

Now, to get past his feeling of missing his kids, Chug forced himself back to jotting down his first-day impressions. The experience was still a blur of teenaged faces, and he knew better than to expect he'd find a hook for the book right away. Still, he wrote everything he could think of, from the sounds and the smells of the building to his impressions of the teachers and the students. Then there was the energetic, almost humming tension a place has when all those young people are jammed into a confined space, even one as large as a school building. His last entry was: *The note???* He'd left the strange note in his desk at school, telling himself that it wasn't important. But maybe he just hadn't wanted to think about it. Each time he did, like now, he wondered what exactly the writer was trying to tell him. Whatever it was, Chug was sure it wasn't something he wanted to hear.

# Chapter Six

Chug first heard about the death around 10:30 that night. He'd spent the last few hours trying to make lesson plans for the rest of the week and was setting the bedside radio alarm, moving the dial to find a better station than the dreary new-age stuff he'd awakened to that morning, when he slipped past a news voice saying, ". . . was found in an automobile at Bryant Pond . . ." It took a few seconds to register and, by the time he'd found the station again, he only caught the "details at eleven" conclusion.

He knew almost anything could have been found in a car out by a pond. And the note had been a little vague about the water. Could've been the ocean, a lake, a goddamn birdbath for all he knew. But his instincts said otherwise, and he paced the narrow confines of the cabin. Out to the little screened porch facing the lake, back in to stare into the fridge, trying to push away the creeping sensation of worry and guilt. He turned on the television thinking there might be a newsbreak. He muted the sound and listened to oldies blaring from the radio while keeping an eye on the television. It was running a movie that had a lot of people shooting at each other in a warehouse.

Television carried the story first, the lead on the eleven o'clock news, and Chug turned off the radio, unmuted the television sound. The opening camera shot was a stand-up with a young reporter at the pond, a sure-enough late-model Volvo station wagon in the background over his shoulder, the police and EMTs moving around. The reporter said the authorities still hadn't released the identity of the victim pending notification of family. Just that he was a male teenager. They also announced there was no immediate evidence of foul play. Chug thought that probably meant they hadn't found a weapon.

The way the shot was framed, all Chug could see was the front of the car, so he didn't know if any hosing was connected to the exhaust. Regardless, as a reporter he'd been around police often enough to know that they'd want to look at the letter describing a death so similar to this setup. And the sooner they saw it, the better it would be for their investigation.

He'd seen a couple of teens dead from carbon monoxide when he had worked on his first newspaper back in Fall River. Two kids out parking on a cold winter night, in a rusted out junker, the engine running to keep the heater on for warmth. Jack Medeiros, his city editor, had called them *cherries* because that's what the kids were losing out there. And that's the color the carbon monoxide turned them. Huddled, permanently cold, they'd been found on an out-of-the-way road near the reservoir. Just a couple of kids cherry red, the naked and the dead.

Among the papers he'd been given this morning and had shoved into his backpack had been a telephone-tree list, who called whom if school had to be cancelled or delayed because of bad weather. Lo, Prosky's name and telephone number led all the rest. Chug's name wasn't even on the list.

Prosky's machine kicked in after the fourth ring, but the principal interrupted halfway through the message, sounding foggy with sleep. The news blew that haze away.

"And what do you want me to do?" he said after Chug had explained himself.

"Did the assistant principal bring that letter to the police?"

"No, he didn't."

"I think you should call and tell him to. As soon as possible."

"Yes . . . well, what was it you said? A teenager died? What's his name?"

"They haven't released that yet."

"And he was from our high school?"

"They haven't said that yet, either. But he was found dead in a late-model Volvo wagon, same as in the letter. Out by Bryant Pond. And the note said it happened near water."

"That pond's in Prescott?"

"Yes."

"And was there any evidence that he had arranged to kill himself? Or that someone had helped him do this?"

He was awake now and fighting the news. Chug had the depressingly familiar feeling of dealing with an administrator who didn't want to hear that a cloud of negative publicity was blowing his way.

"I don't know. They haven't said whether they think it was an accident, suicide, or what. But it's not cold enough to have the engine running for heat. And the car's too new to have the exhaust kill anybody by accident."

"What about some of the other things in the letter? What was it, the duct tape and the hose connected to the exhaust? Anything on them?"

"The reporter didn't say."

The principal was quiet for a while before he said, "I think you're overreacting, Mr. O'Malley. And that paper you're referring to is in my office at school. And it's almost midnight."

"It's ten minutes after eleven. And you told me you were going to give the letter to the assistant principal."

"Yes, well, with all the first-day distractions, I'm sure you can appreciate why I didn't get around to that. Now then, as I said, it's very late, and I don't see how I'd help matters by running over to school. And then down to the police station with a piece of paper that's most likely nothing more than someone's twisted idea of a practical joke. At least not tonight."

"The police might see it a little differently. You probably should call them and ask."

"Well, that's my decision to make, isn't it? And I've decided to call them in the morning, when I have the paper in hand. But you have a copy of it, don't you? Why don't you take it down there and tell them what you think?"

"My copy's in school too."

"Ah, then, I guess that settles the matter for now. I assume you weren't given a key to the building in your orientation packet."

Each answer that flashed through Chug's thoughts would likely result in his being fired, which would end his book before it had begun.

"And I don't suspect that, even if you had a key, Mr. O'Malley, you would've been told the alarm code."

There's a dead kid, he thought, and this jerk-off's trying to win a pissing contest. Probably still burned that I made him wait in the corridor this morning. Should've taken the damned copy to the police on my own. Should've, could've, would've. Didn't.

"Good night, then, Mr. O'Malley," Prosky said into the angry silence and hung up.

Chug had a hard time getting to sleep and, when he finally did, kept waking from troubled dreams full of children and danger. And the children were Sarah and Jason, at earlier stages of their still-young lives. In one of the dreams he'd left them in a van that had belonged to a neighbor when Chug was a boy, and the van was rolling down the street. He desperately ran alongside it, unable to get into it to let them out. In another dream, Jason had somehow managed to seal the outside of the door to his room in the Bradford house with duct tape so no one would know he was secretly playing computer games in there. But, in the dream's twisted logic, he'd only left himself a few seconds of oxygen. Though Chug frantically ran his hands over the silvered surface of the duct tape, looking for a grip so he could tear it off, it had become smooth and seamless with no beginning and no end.

When the radio music woke him, he still felt exhausted, but getting up was better than falling back into any of those nightmares. The morning television news had more details. The boy's name was Donald Parkhurst. He had been, in fact, a student at Prescott High School, but his family had only moved into town last year. He was seventeen, had participated in an evening orchestra rehearsal at the school, had driven to Bryant Pond and had died there of carbon monoxide poisoning. They ran a picture of him. The face was unfamiliar. Still, there had been so many new faces that Chug had to check his class lists. No, no Parkhurst. He felt only a little less guilty than if the boy had actually been sitting in his classroom yesterday.

When he signed in at the office, the assistant principal was waiting at the counter. Walter Traynor, apparently better known as *Basic* Traynor to students and staff alike, was heavyset and fifty-ish and dressed like a cast member from an underfunded road company of *Guys and Dolls.* His bulk was squeezed into a tight, checkered jacket and a baggy, under-the-belly-belted pair of shiny dark pants. White socks peeked out over brown loafers that may have been broken in, but looked as if they'd gone all the way to broken-down. His face, beneath inch-high cropped iron-gray hair, was as loud and loose as his clothing: large ears, thick-browed eyes, a heavy nose and a long-jawed underbite exposing big teeth in a grin that, considering the condition of those loafers, might have been a grimace.

"How ya doin'?" he said cheerfully. Hmm, it was a grin after all. "I'm Walter Traynor."

"Matthew O'Malley," Chug said, shaking hands.

Though Traynor had spoken briefly at the first day's faculty meeting, it was Paul Graves, Chug's basketball buddy, who had told him that "Basic" was a name given with affection and respect, that he was really a good guy: caring, kind, and apparently a lot sharper than his clothing.

"Oh, I know who you are, Mr. O'Malley. Read a lot of your stuff in the papers. Your book, too. Liked it a lot."

"Thanks." Hmm, Paul must've been right about Traynor's brains.

"Dr. Prosky told me to look out for you. He wants to see you in his office."

Chug followed him down the corridor, and Traynor rapped on the frosted glass in Prosky's door.

"Come in."

Prosky was sitting behind his desk looking nattily nervous. Sitting in front of his desk and turning to face the two newcomers was a woman. Raven-dark hair wrapped in a twist, and large, very liquid brown eyes above high and well-defined cheekbones. Her navy-blue skirt framed long, slim legs. She was wearing a navy jacket over a lemon-yellow blouse and held a small spiral notebook open in her hand. Despite the notebook, her attitude looked more take-charge than secretarial. Still, he was hoping she was someone he hadn't seen yet, someone permanently attached to the school.

"Sergeant Cusack," Prosky said, "this is Mr. O'Malley, the teacher I told you about."

She stood and reached out a hand, the fingers long and slender, the flesh against Chug's big hand feeling smooth, but with a firmness beneath it as steady as her gaze.

"And this is Officer Robidoux," she said, nodding over Chug's shoulder.

He turned. It was a tribute to the presence of Sergeant Cusack that he hadn't even noticed Robidoux, who was standing against the back wall. If he'd pushed the door open all the way, Chug would have smacked it into the policeman. Which, he realized, would have been a big mistake in more ways than one. In his thirties, Robidoux had a shaved bullet head and serious lifter shoulders straining at the seams of his gray uniform. Since the policeman's hands hadn't moved from his sides, and the right one still held his uniform hat, Chug just muttered, "How ya doin'?"

Robidoux nodded, his dark eyes narrowed. It was a look Chug had sensed before on some police—everyone's a felon until proven otherwise. Sometimes even then.

"I showed your letter to Sergeant Cusack first thing this morning," Prosky said.

"Do you know why that letter was given to you, Mr. O'Malley?" Sergeant Cusack's voice was as steady and quietly confident as everything else about her.

"No. In fact, until I heard the news last night, I thought it might have been some kind of practical joke."

"What time did you hear about the death?" she said.

"Eleven. It was the first story Channel 23 carried. Then I called Mr. Prosky."

*"He called you?"* She glanced down at her notebook. But, instead of reading her notes, she looked back up to watch the principal's face shift slowly into puzzled concern.

"Um . . . yes, he did. That's right, in fact. He did call. Late last night."

"How late?"

"Oh, around midnight sometime. Pretty late, anyway," Prosky added, backpedaling, Chug thought, faster than a pro-bowl cornerback.

"I called him right after the first news story," Chug said. "And I reminded him, as we were speaking, that it was only ten after eleven."

She was listening to Chug, but looking at Prosky. Traynor, out of the loop, stood at the window looking at the yellow school buses that had begun to caravan in through the main entrance and down toward the junior high below the hill. Chug wondered briefly what Robidoux might be doing behind him. Probably glowering like a bridge troll and taking out his handcuffs.

"That could have been the time," Prosky said, after a few seconds of further forehead contortions. "I was awakened by the call, taken by surprise, you know."

"And you called him about the death and the letter, Mr. O'Malley?"

"Yes, to suggest he bring it to the Prescott police."

"But, as I understand it, you got the letter yesterday morning."

"Yes," Chug said and, knowing what she was getting at, added, "I suggested bringing the letter to the police at the time."

"You also said you thought it might be some kind of practical joke," Prosky said.

"I suggested that as one possibility." Chug felt as if Prosky wanted to turn this into the kind of argument he hadn't been in since he was about nine. "But we concluded that he'd show the letter to Mr. Traynor and they'd decide what to do with it."

"Walter?" she said, Traynor's name sounding both familiar and warm as she spoke it.

He had turned at the window and, smiling at her, briefly shook his head.

"I see," she said, then stared at Prosky for a few seconds. He looked away first and she jotted something in her notebook.

Good, Chug thought, she doesn't mind making the bastard nervous.

"And were you home all last night, Mr. O'Malley?"

Oops, apparently Prosky wasn't the only one she didn't mind

making nervous. But her dark and shiny gaze more than her implication had left Chug temporarily tongue-tied.

"Yes, all night," he said finally. "Alone . . . I live alone."

She jotted a couple more words into her spiral pad but, unfortunately, he was pretty sure the fact that he lived alone, underlined and starred, wasn't part of her notation.

"No contact from the boy? No anonymous calls?"

"No."

"Again, do you have any idea why this letter was given to you, Mr. O'Malley? I understand you're new at the school. Do you know many of the students here? The adults?"

"I don't know any of the students. I'd never met any of them before yesterday. I know a couple of the male faculty from a basketball league I used to play in, but that's about it."

He was tempted to tell her that he might have been sent the letter because of his celebrity, his TV time or the years when he'd had his own column. It was probably even true. But he'd grown to hate that celebrity, and trading on it now would be hypocritical. Still, she was beautiful. And he figured he'd done worse to impress women he'd been far less attracted to. Must be growing up. At last.

"This 'Chug-Chug' reference at the end of the letter," she said, holding up an apparent photocopy, since there were none of the original folds in it. "That was your byline as a reporter. Chug O'Malley, right?"

He nodded, working on looking modest.

"You think that's the reason you received the letter? Because you were a reporter?"

"It's likely," he said. "The writer seemed to be looking for attention."

She nodded, then asked a few more questions—whether he'd noticed anything unusual, had any strange encounters—those kinds of questions. Chug knew he wasn't being very helpful.

Which meant he might not be talking to her for long.

Sure enough, after a minute of reading over her notes, she clicked the ballpoint, smiled and said, “Thank you very much, Mr. O’Malley. I’d appreciate your stopping by the station after school to have your fingerprints taken. So we could eliminate them from the note? Unless they’re already on file.”

“No, they’re not. I pass the station on my way home. I’ll be there this afternoon.”

She flipped over a new page in her notebook disappointing Chug by making no notation of his plans to stop by the station.

Traynor still stared, amiably under-bitten, out the window, though there were no more buses arriving. Prosky was at his computer, mousing his way through something on the screen. Robidoux glared a bullet-headed, bullnecked warning as Chug opened the door. And now that he found himself out in the hall, he had to think about what he’d planned to do with his five classes today.

# Chapter Seven

Though he only had yesterday to compare it to, the school felt quiet, the students subdued by the death of the boy who'd shared this building with them. Still, Chug's homeroom had a lot of *Donald who*? faces following the passing along of the story, and they seemed more confused than upset by the intercom announcement that anyone who felt the need to speak to a counselor could get a pass to guidance.

Since Parkhurst had been a senior, Chug thought he'd better take his cue for his classes from his students. You never knew who might have been his best friend, his cousin, or his girlfriend. At the start of the first period, the AP students seemed quieter, but not especially stricken. Small talk and nodding heads, but a couple of smiles too. And the four silver-key members arriving two minutes later looked much the same as yesterday, just a little more restrained as they sat together in the four seats the others had left in the small circle of seventeen desks Chug had quickly formed at the end of homeroom period.

"Everybody okay?" he said.

They looked okay. Some smiled, a few nodded.

"Anyone want to discuss what happened?"

No one seemed to want to talk about it, so he went ahead with his plan of giving them the test he'd prepared on *Wuthering Heights.* It was only four identification questions, each needing about a paragraph-long answer, just something to check on their reading and see how well they could write, and he suggested they try to finish in twenty minutes.

Brandon Wainwright finished first, in under ten minutes, slamming down his pen like a speed-chess player smacking the clock. Carter Delisle, the sandy-haired boy who seemed to live in Brandon's shadow, was about thirty deferential seconds behind him. Lacey was last, her forehead creased and mouth pouting as she handed in her paper.

"Anybody have any thoughts on the book?" he said as he collected their papers. "Its characters? How about Heathcliff? Victim or villain?"

It had been one of the questions on the test. No response. Well, actually, one student was fidgeting as if he wanted to answer. He sat a few desks to the left, Ernest-something.

Chug had noticed Ernest yesterday because he looked like a building under construction by an eccentric architect. Tall and gangly, he seemed to be all knees and elbows and a bobbing Adam's apple, and his narrow head was crowned by an unkempt thatch of black and spiky hair.

"Ernest?"

His eager face, already red, flushed deeper, the color spreading down to his neck and up to his ears. But he took a breath and screwed his courage to the sticking place.

"I was wondering about the suicide," he said quietly.

The room went silent, as if seventeen people had coincidentally decided to hold their breaths at exactly the same moment. Brandon Wainwright was the first to expel his, in an exaggerated spray of disgust.

"We going to be talking about this all year?" he said.

Ernest, who was sitting almost directly across the circle from Brandon, paled as he nervously shook his head a couple of times and looked down at the floor.

"What?" Chug said.

"Ah, Homer didn't want to talk about anything else in

homeroom," Delisle said from Brandon's right.

A few kids chuckled nervously, waiting for a reaction.

Must've been the name, *Homer,* Chug thought. Some reference he didn't pick up on.

"You know—Mr. Watley. The psych teacher," Delisle said, wanting to show the class he wasn't hiding behind Chug's ignorance.

Chug still didn't get it, didn't care.

"Most of you in that homeroom?" he asked.

"He looks like Homer Simpson. On *The Simpsons*?" Delisle said.

Chug nodded, looked to Brandon who had leaned forward.

"I don't see why we have to spend the whole day bothering about something as insignificant as that flute player offing himself," Brandon said.

It wasn't just what he said that surprised Chug, but the look on his face. He was smiling, a big friendly grin, eyes dancing, ready to share the fun.

Chug had been challenged by students in his adult classes. He considered it a positive reaction, a hint that some interest had been sparked. But this was new. He couldn't figure out what the hell Brandon was after.

"Ernest?" he said, since the boy seemed to represent the opposite view.

Uh-oh, a mistake. Ernest looked up in alarm, even waving his hands a little to signal he wanted no part of this.

"I . . . uh, I didn't even mean Donald Parkhurst," he said. "I meant in the book. Heathcliff. How he . . . Doesn't he commit suicide? I mean, doesn't he will his own death?"

"Well, that's it then, isn't it?" Brandon said, still smiling.

That's when Chug realized what it was about him—the smile. He seemed sincere. It wasn't a nasty smile or an empty one. It was cheerful, pleasant, like a kid looking up from playing with a kitten. And you wanted to smile back. Until you realized that he'd challenged you. Distracting. And maybe, when you looked a little closer, his hands seemed a little tight around that kitten's neck.

"Does anyone want to talk about Donald Parkhurst's death?" Chug said.

Brandon leaned over toward Delisle and said something about a "skin flute" out of the corner of his mouth. Delisle barked out a laugh as wet and ugly as a glob of spit.

Chug waited. No takers. Delisle, grinning, leaned over and whispered something back, but Wainwright just nodded. Apparently, Delisle hadn't mastered all the nuances of toadydom yet.

"Well then," Chug said after the silence began to feel strained. "I've got a few discussion questions here that I want you to look at in small groups." They glanced apprehensively around the circle, all except the one quadrant, of course, who knew which people would be in their group. "For this first one, I want four groups. And they'll be chosen at random."

Nobody seemed pleased with that. Chug either, but he wanted to know a little more about the class dynamics before he let them pick the people they'd work with. And he wanted to break up the silver-key cluster.

"Number off, one to four. You can start," he said, nodding to the girl on his right. He knew he could start anywhere and, because the four of them were sitting next to each other, still completely split up the silver keys. He wondered how they'd respond if he did this enough times. Would they still sit together? It was a thought.

"Mr. O'Malley?"

Brandon, still smiling.

"Getting back to Ernest's question. Do you think Heathcliff intentionally killed himself? Or was it just because he was so obsessed with Catherine that he couldn't bother doing other things, like sleeping or eating? Or was he haunted by her? Or what?"

"I . . . hmm . . . I don't know. Maybe the class can think about that a little tonight. Remind me at the beginning of class tomorrow, and we'll see what people think," Chug said, smiling back as pleasantly as he could.

"But you said yesterday that you wanted to hear our opinions."

Brandon was still smiling, too. Just a couple of grinning fools here, Chug thought.

"Yes, I do. That's why I want to give everybody the chance to think about that question tonight. It's not homework or anything, I'd just like you to let it percolate for a while and tomorrow, we'll hear your opinions."

"And I thought this year was gonna be different," Brandon muttered.

The thing was, he sounded sincere, not sarcastic. And, since his aside was loud enough for everyone to hear, no matter what Chug did, even if he tried to ignore it, it'd be a response.

He asked them to finish counting off, then pointed out different sections of the room for each group. He kept smiling as they scraped their desks into place while he wondered who was in the room below and how soundproofed this floor and the ceiling below might be. But mostly he wondered just how inventive and energetic young Brandon could be. The boy had made his claim, staked out his territory as resident pain in the ass. It was Chug's move next.

When the class ended, Lacey, the beautiful redhead, was the last of the AP students to leave, slowing at the door and leaning in toward Chug with a whispered "Are you planning to do a story about the suicide, Mr. O'Malley?"

"Huh?"

"You know, for television or something? A special, something like that?" She cocked her head to one side and in toward him, so that her green eyes were very close.

"Uh, no. No, Lacey. I'm not involved in television anymore."

Her frown clearly reflected her disbelief, but she decided to be cheerful about it, adding, "Well, if you change your mind, you know, I'd be happy to give an interview. Any time and any place that'd be convenient for you, Mr. O'Malley."

Then, in case he was really slow on the pickup, she began to move in closer. Since he was already leaning against the front board, Chug would have had to execute an extremely awkward sideways getaway, but he was rescued by the first of the 12Bs tumbling into the room for the next class.

"Any time, any place," she said again, her eyes fixed on his and her tongue flicking once, quickly, against her upper lip. Something in there—a silver stud?—winked briefly.

Christ, he thought, even my son would've understood her message by now. As he stood back for the rest of the 12Bs to elbow their way in, Chug couldn't help thinking, *This is gonna be a long year. This is gonna be a very long year.*

Since classes hadn't begun until Wednesday, the first week of teaching should have felt a lot shorter than it did. But when he wasn't teaching, he was planning for his teaching, with random minutes snuck in for writing notes for the book. And there were unexpected problems he had to deal with. On Friday, Brandon and his buddies ignored their silver-key hall duties and showed up with everyone else. Then, when the class formed the circle of chairs, the silver-key guys sat in every fourth seat. When Chug asked them to number off again, Brandon and his pals made a minor ritual of moving their four chairs into a square. Chug wondered how he was going to avoid turning the class into the us-versus-you the silver-key boys so obviously wanted.

Then two girls in his second-period class got into a short

screaming match about which one was the bigger slut. Chug was too busy getting between them to choose, though he thought the one who yelled, "You'd fuck anything in pants!" was the clear frontrunner.

But maybe she shouldn't have been, since the language used around the building was one of the biggest differences from high school as he remembered it. He figured it just went along with everything else that had been happening in society, but it was still a little unnerving to hear "fuck" so often and so liberally sprinkled through the conversations of such young and often innocent-looking kids. They were a little more circumspect in class or when speaking to adults. A freshman girl in Chug's homeroom, for instance, turned and said "Oh, sorry" when she realized he was behind her as she told a friend that some other girl was "such a fuckin' asshole." But her apology had carried the emotional weight of a minor social slipup, a burp, maybe, or an inadvertent bump in the subway.

Even the faculty lounge was full of fucks—well, verbal ones, anyway. Chug had always thought one function of language was as a kind of violence early-warning system and safety valve. At his second newspaper there was a city editor named Devine. When Devine started saying "Now, goddamn it!" at meetings, everyone knew he'd reached his boiling point and, if you were smart, you backed off. Now there seemed to be no clearly marked boiling points. Language could express anger, but it really couldn't release it anymore. Fuckin' shame, he decided.

By the time the weekend rolled around, Chug fell into it as if it were the first oasis in three hundred miles of Sahara, staying up late on Friday and sleeping until eleven the next morning. He worked on notes for his book most of Saturday afternoon. That night, there were a couple of people he considered calling, but no one that was more important than getting ready for next week's classes. And he didn't want to be too tired for Sunday, which he spent with his kids. First at a Disney movie, then at the mall's arcade, and finally, to completely round out the day's cultural overkill, at Taco Bell.

He returned them to Bradford, sneaking away before Connie could find out what they'd done that afternoon and come after his family jewels with a branch lopper. He spent most of Sunday night reading student papers and preparing for the next week, and made it into bed by 11:00, still feeling the results of too much taco meat with extra hot sauce.

That may have been why he slept so fitfully. And it may have been why he woke because of the noise outside his cabin. He lay in the dark not sure what had awakened him, when he heard the movement again out there. It sounded stealthy, but that wasn't too unusual. Hell, he thought, raccoons had probably been rooting around outside the longhouses way back when the Massachuset Indians used to camp by this lake. Raccoons would be out of luck tonight. No one home in the nearby cottages, and he sure as hell hadn't left them any appetizers.

Of course, the more he tried not listening for the next sound so he could drop back to sleep, the more he waited to hear it.

There was another one. Still stealthy, but not as quiet. Not raccoons, either. Bigger. Much bigger. Footsteps scrunching on some leaves. Seemed right outside his window. He knew sounds could be tricky out here, especially at night. So he waited, all thoughts of sleep driven out by the adrenaline rush. Waited, waited, waited.

There it was again. This time—yes, the faint tinkling of someone brushing against the wind chimes Sarah had hung from the small front porch in July. Sonofabitch, someone was—yes, the creak of a floorboard on his porch.

He sat up in bed, feeling around in the dark for the Levi's and T-shirt he'd been wearing earlier. It might be legit.

Somebody lost, one of the other people around the lake needing a hand with something. That beautiful police detective, Sergeant Cusack, who hadn't been around the station when he had his fingerprints taken. Finally succumbing to a desire she could no longer deny, delay, or defuse? No, he corrected, that one would have to be in his dreams.

Just then there was a loud, insistent rapping at his front door. Nothing timid there. His toes found his slippers, and he shuffled into the living room and turned on a lamp, aware of an odd crinkling sound from out front, a little like somebody scrunching up plastic wrap. He flicked on the porch light and nudged aside the curtain on the small window set high in the door. No one there. But there was that strangely familiar scrunching sound, coming from below his range of vision. Going up on tiptoes he stared down. Jesus, there was a fire on his porch!

He quickly unlocked and threw open the door and was relieved to see how small the fire actually was. Some kind of large paper shopping bag, ablaze there at his feet.

Shit! Literally. He couldn't believe someone was pulling such an old stunt. A flaming bag of dog-shit waiting for the victim to smush his foot around in it when he stamped out the fire. Only teens would think he'd be fooled by it and he could think of four likely offenders. Damn. At 12:30, no less. But he'd better do something fast, or the goddamn trick might end up setting the whole cabin ablaze. There was a snow shovel somewhere back in the kitchen catchall closet and, using the reflected light from the living-room lamp, he fumbled around in the closet until he found it and came back to the porch. Hmm, his concern may have been a little premature. The fire had already just about burned itself out.

He glowered angrily into the darkness and turned to scrape under the smoldering pile and remaining bits of burned bag when he heard a cracking sound, and his porch light exploded over his head, showering him with tiny shards of glass. What the hell? He had recognized that first cracking sound, had seen the exploding bulb, but was still a little too stunned to respond when a second shot splatted a hole in the small window of his half-opened door. He dropped the shovel and dove back into the cabin, rolling to the side, away from the opened doorway. Good thing, too, since another shot came through the doorway and shattered the one lamp that was lit.

He crouched, grateful for the sudden darkness the last gunshot had created, and tried to stay calm, figure out what to do about this. No guns in the cabin and nothing but some kitchen knives or hand tools to use as weapons. Wouldn't do squat against a rifle, and he was pretty sure that's what was being fired at him. And not a small one, either. Get out, then. Definitely first priority. And get help. His cell phone was near the bed, and he crawled that way, the darkness in the cabin making him feel a little less vulnerable as he scrambled across the line of fire from the still-open front door. He felt around for the phone, grabbed it and half crawled, half scurried out the back door and through the small screened-in porch. The lake was quiet, unmoving. He crept to the corner of the cabin, peered around toward the woods in front. He was on the side away from where he thought the shots had come, but he really couldn't be sure. Nothing seemed to be moving out there. Still, he raced low, zigzagging toward the trees nearest his cabin, waiting for the sound of another shot. Then he was into the woods, moving as fast as he could with no light, away from the place where the shots had been fired, while sharp rocks jabbed through the thin soles of his slippers and branches whacked at his face and the arms that he'd put up to try to protect himself.

He finally stopped behind a large tree that he thought must be close to Loganberry Lane, the dirt road that passed his cabin. Crouching over to hide the phone's light, he punched in 911.

He didn't want to speak too loudly, but then had to repeat himself to the dispatcher.

"I've been shot at. My name's O'Malley, and I live at Thirty-eight Loganberry Lane, at Lake Metacom. Off Lakefront Road?"

"At Lake Metacom?" the young voice said. "By shots, do you mean gunshots?"

"Yes. Three, maybe four, but definitely three."

"Okay, okay. Three, maybe four gunshots. Uh, Mr. . . . O'Malley?"

"Yes."

"We'll have one of our patrol cars right over there, Mr. O'Malley. Just stay put."

There was no point in telling the dispatcher he wasn't still at the cabin. Any further discussion would just slow down his dispatching that cruiser, and Chug had the very real sense that he'd been speaking to someone who had to have either an L or an R put inside each of his shoes.

He waited, not daring to move. He guessed he'd careened through the woods about as stealthily as a backhoe and didn't want to do anything to attract further attention. Now that he had time to think, he seemed to remember the sound of a car starting up as he was scrambling out the back door. But that could've been anyone. At least there were no noises around him. He figured his galumphing escape had frightened away any of the little woodland critters, which right about now, was just fine with him.

It wasn't very long before he heard the siren, then the squeal of tires as the patrol car turned off paved Lakefront and onto the dirt of Loganberry. He could make out the pulsing rack lights and the headlights bucking wildly on the rutted road, which made the direction to intercept the car obvious. He'd been a little closer to the road than he had thought. The police car was coming around a final turn when Chug stepped out of the woods, waving to get the driver's attention.

It worked. The policeman slammed on the brakes, threw open the driver's door, which was on the far side of the car, leaned across the fender and, with handgun drawn, hollered, "Police! Put your hands up and lower your device!"

Chug spun around, ready to lunge away from the person he was yelling at, but there was no one there.

"Hold it! Don't move, I said!" the cop shouted again, sounding both very young and very nervous. "And lower your device, please!"

Chug turned back toward him.

"I said don't move!" he yelled. And Chug thought that gun sure as hell looked as if it was pointing straight at him. Then he thought to look at the right hand he held out by his side. "And lower your device!"

" 'Device?' You mean my phone? It's just a cell phone, not a device. I'm the guy who called nine-one-one."

"Put that down, sir. Now!"

"Okay, okay," he said, slowly realizing that the cop must have thought the phone might be able to set off an IED somewhere. Helluva place for a terrorist operation.

"I'm putting it down now. And I'm raising my hands. But I'm the guy who called."

"Come over here, sir," the cop said, finally raising himself cautiously from behind his front fender but not lowering his gun. "Put your hands behind your head and come into the headlights."

Once in the light, Chug began to understand why the young guy might have been alarmed. He looked down to see that his T-shirt was torn in a half dozen places and there were streaks of blood on it, as well as on his raised arms thanks to his scramble through the dark woods. *Probably my face too,* he thought. *Crazed and bleeding madman jumps out of the woods at you holding up something that sure as hell might set off an explosion under your car. Should be grateful the cop showed so much restraint.*

"Lean forward, please, and place your hands against the patrol car."

"Okay, I will. But the guy who was shooting at me must be getting away."

He patted down Chug's jeans, could find no other place he might be concealing a weapon, but insisted Chug stay leaning against the car while he backed up to check what had been placed on the ground.

Satisfied at last that Chug probably couldn't have harmed him too badly with the cell phone he was now holding, the cop said, "Okay, sir, if you'll get into the car, we'll see what this is all about."

"You might want to wait for backup," Chug said. "Somebody was shooting at me."

"At you? You sure?"

"Yep."

"Damn. I didn't get that. All I got was reported gunshots down here. Thought it was somebody trying to jacklight deer or somethin'."

He called in, explained that the shots were at a Mr. . . . O'Malley's and was told, yes, he should definitely wait for the backup that was on its way before proceeding. At about the same time they both heard more sirens. Another patrol car came screeching from the pavement onto the dirt. Then a third, which Chug figured probably accounted for most of the night shift.

There were lights on here and there in cabins scattered nearby which he was sure had been dark earlier. Drawn by the sirens, and flashing blues no doubt. He wondered why the goddamn gunshots had brought no lights.

By the time the three patrol cars had driven up to the cabin, they were greeted by a half dozen people who'd responded to the excitement, in hastily thrown-on clothes, wondering what was going on.

One of the policemen went over and began speaking to the gathered neighbors. The second cop, acting on an apparently unspoken agreement among them that whoever had been doing the shooting must certainly be long gone by now, took his flashlight and went over to the section of woods that Chug told him he thought the shots had come from. The third, the one who'd been the first to show up, a tall, young guy with the nameplate *Harrington* on his uniform, shone his flashlight ahead as he walked with Chug up to the darkened front porch to inspect the damage.

"What the hell you got there on that snow shovel?" he said, stepping up on the porch and leaning over for a closer look.

"It's kind of a long story," Chug said.

"So at first you thought it was just a practical joke?"

"That's what I thought then," Chug said. What he was thinking now was how the hollow at the base of her throat looked incredibly soft. "But then he started shooting."

"Three shots," Sergeant Cusack said, writing in her notebook.

"Three. There might have been more after I left the cabin, but I don't think so. I know he shot out the porch light, put a hole in the window in that door, and blew out that lamp over there."

At this moment, Officer Harrington was warily inspecting the lamp in question. *Maybe figures it's some kind of explosive device,* Chug thought. *Maybe just wants to be near Sergeant Cusack. Can't blame him for that.*

"Good shooting," she said.

"I'd thought about that. When I had the time to think about it. Not likely accidental. If he could put out two lights, and a hole just about dead center of that small window, I'm sure he could have hit me if he wanted to."

She stifled a yawn and then squinted in concentration as she jotted something else in her book.

"Want some coffee?"

"Thanks," she said shaking her head. "But I'd never get to sleep."

"You . . . uh, on the morning and the night shift?"

"Huh? Oh, no, no, Mr. O'Malley," she said with a small close-lipped smile. "I was doing some work at home, but I had the scanner on when the call came in."

"And . . . ?"

Chug thought his own smile was just about right, friendly with just a trace of willingness to be the object of someone's curiosity.

She frowned, puzzled apparently by his open-ended question.

"Why did you come down here?" he said.

The frown deepened though there was nothing she could do to spoil that beautiful forehead. "Coincidence."

"You mean, after hearing the scanner, you decided to take a ride and just happened to end up down here?"

"No, no," she said, and he thought her smile lit the cabin. "I mean the coincidence of the two events. I don't know how long it's been since we had a teen suicide in town, and certainly no suicide who's left a note like the Parkhurst boy's. And having somebody shot at, the way you were tonight, is also pretty unusual. And the two events happened within—what, four days? And they both involved the same person, you, Mr. O'Malley. Wouldn't you say that's quite a coincidence?"

"Yes, I guess I would. But that's why we have a word for it. Because coincidence, like that stuff that was on my snow shovel out on the porch, happens."

He realized he must have sounded a little sharper than he'd

intended, if the quick *Watch it*! flash from her dark eyes meant anything.

"Didn't you say that you first thought the letter to you was a practical joke, Mr. O'Malley?"

"Uh, yes, yes, I did."

"And at first you thought this was a practical joke?"

"Right." She had something there, Chug thought, though it may just have been an awareness that he didn't always think too clearly.

"Ah," Harrington said, from the wall behind the lamp where he'd spotted the slug he was looking for.

"That the third?" she said, turning to watch him probing it out with tweezers.

"Yep. Looks like a .30 caliber, same as the other two."

Chug tried, very unsuccessfully, to stifle a series of his own yawns.

"I think we can call it quits for now," she said to Harrington. "Tell the other guys we'll send somebody back tomorrow. Can't find much else in the dark out there anyway. And you can fill out the incident report later."

"Okay, Sarge," he said as he left to get the other two.

"The crime scene's already completely compromised anyway," she said.

"Lots of footprints out in the woods now?"

Chug had noticed that Harrington's two fellow officers had gone stomping around the copse of trees as if they were being paid to level the area.

She smiled and shrugged a what-the-hell as she flipped her notebook closed. "As I said, we don't get a lot of this. You feel all right about staying here now?"

"Sure."

"Well, I'll see that one of the officers patrols nearby. Officer

Harrington. He can be a little too enthusiastic, but he's pretty good."

It was nearly two. She must've been up for a long time herself, yet Chug thought she looked good enough for nine o'clock on any Boston Saturday night.

Hey, she must have caught him staring, as she looked away and smiled quietly to herself with maybe a touch of satisfaction.

"Thanks for your help, Mr. O'Malley. There'll be somebody here tomorrow to check what's left of the woods. Make sure Officer Harrington gets you to sign the incident report."

"Sure enough." He followed her to the door.

As she opened it, Harrington was striding up to the porch.

"Not much to go on, Sarge," he said. "They got a coupla spent cartridges, and Kenny found this out where the shooter was."

He held up a small evidence bag and turned his flashlight beam on it.

"Kenny wanted to know what the hell kinda midget lock you'd use this thing for."

There beneath the light's strong beam, trapped in the clear bag like some rare and delicate insect, was a tiny silver key.

So Sergeant Cusack stuck around while Chug explained the significance of the silver key to her and told her the names of his four students who were members.

"You have to be a rich, white male to join the club?" she said, one brow lifted.

"I don't think so. I've seen girls and black kids with the keys, just not in any of my classes. Those boys all from wealthy families?"

"The three names I recognize are. That Wainwright kid has been a troublemaker in town ever since he was twelve or thirteen. Mostly malicious destruction. Last couple of years some drinking and fighting. But you say he's part of this group that's supposed to help maintain discipline in the school?"

"I'm not sure just what they're supposed to do," he said. "But I think that's about it."

"Must be one of Dr. Prosky's ideas."

"You know the principal?"

"No. First time I met him was the other morning. He's only been at the school a few years. But I was born and raised in Prescott. Graduated from the high school. I've known Walter Traynor all my life, and anything that empowers jerks like Wainwright and Delisle couldn't have come from him."

"You know if Wainwright's a good shot?"

"I never heard anything about him and guns. But Delisle's father's president of the local rod and gun club. I'll look into it tomor . . . later," she said, looking at her watch. "I'd like to interview them at the station. Knowing their parents, though, I'd have a hard time getting the kids to come down. So I'll probably just talk to them in Mr. Traynor's office."

"You think they'd be stupid enough to wear the keys when they came out here? Or careless enough to lose one?"

"They could've done it on purpose," she said, stifling another yawn. "Left the key as a calling card for you, a challenge. Wouldn't put it past Wainwright."

"Yeah, I guess it fits that kind of thinking. The prank with the burning bag of dog crap to draw me out. Then the gunshots. Shows the kind of teenaged arrogance that assumes you can do the shooting without accidentally killing the guy you're playing the joke on. Or without having him shoot back at you."

"You have any weapons here, Mr. O'Malley?" The sleep seemed suddenly gone from those dark eyes.

"No, no I don't. But if I did, tell you the truth, I don't know what I would've done."

If he'd had his gun here, he knew he'd have had it pointing

toward that clump of trees. Would he have fired? Maybe hit one of the kids trying to pull a dangerous, stupid stunt? Jesus!

"Do you own any weapons?" she said, aware that her earlier question had been incomplete.

"I've got a license to carry. Got it a few years back. Still valid, but that's old news. I don't keep any weapons here because my kids come see me a lot . . . I'm divorced."

She nodded, but regrettably didn't write anything about his single status in her notebook. She left a little later, promising that she'd conduct a thorough investigation.

Chug believed her, but he also believed her unstated inference, that these kids wouldn't be easy to shake out of their very comfortable trees.

When Chug came into school early the next morning, he spoke to Irma, a front office secretary with short dark gray-streaked hair and a rail-thin build. Like many secretaries he'd met, she seemed to be much of the glue that held the office together. When he asked if she knew where the silver-key pins were kept, she told him to look in a supply room down the corridor near the guidance suite. Sure enough, there was a cabinet of small drawers, no locks on any of them. In the drawer clearly marked *Silver Key* were about two dozen of the key pins. So much for accessibility.

He didn't know if Sergeant Cusack had had the chance to speak to them yet, but the four boys sure as hell didn't look very nervous first period, three minutes after the bell, as they all marched into his room together. Each had a silver key pinned on his shirt. Two of the key-boys were smirking, but Chug thought that look seemed as habitual to them as the grin on a chimp. Wainwright's face gave no clue. That was no surprise.

Chug gave no clue either, and ran the class as normally as he could, considering he wanted to beat the crap out of four of his students. At least everyone had completed the assignment, rewriting a scene from *Wuthering Heights* by having it narrated by a different character than the one who'd originally described the episode in the novel. Some of the writing was really good. Ernest Abbott, the gangly boy who blushed a lot, had written a particularly funny piece. It was an over-the-top description by Joseph, the garbling old religious zealot servant, of the pivotal scene where Heathcliff first runs off. The class laughed in all the right places and Ernest, his big ears red with pleasure, was clearly enjoying himself.

Lacey McGovern, on the other hand, had simply repeated the scene at the beginning of the book when Lockwood first visits the Heights. It was almost word for word from the book, right down to Lockwood's point of view.

No one said anything about it, though. In fact, no one even looked surprised that Lacey had missed the obvious point of the assignment. It was still very early in the year, but Chug suspected that, between Ernest and Lacey, he'd discovered the beginning and ending links of the intellectual chain binding this class together.

It was late in the afternoon, and Chug was alone in the office, so there was no one to witness his grin when his voice mail issued up the rippling silk voice of the lovely Sergeant Cusack.

When he called the number and extension she'd left, she said, "Thanks for getting back to me. We were at the school for a few hours this morning, but we haven't really got anything yet on the gunshots last night. It's the other matter, the Parkhurst boy's death, that I wanted to talk to you about. You know when you might find a few minutes?"

"Right now," he said. Damn, too eager. "I was just about to leave school. And the police station's on my way." Nope, still too enthusiastic.

"Fine. See you in a little while, then."

He killed a couple of minutes at a faculty bathroom mirror thinking that if the primping didn't help the reflection, at least the time spent might make him seem a little less impatient to see her.

The police station on Main Road was about two miles east of the school. Red brick, white trim, very New England. Very quiet inside, also. The same older desk sergeant who'd been sitting there when Chug had come to be fingerprinted was again bent over some forms. He barely looked up when Chug gave his name and said he was here to see Sergeant Cusack. The older man nodded, pointed to a corridor and muttered, "Last door on the left." The last door on the left was open and Sergeant Cusack looked up at his knock. She smiled politely. Although he'd seen her less than twelve hours ago, Chug still hesitated for a heartbeat, that second of surprise at his reaction to her. He felt a subtle, magnetic pull that he had to consciously resist, or he was worried that he'd just slide right up against her with a click, like one of the two tiny toy magnets shaped like terriers, one black, one white, that he used to play with at his Gramma Rapoza's.

The sergeant was wearing a white, high-collared blouse, the kind Chug thought of as old-fashioned. Not on her! Despite the blouse or the computer terminal she'd been staring at, she had a timeless quality. He sat in the chair alongside the desk as she clicked off the document that had been on the screen. The desk was empty except for the terminal, a file folder, and a small double picture frame. The photo on the left was of a young man, but his clothes were at least two decades out of date. The right frame held a picture of a woman in maybe her late forties, her cheekbones as well as her dark hair and eyes clearly from the gene pool that had flowed into the woman who, as he turned from the frame, was now looking at him.

She held up the file folder. "Thank you for coming, Mr. O'Malley. This is the file on Donald Parkhurst. And there are a number of . . . oh, I don't know, inconsistencies, I guess I'd call them, about his death that bother me."

"Which ones?"

"Well, the boy was new at the school and hadn't made any close friends. Not even in the orchestra, which he had joined last spring. This, of course, fits the profile of a teen suicide. But he had friends where he'd grown up back in Ohio. A few close friends that he kept in touch with through texting and the Internet. He was planning to see them at Christmas, when his family was going to stay at his grandparents' for a week. He was even planning to enroll in a college out there for next year. So it's not as if he might have been thinking that he'd never see his friends again."

"Was one of the friends a girl?"

"Yes." Her brows lifted an appreciative fraction. "But, according to the girl, there hadn't been any change in their relationship. She was stunned, devastated by Donald's death. She said she couldn't believe he'd done that. Said they'd been eager to see each other again at Christmas. His Ohio friends said the same thing. And his parents. There were no hints, no hints at all. And I don't think any of these people are in denial. This was a complete shock to all of them."

"Maybe he didn't want to let them know how lonely he felt here."

"That's possible. But he also didn't give away anything to anyone before his death. You know, his favorite possessions. And he didn't leave any notes to anyone. Except, of course, this one to you." She lifted the edge of the now-familiar letter in front of her.

"Guess he doesn't sound like a typical suicide, teen or otherwise."

"And it's not just that . . ." She shuffled the papers as if one of them might contain something she'd overlooked. "He never seems to have mentioned your name to any of his friends in Ohio or to his parents. There was no indication at his house that he'd ever read anything you'd written. And, since he lived in Ohio until last year, it's unlikely he'd ever seen you on television."

She was telling him this gently, maybe a little cautious with his feelings, although the news actually made him feel lighter, less guilty. As much as he didn't want to take any responsibility for the boy's death, the letter had still dropped the full weight of the suicide right on his shoulders. But then, if her implications were right, and the boy hadn't committed suicide . . .

"Anything else?" he said.

"He didn't own a laser printer."

"He could always have saved his letter and printed it out somewhere else. I'm pretty sure the school has some laser printers."

"It does," she said. "But why go to all that trouble? His parents said he ran off copies of all his schoolwork on the printer he had at home. Why not do the same with the letter to you? And that letter has a different font than the one Donald used for everything he wrote. Also, we've got an officer on the force who's pretty much a computer techie, and he wasn't able to find any trace of that letter anywhere on the boy's computer."

"He check the cache?"

Chug couldn't tell if her look meant he'd impressed her, or if she knew he'd been trying to impress her. He wondered how impressed she'd be if he told her that just about everything he knew about computers he'd learned from his son, who was still three weeks away from turning thirteen.

"Yes, he checked the cache. No references to you anywhere. But our officer says that doesn't mean the boy never tried to communicate with you."

He understood the *what* of what she was saying, but not exactly the *how.* And definitely not the *why.* "What do you mean?"

"Did you ever receive any e-mail from Donald Parkhurst? Or maybe something anonymous that might have come from a young man like him?"

"No."

"Are you sure? Maybe something you thought was spam?"

"I'm not positive, but I don't think so," he said, frowning.

"We have to investigate every possibility, Mr. O'Malley. I'm sure someone with your background would understand that."

"That's okay. I was just . . . taken by surprise, that's all." He knew she had to check his responsibility. He just didn't like it. "No, I never heard from the boy. Now that I'm not in the news business anymore, I only use e-mail with a few people. I'd remember something out of the ordinary. If you want, you can have your computer guy come check my system, see if there's something I might have deleted. I mean, I could have. I don't mind him checking."

"We'll see," she said, but didn't seem interested in the offer. She shuffled a few of the papers in front of her. Apparently her next question wasn't written on any of them. That's when Chug realized what was bothering him about this whole meeting, something that he would have picked up on immediately a couple of years ago even if he'd been distracted by her looks. She wanted something from him, and it wasn't a confession that he'd been in contact with the dead boy. And it wasn't, lamentably, his body. No, it was something else.

"If this isn't a suicide, and it clearly wasn't an accident," he said at last, belaboring the obvious, "then you know what it must be."

"Oh yes, Mr. O'Malley." She looked up at him with her dark and shiny eyes. "I do indeed."

"Wouldn't think you'd get too many murders here in Prescott," he said, though he already knew the answer.

Her head shake was brief, as was the flicker of a smile that accompanied it.

"And this would be—what? The first?"

"Not quite, but I think it's been a few years. If it's a murder. Which the chief doubts. And the state police investigator agrees with him."

Chug thought that if it wasn't a murder, then it had to be a very unusual suicide. And the case was all hers. And, obviously, she'd never dealt with something like this before. He'd been peripherally around a few homicide investigations, but this was a new one for him, too. Still, there was no rule that said he had to admit that.

"Well, if it's a murder," he said, "then why on earth would the killer go to the trouble of sending me this fake suicide note?"

He knew he was playing into her hands, but what the hell, they were really pretty hands.

"That's a good question, Mr. O'Malley." Her pleasant voice didn't quite convince him that she hadn't already thought of that herself. Her smile was open, full-beam. "Any ideas on that?"

It was a good hour—a very good hour considering it was spent right next to her—before Chug left the station. Unfortunately, though they had brainstormed all kinds of possibilities, they hadn't gotten any closer to solving the boy's death.

He had managed to learn a little more about Sergeant Cusack. Her perfume had a slight cinnamon edge to it, and she tended to twirl a strand of her hair around an index finger when she thought. And he learned a lot more about Prescott police politics, which were pretty much the same as politics at any news station or newspaper. Or school, for that matter. Some people spent most of their energies jockeying for position, and the one in charge didn't want a rocking boat. The chief of police felt the case had been solved. The boy had killed himself. No evidence of anyone else there. Clearly not a random act of violence. No apparent motive for murder. The state policeman assigned to the case agreed.

The medical examiner's report was no help either way, stating that the cause of death was carbon monoxide poisoning and that the boy had apparently ingested rohypnol, one of the date-rape drugs, roofies, and must have been unconscious prior to his death. Thorough questioning about roofies of the students who'd been at orchestra practice came up with a blank. No one had seen any, knew of any circulating in the school. Donald had acted, well, normal at the rehearsal, though most of the students seemed a little embarrassed to admit they hadn't been paying attention to him. The girl who'd been sitting next to him during the rehearsal said he'd seemed fine, though he hadn't said anything beyond hello and good-bye. The school's musical director said the boy hadn't been an especially gifted flautist, but he was competent and had played well during the rehearsal. Case closed.

"So," Chug said, "he leaves the rehearsal, drives out to the pond, sets up the hose into the exhaust, tapes the window, takes the roofies, and waits?"

"Apparently."

"And no other prints or evidence in the Volvo?"

"Nothing unaccounted for. Just the boy's, his parents', and his younger sister's. His family is sure he didn't kill himself, and they've been very cooperative."

"How 'bout on the tape he used to seal the window? Duct

tape, wasn't it? Anything there?"

"A couple. Both his."

"Okay, but not very hard for someone else to do. It would just mean the person was thorough. Any evidence of other cars parked there?"

"Hard to tell. That whole area's a popular parking spot for teens on dates or out partying. Though he was parked in a more isolated section."

"And no footprints? I mean, if someone else did it, he'd have to either drive away or walk away."

She shook her head, her smile rueful. "By the time I got to it, the scene was fairly . . . contaminated."

Chug nodded, remembering what had happened to the sniper's roost at his cabin.

And so it went, for over an hour. He didn't come up with many questions that she hadn't already considered and pursued as far as she could. As for the inconsistencies, he knew it was always tough with a suicide, where there were invariably bits and pieces that simply didn't fit. He'd always considered suicide a puzzle with no final solution. Even when someone wrote a ten-page note, you could never be sure exactly why he or she did it. And they'd taken with them all the answers to any extra questions you might have.

Sergeant Cusack was thorough, she was smart, and she was determined. And Chug wouldn't want to be on the wrong end of her investigation. But, as to the cause of Donald Parkhurst's death, he left the station thinking there was no way they could ever declare it anything but a suicide. While he was sorry to lose an excuse to see the sergeant, he was relieved to think that, except for a possible reference in his book, this was the last of his connection to Donald Parkhurst's death. Which, he later considered, just went to show how wrong he could be.

# Chapter Eight

The next couple of weeks passed quickly, although Chug couldn't think of an excuse to see Sergeant Cusack again. At first he had planned to call to ask how she was coming along with the case, but a couple of days after their meeting the Parkhurst boy's death was officially declared a suicide. He got a follow-up call from Officer Harrington explaining that he was still working on the gunshots at the cabin, but the young policeman didn't sound hopeful. Chug told himself that the shooters had been Brandon and his three stooges, and they were just trying to scare him. That way he could stop the incident from immobilizing him and resist the strong urge to ask his cousin Tiago at the next weekly basketball game if he could have his gun back.

The basketball games were on Wednesday nights, fall and winter on a court in a church hall in Fall River. Most of the players were relatives on his mother's Rapoza side of the family and any friends anyone wanted to bring along. Since Chug's mother had three sisters and three brothers, and they all had families, there were usually enough cousins—and now their older children—for four teams. Most Wednesdays they played two games at once on the short side-to-side courts.

Chug and Tiago Silvia were always two of the team captains. Their cousin Paul Rapoza said it was because neither of them could take orders. Although no one in the family had ever mentioned it to his face, they all knew that Tiago had to leave the police force because he had punched out a superior officer. Chug was the only one who knew the argument had begun because the superior officer was trying to make him sign a false report, but everyone else in the family assumed Ti must have had good reason. And no one was surprised when he turned his police experience, his fluency in Portuguese, and his reputation for toughness into the most successful detective agency in Southeastern New England.

Not long after his first book was published, Chug had spent a few months working for Ti's agency. He'd thought the experience might make an interesting second book. Ti had warned him that most of the job was boring and depressing and, unfortunately, he was right. Nothing much to write about beyond a lot of unhappy people.

He got a license to carry a concealed weapon from the experience, although Ti had also told him that the only time he'd had to use one of his own guns was to crack walnuts for a salad he was putting together for one of his dates.

At six feet, with dark and curly hair, classic features and a deceptively easy smile, Ti had a lot of dates. He also had three somewhat longer relationships, and, after Chug's divorce, his cousin sent him a scorecard:

*Ex-wives: Ti-3/Chug-1*

But he also drove up to the cabin in Prescott with a case of beer—Guinness draft cans to honor what he claimed to be his cousin's evil Irish half—and they drank and talked until sunrise.

Chug and his cousin stopped at a Dunkin' Donuts after the next basketball game.

"What's the problem?" Ti asked on the way in.

"Why is there a problem?"

"Because you wanted to come here instead of going out for a

beer with the others."

While they waited for their coffee, Chug told him about the shooting at the cabin.

"You want your Colt back? We can stop by my place," Ti said.

He had taught Chug how to fire the gun, showing more seriousness and patience than Chug had ever seen in him. That was probably why Chug had learned to shoot so well and felt so comfortable handling the weapon.

But he shook his head, explained how he was sure it had just been some students, Brandon and his buddies, trying to scare him. "And if I had the Colt there, I probably wouldn't have realized who it was at first and I might have fired back. Maybe hit one of them."

"Hey, how many times did I tell you . . . ?"

"I know, I know. Never fire unless I'm sure what I'm aiming at. But there was an adrenaline rush, y'know? I *think* I wouldn't have done it, but I'm not sure."

"You change your mind about the gun, let me know."

"That's not what I really wanted to talk about anyway."

"You got a bigger problem than somebody shooting at you?"

"In a way, it is. Different, anyway." He explained how he needed to find his son a birthday present that would stand up to anything Connie and her new husband's orthodontic-enhanced wallet might buy him.

"Jase's gonna be thirteen, right?" Ti said.

"Yep."

"He must still be nuts about computers, video games, that kind of stuff."

"Yeah, but he's bound to get a lot of that from David. And I think David knows more about them, too. Knows what to buy."

He didn't want to give his son a cheap imitation of something his stepfather had bought him. Chug knew his cousin didn't need this spelled out for him.

"I've been trying to think about what Jase needs, you know," Chug said. "Instead of what he wants."

"Thirteen? How 'bout . . ." And his brow shot up toward the pretty waitress who was smiling at Ti as she brought their coffee.

"This is Jason at thirteen, Ti, not you."

It took them almost an hour, two more donuts and an extra cup of coffee each before they finally came up with a satisfactory solution. Chug knew it was what Jason needed and, ironically, it fell well within his crimped price range.

That was why, on the Thursday night of Jason's thirteenth birthday party, after the cake and the predicted altar of electronic excess, like some kind of offering to a young techno-pagan god, that Connie and David had mounded up in front of the boy, Chug told Jason he'd have to come out to the truck to get the gift he'd brought. That way Jason was the one carrying the squirming and happily yipping, mostly black, mostly Lab, sort of puppy back into the house. True, it was kind of a dirty trick to play on spotless Connie and her spiffy spouse, since they'd have to put up with the dog hair and the potential for doggy accidents. But that was just an afterthought bonus of the gift. It was something they'd never buy for Jason, a gift they'd never see that he needed. And, at five months old, the dog was supposed to be already housebroken.

Sarah helped matters along by squealing with delight and joining her brother down on the carpet where the dog was joyfully licking any face in his range.

Connie, arms folded, stared at the rolling clump of kids and dog. She seemed to be trying to regulate her breathing.

"Does he have papers?" David said, frowning down as if ready to examine the alignment of the dog's bite.

"Sure does." Chug handed the certificates to Connie.

"This is from an animal shelter," she said. "In Fall River."

"Yeah. And the papers say he's had all his shots."

"And . . . uh, Chug," David said, pronouncing the name, as always, as if he were trying to clear his throat of some bothersome obstruction. "What kind of dog did you say this was?"

"He's a black Lab. Well, mostly, anyway. You can see that in the face, the nose, and the ears. And the paws. But there's something else in there, no doubt about it. Something pretty big, I'd guess. At least Lab sized."

"Hmm, so he's not fully grown yet?" David's frown spread out across the front of his brow.

True, the dog was sizable for a pup.

"Not quite." Chug knew that saying something like half-grown just might cause a fissure to open there above David's eyebrows.

Connie, who had given up on the breathing exercises and was leaning against a wall for support, hissed out of the side of her mouth, "So he's a mongrel." Her smile was all teeth and no warmth as she added, "From Fall River."

"Hey, that's right. A mongrel from Fall River. Second time you got stuck with one of those, isn't it?"

"Hmm. Maybe this one'll be better trained," she said.

"What's his name?" Sarah rose from a few minutes of leap-and-slather with the dog.

"Well, he was called *Amigo,*" Chug said, "and that's what he's used to. It's Portuguese, spelled the same as the Spanish word, but the Portuguese put the accent on the first syllable and kind of drop the *o* sound at the end. You can change the name, Jase, since he's your present."

His son was looking up from the carpet, his arm wrapped around the neck of the dog who, in all the excitement, had understandably forgotten his training and begun to squirt just a little onto Connie's thick off-white—and, now in one spot, very-off-white—carpeting.

"Does *Amigo* mean *friend* like in Spanish?" Jason said.

"Yep, a friend, a pal. I guess you could say his name in English would be *Buddy.*"

"Amigo's a great name," Jason said.

Jason knew, of course, that *Buddy* had also been the name of the near-legendary mongrel of his father's youth, a mutt whose adventures Chug used to embellish, though only slightly, for his children at bedtime. And Chug would have had to admit that the name was one of the reasons he had chosen Amigo over a half dozen smaller dogs.

"I've always thought that was a good name for a dog." He avoided Connie's laser glare. She'd never been a very cheerful loser. He, on the other hand, considered himself a very cheerful winner.

During this same time, Chug's biggest problem at school was another female with a bad attitude. While Brandon and his buddies had become a permanent pain in the ass, most of their energy went into petty disruptions that were easier to ignore than confront. Since they were all smart and did their work, Chug felt he could live with them though he had begun to think of them as a kind of irritating doo-wop group, *The Four Dipshits.* But it was Lacey McGovern he had become really worried about.

He knew Lacey was popular and was even some kind of student government officer, but she clearly didn't belong in such an advanced class. A couple of students were struggling, and a few others were lazy. Lacey, however, was obviously and completely out of her element. She did the work—that is, she read and wrote whatever he assigned. But she never understood anything at more than the simplest plot level. Even a book like *Lord of the Flies,* a story with symbols that Chug felt were as plentiful and as obvious as the raisins in his morning oatmeal was, according to Lacey's essay, the story of "a bunch of boys stuck on a desserted island who start to act kinda weerd." And classroom discussions invariably had to slow down and maneuver past Lacey's frequent off-center attempts at input as if they were speed bumps randomly scattered around a racetrack.

Yet her classmates, while they didn't seem sympathetic, managed to patiently sit through whatever she had to say and then continue the discussion over or around any intellectual obstruction she'd dumped in their way.

Although he thought challenging a student was a good thing, even in a class this demanding, Chug knew Lacey wasn't up to the challenge. In an easier class, with simpler assignments and more time to complete them, she might learn the rudiments of essay writing. She might even begin to be able to think for herself. In this class, there was no way she'd be anything but lost and confused.

During his free period, he went to see her guidance counselor. There were three office doors off the guidance reception area, and the secretary at the central desk told him that Mr. Davis was Lacey's counselor, but that he was with a student right now. Chug sat with a couple of students at one of the round tables and waited. The placard over the middle office door read *Arthur Davis,* and Chug wondered just what an Arthur Davis would look like. There were many people he'd seen in the building that he still hadn't attached names or jobs to. His prime candidate for someone who looked like an Arthur Davis was a thin little man who favored bow ties and usually looked puzzled.

When the door opened a couple of minutes later and a student left, Chug went up to the office and found that Arthur Davis obviously wasn't the little bow tie man. Big and rawboned, maybe in his late thirties, with thick black hair pulled back in a ponytail, Davis was sitting at his desk, staring at his computer screen. Chug thought he looked like someone who should be out somewhere herding cattle or hunting bear. Grizzlies, maybe.

"Mr. Davis?" he said, tapping at the door.

"Yes? Can I help you?"

Davis's eyes were a very light blue, almost transparent, and his smile, though hesitant because Chug clearly wasn't one of his students, was friendly.

"My name's O'Malley. Matthew O'Malley?"

"Sure," he said, swiveling his chair. "You're the teacher replacing Bill Carstairs this year, right?"

"Right. I'm sorry to bother you, but I wanted to ask about a student in my AP class. Lacey McGovern?"

"Lacey, huh?" He smiled then leaned over and pulled out his desk's file drawer. He ran a fingertip along the folders until he found the one he wanted. "I kind of thought I might be seeing you early this school year, Mr. O'Malley. And I was pretty sure it'd be about our Miss Lacey."

"Why is she in an advanced placement class? She couldn't have been at honors level right along."

"Nobody told you about her suicide note?" He riffled through her papers.

"Her *what?*"

"Her suicide . . . oh, it's not what it sounds like," he said, laughing, as he extracted the paper he wanted. "When students and their parents insist on a level switch that goes against the recommendations of teachers and counselors, we have them sign a note saying that they understand this is contrary to our advice. That they're willing to take the consequences. We call it a suicide note." He held up the paper. "Have to keep the hard copy."

"The suicide thing means they did it themselves, and nobody can bitch if the student fails?"

"Oh, they'll bitch, all right," Davis said with a snort of laughter. "They always bitch. But at least we've got our asses covered. Lacey . . . let's see." He typed her name into his computer and then clicked through a couple of screens. "Right, she was in college prep English classes for grades nine, ten, and eleven, and she barely passed them. Definitely not a prime candidate for your class."

"Yet she was allowed to move up to AP?"

"It happens." He shrugged as he removed the reading glasses. "We like to encourage students to stretch themselves, take a shot at something harder. But this was all Lacey's idea. And nobody thought it was a good one. Considering her poor record at lower levels, I figured this was one fight we could win. But Dr. Prosky signed off on it. Said he'd met with the parents and they were adamant. I don't know, usually he'd fight harder against something like this. Especially since he's really proud of our advanced classes. Still, Lacey's parents are wealthy, even by local standards, and . . . well . . ."

"I see."

"And Lacey, of course," he continued, "gets a few extra perks for being vice president of her class. And she's been involved in the theater here and, oh, a ton of extracurricular activities."

"Well, she's failing English right now, and she needs four years of it to graduate from high school, doesn't she?"

"Sure does." He shook his head. "That'd be a helluva note. Senior class vice president doesn't graduate. Let's see, it's a little late to see her today . . ." He checked the large calendar on the wall to the side of his desk. "I've got a conference to go to next two days, won't be back until Thursday. I don't think I'll be able to talk to her until Friday. That okay with you?"

"Sure. But I want to speak to her first, see if I can convince her."

"She'll fight it. We'll probably end up having to meet with

her, her parents, you, me, the principal."

"If that's what we have to do to get her into the class where she belongs, that's fine with me. But that's a helluva lot of people to convince one kid."

"Oh, I've seen a lot more people than that at one meeting," he said. "About ten years ago, this one boy got an F on an English essay, copied most of it straight off the Internet. His teacher had to meet with the guidance counselor, the principal, the kid, his parents, his psychologist, and the family lawyer."

"You're kidding."

"Uh-uh. True story. I'm sure we won't have that kind of problem with Lacey's parents, but just so you know."

"Jesus. What happened? I mean to the grade?"

"You mean, was the teacher happy he still had his job when the meeting was over? Actually, it convinced him to become a guidance counselor."

"That happened to you?"

"Sure did." He winked. "Again, though, despite what Dr. Prosky said, I didn't think Lacey's folks were convinced she was doing the right thing."

"Well, thanks. I'll let you know how my meeting with her goes. See you Thursday afternoon."

"Good luck," Davis whistled as he slid Lacey's suicide note back into her folder. "You may need it."

Chug called to Lacey the next day as the class was leaving.

"I need to speak to you." He saw a glint in her green eyes and added quickly, "About your work in class."

"My journals?"

That threw him for a second before he remembered the story she'd included in her last writer journal. It detailed a couple of sexual encounters with an older man. Despite knowing how to put leg A over leg B, and being written in green ink, her transparent attempts at eroticism were, except for an occasional inadvertently funny line, neither interesting nor erotic.

"We need to talk about all your work, Lacey. Do you have any study periods?"

"Just this next one."

His second-period class was already elbowing each other into the room.

"I can see you after school, though," she added. "If that's all right with you."

"Sure, that'll be fine."

"Here?"

"What?"

"Here, in your classroom? Or would you rather meet . . . somewhere else?"

Her voice had gained a subtle burr of tension that made her implication clear.

"No, of course this room'll be fine." He pretended he couldn't understand her innuendoes any better than she could follow the themes in *Hamlet.*

"Anytime until . . . oh, three thirty or so. That okay?"

"Whatever's good for you is fine with me, Mr. O'Malley." The throaty ruffle in her voice became softer, more evocative.

He nodded and turned to his desk so he wouldn't have to notice those green, green eyes that were so much older than the face that held them or the way her teeth kept playing with the stud piercing her tongue.

He spent a lot of the rest of the day wondering how best to handle her. She was beautiful and certainly more experienced than the seventeen- and eighteen-year-olds he remembered from his youth. But so were a lot of other students in the school. And if Lacey wasn't exactly a kid, she was still his student. Even in his adult classes at the college, when the occasional student had come on to him, he had resisted. Even after he and Connie had split. Lacey, really just a kid, was strictly a no-brainer. In more ways than one.

She tapped at the glass in his opened classroom door at 2:30, the tentative uncertainty of her smile as fake as his moderately pleased grin of response.

"You want me to close the door, Mr. O'Malley?"

"No, that's okay, Lacey." But the door was already swinging firmly shut behind her.

Her look had shifted to one of total control, a woman who knew her impact, as she walked up to his desk. Her heels clicked confidently, her short black skirt that seemed to be riding lower, exposing even more of her flat belly, swished slightly, swayed lightly as she approached. And her bra seemed to have disappeared. Since she spent most of every class trying to draw his attention to her, he was sure he would have noticed back in class this morning what was now the clear outline of her nipples.

He had moved one of the student chairs out of the circle and left it in front of his desk, but Lacey ignored it and walked right up to him, stopped, leaned a hip against the top of his desk, and smiled down. Warmly.

His first instinct was to back away, heels digging in, rolling that wheeled teacher chair way the hell across the room in full retreat. That would be a mistake. But so would staying put, having to look up at Lacey. Ignore that leg now lifted slightly, heel resting against one of the lower drawer pulls, so that her skirt rode up her thigh.

"Why don't you take a seat, Lacey?" He pointed to the student desk in front of his own.

"That's okay, Mr. O'Malley. I'm comfortable right here."

To prove it she shifted her foot to a higher drawer pull, riding her skirt even farther up her leg. Green, lace-edged underwear. Figures. And, what the hell? Tattooed something? Butterfly wings on either side of her . . .

"Well, I'm not too comfortable with this seating arrangement." He shifted his instinctive, treacherous glance from her inner thighs to her eyes. He saw a quick glint of triumph at his acknowledging both the situation and her effect, but it was soon replaced by an uncertain frown as he pointed again to the chair in front of his desk.

This time he kept his eyes locked to hers, then raised a finger in front of his face and pointed again. After a sigh, she slowly slid her leg from the desk and moved to the chair. Fortunately, it was close enough to Chug's desk so he couldn't see what the hell her lower half was doing down there.

"So, you wanted to see me about my novel?" She sounded chipper now, a cheerleader, if not a seductress.

"Novel?"

"Sure, you know, about Stacy?"

"Oh, right, right." Stacy was the sexually adventurous heroine of the story she'd been writing in her journal. She held up her writing folder, its cover picturing a unicorn grazing in a moonlit meadow.

"Actually I wanted to talk about the rest of your work in class."

That took care of the perky smile, anyway.

"I've been doing my work, Mr. O'Malley. I've been working real hard for your class."

"I'm sure you have, Lacey. Still, I think this class is getting to be too big a challenge for you."

"There's an awful lot to read."

He nodded, waiting.

"And you make us write a lot."

"That's not going to change, Lacey. If anything, there'll be even more to do next quarter."

"Well," she said with a sigh, raising her eyes to his, "I guess

I'll just have to try a little harder."

"Uh, that's not what I had in mind."

"Huh?"

He should have known she'd have a hard time absorbing this, but he had wanted her to arrive at moving down a level as her own solution to the problem. Well, now at least he could see the gears moving behind those deep green eyes. Hey, something seemed to register. She looked up and smiled.

"So what do you think I could do that would help my grade then, Mr. O'Malley? I mean, I'd do anything you suggested. Anything at all."

She had a brow lifted and the pink tip of her tongue running over her upper lip then maneuvering her tongue so that the stud slid seductively up and down. She behaved as if Chug hadn't already rejected the fleshier flash of paradise she'd offered a few minutes ago. But he figured that for someone who was that bad at picking up nuances in literature, anything short of yelling "I don't want to have sex with you!" would be too subtle. Oh well.

"I've spoken with Mr. Davis, your guidance counselor. He told me that you hadn't been recommended for this level. In fact, both he and your last year's English teacher were against the change of class. I think it's just not working out, and you'd be better off if you switched into a section you're better prepared for."

That took a few seconds to process but, when it did, her whole body seemed to go rigid with shock.

"You mean, you want me to move *down*? You don't want me in your class?"

Her eyes were shiny with tears of hurt and surprise. Damn.

"I didn't say I don't want you as a student," he said quickly. "I've got other sections. A fourth- and a sixth-period class, that you might be better prepared for. And there's a second period . . ."

"You mean those morons? That class that comes in here after us?"

"No, you're right. That's the wrong level," he said, though it might be the best fit for her. "But my fourth- and sixth-period classes are college prep. And that's the level you've been in your other years, isn't it?"

It sounded reasonable, but she shook him off, once, twice, like a pitcher unhappy with his catcher's signals. It was awkwardly quiet for a while. Chug was waiting. Lacey seemed to be thinking about it, shaking her head every once in a while. Finally she apparently arrived at a decision. Her head came up, her eyes leveled at him. She stood, smoothing down the short, dark skirt as if he were no longer worthy of even seeing it wrinkled, never mind hiked up to her waist.

"This is not going to happen, Mr. O'Malley." She wrapped her arms protectively around her journal, the moonlight-wandering unicorn now hiding her nipples. "I'm not leaving your AP class."

"Lacey . . ."

"And you're not going to flunk me, either. No matter how much you don't like me."

"Lacey, I . . ."

But she'd spun on her heel and was clicking emphatically to the door. Still caught in her private scenario, she opened the door carefully, turned, and fixed him with an icy anger. "And nothing else is going to happen between us either!" She slammed the door behind her. The glass in the door shivered, but held. Kind of like Chug.

# Chapter Nine

The next day Lacey, dressed in a dark-green skirt and blouse, strode theatrically into the AP class, flung herself into a seat, crossed her arms, stretched her legs out in front of her, and spent the next forty-five minutes either glaring at Chug or staring at her shoes. He did his best to ignore her, though she kept burning and sputtering in his peripheral vision like an emerald candle.

Brandon and his flunkies, who quickly figured out something was up, directed a couple of discussion questions her way and grinned when she shrugged and said, "I don't know."

Chug had planned to speak to her at the end of class, to explain that there'd be some kind of parent conference arranged. He should have told her this yesterday afternoon, but that meeting had gone in every direction but the one he'd intended. And now, when he called to her as the class was leaving, she pointedly turned her head away, flounced her dark-red hair and marched, high heels clicking, resolutely into the hall.

On Thursday, Lacey didn't have her rough draft for an essay completed for class. Because the students edited each other's rough drafts in pairs, the numbers were now uneven, and Chug had to squeeze Ernest, the partner she usually sought out for peer editing, in with two other students.

Since she rarely followed Ernest's advice, Chug wasn't sure if Lacey chose him because he was the brightest and most patient student in the class. Maybe it was because, like her, he seemed an anomaly, isolated as much by his intelligence as she was by her lack of it. Ernest didn't seem to mind the switch, though, flushing the same deep red he usually did when paired with her and working in his familiar quiet but encouraging way with the boy and girl he'd been teamed with.

Meanwhile, Chug asked Lacey to come with him out to the corridor. She followed him slowly and stared up suspiciously as he told her about speaking to Davis and the counselor's promise to arrange a conference with her parents. She wasn't buying it, standing there with her arms folded, occasionally shaking her head back and forth. When they returned to the room, she reclaimed her post near the door, crossed her arms again and fixed her eyes on the board at the front of the room as though with her gaze alone, she could drill a hole through it.

But at least Davis was due back today, and the matter would get resolved as soon as possible. In fact, by the end of the last period Chug was on his way to either speak to Davis or leave him a note about the failed meeting with Lacey, when he stopped first at his mail slot. Two catalogs from textbook publishers addressed to *English Teacher: Prescott High School* and, sandwiched between them, a single sheet of typing paper, neatly folded once. It wasn't until he'd opened it and looked at the familiar printing that Chug realized what the paper was, and he felt a sense of dread creeping through him as he read:

*Her hair was blonde, like a character in a fairy tale. Sleeping Beauty, maybe, or somebody like that. And it glowed in the moonlight. Her skin was white as snow. But she was no Snow White, though she'd probably sleep with all seven dwarfs, yuk, yuk. She'd sleep with anybody and only fourteen years old. Shame, shame. Ain't that a shame?*

*Soon, though, she'd be sleeping alone. Forever (if you catch my drift). Shame, shame. What a shame. Could I do this? Could I? It wouldn't be like the first time. No. I left Donald still alive.*

*All I really did was walk away from him. Had you going there, didn't I, Chug, Chug? Thought it was a suicide, didn't you? But it was all me. And he was alive when I left him drugged out in his parents' boring Volvo wagon. With blondie, though, I'll want it to be different. With her, I'll want to see the life go out of those pretty eyes.*

*We'll meet at the Indian campgrounds. Easy to get her there, just have to know where to apply the pressure. And there can be a lot of pressure from that week she spent in Providence. We'll be waiting, in the bed where I'd never been with her. She'll think she's just waiting for something else, won't know she's just waiting to die. I'll have a candle lit so I can see her eyes as I slip it in. No, no, Chug, Chug—not what you think. I am passionate. But I won't be slipping that in, just the cool, clean blade. I'll see her eyes see her death coming for her, in the blade and in my eyes when she looks through the candlelight at me. Wonder what I'll see in her eyes. Amazement? Fear? Anger?*

*Understanding at last? That'd be good—at the last to be understood. Before I put out her lights for good. And that'll be it, Chug, Chug. That'll be it.*

Son of a bitch! He read it again, but the words refused to change. He breathed deeply, slowly. Son of a bitch!

He realized that he must have already gotten some fingerprints on the paper, but he carefully placed it back between the two catalogs. He took out his cell phone, called the Prescott police and, after explaining who he was, asked to speak to Sergeant Cusack.

When she picked up, he quickly told her what he'd just found in his mailbox.

"Oh my god, are you sure?"

"About what, the wording?"

"Yes. And the paper and everything. It looks just like the other one?"

"Exactly."

"Oh, man." Half sigh, half groan. "I *knew* it!"

"Looks like we've got a real nutcase here."

"Right. A real smart nutcase. I don't believe this."

But there was no denying it and she recovered quickly. "You haven't spoken to anyone else about it, have you?"

"No. I just now found it in my mailbox and called you right away."

"Good. I'm going to have to contact the DA's office about this, but I'll be right over. Tell the principal that I want to meet with you and him right away, and Mr. Traynor, too. But don't tell anyone what this is about. We've got to try to stop this. School gets out soon, doesn't it?"

"In about two minutes."

"Damn! Well, tell the principal I'll be right over."

Prosky was pinned to his computer as Chug rapped on his open door and told him the sergeant was on her way and wanted to speak to him.

"What does she want this time?"

Chug shrugged, which wasn't exactly lying, and added that she'd be there in a couple of minutes.

Just then the release bell sounded. He walked down to the counter in the front office and watched the flood of students heading out to the buses. Eager kids, excited just to be getting out. A blonde girl here, another there, heads bobbing in the rapids. Chug wanted to stop each one, pluck her out of the flow of young people, warn each one of them about the potential danger up ahead. But how could he do it? And what would he say? And this wasn't even the only way to the buses. There were other currents carrying other students with other blondes among them to other exits.

Then he remembered his book, felt guilty about what he was about to do for maybe five seconds, and took a cell phone picture of the letter.

He found Traynor out by the buses in front and told him that Sergeant Cusack wanted to see him and the principal in Prosky's office.

"That girl's a pistol, isn't she?" Traynor's lower jaw hung in that cheerful bulldog grin.

The last of the buses had left the grounds when Sergeant Cusack blew in. She was wearing a tan outfit, skirt and jacket over a white turtleneck. The jacket was buttoned but couldn't completely conceal the lump of her shoulder holster. She was followed by Robidoux, his cap low over his shaved head, his eyes still a-squint, moving from side to side. Looking for likely felons, Chug figured, as he came in the front door. Then came Traynor, as broad as Robidoux, but all lumpy as potatoes tossing around in the plaid sack of his jacket.

Chug showed the sergeant the paper, folded over and resting on one of the catalogs. She pulled a pair of latex gloves from her shoulder bag and asked about a photocopier.

"Down here."

She followed Chug into the copying room, as did Prosky, whispering, "What's that? What's on that paper? What the hell is this all about anyway?" in Chug's ear. She made five copies of the note, then placed the original in an empty folder and handed it to Robidoux.

"Let's see what we've got here." She snapped off the gloves as the four men followed her to Prosky's office. They spread out around the office, reading the copies of the letter. Then reading them a second and third time before anyone spoke.

"What does this mean?" Prosky said at last. "That first boy, that . . . uh, Parkhurst kid. Does this mean he didn't commit suicide?"

"Looks like," she said. "I contacted the DA's office about it. They'll be sending an investigator from the state police over, but we should start on this right now."

"Then there's a killer somewhere in this building?" Prosky said. "And he's threatening another student? That's what this means?"

Ignoring him, Cusack turned to Chug. "You told me this was placed in your mailbox out in the front office?"

"Yep."

"Any idea when?"

"Could've been any time after—oh, about six forty-five this morning, when I got here. That's the last time I checked it."

"And you emptied the mailbox then?"

"Yes."

"Okay. Does one person distribute the mail?" Her eyes skipped quickly over Prosky and stopped at Traynor.

"Usually it's Irma," Traynor said. "But that's just the regular delivery, the boxful the mailman leaves here around ten in the morning. Sometimes she has a student help her, office aides from our business classes."

"Teachers all check their mailboxes every day?" Robidoux said, looking at Chug as if he might be especially negligent.

"Oh yes, they're supposed to," Prosky said. "For announcements, changes in schedule, things like that."

"*Do* they?" Cusack asked, this time pointedly addressing Traynor.

"Pretty much." The assistant principal smiled at her, Chug thought, as if she'd just granted him eternal youth.

She turned to Robidoux. "You'd better ask the secretaries to write down the names of anyone other than teachers that they saw in the office today."

"There are people in and out of the office all day," Prosky said. "Students bringing in notes, leaving late assignments in a teacher's mailbox. Parents are in and out all the time. Students with discipline problems who have to see Mr. Traynor here.

They sit out there waiting to go into his office."

Though it was obvious to everyone in the group that the principal was coming up with more excuses than answers, the sergeant's voice was level and patient. "I'm sure the secretaries won't know the names of many of the students. But it's a place to start. Oh, and if you could, Mr. Traynor, would you get me a list of the students you've seen or had called down to the office today? And I'd appreciate it if I could also get a list from the other people with offices in this area. Anyone they might have seen today." Then she turned to Prosky and added, "That would include a list from you, if you would."

He nodded, clearly knowing an order when he heard one, no matter how politely phrased.

"Now, then, do any of you have any idea who the victim described here might be?" she said.

No one knew.

"She's a blonde," Prosky said. "That much is obvious. And she's fourteen, so she must be a freshman."

"How many students in your freshman class?"

"One hundred and sixty-three."

"Hmm. Figure eighty to ninety, more or less, are girls," she said. "Maybe a quarter blondes. But he's talking about somebody who's very blonde, very fair. You could probably cut that down to ten, maybe a dozen students at most we'd have to talk to."

"Are you suggesting that we should warn a dozen students that someone may—or may not—want to kill them?" Prosky said, leaning back in his chair, brows arched.

"Unless we can narrow it down, yes. That's exactly what I'm saying we should do. Though I'm going to wait for the DA's representative. He'll be in charge."

"But . . . but . . . the alarm that would set off . . . The panic."

The public relations nightmare, Chug mentally added, since

that was what the principal really meant.

"This letter says someone's already murdered one of your students, mister principal," Robidoux said. "Don't you think we should warn people about that?"

Chug couldn't tell whether Robidoux's disdain was for Prosky's position or for the man. Prosky put both hands up, palms out. "Of course we should. Of course. It's just that . . . I don't think we should set off a panic. That's all."

Sergeant Cusack said, "If it takes a panic to prevent a second student from dying, I think we should be willing to take that risk. But maybe we can narrow the field a little. Maybe find out how one of the students here could be connected to the 'week spent in Providence' reference in this letter. Any thoughts on that?"

"That could mean anything." Prosky's eyes avoided Robidoux. "Anything at all. Or nothing. If, as you surmise, the person who wrote this note already killed a student, how can we assume that he's even sane? Come to think of it, the girl he's writing about may not even be a student in our school."

"We have to begin on the assumption that she is," the sergeant said. She turned from Prosky to Chug and Traynor. "How could we find the blonde female freshmen? Walter, if you ran off a computer list of the freshmen girls, for instance, which teachers could pick out the blondes? The fewer teachers involved, the better."

"Everyone takes gym," Prosky said, apparently trying to get back into the arc of her attention.

"Only a couple of times a week," Traynor said. "And it's still early in the year. I don't think the girls' gym teachers would know the freshmen that well yet."

"Might be the same with the freshmen English teachers," Chug said, "since everyone has to take English. But . . ."

"What?"

"Well, almost all these students come here from the junior high, don't they? And that's just down the hill. And they all had to take English there, too. If we talk to the eighth-grade English teachers, they should be able to tell us which girls on a computer printout are blondes."

"Or were, then. Girls that age are prone to changing their hair color fairly often. But it is a start." Sergeant Cusack looked at the principal. "Do you know how many eighth-grade English teachers there are?"

"Three, I think. Four at most."

He called the junior high. There were three women who'd taught eighth-grade English last year. Since their students had all gone for the day, and they were told the police wanted to speak to them, they were all in Prosky's office within fifteen minutes, a little winded by their hurried trip up the hill. Sergeant Cusack introduced herself and Robidoux and told them only that the high school had been informed of a threat to a freshman girl with very blonde hair, possibly long, but not necessarily. That's all. Chug considered it a perverse acknowledgment of where schools had gone that none of the three women even seemed surprised as they settled in to look at the computer printouts of the freshman class and circle the appropriate names.

Thirteen circles.

"Do you know if any of these girls have reputations for being sexually active?" Cusack said.

The women seemed reluctant until she assured them that the threat was aimed at a blonde who might have a reputation and that narrowing the field could help speed up the process. Each woman checked a name and, after a brief group conference, they agreed to circle two others.

"There could be more," the eldest of the three said, a little defensively. "It's not as if we hear all the gossip about the kids."

"Right," another one said. "Any of them might be sexually active. These days and all."

The sergeant thanked them for their help and everyone looked at the list. Five blonde fourteen-year-olds who had reputations strong enough for their teachers to have heard about them last year, Chug thought. Some of the remaining eight might only be more discreet. Welcome to the future.

The sergeant looked at the three teachers. "Do you know of any connections between these girls—or any of these blonde girls—and the city of Providence? Did one of them spend a week there somehow? Some school function maybe? A relative you might know about who lives there?"

Blank stares followed by shaking heads on that one.

"How about any school trips to Providence last year or even the year before?"

No trips. Boston, sure, but that was much closer than the over two-hour round-trip to Providence.

Sergeant Cusack thanked them, and Prosky showed the ladies out of the office. If they were puzzled, it was hard to tell.

The sergeant had Robidoux bring the list of thirteen names to Irma so she could get their addresses from the computer. Then she had Prosky call the junior-high principal to double-check on any possible Providence connection. But he agreed with the three English teachers. No trips there at all in the last few years. No connection he knew of with any of the thirteen names read out to him.

"Any other ideas on this?" Sergeant Cusack said, once Prosky was off the phone. "Any thoughts about the 'Indian campground' reference? I know there's a place out near Lake Metacom, supposed to have been an Indian camp back in Massasoit's time."

"I was there about a month ago," Chug said. He had taken Sarah and Jason out to see it, and they'd all been disappointed.

"The 'waiting in bed' part wouldn't fit. Nothing there but a circle of big rocks, some dead fire pits, and a lot of empty beer cans."

"There's the Y camp down the east end of the lake," Traynor said. "They name the different sections after Indian tribes. 'Least they used to. There'd be beds there. Cots, anyway, though it's locked up for the winter."

Robidoux was back with the addresses.

"The DA's guy is supposed to meet us at the station," Sergeant Cusack said. "If it's okay with him, we'll get as many officers as we can and split up these names."

"Would you please caution them to use discretion?" Prosky said. "There's no necessity to turn this into a media event."

"I understand your concern, Dr. Prosky. The officers would have very specific instructions on what to say. But saving a life has to come first."

"Yes, of course, of course. It's just . . ."

"Thank you, Mr. O'Malley." She cut Prosky off. "You've been a big help on this. And I appreciate the way you've handled it."

Chug smiled, trying for shy and modest.

"I have your home number," she said. "I'll probably be in touch with you later. You seem to be the linchpin here."

"I'll be around."

She nodded, asked for the copies of the note.

Chug felt guilty about the copy on his cell, but not enough to tell her about it.

Sergeant Cusack touched Traynor briefly on the shoulder before leading Robidoux, who graced Prosky with a final angry squint, out of the office.

Traynor watched her leaving, his eyes warm and blinking proudly, a Morse code message as elemental as his nickname, *Ain't she a pistol?*

Prosky sat at his desk, slowly shaking his head.

"Some mess." His smile was weak, his face, as it turned between the assistant principal and Chug, a pasty mix of emotions that Chug couldn't completely decipher. He thought he saw concern there because something was surely going to hit the fan. Maybe a little bit of hope that it wouldn't be too much, or that Prosky could duck when it did.

"Some nut," Chug said.

"She'll take care of it." Traynor rose slowly. "Don't you worry about that."

"Well, thanks a lot, Mr. O'Malley, Mr. Traynor." Prosky took a deep breath and released it slowly as he looked from them to his door.

Traynor nodded, shuffled his broken loafers on out. Chug waited a second, stopped by some sense of concern—not for Prosky, exactly, but about him. Something was just a little wrong here, as if one of the degrees or standard-issue government proclamations he had displayed on his walls was tipped just a half bubble off level.

But the principal's eyes, flat blue coins, shut out any question. Chug knew he wasn't going to get anything here no matter what he said, so all he said was "Take care" and closed Prosky's office door quietly behind him.

# Chapter Ten

Chug moved uneasily around the cabin, his nerves raw, his whole body on edge. Though not the declared target, he had still been singled out by a killer for special attention. His jobs, and especially his brief and reluctant brushes with celebrity, had exposed him to a couple of obsessives in the past, sadly short-circuited souls who thought that grappling onto any notoriety would somehow change their lives. One of them even got a little too intense, with notes and phone calls, but nothing like this. Not even close.

He kept away from the windows that faced the road and the woods. The late-night gunfire a month ago didn't feel connected to this letter, hadn't even been mentioned in it. Still, he wasn't taking any chances. He hadn't gone for his regular afternoon run, which made the nervous and constant patrol of the small cabin feel even more confining. Again, he considered calling Tiago in Fall River to ask for his gun.

When the phone rang, he hoped it was the police with news that they'd found the intended victim and, by extension, the killer.

Instead, the caller was just about the last person he would have expected.

"Mr. O'Malley, this is Lacey, Lacey McGovern. I hate to bother you like this, but I really need a favor."

"Lacey? What kind of favor?"

"I need you to come get me off Sunset Island. I know you

live in one of those little places on the east shore of Metacom. Somebody in class said they saw you out on the lake in an outboard, so . . ."

"I don't think that's a good idea, Lacey. You'd better call someone else."

"No, but you have to, Mr. O'Malley. I don't know who else I can turn to. Y'see, the doctor who owns this island's a friend of my dad. And I check the house for him, you know, clean it and stuff like that. But there's something wrong with the engine of my boat. It was fine coming out here, but now it won't start."

He was about to tell her to call Burnside Marine down the far end of the lake when she said, "And I've gotta get home right away. I'm supposed to take care of Jennifer, my little sister. She'll be dropped off home in a couple of minutes, and nobody'll be there for her, Mr. O'Malley."

"Isn't there somebody you can call to meet your sister?"

"No, there's nobody I can get. Not this late, anyway. It won't take you more than ten or fifteen minutes to get here, Mr. O'Malley, then maybe five more minutes to drop me off at my car. I'm parked at the boat ramp on the west side of the lake, not far at all from the island."

"Lacey . . ."

"Look, I know you're upset with me. And I'm sorry about all of that, and the way I've been in class and stuff. If it wasn't for Jennifer, I'd never ask for your help. She's only six, and she's gonna be really scared when no one's home. She hasn't got a key or a cell phone or anything."

After mulling the options for a half minute, knowing he had already been hooked by her clincher of a scared six-year-old, Chug said, "There's a dock on the island?"

"Uh-huh. That's where my boat is."

"I'll meet you there, at the dock, soon as I can."

"Hey, thanks, Mr. O'Malley. You really saved my life."

"Okay . . . and be at the dock," he added, but she'd hung up.

The sun in front of him had already dropped below the pines, but the twilight would be holding for a while yet, and the October water was still and glittering. He was suspicious as he powered his skiff across the quiet lake. Still, it made no sense that Lacey would go to this much trouble to set up another seduction try after the first one had failed. And her story was believable. She'd even used her sister's name. Somewhere that frightened little girl could very well be sitting outside their house, not knowing what to do as it started to get dark all around her.

There were a few small islands scattered around Metacom, but Sunset stood out. It was the only one large enough for a house. And the house itself was a showplace, all glass and balconies, dormers and decks, sunrise and sunset views and everything in between. On summer nights Chug had seen the house glowing with light and glass like a huge chandelier hanging over the middle of the lake, a gleaming reminder that whoever owned it was having a hell of a better time in life than he was. Now he knew it was a doctor who owned it. Probably a goddamn orthodontist.

The house's two-story sunrise windows were glistening as he approached from his side of the lake. Coming around to the west side of the island, he could see the upper floor's balcony sliders glowing orange, high warm rectangles of falling sunlight. Nearer, at the end of a long dock was a gleaming Formula Sun Sport with the name *Laced Lightnin'*. Figures, he thought. Too big and too fast for this lake. Kind of like Lacey.

He cut his engine and gently eased up next to it. Above him a large sign declared, *Private Property—Police Take Notice*. No one seemed to be noticing much right now.

"Lacey?" He cupped his hands over his mouth. "Lacey?"

No movement at the windows, on the balconies, or at the

huge front door down below. Nothing. Not good. Not good at all.

He tied up and climbed onto the dock, calling Lacey's name three, four times, waiting each time for a response.

No response. No way was he going up to the house. He could see it, so she could see him. If something had delayed her, she could call down. He'd be able to hear her.

"Lacey?"

Part of him wanted to just go back to his cabin and use the callback on his phone to see if he and Lacey had crossed wires somehow. His cell phone was no help since she'd called the landline. Still, the house was only about a hundred yards away. And the parent part of his mind imagined the encroaching darkness and the six-year-old sister waiting for someone to come get her.

Then he heard the scream. It cut through the twilit island, ripping apart the serene fabric of evening, water, and pines. It sounded female, and it sounded terrified, but he was shaking his head even as he ran along the dock and up the path. He was sure he was being manipulated, maneuvered. Yet each step offered no acceptable alternative.

The front door was open a crack. He knocked on it anyway. "Lacey? You here Lacey? You all right?"

He poked his head in. The curtains on the two-story wall of windows facing the sunrise side of the lake were opened slightly, letting in enough light to see that there was no one around. He stepped onto thick, dark carpeting, vaguely aware of large couches and chairs in the huge and open room, the bright splashes of paintings on the walls. And there, in front of one of the couches, on a broad free-form slab of marble coffee table, a thick red candle sat burning. One of those scented gift-shop candles, the spicy smell of it suffusing the living room. And under the candle was a white sheet of paper, large letters written in black Flair:

*Hey, Mr. O, I'm upstairs. First bedroom to the left.*

"Mr. O"?! "Bedroom"?

Shit! Shit, shit, shit! No way. No way!

The staircase, hugging the far wall in open, dramatic fashion, stretched like an arm raised and pointing to the second floor, where a door just to the left, was ominously ajar.

"Lacey? Lacey, you up there? It's Mr. O'Malley. Come on down now or I'm leaving."

No answer.

"Lacey?"

Silence. This was not good. The scream had sounded genuine enough, but the timing was too perfect, too coincidental to his calling her from the dock. And the scream sure as hell didn't go along with the invitational tone of the candle and note on the coffee table. And the note didn't go along with her phone call. But everything would go along if someone wanted to fit it into a neat package labeled *Entrapment.* Get him up to that bedroom, take some snapshots or video, and he'd have a hard time not getting his ass bounced out of Prescott High. Like as not into a ton of trouble, one way or the other. Which meant he'd never get to write the book. Which meant he'd be right back at square one, financially, but now he'd be stuck with the reputation of having had sex with one of his students. One thing news work had taught him was: if you're ever accused of something, especially if there's a sex angle, most people secretly think you did it.

And yet . . . he couldn't just leave. There was still the possibility of a six-year-old all alone somewhere. Even more, he had to find out if that scream had been as real as it had sounded. And, if so, what had triggered it.

He looked around for something heavy. Monstrous fireplace along the left wall—must be—yep, a poker, half sword, half club and plenty heavy. Chug held it at his shoulder like a baseball bat, ready to jab or swing as he slowly climbed the carpeted stairway toward the quickly darkening second-floor corridor. He called Lacey's name as he drew closer to the top. No answer.

He stood against the wall near the half-opened door. Couldn't see into the damned room, couldn't hear anything. He pushed the door with the poker and it swung silently open.

Nothing. No explosion. No fusillade of bullets. No velvet voice cooing, "Hello, sailor."

"Anybody in there?"

No answer. He looked around the frame, the poker ready. There was a large bed near the curtained sliders that must lead out to one of the sunset balconies. Another fat red candle burned feebly on one of the nightstands. And there was definitely a shape in the middle of the bed although, in the dimmed light from the candle, he couldn't see who it was. He fumbled for the wall switch, flicked it up.

Lacey. She seemed to be sleeping, her head turned away from him, her auburn hair fanned out on the pillows. Her creamy shoulders, defined by two silky green lingerie straps, were exposed above the sheet and blanket drawn up just over her breasts. Her hidden hands, steepling the blanket away from her, looked to be folded in prayer. *Now I lay me down to . . .*

"Lacey. Lacey. Wake up, Lacey."

No response, but by now he hadn't really expected one.

"Lacey!" Louder, a little hopefully now. "Wake up!" Still nothing. "Lacey?" Almost a whisper now, and definitely a question because the scene had been gradually refocusing for him, the room looming heavily with her silence as Chug finally, reluctantly, entered it. But his reluctance was no longer because he was afraid of someone with a camera snapping his picture.

The room no longer felt like a place where one person was going to try to seduce another, or where two people were going to have an argument. It wasn't even a place where there were two people anymore. He was alone, and facing a huge bed that held a body that used to be a teenaged girl named Lacey McGovern. Holding the poker out at his side, he cautiously approached the bed and felt for the carotid on the exposed side of her throat. He already knew there'd be no response. And when he folded back the blanket to see what might have stopped that pulse, he saw that her hands weren't clasped in prayer at all, but were actually by her sides. What had kept the blanket raised above her body was the long bone handle of the hunting knife imbedded to the hilt just below her breast.

# Chapter Eleven

"Prescott police."

"Hi, I'm . . . my name is O'Malley. Is Sergeant Cusack around? I'm connected to a case she's working on."

"Oh, sure. Just a sec, I think she . . . Hey, Sarge?"

He must have told her who was calling because her voice sounded tense when she came on. "Yes, Mr. O'Malley?"

Chug knew he was not about to make her life any easier. "I'm calling from Sunset Island. In Lake Metacom? I found a body here, a girl from the high school. She's been murdered."

There was a pause of a second or two, but her voice, when she spoke, was controlled. "Is she a blonde?"

"No. Definitely not a blonde. But she was stabbed, and she's in a bed. And there's a candle here, same as in the note, so I'm pretty sure it's connected to that letter."

"Where'd you say you were? Sunset Island?"

"Yes, the one with that big house on it."

"Okay, we'll be right there. You'd better . . . lock yourself in a bathroom or something until we get there. Just to be on the safe side."

"I don't think the killer's still in the house. I've, uh, looked around a little."

"Mmm," she muttered and then was silent for a few seconds.

"I didn't mess up the crime scene, Sergeant. And I haven't been in all the rooms."

"Have you looked around the island yet?"

"No."

"Okay. Don't. Just wait in the house until we get there. And don't touch anything."

Chug sat on the edge of the couch and stared through the wall of windows toward the darkening waters. A few scattered cottages on the far shore, the sunrise side of the lake, had lights on. His cabin was out there somewhere in the darkness, a single light shining over his table. And on that table was his rank book. And in that rank book were all of Lacey's lousy grades. And not one of them had any meaning anymore.

"Death was probably instantaneous," Sergeant Cusack said, taking a sip of the coffee Chug had made for them. It was 9:30 that night, and they were sitting at Chug's kitchen table under the single light. "There was only the one knife wound visible, though we'll know better after the autopsy. Whoever did it apparently found the space between the third and fourth ribs on the first try."

Sergeant Cusack, Robidoux, three patrolmen, and a Sergeant Cassidy, a state policeman working out of the DA's office, had gotten to Sunset Island within a half hour. After they'd done a quick and futile search of the house and the island, Sergeant Cassidy had taken Chug's statement. Cassidy was tall and lean with prematurely gray hair over black brows and a youthful face. He and Chug had been sitting in the sumptuous living room while the tech people who had shown up within the hour moved everywhere with their vacuums, brushes, powders and evidence bags. Then a couple of men from the Boston ME's office had come in with a gurney for the body.

It had taken a while for Cassidy to get all the details, but once he was satisfied with the answers, he had a lengthy discussion with Sergeant Cusack. Chug couldn't hear them, but they both glanced his way enough to convince him he was the subject. Then Cassidy came back, thanked Chug for his assistance and excused him to motor back across the lake. Which Chug did while cursing himself for not stopping this from happening and wondering how the hell his involvement in this was going to look when the news broke. And, like Cassidy, who had discussed it with Chug, he was wondering why the killer hadn't followed his own bizarre declarations in that note. There was a bed, sure, and a candle. And he'd used a knife, apparently killing her just the way he'd said he would. One quick and deadly thrust. But what about the Indian camp? And why Lacey, rather than the blonde fourteen-year-old?

"We contacted the owner of the house," Sergeant Cusack said, raising her coffee cup again. Chug thought she might be making a mistake, drinking real coffee this late at night. But he didn't like decaffeinated coffee, and, because he no longer lived with fat-free, caffeine-free, odor-free, joy-free, Chug-free, Connie, he didn't keep the damned stuff in his house.

"His name is Dr. Ishrish," she said, her lips turned down a bit, her head shaking slowly.

"What? Whose name?"

"The man who owns the house. Dr. Ishrish. He's a neurosurgeon in Boston."

But there was something else in her look, something Chug had missed.

"He's from India," she added. "He's an Indian. And that's his summer house."

"Oh, Jesus! An 'Indian campground'!"

"Just what we needed," she said. "A psychopath with a sense of humor as twisted as the rest of his mind."

"But Lacey was the wrong age. And she definitely didn't get that auburn hair from a bottle."

"An inconsistent psychopath, then. Anyway, we've spoken to her parents. They're friends of Dr. Ishrish. That part of what

Lacey told you is true. They have a key to the house, and Lacey knows the code to turn off the alarm. But she doesn't clean the house, she wasn't supposed to be there. And she doesn't have a"—she bent to her notebook—"six-year-old sister. No siblings, in fact."

Chug nodded, wondering what kind of pain her parents must be feeling. Unimaginable. No matter what kind of person Lacey was or was likely to become, she must have once found the same kind of joys his daughter, Sarah, had in snowflakes and chestnuts, the same excitement in looking out her bedroom window to find the moon riding clouds across the night sky. Like Sarah, she must have done something like sneaking downstairs when she was little and couldn't sleep. Creeping along in her Dr. Dentons while her father was watching TV and curling up next to him on the couch, where he found the kid-warm, trusting weight of her leaning against him too sweet to ship back off to bed right away.

"Anything else?" he asked.

She nodded, squinted a little farsightedly at her pad. The lights weren't any too good in here, and he could have turned on another lamp, but unlike Robidoux, she looked damned cute when she squinted. And if she needed glasses, she should wear them, right?

"You're sure it was Lacey's voice on the phone?"

"Yep. We only talked for about a minute, but I'm almost positive it was Lacey."

"And you were there in twenty minutes?"

"About that. You can see how close the island is."

"So, she was alive at five ten and dead by five thirty."

"If it was Lacey screaming, then she was still alive at five twenty-five."

She nodded, jotted something in the notebook.

"Of course, the scream I couldn't be sure of," he said. "I

mean, whether it was Lacey or not. It just sounded female and frightened."

"Well, it could've been Lacey screaming in fear or screaming to try to get you to the house. If that was her plan."

He had already explained the confrontation they'd had about Lacey failing the class, her threat as she'd left his classroom, and his first guess that she wanted to get him to the island to try either seduction or blackmail or both.

No little sister. Nothing wrong with her boat, according to the sergeant. Lacey knew the owner of the house, but what the hell was Chug's excuse for being there? And she was a student of his, a kid. She wouldn't have gotten him in bed, but a picture of her in the green teddy and Chug in anything that showed his face would sure as hell have gotten him in trouble, gotten him fired. Which would have been just fine with Lacey. Still, regardless of her motives, she'd paid too high a price for him to feel anything but sorry for her.

"You figure she was working with whoever sent the notes? I mean, when she was calling?" he said.

"Seems likely. Only one boat there, no signs of a struggle, nothing upset in the house before she was killed. My guess is she was waiting with an accomplice. Maybe she screamed to get you to come into the house, then, once they saw you coming up the path, she got into the bed. The accomplice could have been there to videotape the encounter, or perhaps to find the two of you together in a compromising situation. That could be when he stabbed her. Or his stabbing her may have caused the scream. Whatever the plan was, Lacey couldn't have suspected a knife would be part of it."

"And the killer snuck out the back stairway as I was coming up the walk."

She nodded. "Since Lacey's boat was still there, we're assuming the killer had his own boat hidden somewhere on the island.

It could've been a canoe or a rowboat, since you didn't hear any boat engines after you entered the house," she said, checking her notebook.

"And this accomplice is my mysterious letter writer? The same one who killed Donald Parkhurst?"

"Looks like it. I don't see Lacey knowing her accomplice was Donald's killer. But if she did, that could be one more reason to kill her."

"To keep her quiet? I dunno. Lacey didn't seem the type who'd keep that kind of secret very long. If she knew who'd killed the Parkhurst boy, she'd've told somebody . . . Want some more coffee?"

"Maybe a half cup. You mind?"

He shook his head, watching her nose. When she asked questions, her nose scrunched up. It distracted him, made him think about that instead of the question she'd asked, so he sometimes found himself a half beat off on his answers.

"Going to be up late." She stretched as he refilled their cups. "We've got to talk to Lacey's family again, to neighbors, to people along the west shore of the lake. Then, tomorrow, to her friends at school, her other teachers."

"I guess a few people are gonna be wanting to talk to me, too."

He had seen too many half-truths bury people in the past. If the media were going to be told about his being on the island with Lacey, then they'd better get the whole damned story: Parkhurst, letters, gunshots at night. All of it.

Sergeant Cusack thought about her answer for a little while. She seemed to be trying to buy time with stirring her coffee and taking a tentative sip, though she only piqued his curiosity.

"What are you not telling me?"

"I'm not sure about the wisdom of this approach, Mr. O'Malley, but Sergeant Cassidy says the DA's office wants to keep a very tight lid on this."

"You mean a tight news lid?"

"That's the plan. Sergeant Cassidy doesn't want to give out any information about the letters or your involvement in any of this. As I'm sure you know, the more information we keep out of the news, the easier it will be to filter out the cranks. And to find the real killer."

"The press isn't going to like this much."

"No, I don't suspect they will. Oh, and Sergeant Cassidy would like you to cooperate as much as you can with us on this. I think he was concerned because of your news background, but I told him I didn't think you'd mind keeping your name out of this for a while."

"You've got that right. 'Course, handling the press can be a little like tracking a tornado. It's not too hard to do, but if you make the wrong move, you can find yourself wondering how the hell to get away."

She smiled as she put down her cup.

"What about the blonde girls, though?" he said. "Haven't you already been speaking to . . . ?"

But she was shaking her head. "The DA's office overrode that approach."

He realized now why her first question had been about the victim being a blonde.

"Why? Politics?"

"Probably. Sergeant Cassidy didn't say."

He felt a little guilty because the politics that seemed bent on not triggering a panic or making the school look bad were also what was keeping his name out of the spotlight.

As if reading his mind, she said, "You know, I'm a little concerned about the level of your involvement in all this."

"Meaning . . . ?"

"Well, there's your safety to consider. Obviously the killer has a fixation on you. He—or she—is showing off for you. And this is someone who's already taken two lives. And it's probably the same person who shot at you last month."

"Shot at the lights, not at me. And I don't think that was the same person. I think that was what you might call a genuine coincidence."

Hey, she smiled, which meant she had remembered their earlier talk about coincidence. Good sign. "I think what this person really wants is publicity more than my approval," he said. "Just somebody else who thinks being on television will bring immortality or something."

"Then you don't feel threatened? Don't feel you need any police presence?"

"Are you talking about a bodyguard?"

"Something like that. Just for a while. Unobtrusively, of course. Maybe we can even catch the killer if there's another attempt to contact you."

"The notes weren't delivered when I was around." He was shaking his head, when another thought leaped off his tongue before his mind had time to process it. "Uh, who would be doing this . . . police *presencing*?"

He saw a quick blush there in the poor lighting, and a small smile on the pressed lips as she bent over her cup.

"Some of the officers." Her voice was quiet but even. Still, the blush had acknowledged that he wasn't disguising his interest very well. And the smile. What had that meant? Yes, what indeed?

"We haven't got the manpower in town to do the job right, but we could probably convince Sergeant Cassidy it would be worthwhile to get some state help. Especially at night, when you're alone here, Mr. O'Malley."

"Matthew." He figured he'd see if he could narrow the reason for that smile a little more. "And, as for the bodyguard, I don't think so. If you want to put a trace on my phone or something like that, it's fine with me. Just let me know. You want to put somebody undercover in school, that might work. Though the students'll probably know about it within a couple of minutes. But nobody on me, okay?"

"Okay." She took a final sip of her coffee and placed the mug carefully on the table.

"I'm not trying to sound melodramatic," he said, though he knew he was going for at least dramatic, "but I've had to deal with some threatening situations before. When I worked newspapers. I can handle it."

"Two people are dead . . . Matthew."

"I can handle it."

"Still no guns in the house?"

"No."

She rose from the chair in a single smooth movement. "If you need to get in touch, especially if you hear again from the killer, these are my work and cell numbers."

The card read, *M. Cusack/Sgt./Prescott PD.*

"These numbers are just for . . . like, the case, right?"

She nodded seriously, but he'd caught a glimmer of that small, almost shy close-lipped smile flickering like heat lightning on the edges of a summer night. He could see where trying to raise that smile could become habit-forming, something a man could spend hours at, honing his skills. Or he could watch her brow pucker, her nose scrunch. He could squander days, weeks, months admiring the curve of her neck, the way her white blouse tucked in beneath the swell of her probably perfect breasts. Had we but world enough and time.

He opened the door, and she hesitated beneath the wind chimes on the small porch, not too close, but near enough so that he could smell the spicy edge of her perfume, that subtle cinnamony smell that he remembered from sitting near her in the police station. He wanted to dip his nose in beside her ear to get a better sense of it.

"Be careful," she said. "Matthew."

"You too . . . what?" He looked down at the M on her card. "Mary? Margaret? Matilda? Or is it just M like the old German movie and . . . uh, James Bond's boss?"

Her smile spread slowly, like a sunrise, until it lit her dark eyes shining in the dim yellow wattage of his replaced porch light. "Miranda."

"Really? Well, you be careful too, Miranda. That brave new world out there can be just as dangerous to you."

"Ah, but it hath such creatures in it," she said as she turned and walked away.

Hey, Traynor had said it best. She was, indeed, a pistol.

Chug had a very hard time getting to sleep. His insomnia was part coffee, part Lacey's murder, part a new and acute awareness of all the goddamn noises around the cabin. But there was another element to his sleeplessness also and, when he finally dropped off, out of exhaustion more than anything else, he was thinking about Miranda's dark and shiny eyes.

# Chapter Twelve

The radio, screaming mid-commercial for a car dealership in Somerville, shook Chug out of troubled dreams, shattering his memory of everything in them but a vague sense of dread. He was heading for the shower before his fragmented brain focused and, with a shock like icy water, he remembered Lacey, the knife stuck through that green, silk teddy.

He watched the early news as he dressed and tried to spoon down some cereal. Sure enough, Channel 23 led with a live feed from the mainland boat ramp, Sunset Island framed behind a young woman reporter he didn't recognize. She began by referring to Lacey as the second Prescott High senior to die this year, and then went on to present an outline of Lacey's death, but was a little vague on the details, not even including the kind of weapon used. A picture of Lacey flashed on the screen—posed, poised, a yearbook kind of picture—followed by a return to the closing out by the reporter at the ramp. The studio anchor asked her if the police had made any connection with the first death. The reporter explained that neither the Prescott police nor the DA's office had any statement on that at this time, but promised that more information would be forthcoming.

Most mornings Chug stopped at a small coffee and muffin place called Cap'n Bill's Java. Though he didn't read the papers much anymore, he picked up a copy of the *Boston Globe*. It had a front-page picture of Lacey. Same photo the TV news had used. And above the fold. Probably a slow news day anyway, he thought, but it didn't hurt that the victim was a beautiful girl from rich Prescott instead of some poor kid from Chelsea or Roxbury caught in a drive-by.

As he turned into the school drive, he saw that three different television stations already had crews at the school, and there were still forty minutes before the buses were due to arrive. Two of the stations had sent mobile vans, but Channel 23, his alma mater, had one of their live-remote cherry-picker trucks. The reporters, busily checking clothes and makeup prior to their shots, were all women. He didn't recognize the blonde or the Asian, but 23 was represented by Tesha Dunbar, their six o'clock anchor. For their live remote. Christ, Tesha Dunbar live at this time of the morning. Tesha was always angling for a bigger market. If she was here, then she thought the story had good legs. What the hell, good legs hadn't hurt Tesha's rapid advance.

Walter Traynor, who arrived early, was just lumbering from his red Cherokee Jeep. Chug could already recognize the Jeep because its back window was ablaze with decals from ski areas, and it was here before Chug most mornings. Walter seemed just the type who'd buy a used Jeep and never get around to scraping off the decals. Chug noticed the reporters perk up, their carefully coifed heads turning towards Traynor like three hungry lionesses out on the veldt who had just noticed that one of the Cape buffalo, the one in the ugly sports coat, was looking a little old and maybe a touch slow.

Traynor's jacket may have been a different one than he usually wore; at least its pattern seemed darker. But his pants had the same indeterminate dark sheen and his painful, splayfooted walk probably meant he was wearing the same broken pair of brown loafers. His lower jaw popped open in a tentative smile and a wave toward Chug, who kept his head turned toward the assistant principal as he slowly drove between him and the waiting women. Chug was tempted to slam on the brakes, open the passenger door, haul the poor bastard in and blast him the hell out of there. But he knew Traynor wouldn't understand. Like anyone else in that kind of situation for the first time, he'd have to experience it himself. He might be all right, or he might realize that, rather than face those reporters, he'd have been better off just doing an Anna Karenina under the wheels of Chug's pickup.

No reporters at the gym/auditorium entrance in the rear of the building, thank god. Though it was the way the teachers came in every morning, Chug now felt as if he were sneaking into the school. He hurried down the hall, slipped into the front office and signed in quickly, reluctant to talk about the death with anyone. There was no one else around anyway, except Irma, alone at her desk. She was looking frazzled and preoccupied as she answered two phones at the same time. Out through the front windows Chug could see Traynor ringed in by the three women reporters and their crews. The assistant principal wasn't grinning anymore and his eyes sought the heavens. But heaven didn't seem to be responding to any early-morning requests.

The upstairs corridor was empty, the classroom doors all closed, the only sound the squeaking of his Nikes as Chug padded down the hall. He finished the Cap'n Bill's coffee at his desk as he read the newspaper. It had more details than the television report, including the knife as murder weapon. They didn't mention the teddy, but that may have been discretion on the newspaper's part. Hell, if *Action 23 I-Squad* had found out what Lacey'd been wearing, they'd have led with a shot of lingerie, the more provocative the better, as a kind of visual aid for the imagination-impaired. The newspaper article quoted Prescott's Chief Everly, who presented them with the familiar "You'll-know-more-as-soon-as-we-know-more" police response. According to Everly, the police had been brought to the island by a call from a nearby resident concerned about suspicious activity on the island. Chug thought that was the truth stretched so thin it was almost transparent. The paper also explained that Lacey's family had been friends with the owners. There was no indication that robbery had been the motive. Responding to questions about sexual assault, Chief Everly had turned it over to Sergeant Cusack, who said they'd have to wait for the medical examiner's report.

There were also a couple of paragraphs detailing Lacey's involvement in school government and drama. The article ended by making a reference to this being the second death of a Prescott senior this school year. When asked for comment on any possible connection, Sergeant Cusack had said, "That's one avenue we are investigating."

And, thanks to a DA's office that had decided to play their cards so close to the vest that they seemed glued there, Chug hadn't been mentioned at all.

As he was folding the paper, there was a tentative tap at the opened classroom door. A woman he didn't recognize: hefty, middle-aged, smiling, was standing there, her head cocked to one side.

"Can I borrow one of your desks?"

"Sure."

"I'm Gail. Here for the day." She scraped the nearest chair-desk toward the door.

"I'm Matthew. Here for the year." He got up to help her move the chair.

She nodded, still smiling, as she set the chair in the hall next to the opened door. "I'll be in the library. I understand there's a listening room there I'll be using."

He nodded again, slowly.

"If you need to talk to someone," she added.

"Okay . . ."

Then she reached into a shopping bag she had hooked over her arm, extracted a small, square box of Kleenex, opened it, popped up the first one, centered the box on the chair's writing surface, smiled encouragingly one last time, and moved on down the hall.

All along the hall student desks had been brought out of rooms. Each held a Kleenex box, one tissue raised like a banner.

Paul Graves, on his way to his room, stopped to pluck a tissue from the box at Chug's door. In his mid-thirties, Paul was short and going to stout. His tonsure-pattern balding made him look like a medieval monk, although Chug thought Paul's basketball game was a little more along the lines of Attila the Hun.

"Terrible about Lacey," Paul said.

"Sure is."

"Are these compliments of the Grief Patrol?" Paul said, before blowing his nose.

"The what?"

"Grief patrol. It's not really funny, I know, but that's the way I think of them, the counselors, brought in to help in cases like this." He shook his head slowly. "They were here a couple of years ago, when one of our kids was killed in a pileup out on 128."

"Oh." Oh. So that's what Gail had meant about being here for a day in the library listening room.

"It's a good thing to have them here." Paul reached for a second tissue. "But I think it confuses a lot of the kids. I mean, like these chairs and tissues at every door. It's like they're telling the kids how they're supposed to behave. Politically correct grieving, know what I mean? Last time, I had a couple of kids really bothered because they didn't feel as bad as they thought they should've, about the boy killed in the crackup. 'Course, they didn't know him anyway, but they still thought they were some kind of monsters for not feeling worse."

Chug nodded. The desks did seem a little emphatic, kind of like a row of confessionals. He didn't know how he'd feel about it all if he were a teen again. He just knew he wouldn't have wanted to talk to Gail in the library.

"You know anything more about this from your friends in the press?"

Chug shook his head, committing what one of the nuns who taught him back in Fall River would label a sin of omission.

Paul shrugged, muttered, "Meanwhile, the poor kid is still dead," snatched two more tissues and stuck them in his pocket as he shook his head, mumbled "Jesus Christ!" a couple of times under his breath, and walked down to his classroom.

Chug's freshman homeroom students had all heard about Lacey's death—if not at home, then from each other on the school buses this morning. And, though she probably didn't know many of them, they all knew who Lacey was. She turned heads as she passed, maybe sat at a nearby table during lunch. Now she'd been murdered. Someone they knew.

Chug didn't immediately recognize the voice that came over the intercom asking the students to stand for the Pledge of Allegiance, except it wasn't the familiar clipped drill-instructor sound of Prosky. This new voice was deeper, spoke slower, and was all the way up to "under God indivisible" before Chug realized it was Walter Traynor. There was a sepulchral sadness in the voice that was unmistakable and very moving as it seemed to echo into the room from the speakers out in the corridors. When he finished the pledge, he said, "Please remain standing for a moment of silence in memory of our student and our friend, Lacey McGovern." The brevity of his statement made it all the more poignant, and in the silence, muffled sobs bubbled up from a half dozen people in the room. Traynor ended the silence by saying, "Any student who feels upset about Lacey's death can sign out of class and go to guidance, the cafeteria, the auditorium, or the library, where counselors will be available. Lacey's parents have not announced preparations for her wake or funeral, but we'll pass on that information as soon as it becomes available."

Traynor added that homeroom period would be extended an extra ten minutes because some arrangements for counselors had to be completed. He skipped the morning announcements, the everyday reminders about team practices, sports physicals, club meetings, and drama tryouts. Homeroom teachers got a list anyway, and Chug tacked his up on the bulletin board. As he did, he could see students in the room across the hall gathering at the windows facing the highway. Another live-remote cherry picker was turning in. And there'd be more. No doubt about it, the circus was coming to town.

The difference between his freshman homeroom and the AP class was both stark and painful. Lacey's classmates were stunned, still unfocused and in shock, coming into the room distracted and distraught. There was nothing he could say to them, nothing that would help, so he told them they could read or speak quietly among themselves. They ended up gathered in small groups, groups not very different from the ones he usually formed. Except these were more natural, a little quieter, and more supportive. Even Brandon and his satellites were in-gathered and pensively quiet.

Chug was late for his fourth-period study hall. To make matters worse, it was down in the B-wing, about as far away from his regular classroom as he could get and still be in the building. He was passing through the lobby when he saw Tesha and a camera crew he didn't recognize hovering in front of the office, stopping kids to ask them how they felt about their classmate being murdered. Chug didn't understand why someone still hadn't told them to get the hell out of the building, but there they were. He hunched and hurried, hoping to slip by Tesha, but she spotted him anyway, calling out, "Hey, is that you? Chug! Chug O'Malley!" The few students around him stepped back and away, the cowards, leaving him alone like the fall guy in a bad western, trapped out on Main Street smack dead in the sights of Tesha Dunbar, the fastest mike this side of Laredo.

Running for it could be a big mistake. Even in heels, Tesha was quick. And if she didn't catch him, she'd probably open the six o'clock news with footage of his butt scooting ignominiously down the B-wing. Maybe he could talk his way out of this.

"I don't want to be interviewed, Tesha." He waved his hand at the camera like the latest mob boss doing the perp walk into court.

Still, she held the mike and her expectant smile poised before him, her startling dark-blue eyes concentrating on her question rather than on what he had just said.

"You are . . . ?" she began.

"Me? I am someone who doesn't want to be interviewed by a television station milking a tragedy for everything they can get out of it."

Hey, that got her attention. Her mike hand hesitated, seemed to tremble a bit.

"You don't want to be on camera, Chug?" Her eyes looking pained though there was no tremor or change in her voice.

He noticed that, despite the fact that the bell to begin fourth-period classes had rung at least a minute ago, they had drawn a considerable crowd of students and, hovering guiltily at the edges, a few faculty.

"No, I don't want any camera exposure." He covered her mike. "I'm new here. I don't know anything, and I haven't got anything to say."

"Well, I hope somebody does," she said out of the corner of her still-smiling mouth to him, as she gave the cut sign to her crew. "We're not picking up anything around here."

"No?"

Her voice dropped to a confidential hush. "What's the story with the principal here anyway, Chug? He announces the press conference, then he doesn't show up. The fact is, I don't think anybody's seen him yet."

By anybody she meant, of course, the media people.

"No kidding? I dunno anything about him, Tesha. Or where he might be. I'm just a sub here, and I've only been around since September."

"Yes, I'd heard somewhere that you were teaching, but I thought it was at a college." She frowned as she looked around at the walls, the halls, the students.

"Did you know the girl?" She quickly fixed him with a bright, birdlike, predator's eye.

"Just who she was." He didn't even blink and realized that if Tesha hadn't sniffed out any hint of his connection to the killings, nothing about the two letters or even the call from Lacey, then the police lid on this investigation was very tight indeed.

She took Chug's elbow, tugging him close to her into an intimate, hushed conference.

"I also heard that you and ol' whatsherface have split." Her whispered breath was warm and pulsing in his ear, her very expensive perfume beckoning him closer.

"Connie. Yes, a coupla years ago."

"And you've never *called*?" she whispered.

He tried to back away, still smiling, not sure how it looked to the students gathered around, but pretty sure how it felt to be ringed in by her.

"Aren't you and Dave still together?"

She shrugged, gave a you-know-how-it-is smile. "You can be committed to someone else without being obsessive about it, you know."

He smiled. "Well, I've gotta go now. Got a bunch of kids waiting in a study hall. See ya later, Tesh. And no footage of me, okay? I've had all the television exposure I need for a lifetime."

She patted him on the arm, whispered a final "You get in touch with me now, okay? You've got my number."

"Yep, I do." No doubt about that, he thought.

He didn't see any media around at the beginning of fifth period, when he went to lunch or for the rest of the day. Their absence seemed to have a calming effect on the school atmosphere.

Detective Cusack came by his room just after his last class had left. "Got a minute?"

Superfluous question. He knew she'd been around the building all day, along with as many town police as they could gather. But they were interviewing staff and students, and he didn't have any excuse strong enough to break in on her.

"How's it going?" he said. "The media been after you?"

She shrugged. "Sergeant Cassidy held a news conference down at the station. At least it got them away from the school, with plenty of time for them to make the evening broadcasts. He didn't tell them much, though."

Which, he thought, was her way of telling him his name had still not been connected to the case. She leaned back lightly against a student desk.

"You find out more about Lacey?" he asked. "That you can tell me?"

"Chief says I'm supposed to keep you 'up to speed.' I think he sees it as a payback for your keeping quiet about the case." She hesitated before adding, "There's a rumor around that you're writing a book."

"Yeah, I've heard that."

Her smile acknowledged that he'd sidestepped an answer. "Anyway, it'll be a while before we hear officially about cause of death and such. Being hot local news doesn't make us a priority in the Boston ME's office."

"They're usually pretty busy."

"We're not getting much from the interviews. No enemies. No intense love interest, though I do have a couple of kids I want to talk to again about that. They seemed like they wanted to say something, but . . . I don't know."

"When I was reporting, I usually followed my instincts."

"Mm. I plan to. I just felt the setting was wrong. That maybe if I talked to them somewhere else, more informally, I could get more out of them."

"Anything on the notes?"

She shook her head. "The paper's the same on both. A common brand, sold everywhere. No fingerprints beyond yours on both and the principal's on the first one."

"How about the contents? Any ideas on why the killer murdered Lacey and not a blonde?"

"We've got nothing on the whole blonde thing. We've had all the girls on the list come downstairs today for interviews, mixing them in with the other kids we talked to. We didn't tell them about the note, though we did ask if they'd spent any time in Providence, something we didn't ask all the other kids we interviewed. It was no help anyway . . . from them or from anyone else."

"Cassidy still saying you can't warn the girls?"

"Yep." She cut off the word with a firm press of her lips. "He's following orders, and I don't think he completely agrees with them. I know I don't. I'm worried sick that something might happen to one of those girls because we didn't warn them."

Chug figured the smartest response was none. She'd have to find her own way of dealing with this.

"We're right to keep a lid on it," she said. "I can see how telling the girls would open the whole thing up. And maybe it would make it much harder to catch the killer. But—and I think this is a big but—if we find the right girl, she might be able to lead us straight to the killer."

Maybe, but he didn't think it likely. Someone who could play everyone so easily on the death of Donald Parkhurst and then set Lacey up for her own murder, might not be that recognizable to a fourteen-year-old.

"One other thing, though it may be coincidental." She checked off an item in her notebook. "Lacey actually had a connection with the reference to a week in Providence. Her mother told me that Lacey had been there last summer, at Brown, at some kind of student government leadership conference. I've still got to check on whether or not anyone else from the school attended. Don't know who'd have that information. The registrar, maybe. Is that still Mrs. Carpenter?"

He shrugged.

"I hope so," she said. "Mrs. Carpenter always kept track of everything. I'll stop down her office before I leave."

"Have you tried any other connections of Lacey to the second note? Found out if she ever dyed her hair or something?"

"I asked her mother about that." She shook her head. "No way. Lacey was very proud of her hair. It doesn't matter anyway. She sure as hell wasn't fourteen."

"No. But she was killed in the way the note had described. And she had spent time in Providence."

She nodded, but said, "I still think I should talk to the blonde girls on the list. I don't know. I may be about to do something that will force me to look into alternate career opportunities."

He could see her point. Sooner or later this all had to rise to the surface. And, when it did, the fact that secrets had been kept from the media could have a devastating backlash. For her, for him, for the case if it wasn't solved. At the minimum, he thought he'd definitely have to stay out of hand grenade range of Tesha Dunbar. At maximum, Miranda's career and his plans for the book could be scattered like so much shrapnel spewed out by the evening news broadcasts.

"So where do you go from here?" he said. "I mean, after the registrar's office?"

"I'm not sure. I thought about setting up a discreet surveillance camera in the front office, something with a view of the mailboxes, in case you get another note. Walter Traynor's in favor of it, but I haven't gotten to see Dr. Prosky yet."

"I heard he's been hiding out."

"Apparently with the superintendent, Dr. Mackey, all morning. I don't know about this afternoon. He's just not available."

Not what Chug would have expected of him, but different people handle crises differently. A guy like that, always so crisp-looking and on top of things, might just freeze at the wheel when something this messy splattered unexpectedly all over his windshield.

"You know, I've been wondering something else, Mr. . . . Matthew. Why . . . why are you here? In the school? *Is* it a book?"

He nodded, told her about the series the publisher was developing.

"This is hardly what I'd call a typical year in the life of a school like this," she said.

"I know."

"Are you still going ahead with your original plan, even with all of this other angle opening up?"

"I dunno. I'm pretty much doing both right now. I'm still keeping a journal that describes the day-to-day of the school year, but I've also begun a separate notebook on all of this."

"Would that include any copies of the notes you got?" She raised one brow.

"Not unless the case was closed. Or I had your okay."

She was fast, he thought. No two ways about that.

"Are you planning to name names this time?"

"I don't know about that, either. I've . . . how'd you know I didn't name the people in my first book?"

"I read it," she said, with that unwavering gaze fixed on him.

"You did? When?"

"A couple of years ago, when it came out."

"Oh." He was disappointed because he had hoped she'd read the book sometime after they'd met.

"I thought it was a very good book."

"Thanks. Y'know, you never let on that, beyond my name, you really knew much about me."

"I don't know much about you," she said. Then, after waiting a couple of heartbeats, with a perfect timing that left Chug frozen with expectation and delight, she added, "Yet."

He waited a few seconds, working on his own timing, before he said, "Well, do you think going out for a meal, say, tomorrow night, might be a way to get to know me better?"

Whoops! She had hesitated there, her nodding seemed to be a gradual evaluation of what he had asked, rather than an agreement.

"Uh, if that's a problem," he said. "It's all right with me. I just thought—maybe I misunderstood. It's okay. I'm sure you've got other plans. I shouldn't have bothered asking."

He figured about the only thing he didn't do was call himself a worthless slug for even asking her.

"No, it's not that, Matthew. I've had a couple of dates with somebody in the last few months. But it's nothing too serious. No commitment, except for symphony tickets for tomorrow night."

"And we do need to talk more about the murder."

"I've got a friend's baby shower to go to on Sunday. No idea when that'll end."

"Oh, okay. I understand."

What the hell, he'd given it a shot.

"I'm free tonight." It sounded as if she were asking a question, a question that he answered without even pretending he had a full social slate—which he would have wiped clean for this chance anyway.

"How about dinner? I make this very special spaghetti sauce. Much praised. Near as I can tell, it's my only affectation."

"That sounds good. I've never met a pasta I didn't like. I'll bring wine."

"Seven?"

"Seven's fine. But I've got to get back to work now. Got to go find the registrar. Then decide whether or not I'm going to talk to those ninth-grade blondes. If I do, I won't tell anyone about the notes to you, but if this all blows up, so be it. I'll see you at seven."

One final slow smile and then she left, carrying herself like someone who knew she was being watched. And appreciated. Sharp detective like her, he thought, must've also known she'd left him feeling very good about himself, about this day, about this universe. Yessir, life does have its moments.

He spent the next hour or so trying to concentrate on student work, but kept finding himself distracted and looking suddenly up at the open door, expecting to see someone standing there. And, oddly, about half the time he thought it would be Miranda with her enigmatic, flickering smile. But the other times he expected Lacey, confidently sashaying into the room, ready to try something else to change his mind. Finally, tired of being caught between desire and depression, Chug just gave up, shoveling the student papers into his backpack with the vow to get to them at some undetermined *later.* Besides, he still had to drive through the Friday afternoon Route 128 traffic to get to Newton, to the gourmet deli that carried what he had told her was his original spaghetti sauce.

He was downstairs, hurrying through the lobby outside the main office, when he noticed one of the display cases along the far wall. Most of the cases had their usual collection of trophies or plaques won by various student groups, but the top of this one case was now covered with flowers. Inside, some of Lacey's friends had arranged an impromptu memorial. On the glass shelf running across the middle of the case was a posed head shot of Lacey. Someone must have gone to her parents for it and for Lacey's ribbons, trophies, medals, and citations for student government work and theater that surrounded it. The back wall of the case had been covered with black poster board, and mounted on the backdrop were snapshots of Lacey with friends—at the beach, at parties, yearbook shots of her smiling in a classroom. She was usually at or near the center, cushioned by her popularity, her smile as confident as her beauty. Near the bottom were pictures of her in various theatrical productions, both musical and dramatic, with the title and date of presentation listed below each.

Even as a freshman she'd been an incredibly attractive girl, though there was one picture from that year that at first confused him. It was obviously taken during a play. There was only one person in the picture, a girl, but it didn't look like Lacey. She was leaning out a window of a stage-designed tower, but her hair was what had initially thrown him off. When he looked more closely, he realized she was wearing a wildly exaggerated burlesque wig from a production of *Into the Woods* that had been put on during her freshman year. It really made her look different. He'd seen the musical years ago, but it wouldn't be hard to recognize which of the fairy-tale characters she was playing in the photograph—Rapunzel. Not the biggest part in the musical, but Lacey had only been a freshman, and the production date was early in the year. She had probably been about . . . fourteen years old. And, in keeping with the more comic and slapstick tone of the musical's first act, she was letting down from the tower window one of the longest, most exaggerated heads of heaping blonde hair that had ever graced a high-school stage.

He checked down in the registrar's office. Locked. As was the guidance suite next door to it. He took Miranda's card from his wallet and called her cell.

There was a lot of background traffic noise as he told her what he'd just seen in the lobby.

"Damn!" she said. "That bastard! That sadistic, sneaky bastard."

"Yep, it was Lacey all along. Everything in the note was about her. The week in Providence, blonde, and fourteen at the time she was a blonde."

"And she died at the Indian doctor's summer home."

"Y'know, there was even a hint about when she'd been a blonde, with those references in the letter to Snow White and Cinderella."

"Jesus, that's right!"

He waited while she fumed.

"Well, I'm not sure where this leaves us," she said at last. "Right now I'm almost at the house of the first freshman on our list. I already called them to say I was coming over. I guess I'll just cancel it now, tell them I had the wrong name or something, since we already spoke to her in school."

"It doesn't mean you were wrong to go speak to them."

"Yeah. It's just . . . Jesus, Matthew, thanks for calling me. The chief would've had my hide, especially when it came out the blonde freshmen weren't the targets in the first place . . . Is Prosky still at school?"

Chug walked over to the front office window where he could see the reserved parking spaces.

"No, he's gone."

"Walter Traynor?"

"His Jeep's gone too."

"Damn. I wanted to find out more about that time Lacey spent in Providence. Mrs. Carpenter, the registrar, didn't know anything about it, had no information about a student government conference in her files. And that woman has kept everything since day one. But there's got to be some connection there if the killer knew about it and could use it as leverage on her."

"You plan to talk to the mother again?"

"Uh, no, not yet. She's too confused, in too much pain. Maybe I could see Prosky at home. But I planned to talk about the case with a friend who's a Boston police psychologist. I'll give him a call, see if he can fit me in this afternoon. I'll get back to this Providence thing later."

"You're not writing yourself notes while you're talking to me and driving all at the same time, are you?"

"What? No, 'course not." But her surprised and guilty squiggle of laughter told him different. He usually referred to people who talked on phones or texted as they drove as CPA's—cell phone assholes—but decided not to share that with her just yet.

"And we're still on for tonight?" he said. "I'd understand if this case got in the way."

"Well, our meal's a kind of continuation of the case. There's still a lot about this I want to discuss with you. But I won't put in for overtime."

"Oh. Uh, good. Fine. See you then."

From the other end he could hear the nervous-sounding double tap of a car horn.

"And stop writing yourself notes while you're driving."

# Chapter Thirteen

Route 128 was running under its usual Friday afternoon battlefield conditions: five minutes of cars playing no-blinker, lane-switching, seventy-five-mile-an-hour bumper tag, followed by inching forward boredom in backed up traffic. Fortunately, the Newton exit wasn't too far, and Chug bought his groceries and was back at the cabin and showered by six. That left him an hour to clean the place and cook the meal. The pasta wouldn't take long and heating the sauce and the garlic bread would be even faster, but the cabin was another matter. On the plus side, at four rooms, it was a small place. On the minus side, it was a big mess. Examining it now from the perspective of a stranger, he could see that he'd been ignoring the place, treating it as temporary because that's what he wanted it to be. He didn't even own a vacuum cleaner, making do with a broom for the big stuff and a Dustbuster for everything else. Sarah and Jason were his only regular visitors and, as teens, they moved through clutter as naturally as hamsters in a Habitrail.

But Miranda wasn't a teen and neither was he. He opened the windows to air the place, took the couch cushions out to the picnic table and whomped them with his tennis racket, cleaned the bathroom and, with a last surge of optimism, put fresh sheets and pillowcases on the bed. *Hey,* he thought, *stranger things have happened.*

He heard the car turning into the ruts of his driveway at exactly seven. It was a late-model red Accord and was barely clearing the ruts now. If this had been March, she might have had to walk the last half mile of Loganberry Lane.

Watching her get out of the low-slung car was a pure visual pleasure. He saw the red high heels and the long, lovely legs sliding out first, then the mid-length cream-colored coat. There was a hint of a red dress matching the heels—no suit this time—beneath the coat. Her hair was done up, and she had a small beaded bag tucked under one arm. She looked like an ad for a Rolls, and moved across the rutted path as if it were the entrance to Symphony Hall. Still, as she got closer he could see something in her eyes, a trace of nervousness, maybe, some tentativeness. Good, at least he wasn't the only one.

The meal went well, although through most of it they talked about the murders.

"This whole manipulating aspect of the case really bothers me, Matthew. His manipulating us, manipulating his two victims. He must've already planned exactly how he'd kill Lacey when he sent you the second letter. Right down to you being the one to discover her body."

"He knew he could convince Lacey to have me come to Ishrish's house?"

"Looks like. You got the note—what, two days?—after you told her you wanted her to change classes? He must have set the whole thing up with her to entrap you somehow—maybe, as you said, with a video camera. Then he double-crossed her at the end."

"What bothers me even more than the manipulation," he said, "is the escalation. The second note said the boy, Parkhurst, wasn't dead when the killer walked away from the truck. But he killed Lacey in cold blood. Maybe even looked into her eyes as he did."

"And what's going to happen next?"

"Yeah, that."

But, no matter how casual he tried to sound, how much he used words like *manipulation* and *escalation,* he knew there was no getting away from what they were really talking about. It was murder, and Miranda hesitated a long beat before speaking slowly, as if reading from a prepared statement.

"I explained the case and showed the letters to my friend, the Boston PD shrink this afternoon. He agrees that they're written by a male, a fairly bright male. Though it might also be a very smart woman, trying to make us think a male's doing the killing. He's not sure about the age of the killer either. A high-school student would be a little young to become a serial killer, though it's not impossible if he's driven enough. And my friend doesn't think a teenage boy would be able to kill Lacey the way it was done, with a single knife thrust."

She was concentrating on twirling a forkful of spaghetti against her spoon as she added, "He insisted on seeing it in sexual terms, of course, with premature ejaculation or sexual frenzy being the marks of kids. But, there was no indication of semen anywhere at the crime scene."

"Which could support the female killer thesis."

"Yes, it could. It certainly could."

"What do you think?"

She shrugged, stopped for a sip of wine, still seemed to be feeling her way. "I don't know. My friend's a Freudian at heart, though he says he's not. So you have to filter everything he says through that. He thought the pathology's pretty unusual regardless of the killer's age. For one thing, there's not a lot of time between the deaths of the two victims."

"And the victims are very different from each other." Chug realized that fact had been bothering him subconsciously. "I mean, there's an apparently passive boy, followed by a fairly aggressive female. Not much of a connection."

"No, you're right. He didn't mention that, but he was

concerned about the increased interaction of killer and victim. Said he wouldn't be surprised if the level of interaction was even greater with the next attempt."

"By interaction, he meant what, violence?"

She nodded, pausing to gauge Chug's reaction before saying, "That's the part I definitely agree with. Both that this person's going to be looking for another victim, and that it's likely to get worse."

Chug had thought as much from the time he had found Lacey's body. But hearing it was still chilling. "And . . . ?" Having asked so many questions in his career, he knew there was another unspoken one coming at him.

"And I asked him about you."

"Me?"

"If he thought you might be in danger."

"Oh."

"He wouldn't commit." Just a hint of humor in her eyes at her verb choice. "At least not on the limited information I could provide. But he didn't think you'd be the next target anyway."

"That's reassuring."

"He thinks that the killer probably sees you as a conduit to the authorities as well as a ticket to fame."

"Even if I don't know who he is? Or does your friend think the killer's going to reveal his—or her—identity?"

"I asked about that, too. He said that doesn't happen as often as people think. A lot of serial killers just don't get caught. Or if they do, it's because of a fluke, a stroke of fate, not some subconscious screwup. Now, I think our guy's going to get caught just because his plans are so elaborate. He thinks he's so smart, but too many things can go wrong for him. Something will, soon. Hell, I'm hoping something already has, and we can find out what it is before he decides to do something else."

"And the killer gets his kicks out of manipulating people?

Keeping me and you guys running around after him?"

"Well, that and the killing itself. My friend thought that killing Lacey, much more than the first murder, marked a new plateau for him."

"Hmm."

"What?"

"Oh, I was just wondering what happens when the killer realizes I'm not going to write about him for the newspapers or do a television special for *Action Twenty-three I-Squad.*"

"I never thought to ask about that." She reached into her purse for her ubiquitous notepad and pen. "Anything else you want me to ask?"

"When are you going to see the psychologist again?"

"Tomorrow night. I told you, we've got tickets for the symphony."

"Oh."

As she began to squeeze the pen and notebook into her purse, Chug noticed that she was squeezing them in around a pistol.

She saw where he was looking, shrugged and smiled. "I didn't think I'd need it, but I have it just in case. And not to protect me from you."

The transition from talking about the murders, which meant also discussing her recent boyfriend's theories, to talking about each other was easier than Chug had expected. He later realized she must have managed it, when he'd been distracted by her eyes shining over her raised wineglass. Somehow, he found himself explaining, as objectively as he could, how he and Connie had split.

"She left you because you quit your job?"

"Well, that's when it happened." He put their plates in the sink and turned his attention to the coffeepot. "The air had gone out of the relationship a long time before that."

"But quitting Channel 23 was the trigger?"

"Yeah, that and telling her I wasn't going to be doing television anymore. Or a newspaper column. I didn't want to go back to that either. She was really concerned about having a secure life. Her parents' farm went bankrupt when she was about ten. She never wanted to be broke again."

Chug had been on a fast track when he met Connie. He had a feature column and appeared every once in a while on a small television station's weekend talk show. He knew a lot of people and, what he found really strange at first, more people—even some famous ones—seemed to know him.

Connie liked that. She was, easily, the most beautiful woman he had ever dated. She reminded him of Grace Kelley in one of his old favorites, *Rear Window*—that kind of tall, cool, blonde beauty. Chug found himself smitten by it, befuddled, bedazzled. Bewitched, bothered, and bewildered. Every once in a while he still just liked to step back and admire her beauty. But he didn't want to be married to it anymore. No thanks.

"So why *did* you walk away from it all?" Miranda asked.

He shrugged. It was a fair question and, for him anyway, a familiar one. "There were some moral choices involved. And I didn't much like the kind of person the pressure and attention was turning me into."

He knew it wasn't much of an answer. He was sure Miranda knew it, too. But she was nice enough to let it slide.

"And you've got two kids?" She was looking at their pictures on a shelf over the table.

"Sarah and Jason. Great kids."

"Did your wife remarry?"

"Yeah. Well, that's why the separation became a divorce, so she could get remarried. To an orthodontist in Bradford."

"Ah, security and straight teeth."

"Something like that. He's a pretty good guy, though. And

the kids like him."

Still, Chug had once heard Sarah referring to David as her *pa-rental.* The girlfriend she was talking to, out on the cabin's porch, had joked back about the *ma-rental* she and her dad were living with. Just a couple of sad little wiseguys trying to sort things out. Name it and you can claim it.

Miranda was standing beside him at the sink, both waiting for the coffee to finish dripping into the carafe, when she put her hand on his arm, gently, reassuring. Chug was surprised, impressed. She had understood his silence after he had mentioned his children and had offered Chug the one thing he hadn't realized he needed just then—friendship. In a heartbeat he realized they had gone right past the physical to some other area of intimacy he hadn't even been expecting. *You just never know what life's gonna bring you.*

He found out more about her over the coffee and during a walk out along a stretch of lakefront where she had kept her small purse tucked heavily under one arm. She'd been born and raised here in Prescott, graduating from the high school ten years ago. She'd lost her father even earlier than Chug had lost his, when she was eight, to cancer.

"Walter Traynor helped with Sunday school at our church," she said. "And he was always there for me, especially when I got to high school. I practically lived at his place for those four years."

After high school, she'd gone to U. Mass Amherst and majored in English. During her junior year of college, her mother had been killed by a hit-and-run driver on Commonwealth Avenue in Boston in the middle of a Saturday afternoon. The police never found out who had done it.

"When I graduated from college, I thought about teaching at the high school, but I had to take some education courses first. When I went to sign up for them at U. Mass Boston, I suddenly decided to take criminal justice instead."

"Your mom?"

"Sure, what happened to her was part of it. But I also just wanted to help people in a more hands-on, day-to-day way. And I like solving problems."

"Well, you've got a helluva problem to solve now."

By the time they were back standing in his small living room, their conversation had trailed off into that silence that signals the end of one thing and the beginning of another. He knew they could force their way into a new, friendly chat, they could recognize that it was time to call it a night, or they could do something else. They just couldn't remain standing facing each other silently, although it didn't feel as awkward as it should have. He smiled at her, shrugged. *Your move.*

Her eyes looked down. Chug noticed a deep intake of breath, then a slow exhalation. Just the way he had been taught to fire a gun or shoot a free throw. Calms the nerves. Squeeze the trigger or release the ball halfway through the exhale.

She looked up, smiled, raised a hand to the side of his face. He knew he felt cool from the night walk, but the touch of her fingers was so warm, so right.

"I'm not in a rush, y'know," he said. She'd been seeing that shrink, had a date with him tomorrow night, all that. She was too good for him to chance messing up by pushing too hard, too soon.

"I'm not in a rush either, Matthew." She slipped up against him, her deep eyes staring unblinking into his. "Believe me, I think we should take our time." And her lips were brushing lightly on his, the softest touch before he felt them leave and then heard her, unbelievably, whisper, "After all, we've got all night."

She actually didn't stay all night. Good thing, too, he later decided, because he probably would've kept himself awake just to watch her sleeping, lying on his clean sheets, dark hair fanned out on his fresh pillowcase. Their journey to the bedroom had been frantic, scrambling and damn near slapstick. When she'd tossed the purse with a heavy clunk on his table, Chug had flinched at the sound.

"Safety's on," she'd whispered while bringing her now-free hand up behind his neck.

Could be a different gun going off accidentally, he thought as her pelvis moved up against his.

They reached the bed, and he was struggling to get his shirt unbuttoned as she bent to remove her shoes.

"Oh, that drawer there," he said. "In the nightstand. Something in there." Then, remembering what she'd said about bringing her gun, added, "I didn't think I'd need one, but I have one just in case." Despite his passion, he was pleased by her smile as she reached for the drawer pull.

Later, grateful that the other weapon hadn't discharged prematurely, he lay spooned against her. Indirect light from out in the living room shone through her dark hair. They spoke quietly, warmly. He told her he had hoped this would happen, but hadn't really expected it.

"Well, I'm not exactly a first-date woman, Matthew."

She turned and, as he fell onto his back, laid her head on his chest and traced a fingernail lightly down between his ribs. "Fact is, I'm not a second-date woman either. Sure, I thought about you like this. But I didn't know if it would happen. And I never thought it would happen tonight. Not until it happened."

"I don't want this to be just . . . *this,* y'know? That's what I meant about not being in a rush."

She'd lowered her head to his chest, and he could feel her lips forming a smile just over his heart. Then she sat up and smiled down at him, while her long hair fell across her firm and perfect breasts.

"How do you feel now?" he said.

"Now? About what happened? I feel good about it. Very good."

"And you don't think it was a mistake?"

"No." Her smile wavered uncertainly. "Is there a reason you're asking?"

"Uh, yes." He sat up and gently parted her hair away from first one breast and then the other. "I wanted to make sure you felt good about it because I think it's about to happen again."

She left around two, concerned about an eight o'clock meeting she had scheduled with the state cop, Cassidy, and the task force he'd assembled. "If I stay, we may not get any sleep at all."

"And that's supposed to be a reason for leaving?"

"No," she whispered at the door as she rose on tiptoes and pressed her lips softly to his. "But it's the one I'm using for now."

He had pulled on some sweats and a T-shirt and stood in the doorway watching her walk to her car, her heels steady even at this late hour and on that uneven earth. He could feel the cool, October breeze rippling in off the lake, could see it ruffling some stray strands of her hair as she ducked into the low car. She leaned once against her steering wheel as if taking in a deep breath before looking over to him and smiling, waggling her fingers and then turning on the ignition. There was no moon. No stars. No matter.

He stood in that doorway long after her car turned onto Lakeside Road and faded away toward town. The warmth that he'd brought with him from the bedroom chilled through the T-shirt and onto his chest; his eyes watered from the breeze off the lake and his cheeks began to feel numb. But his lips still felt warm with the sweet pressure she'd left on them. He must have stood there fifteen, twenty minutes, just savoring.

# Chapter Fourteen

Lacey's wake and funeral were Saturday afternoon. The line of people stretched out the door of Gaither's Funeral Home and all the way down the block. Lots of students, girls supporting each other, boys nervously adjusting their unfamiliar and poorly knotted ties. Many of his seniors were in the line and, as Chug walked to the end of it, they greeted him soberly. A couple of boys, unsure of the protocol, reaching out to shake his hand.

Ernest and another tall, thin boy came up behind him. Both looked solemnly uncomfortable.

"Mr. O'Malley," Ernest said, nodding.

His friend smiled, muttered, "Hi."

The line inched slowly, quietly forward, conversations muted, hushed, as if anything louder would indicate disrespect for Lacey.

Finally, Ernest whispered, "Mr. O'Malley?"

"Yes?"

He was blushing dark red, and his whisper took on a croaking, desperate edge to it. "What . . . what are you supposed to say? I mean, to Lacey's parents and all?"

Good question, Chug thought. What could you say? How could you try to address the unthinkable that had happened to their daughter, that had happened to the rest of their lives?

"Just tell them how sorry you are about what happened and you're sorry for their loss. I don't think there's much else anybody can say."

Both boys nodded and thanked him.

Just then the line perked up, with a buzz of conversation coming from the people behind and the people in front turning around to see what had caused it. As Chug turned, he saw the source—a TV news crew approaching. The reporter was the Asian woman who'd been in front of the school, and she took up position so her opening shot would show most of the line behind her. She patted her jet-black hair, took her coat off to reveal a bright-pink suit, and tossed the coat in the van, took a deep breath, and signaled her crew. Chug assumed she was speaking into her mike, but he was too far away to hear and had turned his back as soon as she'd given the cameraman the signal.

He had reached the stairs of the funeral home when the news crew came up to what was now the front of the line. He turned his face to the side, trying to avoid eye contact, but the reporter wasn't interested in him anyway.

"Was Lacey McGovern a friend of yours?" she asked the two boys behind him.

They must have nodded because he didn't hear anything and the reporter continued, "And how do you feel about this?"

"I think it's terrible," he heard Ernest say and could imagine the red edging out to his floppy ears.

"Yeah, awful," his friend said.

"And this is the second of your classmates to die this year. How do you feel about that?"

"Awful," said Ernest.

"Terrible," said his friend.

Inside there were two men in suits and ties standing near the sign-in book. They might have been funeral-home workers, but Chug figured them for police checking out the mourners. In the room past the guest book there were kneelers in front of the casket, so Chug knelt, folded his hands in front of him, and looked at Lacey. Flawless skin, every hair arranged, delicately made up, her final image would be one of perpetual beauty. But she wasn't beautiful anymore. This was a dead body, and whatever had inhabited it, driven it, given the body its substance and meaning, was gone. He tried to pray, but couldn't come up with anything more than the phrase he'd given Ernest and his friend to say to the parents, *I'm sorry.* He blessed himself, took a deep breath, and stood to face the receiving line.

Lacey's parents looked shell-shocked. They were shaking hands and smiling at people although, in a way very much like their daughter, there was no one home behind their eyes. Chug imagined that, whatever sedatives they'd been given, their minds were off screaming somewhere in a dark and jagged abyss. The difference was that, unlike their daughter, they could return. But they'd never be the same again.

Chug had met them on parents' night over a month ago. He could see they didn't recognize him as he told them he had taught Lacey and how sorry he was about everything. Each took his hand and held it briefly, smiled and thanked him for coming. He was grateful that they didn't know he'd been used as the bait that had lured Lacey to the room where she had been murdered.

Mr. McGovern numbly, automatically, told him that the next two people in line were Lacey's grandparents, and Chug moved on to them, while behind him he heard Ernest saying to the McGoverns, "I'm really, really sorry about what happened to Lacey" and his friend echoing, "Yeah, it's terrible."

After Chug made his way through the rest of the line, he turned to find a seat. All the chairs in this room were filled. There was a large arched opening into the next room, and there the chairs, arranged in even rows, were nearly all filled also. The people in them looked as if they were waiting for some kind of performance to begin. If that was the case, then Brandon and his satellites were the warm-up act. They sat dead-center, the faces of the three flunkies so contorted by trying to hold back their choking laughter that they might have been mistaken for being in excruciating pain. Brandon, the master artist, looked blank, uninvolved in his creation, and his eyes didn't blink as they followed Chug.

Walter Traynor was sitting in the next-to-last row beside a good-looking woman, who was maybe in her late forties and had hair the color of a mahogany sideboy Chug remembered from his Gramma Rapoza's apartment. Traynor had his head lowered. There were a couple of empty seats next to him, so Chug sat in one of them. Walter looked up and nodded, then dropped his head again. For a second, the way his head was lowered and his jaw muscles worked, Chug thought he was praying. Then the head lifted again, the eyes fixing on Brandon and his buddies as if taking aim.

A few minutes later Arthur Davis, Lacey's guidance counselor, came in with his wife, though Chug lost her name while Davis was introducing her. She shook Chug's hand and then leaned over and hugged Traynor and the mahogany-haired woman, kissing them both.

Davis said, "Walter, I thought you two were coming over last night."

Chug didn't hear the answer, shifting places with them so they could sit together. The two couples spoke quietly, comfortably, their conversation a pleasant humming offset by the occasional coughs of laughter from Brandon's claque a few rows ahead.

After about fifteen minutes, an old priest came into the room and looked around, black beads dangling from his hand, and Chug, who had said too many unanswered rosaries in his life, figured it was time to leave.

★ ★ ★ ★ ★

He tried writing notes for his book on Saturday night, but found himself thinking about either the murder or Miranda, so he switched back to schoolwork. His mind-set didn't switch with the task so he took a walk along the lakefront, hoping to clear his head. Ishrish's house on Sunset was turned on. Despite its festive appearance, he didn't think the doctor was entertaining tonight.

His Sunday father thing with Sarah and Jason was the usual exercise in joy and frustration. The joy came from just being with them and from seeing the changes taking place in them. But that was part of the frustration, too: being able to actually see the changes. They were subtle, week to week, yet much stronger than the day to day of their childhoods. He felt as if he were watching their lives progressing if not at fast-forward, then at least at double speed, and it was disconcerting. Jason may have already firmly established a new hobby, and his father wouldn't even know he was interested in it. A crush of Sarah's could be come and gone before Chug had so much as heard the new boy's name.

Then, too, there was the frustration of the three of them trying to confirm Chug's place in their lives. Connie was the continuum, the house in Bradford their foundation, their core. He knew they'd never confuse ortho-David with Dad. Still, David was there every day. He could help them with their homework, talk with them at breakfast, pick them up after soccer practice and give the evil eye to any boys hanging around Sarah.

And Chug? He felt he had become Mr. Weekend, a kind of indulgent bachelor uncle. His cabin was a place they came to visit, a place not outfitted for the needs of two growing kids, one of them a female. He worked at it, but he was always one step behind their growing and seven days behind their interests.

Sarah, as usual, was first out of the house when he pulled into the driveway.

"Hey, Dad," she said, giving him a hug as she barreled her ponytailed self in beside him on the bench seat. "Jase'll be along in a minute. He's downloading something."

"Must hurt like hell. Kid needs more fiber in his diet."

Her gray-eyed smile was appropriately pained, but then Jason was at the side door, calling something about Amigo's training back to his mother.

As he got to the truck, he said, "Celtics won last night, in overtime."

As usual, Chug was tempted to tell him he needn't bother faking an interest in sports, but again reminded himself it was a gift his son gave out of love, so he should accept it the same way.

"Well, what's it gonna be, you two? MS or MFA?" Chug asked, repeating the alternatives they still hadn't resolved when he had called them during the week.

"I vote for the Museum of Science," Sarah said. "Wanda told me they've got this great laser show there."

Jason, strapping himself in next to her, said, "Okay. Either one's fine with me."

"Science it is, then," Chug said. He knew Sarah would have preferred the Museum of Fine Arts, but she must have picked up Jason's undertone of yearning when he casually mentioned the special exhibit on computers at the Museum of Science during their three-way midweek phone conversation. For Jason, that was nirvana. They'd fit in the laser show if they got the time, but Chug knew it was definitely not her main reason for suggesting they go there. That was Sarah.

"So, I heard you say something to Mom about Amigo's training," Chug said to Jason. "What's up?"

"He's getting there," Jason said, his smile eager as he leaned forward to look over.

"It's incredible, Dad!" Sarah said. "Y'know how Mom's so worried about the neighbors being bothered by his barking . . ."

Chug nodded as if he did, in fact, know this.

"Well, Jase has trained Amigo so he won't make a sound, not a sound, for . . . what, Jase, fifteen minutes?"

"Almost twenty so far," Jason said, shrugging, though obviously pleased with himself.

"You just have to say 'Quiet' to him every once in a while, to remind him, y'know," Sarah said.

"That must make Mom happy," Chug said.

"Sure, but she's not too crazy about the release phrase."

"The what?"

"The words that tell him it's okay to start making noise again," Jason said.

"And for Amigo, that can mean barking like a madman," Sarah said, making her brother squirm a little uncomfortably. "Though it's changed the way David acts around the dog."

"And that 'release phrase' is?"

"Bad Dog," Jason said, squinting out the windshield at the expressway traffic as if suddenly fascinated by the cars swooping in and out of the lanes. But the corners of his mouth were turned up and there was a very satisfied glint in his eyes.

Way to go, Jase! Chug thought. Train Amigo and David at the same time.

The traffic through Boston was light for once. Big turnout for the computer exhibit, though. Tough parking outside. Nerd Central Station inside, with kids that looked to be as young as five or six blathering knowledgeably about gigabytes and megahertz, and teenagers drooling over the latest software with all the ardor Chug used to have for a rebuilt '65 Mustang convertible.

Jason blended in seamlessly. Sarah, who did very well in math and science, thank you, mostly kept her father company.

During one of the lulls in the afternoon, she asked, "Did you know that girl from your school who was killed, Dad?"

"Uh, yes, I did. She was a student of mine."

"No kidding! Wow! Justine told me her older brother—you know, Mark?—had dated a friend of hers. But you knew her, huh?"

"Yes, I did."

"What was she like?"

A dozen answers presented themselves to him, everything from his real estimation to a warning about the personality traits that he thought had helped doom her. In the end, all he said was that she was a nice-enough kid.

"They have any idea why she was killed?"

"They're apparently not sure yet."

"Wow, she was in your class."

He could tell by her voice that his daughter had just accumulated some big points in the game of school corridor one-upmanship. And he understood her obvious interest in the murder. It was mixed with distance since Lacey was no more than a face in the newspaper.

Jason, who had joined them in time to get most of what they were saying, looked concerned as he asked, "But you didn't know the other one, that guy who killed himself, did you, Dad?"

"No, Jase. I didn't know him."

Jason seemed relieved. It was one thing to have a father who knew a murder victim. Knowing two who had died would be cutting it a little too close. Chug thought his son might get an ulcer if he knew just how connected his father had become to both of these deaths.

On their way back they stopped at a McDonald's in a strip mall near the Bradford/Prescott border. The parking lot was full at 5:15, the smell of fries its usual overpowering presence as soon as they stepped inside. Four lines at the registers, each line about four deep.

"I'll take a number three," Chug said, giving Sarah the money. "I've got to make a pit stop first."

By the time he got back, Sarah had already paid for their order. She and her brother were out of the line, leaning back against the counter, waiting. It was what he had expected to see. What he hadn't expected were the two boys in Prescott varsity jackets, standing facing his kids. Both were big, one a little bigger than the other. Chug could tell by Sarah's eyes that she was all right. Their attention made her a little nervous, but she was handling the situation. Jason, his back against the counter, his arms crossed, seemed less comfortable. He was a seventh grader. Compared to him, these high-school seniors were men. But not compared to Chug.

"Brandon, Carter," he said as politely as he could muster. "How ya doin'?"

"Mr. O'Malley!" Brandon said, turning his head. "Carter, look who's here."

Delisle faked surprise about as well as Chug faked being happy to see them. "Thought you spent all your leisure time at home correcting our papers, Mr. O'Malley," he said.

"Not quite."

"The order'll be here in a minute, Dad," Sarah said.

" 'Dad'? Did she say, 'Dad'?" Brandon said to Delisle and looked from Chug to Sarah and back again. "I don't believe it! Beautiful young lady like this? Your daughter?"

"Don't be a jerk," Jason said, rising to the bait his sister and father had easily ignored.

"What? You talkin' to me, runt?"

Chug began to feel that Brandon was now trying a bait that would get his attention. Fortunately, their food arrived, and Sarah and Jason turned to pick up the two trays. When they turned around again, Wainwright and Delisle were standing in front of them, backs to Chug again, blocking them. But only for a second.

Chug gripped Wainwright by the back of both his arms, just below the triceps, and lifted him back on his heels, as he said, "Excuse me, but I think they're trying to get by."

Delisle looked stunned and, as Chug had expected, had no idea what he should do next. Wainwright tried to shake himself free, but realized that, without footing, he had very little leverage, and Chug would probably only apply more painful pressure. Which he did.

"I think it'd be best if we let them pass," Chug said, smiling kindly at Delisle as he swung Wainwright out of Sarah and Jason's path.

" 'Fuck's the matter with you, man?!" Wainwright growled out of the side of his mouth, still pulling, but still not going anywhere.

"That's my son and daughter," Chug hissed into his ear. "And whatever games you want to play with me are one thing, but they're out of bounds. You mess with them, I'll stick your head in the French fry oil. Y'understand?"

Chug released him, and Brandon shrugged his shoulders the way he probably did on the football field to show that some particularly hard hit hadn't bothered him. Then he started for the door.

"Hey, what about . . . ?" Delisle began, but then followed his leader out the door.

Chug had to admire the fact that Wainwright hadn't even reached to rub his sore arms.

He turned and walked into the dining room, watching the boys' reflections in the window in case they decided to come after him. The one thing he didn't want was to duke it out with a couple of teenagers, rolling around on the floor tiles in a McDonald's.

Sarah and Jason were at a table down near the back window. They both looked a little concerned, but then eased up as they saw the two boys going out to Brandon's car.

"They were sitting at that corner table, Dad," Sarah said. "I saw them watch you go to the bathroom. Then they got up and came over to talk to me."

"They bother you much?"

"No, not really. They were just being, you know, like senior guys hitting on a freshman. But I figured out pretty quick that they must be students of yours."

*Senior guys hitting on a freshman?* he thought. *Wonder just how much she knows about that!*

"Jerks," Jason said. "Jerks."

"They left some of their food there," Sarah said.

Must've been what Delisle was concerned about, Chug thought, but he just shrugged.

"Maybe they lost their appetite," Jason said with a chuckle. "Bad Dog!" And he snickered into his milkshake.

Chug reminded himself that the boys were only high-school seniors. Grown pretty big, but not men yet. What he had done to them had been immature. He could have talked them into behaving. But they were all out of the classroom here, out of the school. And this was about his daughter and son. He knew he got a little crazy where his kids were concerned.

He popped the lid on his Big Mac, grabbed a handful of fries, took a deep breath and let it out slowly before he began chowing down.

He called Miranda when he got back to the cabin, and they talked for a while about their separate weekends before she suggested that they could carry on this conversation in person.

"I was kind of hoping you'd say that," he said. "Your place or mine?"

"Be there in a jiffy," she said, hanging up.

She was true to her word, out of her car and into his arms within twenty minutes, a jiffy even by Chug's currently impatient standards.

# Chapter Fifteen

Monday evening, though they had both assured each other that they were in no hurry to rush their relationship, Chug called Miranda after supper, got directions, and drove over. She lived in a cottage set back on a lot that was ridiculously big for Prescott. She explained that it had originally belonged to her great-grandfather back before the town was considered such a desirable suburb. The cottage was small, three rooms downstairs, two and a bathroom up. The living room had full bookcases and a fireplace across from the couch. He followed her upstairs where she showed him the bedroom that she used as an office. More full bookcases. Then she opened the door to the other bedroom. *Best for last,* Chug thought. And it was.

On Tuesday school got back to as normal as it could be under the circumstances. At least there were no news people around the building and no Kleenex stations in the hall, though Chug knew that Sergeant Cassidy and his task force were still talking to students down in the guidance suite. The AP class, which hadn't met on Monday, was still feeling a lot of pressure from Lacey's death, but they got to work anyway.

Brandon was quiet. So were Delisle and the other two flunkies. Chug thought it just went to show that if you mix a little Mr. Macho in with Mr. Chips, you've got students who behave. In retrospect, though, considering the way he had acted at McDonald's, Chug felt a little too much like the backside of that old sitcom character, Mr. Ed.

At noon most of the subdued conversations at the long teacher lunchroom table seemed to be about Lacey and her death, though a few people had begun wondering what was wrong with Prosky. According to Irma, sitting up near the head of the table, Prosky had barricaded himself in his office all Friday. Part of the time with Dr. Mackey, the superintendent, but most of the day alone. Not taking any calls. He'd phoned in sick yesterday, and he was out sick again today.

"I guess this murder is just not part of the game plan," Irma announced to a few snickers.

"No, it's not the best way to go out and up," someone else said, and the solemnity of the room lightened with a few smiles.

"What the hell's that about?" Chug asked Paul Graves, who was sitting diagonally across the table.

"It's something Prosky said at a party, about a month after he first got here," Paul said, his bald tonsure gleaming as he frowned down at the school lasagna in front of him. "Said he had a game plan for his future in education. Said Prescott'd only have him three years, four at most. Then he'd be out and up."

" 'Out and up'?"

"His very words," Paul said, cautiously lifting a forkful of lasagna toward his mouth.

"Where would he go?"

"Oh, a bigger school," he said around chews. "Or a small superintendency somewhere if he got lucky. Maybe a midsized assistant superintendency. Then something bigger. He's on that track."

"I never knew there was a track like that."

"Oh sure," Mark Gruyer, a French teacher, said. "We've had a few of them come through here. Remember that guy, who was he? Ray Roylance?"

Most of the people at the table smiled, and someone said

something about watermelons, obviously a reference to a story about Roylance, which got a small but genuine laugh. Then someone mentioned somebody else who used to be in guidance, and the discussion for the rest of the meal was pretty much about people Chug had never heard of and situations where you had to have been there to catch the humor or get the point. At least the mood had lightened a little.

But now Chug knew what had bothered him about Prosky. He didn't want to be here, in this school. He didn't even want to be a principal. This was just a stop for him. Though Chug had seen his share of the type working on papers, and they were as common as cosmetic surgery on television, it was strange to think of people like that in education, men in three-piece suits and women dressed for success, wandering the countryside looking for interviews, letters of recommendation and résumés in hand—well-dressed briefcases zipping up and down the education highway.

The telephone message slip was in his mailbox after school. Prosky's name and telephone number. He answered on the first ring.

"Yes, Mr. O'Malley. Thank you for returning my call. I was wondering if you could stop by my house this afternoon. There's something I'd like to discuss with you. About the murder of Lacey McGovern."

It wasn't hard to find Prosky's house. It was on one of the better streets in town, an impressive colonial set on a large lot. The house, like the oaks fronting it, looked solid, long-lived. Someone at lunch had once said it was a rental, and that made sense considering Prosky's career plan. Someone else at the table, a science teacher who seemed to have a prissy, nasty intensity about other people's business, had referred to Prosky's wife as the "money mouse" and said maybe she'd bought it for him.

Chug parked in the driveway. When he turned from the car, Prosky was already standing at the opened front door. If he thought the principal had looked bad the last time he'd seen him, it was only because he had nothing to use as a comparison. Now, as Prosky stepped back to let Chug enter the cool, dark foyer, he looked terrible. His eyes were bloodshot and drooping. He had beard shadow that might look okay on some men but on him gave the appearance of dirt smudged along his cheeks and chin. His hair was scraggly, his shoulders slumped.

"Thank you for coming over," he said quietly, his voice as drained as the rest of him.

Just then small, thumping footsteps approached from the back of the house and a little girl, not much over a year old, plump with a head full of curly blonde hair, clumped unsteadily out to see her father. Walking must have begun recently because she still had that half nervous, half delighted look children bring to their first attempts at vertical mobility.

"Ashley! Ashley!" a small voice called, and a thin woman with mousy brown hair and little beady eyes came hurrying in, smiled apologetically toward the two men, scooped up the toddler, and skittered into a back room.

"Maybe we could speak down here." Prosky opened a door near the staircase. He flicked a switch and led the way down narrow, carpeted stairs that opened to a huge, high-ceilinged and brightly lit rec room. Dead center under a clear plastic drop cloth was a nine-foot pool table with leather basket-pockets. Four raised pool-hall chairs, also covered, lined the wall near the table, comfortable couches and chairs scattered around the rest of the room.

The whole cellar was a game room in storage. Along the far wall ran a dark oak bar with five stools fronting it. Against the wall immediately at the foot of the stairs was a classic Wurlitzer jukebox, also covered by a transparent drop cloth, as was the elaborate pinball machine, that displayed scenes from an Arnold Schwarzenegger movie on its back glass.

Prosky slumped onto one of the couches, his eyes staring blankly toward the rich beige carpeting at his feet. Chug took a bar stool. The decorations behind the bar, like everything else down here, were turned off, even the couple of beer clocks that would have had bubbling lights and one beer-ad sign Chug had once seen years ago that, when lit, showed cars that seemed to drive through the evening streets in a city. Lookin' for the heart of Saturday night.

"I'm sorry for the . . . ," Prosky began, but then stopped, unable to find the word and waving his hand around the room as if it embarrassed him, but he couldn't explain precisely how. "I thought we could speak more privately down here."

"You shoot pool?" Chug asked, thinking that whatever Prosky had to say might go down a little easier over a game or two—especially on a table as nice as that one.

"No, no. The house came like this . . . with this room."

Again, a sense of distaste. Hell, Chug thought, it wasn't as if there were paintings of poker-playing dogs on the walls.

He swiveled idly on the bar stool, checking out the ceiling. Soundproofed tiles. Now he understood what Prosky had meant by their speaking "privately."

"Oh, can I get you a drink, Mr. O'Malley?" he said. "Coffee? A beer? I think we might have some."

"No, nothing, thanks."

Chug waited, deciding silence might best move the principal along. Prosky examined the carpeting for a minute or two more before looking up.

"I . . . I received a note. In the mail three days ago. On Saturday." He extracted a tightly folded piece of paper from his shirt pocket, opened it, read it one more time as if to be absolutely sure of its contents, and then handed it across to Chug.

The print looked the same as the other two. So did the paper.

*If you want to know who was nailing the slut in the green lingerie before she was finally nailed once and for all, ask Prosky at the high school whose juice it was she had in her. I may have put her lights out but, as for the rest, it's not my baby. Right, Vic-Vic?*

*Cc: Detective Miranda Cusack*

*Chug-Chug O'Malley*

*To be sent in four days (I am serious)*

Chug read it a couple more times, carefully. To absorb the message. To see if there were any hints about future actions. To stall looking back at Prosky. When he was a kid, the nuns had told him that confession was good for the soul. When he grew up, he discovered that listening to one wasn't.

"You, uh, you seem to be involved to a considerable degree in this case, Mr. O'Malley. I think that you may know some things, have some information that not everyone else is privy to."

"Well, you know the other letters were sent to me, so I couldn't *not* be involved, even if I wanted to."

"Do you know if, in fact, Lacey was wearing green lingerie when she was killed?"

Chug nodded, though he wasn't planning to explain how he knew. Let Prosky think the information had come from Miranda.

"The green, uh, lingerie," Prosky said, very quietly. "Was it what they call a teddy, with thin shoulder straps?"

Jesus. "Yes, it was."

What the hell, the note had already told Prosky what she'd

been wearing. Giving away the style wouldn't make much difference.

"Can you tell me why she had it on?"

For the first time Chug saw a spark of something—curiosity, anger perhaps?—in those dulled eyes.

"No."

"Can't? Or won't?"

Chug ignored the questions. They came to the same thing anyway.

Prosky sighed, got up, walked over to the other end of the bar and plunked himself down on the last stool, looking about as natural there as a bishop on a Harley hog. Upstairs, even through the soundproofing, they could hear the distant thumping of his infant daughter's clumpy running across the floors.

"Lacey and I were having an affair," Prosky said abruptly.

Chug nodded. No shit. What the hell other conclusion was he supposed to reach when the man had just described her lingerie?

"We were . . . lovers," he added, looking up at the acoustical tiles as if to confess it finally to his wife, the money mouse.

Chug waited, silently, understanding his role by now.

"I . . . I don't know how it began. I don't think it was my fault. I really don't. I mean, I didn't start it. I didn't suggest it. It just kind of happened."

He made it sound a little like taking your eyes off the road for a second and bumping into the car in front of you. Then Prosky finally got down to it and told the story.

It had begun last year, when they were working together after school on a student government project sponsoring a school assembly on STDs. She had initiated the affair, he insisted, and he insisted on repeating the term "initiated" at least three times as he unfolded his tale. Chug thought he may have been subconsciously trying out his testimony. They'd had sex in his office. The door was locked and the curtains drawn on the windows, but there were still people in the building, even the two secretaries in the front office just down the short corridor.

"We had to be quiet." His eyes were bright with the memory, but not with any apparent remorse. "Or people would hear us. It was unbelievable. Very slow. Very silent. She was so beautiful and so intense. It was the most incredible, most daring and erotic thing I've ever done."

Chug was tempted to suggest that maybe the fact he was committing statutory rape with an underage student had added a little spice to the proceedings, but he doubted at this point it would have even slowed Prosky down.

"After that, we just met wherever and whenever we could. She even stayed here in the house while Margaret took Ashley out to visit her mother in California last summer for a . . . uh, while."

He'd hesitated there for a second, stumbling over something, but then hurried on. Chug put a mental checkmark on that stumble.

"Lacey wasn't like anyone I've ever known before. She may have been young chronologically, but she was the most exciting woman I've ever met."

"Did she ever mention anyone else? Someone she might have confided in about this affair?"

"Hmm? Oh, no." Prosky came back to reality. "No. She never talked about anyone else. She said I was the only one she was . . . uh, lovers with, but I never completely believed her."

"Anyone catch you together, almost catch you, anything like that?"

"I don't think so. We were careful. The only times we ever made love at school were the first time, once again on opening day this year and . . . the day she died."

Chug took a few seconds to absorb that before going on.

"Ever check into motels, anything like that?"

"No, no. Of course not. My wife has commitments a couple of nights a week, and Lacey used to come over then. While I was babysitting Ashley. But we were careful. She'd leave her car up on North Street, in the Wal-Mart parking lot. Sometimes she'd pretend to be jogging, so people wouldn't pay too much attention to her going up and down this street. She'd wear a tank top, shorts, sneakers. She used to show up with a little—you know, a little film of perspiration."

He wore a smile of reminiscence, a glint in his eye.

"But you didn't use condoms?" Chug said, reminded of the letter's contents and consciously tossing a little cold water on Prosky's Mr. Clean-meets-Sweat Patina memory.

"She said she wouldn't do it with condoms, that they made the act artificial and unnatural. And she was taking the pill. You know, for birth control."

Jesus. And they'd started having sex while planning an STDs assembly.

"And you say you had sex with her in your office on the day she died?"

"About four o'clock. After you'd gotten that note, the second one. After the police had gone. The building was nearly empty, so it seemed safe enough."

"And what time did she leave?"

"Around four twenty, I'd say. We had to hurry because she said she had somewhere she had to be."

"And you didn't see anyone around?"

"No. I was very careful about that. I even watched her drive past on her way out. There was no car following her."

"You thought somebody might be following her?"

"No, no," he said quickly. "Nothing like that, really. I was just being cautious."

Nope, he answered too fast. File that, too, Chug reminded himself.

"So, what we've got here," he said, holding up the note Prosky had given him, "is her killer knowing she had sex with you. Knowing it was unprotected sex at that. He also knew it would show up in the autopsy, even though it happened more than an hour before her death."

It was a little more information. For the killer's note to be that confident, Lacey must have told him about her and Prosky.

"Why are you telling me this?" Chug said. The question had been bothering him from the beginning.

"Well, the letter." Prosky nodded toward it.

"Yes? So?"

"There's a copy going to Detective Cusack. Tomorrow."

"And?"

"Well, you must have been around crimes before, as a reporter, right? What do you think she'll do about it? The letter?"

"I dunno. I'm sure she'll speak to you. Or Sergeant Cassidy will."

"But what should I tell them?"

"You should tell them what you've just told me." The principal was already shaking his head when Chug added, "And if you don't, then I will."

"What?! You can't! I've been speaking to you in complete confidence."

"Confidence in what? I'm not your lawyer, and I'm not your priest, and I'm sure as hell not here as a reporter receiving privileged information."

He had never liked Prosky, and this only made his dislike turn to disdain, but he tried to cushion his anger. "Look, in cases like this, the more information you give the police, the easier it is for them to solve the murder."

"No." Prosky's eyes were narrowed, betrayed-looking. "It'd be in the news. It'd end my marriage, my career. No, not unless the police promised no one would find out."

"You'll have to speak to the police about that." But he was sure they'd never give the principal that kind of guarantee.

"They can't make me take a DNA test, can they?"

"Not if they haven't charged you with a crime, I don't think. Do you have an alibi for the time Lacey was killed?"

"Yes. I explained it to the police when they interviewed me. We were low on milk, and I took Ashley with me to a Seven-Eleven two blocks away. There was an older woman at the register who I thought would remember us because she was so taken with Ashley. And when the police double-checked, she told them we'd come in shortly after she had begun her five to eleven shift."

"I don't see how the police could charge you anyway. Since the killer sent the letter, it would make no sense that you'd be the killer."

Of course, it would make a perverse kind of sense if Prosky had ratted on himself. But Chug knew he wasn't the kind of guy who'd do that. He had no guilt, just fear of discovery.

"And all the DNA would prove," Chug said, "was that you'd had sex with Lacey."

"Well, wouldn't it also prove I was the father of the baby?" he said. "DNA can do that, can't it?"

"Baby? What baby?"

"The autopsy must have shown she was pregnant."

"What?"

"Pregnant. A . . . a couple of months pregnant." Prosky's lips looked dry, his face even paler than before. "Isn't that what the 'not my baby' line refers to?" he asked, but his voice lacked conviction.

"I don't know," Chug said. "I don't know if the police even

have the autopsy results yet."

Prosky's eyes darted about the carpeting as if desperately looking for something he'd lost. "I must've misunderstood," he said at last, very quietly.

"Lacey told you she was pregnant?"

"No. Uh, no, of course not. It was the letter. This goddamned letter! That's all."

But Chug knew he was lying. Of course! A maneuver like that was pure Lacey. She mightn't be all that smart, but she was cunning! It would give her a couple of months of power over the principal, especially if she said she didn't want to abort the child. Then she could just come back from Christmas vacation and tell him she'd gotten rid of it. She'd done it for him. Which meant she'd have even more power over him.

Come to think of it, he realized Prosky now had a motive for killing her. Well, some of the police might see it that way despite the 7-Eleven alibi. But he knew Prosky hadn't killed her. He wasn't the kind of guy who'd do something like that himself. Though he must have seen her death as a reprieve from the emotional blackmail she'd been putting him through.

That's when the other thought, that mental checkmark with its accompanying realization, popped into Chug's head. And he knew the answers before he even started asking the next question.

"That week you told me you spent with Lacey, when your wife was gone. How was Lacey able to get away like that? I mean, her parents seemed the type who'd want to know where she was for a week."

"I don't remember what excuse she used," he said rapidly. But Prosky didn't realize that his earlier mention of this had not included the fact that a week had been the amount of time he'd spent with her. Gotcha, you bastard.

"Maybe she said she was staying with a friend," he said.

"You don't remember? It was only this past summer, a few months ago. How could you forget something like that so fast?"

"I don't know."

"Lacey's mother told Sergeant Cusack that Lacey had attended a student government conference for a week in July at Brown University. That couldn't have been the same week, could it?"

"I . . . I don't really remember. It might have been."

"I'll bet it might. Funny, though, that the McGoverns would let their daughter leave home for a week on just her word alone. Yet Sergeant Cusack says there's nothing about any such conference in the registrar's office. So how were her parents convinced?"

"Oh, that's right," Prosky said, brows lifted at the memory. "I sent them a letter. On official stationery. Explaining the selection and congratulating them on Lacey's being chosen."

If he thought saying it fast would gloss over the ramifications, he was dead wrong. Chug knew this was Prosky's fourth year at the school. During his first year as principal, wanting to make a good impression, he must have gone to as many student events as he could fit in. Including one with a freshman playing the part of Rapunzel in a long, comic blonde wig. But three years later, that freshman had told him she was pregnant, goddamn it! Chug now realized that when the police gave Prosky the killer's letter to read, he had immediately understood its references to the week in Providence and had made the quick connection to the blonde fourteen-year-old. Then, later that same day, he'd had quick sex with her one last time, had watched her drive away, making sure no one was following her, and he had never whispered even a word of warning. To her or to anyone else.

Prosky looked up from the carpeting to meet Chug's disgusted gaze, saw that Chug understood exactly what he'd done and why. The principal's gaze shifted back to the floor without any change of expression.

"You son of a bitch. You dirty bastard." Chug slid from the stool, walked over to the stairs, and left.

By the time Chug told Miranda about his meeting with Prosky, the principal had already called her, pretending he'd just gotten the note in the mail that day. Later, when she spoke to Prosky again and brought up the possibility that he'd known Lacey would be the blonde victim in that note, he denied everything. He claimed that Chug had misunderstood him during their rec-room conversation, that he'd never had any inappropriate contact with any of his students, that there wasn't an iota of proof against him, and that he'd sue everyone in sight if anyone had the audacity to suggest otherwise.

After speaking to Lacey's parents about the week at Brown and later discussing it with Cassidy, Miranda was told to back off. The autopsy had determined Lacey was not pregnant, there had been no usable cause to check for sperm, much less DNA. She double-checked Prosky's alibi for the time of the murder and it held up, and there was no proof except Chug's testimony to charge him with statutory rape or, at best, depraved indifference in the girl's death. But Miranda assured Chug that, when they found the killer, with everything he—or she—seemed to know about Lacey's affairs, then that might provide them with enough evidence to go after Prosky, possibly on both charges. Chug didn't mention it, but he was pleased that she so confidently had referred to "when" they caught the killer.

And Prosky was back in school the next day, all flu symptoms gone, not a pants crease or an emotion out of place. He did, however, tend to avoid all eye contact with Chug, whose copy of the killer's note to Prosky arrived, as promised, right on time.

# Chapter Sixteen

Getting more information on the killer, however, proved elusive for the task force. October trudged into November, and still there was nothing new, though Miranda dedicated all her days and big chunks of her nights to the case.

Chug's days were also long, between preparing for and teaching his classes and working on his book. And the book was clearly taking on a direction all its own, more and more about the two deaths rather than a typical year in a typical suburban high school. Jeremy, his agent, had called to say he'd spoken to Alice Bainbridge, his editor, who had called to make sure Chug was following up on Lacey's murder.

Chug couldn't tell Jeremy that there were actually *two* murders, both the work of the same person. And he couldn't mention just how entangled he'd become in the web of events.

"I'm working on it, Jeremy," he said. "I'm getting as much information as I can."

"I see that murder as your book's centerpiece."

"Right."

But Chug had no real sense of where the hell he was going with the book. He knew what Alice and Jeremy wanted, but they didn't know there was someone else who also wanted to influence his writing. He often had the chilly sense of a pair of eyes looking over his shoulder as he sat at his computer, eyes that checked everything he wrote and, though he resisted, kept trying to guide his thoughts.

At least he managed to break away from the book to spend some of those late nights and parts of the weekends with Miranda. And, when she met Sarah and Jason, they got along so well that Miranda also became a semi-regular part of their Sundays. And she was a big hit with his family, which included all the aunts, uncles, and cousins, at his mother's Thanksgiving gorge-out.

December began a little warmer than normal, deceptively so, but it had settled into some steady cold by the time Chug drove into school on a Friday, a week before Christmas. He was early, as usual, and, as usual, Traynor had beat him in, the red Cherokee with the ski area decals parked in its *Assistant Principal Traynor* spot in front of the school. There was another car parked around back, in the first row reserved for teachers. He knew that one, too, because of the "Sparks" vanity plate. Bill Sparkman, a gym teacher, had led the Prescott Panthers to the Division Three state finals fifteen years ago. He'd gone on to a so-so Division Two college career sidetracked by a fondness for beer that kept his grades down and ballooned his weight into the upper two-hundreds on a six-five frame. A few years out of college he found religion, quit drinking, and became a pretty good high-school gym teacher and coach.

Right now, though, it looked as if he'd swapped his religion for alcohol again because, as Chug was turning off his ignition, the locker room door slammed open and Sparkman came lurching out. He turned to some bushes growing near the door, bent over, and began vomiting monumentally into the shrubbery.

Chug sat in his truck wondering what to do. Confronting him didn't seem to be a good idea. What the hell could he say to Sparkman? Over the years Chug had hung out with enough drunks to know there were no philosophies that work when they're still bouncing from having fallen off the wagon. Didn't want to walk Sparkman down to the office and turn him in to Traynor. Wouldn't be right to ignore him either, since the students would be here soon. So he sat there uncertainly while the gym teacher continued to retch on the rhododendrons.

After a while Sparkman stopped, looked up and around, and his face seemed taut with . . . fear? Chug thought it sure as hell looked like fear. And it was stretched across his face before he saw Chug sitting in his truck. In fact, when Sparkman saw Chug, he beckoned eagerly, maybe a little desperately.

Chug was reluctant to respond. Sparkman had turned for one more go-round of regurgitation, and, though his hand came up again in an urgent come-here gesture, he was still bent over when Chug got to his side.

"Uh . . . is there something I can do?"

But Sparkman just pointed at the locker room door and continued shaking his head at the ground and gagging.

"In there? Something in there, Sparks?"

It felt a lot like talking to Lassie.

Sparkman nodded, coughing and choking and still pointing.

Chug didn't know what he meant, didn't know how long it would be until Sparkman could tell him, didn't know what he should do next. There was only one thing he did know. He knew he didn't want to go into that damned locker room.

"Is somebody in there?"

Again, a nod.

"Somebody hurt?"

Now Sparkman's head bobbed as eagerly as someone in his situation could manage.

Damn! One question too many. Now he had to go in.

He reached for the door latch, pushed it down slowly. The small cleat room corridor with its rubber matted floor and wall-hugging wooden benches, was empty and quiet. It smelled familiar, that reassuring mixture of musty dried sweat and sinus-clearing Ben Gay. But he could only see one small section of tiled locker room wall up ahead. Somebody was hurt, though, so he forced himself to walk through the cleat room. At the doorway, he turned into the locker room and got his first clue.

There was a spray of red so dark it was almost brown up ahead on the white-tiled wall. It looked like an abstract design, a cresting wave or the Nike swoosh painted large. Appropriate for a locker room maybe, but not when painted in blood. And this was definitely blood, dried now, but sprayed up there from a deep wound. He turned toward the lockers. There were four rows of them, like a series of short alleys off the main corridor that led to the showers. The color that had produced the wave on the wall continued near the first row, where the green lockers close to the corridor were smeared with more ominous splatters. Blood was everywhere, spread in spots and splotches, and it seemed to form a path along the rows of lockers, with now and again a thicker congealing puddle, as if whatever had been crawling had been struck again and again while trying to drag itself along the floor. The last locker, in the last row, had the dark imprint of a couple of fingers, down near floor level, where the crawler must have reached up in agony. Chug edged along the rows of lockers, listening desperately for some sound of whoever had suffered here. He could see that the bloody trail turned after the last row, in toward the boys' large communal showers. He didn't want to go there, didn't want to turn that corner.

He slowed his breathing, measured it out. No time to find a weapon, the way he had at Lacey's death. And the blood had dried in many places, so he didn't think it had recently been spilled. Then there was Sparkman, who must have seen more than what Chug had encountered so far to turn his stomach so violently. He took a deep breath and turned the corner.

The trail of blood became a path. The path ended at the far

wall, down near the boys' communal shower entrance, where the crawler had gone in a desperate and futile attempt to escape whoever it was that had been hitting him. The victim's legs were buckled under him, socks streaked with blood that spattered and spotted the shoes. Even the shoes' soles and heels were smeared with it. The last of the blows must have come after he'd reached the far wall, because he might have been able to crawl with a left arm half hanging off, and maybe even with his jaw carved open like a badly botched jack-o'-lantern, mouth suspended in gaping horror. But nobody could have kept moving with the side of his head caved in the way Walter Traynor's was, one eye half out and turned down as if it couldn't believe what had happened to the rest of his body. In fact, his head was such a mess that, if it hadn't been for the loafers and bloody white socks, the tightly belted belly hanging out below the ill-fitting shirt wrapped in the blood-smeared checkered sports jacket, Chug never would have known who it was.

The smell here was stronger, more cloying than in the rest of the room, and Chug tried to breathe through his mouth. It looked as if Traynor had been dead for a few hours, the blood coagulated and dried like large and ugly scabs.

There was nothing Chug could do for him, nothing he could do in this place, so he hurried out to the main corridor and down to the office. The students would be showing up soon, and many of them stopped in the locker rooms first to leave things in their gym lockers. Couldn't let that happen.

Down at the front office Irma turned, her smile perky but quickly wiped away when she saw the look on Chug's face as he came through the door.

"Call the police," he said. "Get 'em here quick! Walter Traynor's dead. He's been killed—down in the boys' locker room."

He probably should have said more, but then, through the

front windows, he saw the first of the yellow buses come along the highway and turn in at the junior high. That meant they'd be here as soon as they dropped off the younger kids.

"The principal here?"

She shook her head, her mouth still open.

"Call the police," he repeated, and took off back down the corridor toward the gym and locker room. Had to stop the students from seeing this, seeing Traynor's body. *Jesus Christ, Traynor's body! That poor bastard!*

And this killing was different, much too different. And no note. There'd been no note. Was it somebody else? What the hell kind of nightmare had been unleashed here?

He went out the back doors where a couple of teachers were already gathered around Sparkman, who was sitting against the wall, his head between his legs.

Their faces were lined with shocked disbelief, so Chug assumed that Sparks must have found his voice at last. One woman, a foreign-language teacher, he thought, had begun to open the cleat room door.

"You don't want to go in there," Chug said.

"It's true, then?" She let the door thump closed again. "Walter's been killed?"

Chug nodded, noticed a couple of cars parked back in the student rows, and a few upperclassmen were clustered there, looking toward the teachers and talking quietly, their faces puzzled. Then they started walking toward the building carefully, hesitantly. And those buses would be here any minute.

"Look, we've got to keep the students away from here," Chug said. "We should send the buses around to the front entrance. And somebody should go down to the other end of the corridor to make sure the students don't come up that way to the locker room."

Nobody moved.

"Why don't you two go to the front door, you two go down to the other end of the corridor, and the rest of us will reroute the buses and the kids."

It was arbitrary, but it worked. The woman foreign-language teacher went over to the parking lot and told the students leaving their cars to walk around to the front door. Luckily, they still had four teachers for the buses because the drivers were opening the bus doors as soon as they stopped, and buses four and five places back in line were letting students out. The teachers had to run down to them and herd the students back on, telling the drivers to drop them off at the front doors. Eventually, the drivers further back in line caught on, and the later buses only slowed down momentarily and then followed the others as the teachers waved them around to the front of the building.

Then three Prescott police cruisers came screaming, lights and sirens on full, into the parking lot. The dramatic arrival of the cruisers brought the students who were being dropped off at the front of the building running around to the back, zigzagging between the later buses and the student and teacher cars still coming in to park in back. But there were only a couple of doors to watch, and the teachers at least managed to keep everybody outside, away from the locker room.

A policeman came up to the back doors and asked what the hell was going on just as the doors opened from within and Prosky came barreling out, carrying a bullhorn and ordering everybody to homeroom.

It took a while to clear the area but, eventually, everybody was away from the gym although not quite in homerooms. The bells, still running on their programmed schedule, sounded for homeroom, but the halls were chaotic with groups and rumors, students and teachers alike, all talking at the same time. Chug moved through them without speaking. They'd find out soon enough. As for him, only two thoughts kept going through his head: Why the hell had there been no note this time? And how was Miranda going to take Traynor's death? Over the two months they had been dating, she'd filled him in with bits and pieces of her background, and Walter Traynor was so important to her that Chug had begun to see him through her eyes. He kept meaning to have this long, grateful talk with Walter for doing all he'd done for her, for helping her become the person she was. Now, of course, he'd never get that chance. And she had lost her second father.

Prosky, his voice hoarse, came over the intercom. "Students have one minute to get to homeroom. One minute!"

Amazingly, people rushed to get to their rooms. Apparently, no one wanted to be left alone outside when the bell rang. Chug's freshmen stood around the classroom in defensive knots, as full of guesses as everyone else, talking about the police cars and the cordoned off gymnasium end of the building. The most popular rumor Chug heard, or at least the most hotly defended, was that the police had Lacey's killer trapped in the gym. If only.

Still, he remembered the school had a security system with cameras all over the place. He knew there wouldn't be any actually in the locker rooms, but still the killer's face must have been caught on one of the outside ones.

The intercom was silent as homeroom period stretched out to five, six, ten minutes. Someone must have shut off the bell program. Then Irma's voice came over the intercom. "All students are to remain in homeroom until further notification."

It made sense. They couldn't just send everyone home. It would've been impossible anyway, since the buses right now were out picking up the elementary schoolkids. And they sure as hell couldn't carry on a school day as if nothing had happened. So they waited.

Kept among themselves, Chug's homeroom students seemed mostly befuddled, maybe a little frustrated by a lack of new rumors. They were sitting now, but still clustered around the room in protective circles.

As a reporter Chug had seen a few murder victims before encountering Lacey on that bed. Most of them looked a lot worse than she had. But none of them had suffered the vicious ferocity that had been inflicted on Walter Traynor. It didn't seem possible that the same person could have killed the two of them. But if it had been the same killer—and Chug could only hope that the first one hadn't unleashed a second—then he'd stopped following his own rules. He hadn't announced the murder ahead of time, hadn't even brought the killing to Chug's attention.

Just then the intercom clicked on. Everyone expectantly faced the hum coming from the speaker grill beneath the clock. After a few seconds of hesitation, Prosky tersely announced, "All teachers are instructed to take special care with homeroom attendance today. No locker passes are to be given, no passes of any kind are to be given except in extreme emergency. Any students leaving classrooms must be accompanied by one of the adult monitors in the halls. Students are to remain in their homerooms until further notice."

Chug wanted to find Miranda, try to comfort her if he could, but he couldn't leave these kids alone. And a couple of girls began to seem really alarmed. He spent the next ten minutes reassuring them, while the rest just kept spreading the same rumors, more and more emphatically, as if the stories were some bizarre, accelerated strain of virus.

After a while the room was calmer. A woman he thought might be a library aide appeared at Chug's classroom door and called him over.

"You're supposed to go downstairs and speak to the police,"

she whispered. "I'm supposed to cover your homeroom."

"Just keep them in the room." He was going to add something about keeping them calm, but a closer look at her taut face changed his mind.

Paul Graves and a few other teachers who didn't have homerooms were on duty in the hall. Paul looked as if he wanted to stop Chug, ask him about what was going on, but Chug just shook his head and kept walking. A uniformed policeman with a clipboard was patrolling the far end of the corridor, and when he asked for ID, Chug showed him his driver's license while the man checked for his name on the clipboard. Two more police were downstairs in the main lobby.

Five other teachers waited in the front office, sitting in the chairs normally reserved for students in trouble, students who had to go see Basic Traynor. Sparkman was there, still looking pale, and the woman who was maybe a language teacher, and a couple of other people who had been outside with Chug this morning. He sat in the last seat and waited. One of the teachers told him there were three policemen in different rooms down that corridor taking statements from witnesses.

Just then Irma looked up from the telephone she was holding, frowned, and called, "Mr. O'Malley! You're supposed to go straight to the guidance offices and speak to Sergeant Cusack."

The corridor down past the administrative offices led to a side door into the guidance suite. As Chug opened the door, he saw Miranda sitting at the receptionist's desk. She had her head turned away as he came in. She was speaking to young Officer Harrington, her red-nailed index finger emphatically making each point on the top of the desk where she sat. As much as he liked being near her, Chug wouldn't want to be Harrington. Not right now. The young policeman, who must have regretted his change to the day shift, had been nodding nervously all along and now made a final rapid cluster of "yes sir" nods.

Then he hurried past Chug out of the room.

Miranda turned and her eyes flickered uncertainly over Chug before she said, "Jesus, Matthew. I don't believe this."

"I know. I'm sorry, Miranda."

"Did you see him? Did you see what that bastard *did* to him?"

"I know, I know."

"How could they *do* that to him?" Her voice was hoarse. "I'll get the bastard who did this. I'll *get* him!"

He leaned over the desk, put a hand on her arm, but the warning look in her still-angry eyes held him back.

"I've got to get to work, Matthew. And I need to get your statement. Don't know why it wasn't taken sooner."

He sat in the chair still warm from Harrington.

She sighed, smiled to soften the look she knew he must have seen. "It's just that I can't believe he's gone." Then she told a few more stories about Traynor. How he'd helped her mother find a better job, how he'd helped Miranda when she was in college.

"And it wasn't just me. He was always helping kids. There was always some kid who'd been kicked out of the house staying at Walter's."

"Still?" Chug said.

"Sure. In fact, once I was on the force, Walter would send students to me when he thought I could help. Sometimes I sent them to him. He's something else, Matthew . . . he was really something else."

She had hesitated as the reminder that Walter Traynor had become past tense, gone permanently, struck home again.

"And . . . uh . . . about these kids staying over . . . ," Chug said awkwardly, reluctant to bring up the subject. But Traynor sounded like a textbook case.

"No, Matthew. It wasn't like that at all. And, believe me, if anybody'd know, it'd be me. I wasn't exaggerating when I said I practically lived there."

"It's not him, Miranda, it's just—you say there were teens staying at his place, boys and girls hanging out there. There's the virulence of his death. And, it doesn't seem connected in any way to the other killings. So much more violent. No note sent to me ahead of time."

"No note?"

He shook his head.

"Well, if it was some kid he tried to help who did this, then it wasn't because of anything Walter did wrong. You can count on it. He was . . . I don't know how to put this, but I know what people can do to each other, and to children. And when I first began studying psychology in college, I thought a lot about Walter, wondering what drove him. Then I finally smartened up enough to accept what he was . . . very simply, a good man. Kind to others, caring, trying to do the right thing. And it didn't matter why. Walter Traynor was the most moral person I've ever known."

She opened her notebook, flipped through a few pages, then asked again, "No note?"

"None."

"Nowhere? You check your mailbox at home this morning?"

"No, but mail isn't delivered out there until mid-afternoon. I looked in my mailbox here, all through my desk during homeroom. I would've passed anything on to you right away."

"Jesus."

"The school's security cameras pick up the killer?"

"I've got somebody checking them. Nothing yet, but there's got to be something. One of the outside cameras. Something. Hell, I don't know whether I'm more afraid that it's the same person or that it isn't."

"Your psychologist friend didn't predict this level of violence, did he?"

"Matthew, this is a quantum leap beyond what he suggested might happen. And no note, no game-playing with you. Uh-uh, this has to be somebody else. When Cassidy saw . . . what had happened to Walter, first thing he said was, 'Christ, now we've got two psychos. And this one's worse.' "

"I think he's right."

Her small recorder trembled slightly in her hand as she placed it on the desk to take his statement. Her voice, however, was steady as she asked questions.

"You were the second person to see the body?"

"Right. Ordinarily, I'm one of the first ones to get here in the morning, usually before Sparkman. But the thing is, I never go into the locker room. So there's no way I'd have even known the body was in there. Sparkman's got a key to the locker room, of course, but if he hadn't been early, and I hadn't seen him outside, I would've walked right past the room."

She sighed, shaking her head as he described what he'd seen in there.

After she finished the recording, he said, "It looked like it happened a few hours ago."

"We won't know for sure for a while yet. I checked the patrols. One of our officers said he saw Walter's Jeep parked out front of the building around nine, and another guy saw it when he swung by at one a.m. The light was on in his office, they both said, but that's nothing new for him so they didn't check it out. It wouldn't be the first night he worked late here and slept on the cot in the nurse's office. There's a shower in there, too, and I think he kept extra clothes in his office. 'Course, the way he dressed . . . ," she said with a small, sad puff of laughter, and let the thought slide.

"Was anybody else around?"

"Not that we know." She turned back a couple of pages. "There's a maintenance crew that works until eight thirty. After that, no one was supposed to be in the building. It's unusual, too. Most nights this time of year there are people here later, what with basketball games, play and orchestra rehearsals, school committee meetings and adult-ed classes. Last night was just one of those empty spots in the schedule."

She shook her head and muttered, "Poor Walter. Poor, good, sweet Walter."

After another minute or two of looking at her notebook, she stood. "I'd better check in with Sergeant Cassidy."

As they stood, he held her arm. "I'm sorry, Miranda."

She nodded, smiled, and reached up to kiss him on the cheek. "Thanks, Matthew." She breathed deeply, let it out slowly, and opened the door. They walked the short corridor.

The main office had seemed busy earlier, but now it had shifted all the way across the spectrum to near-chaos: parents, police, students, teachers, all milling and asking questions at the same time. But there was no one to ask except each other.

"Where's the chief?" Miranda asked Robidoux who was leaning against the counter, thick arms crossed, head lowered, his eyes narrowly scanning the milling mob. He shrugged, said he thought he was in the principal's office.

Then, as if responding to a command, Prosky came out of his office with Dr. Mackey, the superintendent, and Chief Everly. When they saw the broiling masses, the superintendent took a step back, and even the chief seemed to be looking around for a SWAT team. Prosky looked more disgruntled than alarmed. He turned back into his office and came out with his bullhorn.

"May I have your attention, please?" he said into the horn. "May I have your attention?"

After a few seconds, things got fairly quiet.

"In the face of the tragedy that has struck the school, we have decided to take some unusual steps. I'm going to announce over the intercom that students and teachers are to report to the gymnasium. We'll explain everything there. Parents who've come for their sons and daughters should sign the names of their children on a list we'll place on the counter. Be sure to show photo identification when you sign. You should remain here. Once I've spoken to the student body in the gymnasium, the students on the list will be sent down here. We've decided to keep the rest of the students in the building. Although there won't be any classes today, releasing them is probably not in their best interests, especially since many working parents will not be aware of our tragedy. We've made arrangements for trained counselors to come in to help them deal with the terrible situation. Also, Dr. Mackey has decided that the high school and all the schools in town will be closed for Christmas vacation starting at the end of the day."

Once everyone was assembled in the gym, the students sitting in nervous silence, the staff scattered around, Prosky slowly and carefully explained to the assembly that Walter Traynor had been killed. Although he didn't go into details, as the principal's message sank in, a growing gasp began to spread like a ballpark wave through the students in the stands. This wasn't the Parkhurst boy whose death they still thought had been a suicide, or even Lacey, who'd been killed away from the school. This was everyone's favorite eccentric uncle, an adult that many of their parents had remembered fondly from their own days at the school, the assistant principal, the legendary "Basic" Traynor. It was as if a curtain of safety held in place between the students and the world's mayhem had suddenly been torn down and exposed as something temporary and fragile. There were a few scattered screams, and sobbing broke out in little clusters of students. It never really spread to everyone, but the combination of loss and fear were potent, palpable.

The whole day felt like an extended wake, heavy with sorrow and small pockets of subdued conversation. During lunch period, when Chug had cafeteria duty, he could see the reporters through the large wall of windows, as they circled the parking lots, beyond the patrolling police. Television cameramen roamed out there, lenses trained on the building, on the police, on the reporters doing stand-ups, and Channel 23's "Action Chopper 23" hovered over the school.

The students were released to their buses at the regular time and police were at all of the exits. But out in the back lot, where the seniors parked their cars, television crews were waiting. After the buses had left, Chug waited until the seniors went out to their cars where clusters, as if by magnetic attraction, formed around the reporters.

Head down, Chug walked quickly to his truck in the front row. He slipped into it and left the lot. Although his thoughts were light years away from peace on earth and good will to man, it seemed that Christmas vacation had begun.

As he drove down toward Lake Metacom, Chug's head felt spiderwebbed with theories he'd been trying out, hoping to reconcile what had happened to Walter with what had happened to the two students. Still, he opened his mailbox with trepidation. Nope, two catalogs and two bills. But right next to the mailbox was a *Boston Globe* newspaper tube, left there from the last owner of the cabin. And inside the tube was an envelope, a business envelope, no return address, no stamp or postmark, just his name printed dead center in a now chillingly familiar font.

He carried it in on top of the rest of his mail and placed it on the table. He knew he should contact Cassidy and wait for him before opening it. But he also knew, as he took out his small penknife, that it wouldn't make any difference. But just in case, he held the envelope down with an elbow and slit the top, slid out the folded letter with the tip of the knife and opened it with the same tip.

The letter writer must have known that the *Globe* was delivered to the subscribers down here around six each morning. Since there was a tube next to Chug's mailbox, the killer must've thought he was one of the subscribers, that he'd find the envelope when he got his morning paper. First thing he'd gotten wrong about Chug so far.

*Hey, Chug-Chug! Got a little surprise for you in the boys locker room at the school. Stop in for a look-see. The display's a little basic, but I think it was a bloody good try. Hey, aren't you from that city that's famous for Lizzy Borden? If I could, I'd leave you a token of what's to come, Chug-Chug, but I can't. I'm the pledge. Next time you hear from me, I'll be sure to pay for a stamp. This time I was in a big hurry, chop-chop, you know?*

Well, that settled the copycat psycho question. There was only one killer, but this one had gone completely out of control.

# Chapter Seventeen

Chug was about to call Miranda when his phone rang. Jeremy, his agent.

"I've been watching your school on the news. Live," he said. "How are you?"

"I'm okay."

"This thing's really exploding, isn't it?"

"Looks that way." Especially if Jeremy was watching it live in New York.

"This changes everything. But you know that."

"Right." Actually he'd been too concerned about the murder itself to really consider any effect it might have on his project. But he couldn't tell Jeremy that without going into his close connection to the case.

"Alice may want your book to be a stand-alone now," Jeremy said, "and not part of that series. I'm going to talk to her about it."

"Fine."

"What can you give me on that?"

"I don't know. I'll think about it, e-mail you some ideas a little later."

"It will mean more money."

"That's good." He had to strain to sound enthusiastic.

"Did you know the guy, the victim?"

"A little. He was a good man."

Jeremy offered condolences, then told Chug he'd wait for the e-mail before talking to Alice, but they needed to be quick about it.

After hanging up, Chug called Miranda, explained about the note and told her he'd bring it in. Before he left, though, he used the cell to take a picture of the note. Ultimately, the killer would get what he wanted. The notes would all appear in a book, and the book would be about the killer. And Chug would be the one who wrote this goddamn book, whether he wanted to or not.

The medical examiner's office didn't release the body for a couple of days but, in keeping with his wishes, Walter Traynor was cremated. Also, following the specific requests of his will, the only people invited to the cremation ceremony were his brother and his brother's family, Dorothy Bramwell, who was the mahogany-haired woman Chug had seen with him at Lacey's wake, and Miranda. A memorial service was scheduled for the last Saturday of the Christmas vacation.

Chug had been looking forward to the vacation as a time to spend with Miranda and to do some concentrated work on the book. The latest murder had changed all that. Miranda spent almost all of her waking time working on the case. Two of the school's security cameras had been spray painted by someone who knew how to sneak up on them, and the other cameras had nothing on them, no one coming or going until Sparks entered the building in the morning. So Miranda went over every word that every investigator had written down, interviewing people a second and third time. When Chug was with her, he found himself trying to reassure her that the killer would be found. But each time he saw her, she seemed a little less sure of herself. Or maybe just a little closer to despair.

As for working on his book, that now meant developing a section on Traynor, how he had lived and how he had died.

Miranda had told Chug a lot about him, and he could get more details from her later, when she'd had more time to deal with her pain. But he also wanted other people's impressions. He began on Monday by calling Art Davis, the guidance counselor, since it had been apparent at Lacey's wake that he had been a friend of Traynor. But Davis apologized, explaining that he and his wife were leaving in an hour to spend the two-week break in Florida.

"Paid for the condo months ago," he explained. "Even though we've got a coupla extra days, I don't think we'll enjoy it much. We'll be back for the memorial service, though. Get in touch with me then."

"You know anyone else who'd be good to speak to?" Chug said.

"Well, there's Dorothy, of course. She and Basic've been together—oh, must be ten, twelve years."

"Maybe I'll get to her a little later."

He had never felt comfortable as a reporter probing somebody's bleeding wound, all the while asking them how much it hurt.

"Let's see," Art said. "Hey, there's Bill Carstairs, the guy you're subbing for? Hell, he knew Basic about as well as anybody. You must've met him already, to talk about your classes."

"No, never got around to it."

"Oh . . . Well, if you're writing about the school, then Bill's somebody you really should talk to. He's an interesting guy. Though I'm not too sure why he took this year off."

Couldn't blame Davis for being surprised he hadn't already spoken to Carstairs. Chug had thought about it from the day he'd accepted the job, but he just hadn't wanted someone else's impression of the students before he'd formed his own.

He called the number Art Davis had given him. Carstairs's

voice was dry, nasally, the tone impatient but, after Chug explained who he was and what he was writing, his tone became more agreeable.

Carstairs lived near the border with Bradford, halfway down a tree-lined street of midsized homes that looked pretty much the same except for one thing: it was dark when Chug arrived and Carstairs's house, a cedar-sided gambrel, had no Christmas lights. Every other house on the street had decorations inside, outside, on the roofs and on the shrubs. Carstairs didn't even have a candle in a window. The man who opened the door to Chug's knock didn't look much like Scrooge. He was average height, with a wiry frame, in his early fifties, his hair dark-brown sprinkled with gray. His brows were Dickensian though, dark and bushy, and beneath them were large and watery, brown hound eyes that didn't seem very happy to see Chug, though he shook hands and held the door open.

Chug followed him into a large living room and sat on the couch Carstairs waved at while the owner settled gingerly on one of the chairs, wincing as if the effort had pained him.

"It's very hard to believe this happened," he said. "Or that he's gone. And the way it happened. Did you get to know Walter?"

"No, not really. Just spoke to him a couple of times."

"He was a good man." He glared at Chug as if his answer had been both inadequate and impertinent.

"That's what I've heard."

"I knew Walter Traynor for twenty-five years. I can't understand why anyone would want to so much as look askance at him, never mind do what that psychopath did."

Chug nodded, sat back and, for the first time, took a look around the room. It wasn't as large as his first impression, though their voices seemed to echo. Probably because the room was nearly empty. There was the beige couch he was sitting on and two matching chairs on a tan carpet. That was it. No television, coffee table or end tables. Nothing on the walls either. No photos, hangings, paintings, mirrors, or anything else. Just the lighter silhouettes of where things had been. The carpet had darker patches of original color, the ghost shadow of what might have been an entertainment center directly opposite the couch, and in a corner a circle that had probably been left by the round base of a standing lamp. Even these markers were fading as if the furnishings had been gone for a while.

The only color in the room came from thick rust-colored curtains covering the windows, but their function seemed more to keep out the neighbors' Christmas lights than to add anything positive to this man's world.

"I'm divesting myself," Carstairs said quietly, apparently responding to Chug's appraisal.

Since he didn't know what the hell Carstairs meant, Chug just nodded.

"That was terrible news, those other two students," Carstairs said. "I didn't know the boy, but everybody knew Lacey."

Then, as if to show he also knew her personality, he shook his head again and added, "Still, she was only a child, just a child."

"She was in this year's AP class."

"Really? Lacey? Now that's a surprise. I never taught her, but I knew her from study halls. And she was a member of the ski club, of course. But she never did seem to be the advanced placement type."

"Ski club?"

"Sure. In fact, her parents and some of their friends owned lodges near Loon Mountain large enough for the whole club to use for a couple of weekends each winter."

"Were you connected to the club?"

"Indirectly. I chaperoned a few trips. Walter roped me in. He was the ski club advisor."

"Walter? Walter Traynor?"

"Sure."

"Really?" Chug had to think about that. Traynor on a ski slope. Though Miranda had told Chug she was looking forward to teaching him how to ski, she hadn't mentioned that Traynor skied. Apparently, he hadn't bought his Cherokee with the mountain stickers already on it. Chug couldn't help picturing him in a loud, checkered ski parka and down-at-the-heel boots, smiling cheerily as he gulped in mountain air.

His thoughts must've been showing though, because Carstairs said, "Walter was a very good skier, Mr. O'Malley. You'd be surprised."

"Did they get along? Walter and Lacey?"

"Walter treated her the way he treated everyone. With care and respect. I don't believe their relationship had any other element to it, if that's what you mean."

"I didn't mean anything," Chug said, lying with as straight a face as he could manage. "I just wanted to know if there was any way to tie the two victims together."

Since the Parkhurst boy had transferred to the school last spring, it wasn't likely he'd had anything to do with the ski club, but this was the first time Chug had heard of any connection between Lacey and Traynor.

"Thirty, forty, sometimes fifty students would go on those ski club weekends," Carstairs said. "And there'd be a half dozen adults—parents, faculty chaperones. Paul Graves, Wendy Johnson, Art Davis, myself early on. We always made sure the students behaved and, believe me, Walter wouldn't even let the parent chaperones drink on school-sponsored trips, never mind the students. Adults couldn't even have wine with their meals, couldn't smoke. So there was nothing else going on, if that's what your look means."

"No. I was just surprised that so many faculty members would be willing to go out of their way like that. I mean, a whole weekend."

"Skiing is expensive, Mr. O'Malley, and teacher salaries are still a joke. Faculty chaperones got free lift tickets; spouses did too, if enough students went. We took a lot of day trips, which meant the only thing the chaperones had to pay for was their meals. And later, when they stayed overnight at the parent condos, the lodging was free too."

"Did Dr. Prosky ever go along on any of the trips?"

He frowned, shook his head. "I'm sure you're not here to talk about ski weekends. What else did you want to know about Walter for your book?"

"Can you remember any specific anecdotes about him, stories that'd highlight his personality?"

Carstairs thought for a while, tapping his fingers on his knees. After a couple of minutes, Chug thought he'd forgotten the question, maybe even forgotten he was there, but when Carstairs finally looked up, he shook his head.

"I can't think of a single damned one, Mr. O'Malley. Isn't that funny now? Twenty-five years I knew that man and . . ." He shook his head again, looked past Chug, his eyes focusing, and Chug half turned, expecting to see someone out in the kitchen. But there was no one there and, from what he could see, that room was as stripped down as this one.

"If you want to talk about those classes of mine you've got, I can't be too much help either," he said. "I hadn't taught senior English before. And I've never taught an AP class."

"Well, that's not why I'm here anyway."

"Of course, that didn't make any difference to Dr. Prosky."

"You mean he assigned you the classes that I'm teaching now?"

Carstairs nodded his head, his lips turned down.

"And this was—what? Some kind of punishment?"

"Dr. Prosky is a miserable son of a bitch."

*More than you know,* Chug thought.

"Did those classes have anything to do with your taking a leave of absence?" he said, cautiously, feeling that he was probing a sensitive area.

Carstairs cocked his head to the side, like a dog suddenly hearing something outside of human range. Those brown hound eyes narrowed as he turned back to Chug, before he spoke.

"I remember you from the newspaper. You used to write a lot of stories about eccentrics, character pieces on the human flotsam drifting around Boston."

"I sometimes wrote about people I met," Chug said. "But I never considered the people flotsam, and I don't think I wrote about them that way. I asked you about taking the year off because I need to ask a lot of questions to write a book. It doesn't mean I'm looking for anything in particular, or that I'm trying to work an angle. And you can refuse to answer any question I ask. No hard feelings."

He absorbed that, nodding his head, though Chug had no idea whether or not he agreed with anything he had said.

"I'm not sick, you know," Carstairs said quickly. "That's not why I'm taking the time off."

They were both quiet for a while longer. Carstairs had his fingers laced together, his head bowed toward the carpeting. "And it wasn't just concern about teaching all new classes after I'd been at Prescott for twenty-five years."

Chug waited some more.

"Are you having any problems with your students?" Carstairs said, looking up at last.

"Some."

He nodded, satisfied. "I thought that you might be. I've needed to get away from the school for a while, but knowing I'd have the same students again this year was the last straw. The messages definitely didn't help, I'll tell you that."

"Messages?" Chug tried to restrain the sudden rush of anticipation, hoping Carstairs's messages weren't warnings written on the clouds or whispered in his ear as he slept.

"There were a couple of practical jokes earlier in the year," Carstairs began. "Nothing too serious. Once I got a manila envelope filled—well, I'm not much of a naturalist, you know. I suppose the envelope's contents could've been dropped from the back end of a horse, but I suspect it was intended to be bullshit."

He snorted, added, "After full consideration, that wasn't really a bad one. There was a label on the envelope as if it were a research paper prepared for me and, of course, I've read more than my share of legitimate papers that smelled much worse."

Chug thought about his own little excremental doorstep delivery.

"Later there were less pleasant surprises. A dead rat was mailed to me. And there was a garter snake, very much alive, I might add, left in my desk drawer in school. But then, sometime later, the messages began, and they really began to bother me. They were perverse, twisted notes, disgusting and mean-spirited."

"Do you still have any of them?" Chug asked, his voice a little wobbly with growing excitement. But Carstairs was already shaking his head and a shudder rippled through his shoulders.

"Many of them were threats. Obscene, bizarre threats. They'd show up in my mailbox at school, on my desk in my classroom, mailed to me here. Terrible. Terrible things."

"Were they handwritten?"

"No, none of them. This writer was much too smart for that. They were computer printed."

"What was the style?"

"I'd describe it as manic, over the edge, a little like Poe on a very bad day, with a *Tell-Tale Heart* narrator kind of voice? Sometimes it felt as if some madman in a bar had just grabbed my sleeve, and I knew my night was going to be ruined unless I could get out immediately. But there was no getting away from them."

Chug nodded. He knew, he knew. Both the notes and the whack jobs in the bars.

"How did he address you in the notes? Teacher? Mr. Carstairs? Hey, you?"

Carstairs turned his head to the side, aimed one narrowed eye at Chug. "So, you've been getting some too. Is that your real reason for coming to see me?"

"Maybe one of them."

"I suspected as much. It's too much of a coincidence that you should ask about the way he addressed me. I think that bothered me almost as much as anything else about the whole deplorable situation. He addressed me as Willy-Willy. My name's William, and no one's ever called me anything but Bill or Billy when I was a kid. That Willy-Willy reference began to get to me after a while. Guess you could say it gave me the willies, no?"

Chug smiled, though Carstairs seemed to still have no idea how far beyond the threats the writer had gone.

"Any letters since you retired?"

Carstairs shook his head. "What does he call you?"

"Chug-Chug."

"Hmmph," he snorted, apparently deciding Willy-Willy hadn't been so bad after all.

"Any special reason you think a student did this and not somebody else on the staff?"

Again, Carstairs gave Chug a look that made him feel as if he were definitely going to fail this class.

"No one on the staff would do that to me," he said, slowly and precisely.

There was something else there, something unspoken, but Chug's gut reaction was to not pursue it.

"Was there anything in the notes that *had* to be from a student, maybe even from a student in a particular class? A reference to something that had happened in one of your classes, an assignment you'd given, an argument you had with a student, something somebody said? Anything like that you can remember?"

Carstairs was shaking his head. And he didn't have the notes. Jesus, most of the teachers Chug knew saved everything they'd ever put their hands on. And half of them had it organized alphabetically. But you couldn't really expect a man who seemed to have cleared every lamp, picture, and mirror out of his house to keep some nasty notes.

"If I had to narrow it down," Carstairs said, "it would be the eleventh-grade honors students, the ones in your advanced placement class this year. But that's just a feeling. There was no one thing I could put my finger on, even when I was receiving the notes. But . . . well, whoever was sending them was fairly bright. I don't think it could be many of the other students."

"Did you have any special problems with the kids in that class? Confrontations? That kind of thing?"

"Well, there's Brandon Wainwright and his friends, of course. I'm sure that you've already found out what a flaming boil on your backside old Brand can be. He was my prime suspect for most of the earlier pranks. But the notes, well, I just wasn't too sure about those. And I could never prove anything, anyway."

Chug nodded. He shared Carstairs's doubts about Brandon. Something just didn't jibe. The style of the crimes and even of the notes, that manic insistence that just didn't seem to fit Wainwright. Someone just doesn't go from taking careful, long-distance shots meant to scare the target to slaughtering Walter Traynor that way. At least not in a couple of months.

He couldn't think of anything else to ask Carstairs, and both the man and his echoing house were starting to get to him. Come to think of it, this was a helluva big house for one person. But he didn't want to go there, so he thanked Carstairs and got up to leave.

"Thank you for coming over," Carstairs said, almost as if he'd tendered the invitation, and Chug had been doing him a favor. "I don't get many visitors anymore. It's ironic, since this house used to be fairly lively. I was a popular teacher and . . ."

Carstairs looked around at the bare living room, and Chug thought he saw a shudder ripple through whatever he'd left unsaid. The man seemed to become aware for the first time just how empty his house was.

"I remember an old English professor I had in college," Carstairs said. "He invited a group of us who worked on the school newspaper over to a meal one night. After the meal, he began telling this long, extremely convoluted story about a rare bird he'd once seen in Brazil back when he was young. And we, well, college kids were polite back then, so we listened respectfully, while his old wife kept pshawing at him, and saying, 'Now, now, Marvin. Not that story.' But he kept telling it anyway about his tracking down this rare Brazilian bird that had a peculiar flight pattern. It seems that it flew in smaller and smaller circles. Then he kind of caught us off guard, fixing us with one of those wild old-man stares, and he said, 'Guess what happened to it finally?' And we, well, we just shrugged our shoulders, politely. 'Flew up his own ass!' he said and started cackling like a crackpot. His wife slapped him on the shoulder, but you could see she enjoyed the way the old man was having a little fun at our expense."

Chug stood at the door. Carstairs had a very small, very

painful smile on his face, as he looked at the empty walls of his house, and then stared out at the festive, blinking and winking neighboring houses.

"I always thought that was just a joke," he said, shaking his head and wincing one last time.

"So that's it?" Miranda said. "He thinks it might have been a student in his eleventh-grade honors class who sent him the notes, but he doesn't know why? And he didn't keep any of the notes."

Chug nodded, watching the disappointment spreading slowly from her eyes to her down-turning lips. But then with a quick twist of her jaw she flicked it off, as if it were a live thing that she didn't want hovering around her.

"Even the suspicion's just a feeling," he added. "Nothing tangible. And this from a man who doesn't seem all that tangible himself."

"He used to be tangible, you know." Her smile echoed the sadness that had been in her eyes when Chug had described the man's house and his "divesting" explanation.

"He was one of your teachers?"

"Sure was. A good one, too."

"What happened? I mean, it couldn't've been just the letters or Prosky forcing him to teach the same students again. Though that would probably mean more of those letters."

"No, no. About eight years ago, he was driving his family home from Cape Cod, late at night. He fell asleep at the wheel, crossed the median and was broadsided by a truck. He got a broken wrist. His wife had a concussion. But their two kids, eight and ten years old, were killed."

"Jesus."

"Yeah. Jesus. He was never really the same after that. His wife . . . she took her life a year later."

So that's what Carstairs had meant about no one on the staff sending him the letters. But students might not know his history, or even care. After all, if they were seventeen, the accident had happened when they were nine, a lifetime ago.

"I wish I'd known that before I'd gone to see him."

"I'd have told you."

Chug thought she was tempted to add, *If you'd asked me, you big jerk-off.*

"So what happens now?" he said.

"I don't know. The fact that he got those notes helps. No doubt about that. I'll give the information to Sergeant Cassidy. He may want to see you about it too, I don't know. And I'll ask him about my talking to Mr. Carstairs. See if I can get anything else."

She sat back, rubbed her eyes. "Chief wants to take me off the case," she said finally, flatly. It was a statement with defeat in it, but delivered rationally, as if she had said, I think this car just ran out of gas.

"He thinks you're too personally involved, because of Walter?"

"That's what he says. I don't know, Matthew. It feels more like something else."

"He thinks you can't do it?"

"Something like that."

He could see her problem. Chief Everly had included Miranda at all the press conferences, had deferred questions to her. Even Cassidy had given her nearly equal response time. The media, of course, had loved her: attractive, articulate, confident. If she were taken off the case now, no matter what reason was given, it would clearly be seen as a failure on her part. The media would think that she was the reason the case, that now included three dead people, wasn't getting anywhere. She was definitely in a jam.

A writer friend of Chug's had once inadvertently found media fame by having an affair with a senator's wife, an indiscretion which came out during the senator's messy divorce. After the smoke had finally cleared, the writer told Chug that the red lights on the TV news cameras trained on him had reminded him of the eyes of wolves closing in on a Russian troika. As seen by the person about to be heaved out into the snow.

No, Chief Everly's paternal bulk wouldn't end up bouncing over the sleigh ruts. Nor would sturdy Robidoux's or Cassidy's lanky gray-haired height. If there was another killing, or if they didn't solve the crimes very soon, then Miranda Cusack was going to be the first one served up as the media's breakfast. No two ways about it.

# Chapter Eighteen

Since Carstairs's hunch was just about all he had left to go on, Chug stared at his five class rosters for over an hour, most of the time spent on the fifteen names on the AP list. As much as he wanted to eliminate at least some names, he couldn't. They were all possibilities. The sweetest girl. The shyest boy. His early years of interviewing teary-eyed, hoarse, sincere people who kept insisting, "Oh, no! He/she could never do something like that!" while all the time that was exactly what he/she had done had left Chug with the cynical belief that, given the right set of circumstances, almost anyone could do almost anything.

And though Carstairs was sure it hadn't been a staff member, he didn't know that the letter writer was the same person who had later gone on to murder three people. Someone who could do that could certainly have been cruel enough to start out by playing head games with Carstairs's fragile psyche. So the killer could just as well be any one of the adults on the police's extensive lists, most of whose names Chug still hadn't connected with faces. Teachers, custodians, secretaries, aides—each as likely as anyone else.

But Carstairs thought it was a student, so Chug looked at his class lists and checked out his bootleg copies of the killer's notes.

Nope, nothing leaping out at him. The diction, the random slipping in and out of slang. The repetition. The repetition. Maybe something there? Something, somehow . . . ? No, too vague. For a second there, he thought he had the edge of an idea, something about repetition, but no. Nothing.

Anything else about the letters, then? Miranda told him that Cassidy had a couple of profilers examine them and the murders, looking for any clues to the writer or his psychological makeup. Mostly they came up with conflicting conclusions, one of them adamant about the writer wanting to reveal himself, to exult in his superiority, while the other was just as sure the killer was determined to keep his identity a secret.

So what, then? What the hell could he hope to do about this? If the content offered no clues, then how about the style? Carstairs had called the letters he had received manic, and that seemed about right. Lots of short questions, both to himself and to Chug or to Prosky. Lots of complex and compound sentences. Few simple declarative sentences. Repetition. Repetition. Again, that thought drew him up short. But he didn't know what to do about it, so he did what came naturally when confused. He went out for a run.

Because he was acutely aware that someone much too interested in him had already killed three people, it was a strange run, marked by more alertness than normal, less cruising along hoping the right side of his brain might come up with a creative solution to a problem while the left side went to sleep. That's why it was such a surprise when the thought "sentence structure" blinked on in his brain like a fluorescent light just turned on in a dark basement. That's what the notes all had—sentence structure. He'd already looked at them from a stylistic angle, but he hadn't thought to look for a pattern.

Although he had only covered about a third of his usual running distance, he turned, and ran back. And though he was sweating, he didn't even try to cool down, just grabbed the letters as soon as he came in the door.

He stared at the letters lined up on his table, his breath still coming in gasps. They were similar lengths, with Prosky's the shortest. He could probably scan the sentence structure of the damn things, like a poem. What the hell, why not?

He grabbed an envelope and used the back to write out the pattern of sentence structure for the first letter, the one about Donald Parkhurst's future suicide. As he had already known, the sentences were mostly interrogative, a few complex and compound, only one simple declarative sentence.

There was just enough room on the envelope to write out the structure of the second. It wasn't exactly the same, but the rhythm of the sentences was: interrogatives, complex and compounds, and, somewhere in the middle, one simple declarative.

Chug didn't have to write out the structure of the third, Prosky's letter. He could see how, basically, it followed the other two, and though the declarative sentence was now at the end, there was something singular about it. Something repetitive. But it wasn't until he got to the fourth and saw the writer had included another declarative sentence that Chug began to sense just what the writer was declaring. Jesus Christ!

"I think I found something in the letters," Chug said, as Miranda stood next to him, staring down at the four pieces of paper lined up on his kitchen table.

He had been a little cryptic on the phone when he asked her to come right over, saying just that he thought he might have something on the case. She turned from the letters to him, one brow arched, but didn't otherwise seem surprised that he had copies of all of them.

"What have you found?"

"I thought I'd need them for the book," he said. "That's why I made copies, some from pictures I took with my cell phone."

"What have you found, Matthew?"

"There's a repeating pattern in their structure. I didn't notice it until I looked at the sentence structure of all four of them. At some point in each message, the killer throws in a straight declarative sentence, a statement aimed at the reader—me or Prosky. See the first one?"

He had it highlighted in yellow.

" 'I am sincere, too,' " she read.

"And the second?"

" 'I am passionate.' "

"And the one to Prosky, here?"

" 'I am serious.' "

"Now the last one."

" 'I'm the pledge.' "

She shook her head, shrugged.

"In the first three," Chug said, "he uses adjectives to describe himself, saying he's sincere, passionate, and serious. Then in the last he uses a noun, saying he's a pledge. The first three are such familiar words and more or less appropriate in context that I didn't really think anything about his choice of words. Not until I started looking at the last reference, calling himself a pledge. That's a stretch for the situation in the note. And it's enigmatic enough to be one of his clues, though I couldn't quite see how it fit Walter's murder. But, then the other declarative statements weren't directly about those incidents either. They were about the writer. So I isolated those sentences, looked just at those words. Y'know, there are any number of synonyms for sincere, passionate and serious, but there's only one word that's both synonymous with those three and also means a sort of token, like the pledge that he refers to in the last letter."

She waited, allowing Chug his dramatic moment.

"Earnest," he said.

"Okaaay," she whispered softly. "And?"

"Look at my AP class list. First name."

"Ernest Abbott! You really think so? It seems a little thin."

"He fits the clues. He knew Lacey. They worked together a lot. And as for smart enough, he's the smartest kid in the school. There was something in the school paper a couple of weeks ago about Ernest being a National Merit scholar and getting early admission to Harvard."

"And you think he's telling us that he's the guy committing each murder?"

"That's what those sentences say. If not him, then someone with the same first name. The first three are obvious synonyms for the word *earnest,* but the last is more obscure. It's a promise you give, a token or a pledge for something to come. So, what he's saying, in each letter, is 'I am earnest.' Have you found anyone else named Ernest in your investigation of the case?"

"No one comes to mind," she said, flipping through her notebook until she found the page she was looking for.

"He has a part-time job, nights five to nine, Monday through Friday. He was on the job at the time of each of the murders."

"He's alibied out for all three of them?"

"No, that's just it, Matthew." Her voice took on an excited edge. "He doesn't have an alibi for the time of the deaths, not really. His job's at . . . Let me see . . . Baines Computers. It's a small place over in Braintree. Ernest checks in at five, when the owner closes, and the boy is alone there until nine, doing repairs on whatever's been brought in. The owner says the kid's some kind of computer genius, he can fix anything. He works alone in the back of the shop. Supposed to leave at nine, but I doubt that there's a time clock or anything, and sometimes he stays later. He's got a key. He could have left on the nights of any of those murders, no problem."

"Wouldn't the owner know if he hadn't been working?"

"I don't think so," she said. "I've talked to so many people about this case that some of them are starting to blur. But I remember Ernest's boss because I thought at the time that, if he really appreciated the kid as much as he said he did, he'd give him a better alibi. The owner says he's got a priority list of repairs, but they're the kinds of jobs that might take three hours or they might take ten minutes. And I got the feeling that a lot of times the owner himself had no clue how long a job might take. I'm sure he lets Ernest work at his own pace."

Chug was nodding, listening, but all the time also thinking about Ernest. *Right, right,* he reminded himself, *almost anybody can do almost anything. My own goddamn motto. But that doesn't mean I can't still be surprised.*

And for these murders, Ernest was a surprise. Not his silences or embarrassments, or intelligence—Chug didn't think those things were important markers in the long run. But a couple of times he had seen the boy being kind when he didn't know anyone was watching and when there was no apparent payoff. 'Course Dr. Jekyll was supposed to have been a helluva nice guy, too.

"I've got to speak to him," Miranda said. "And I'd like you nearby, listening. Looking on, but not so he's aware. You know the boy, and maybe you can pick up on something I miss."

"At the station?"

"Well, since the school's closed, there's really no other place."

"He's a very bright kid. If he did these killings, and you single him out to speak to again, he'll be pretty wary."

"I may be able to find some way to catch him off guard," she said, then graced Chug with a smile warm and seductive enough to convince him he should confess to being on that grassy knoll in Dallas when JFK was shot. Still . . .

"Still, you want to be careful."

"It will be fine, Matthew."

Her eyes now assured him that was all there was to be said about that.

After explaining to Sergeant Cassidy why she thought Ernest needed to be questioned again, Miranda arranged for the interview to take place in a small room at the back of the police station. They had an interrogation room, complete with a one-way mirror, but she didn't want to use it. She was sure the mirror would put Ernest on his guard. The room she led him into had nothing but a table, a few chairs, and a video camera mounted in the corner with a feed to the monitor in another room where Chug sat watching.

It was a cold morning, and Ernest came into the room wearing a parka that looked about right for Antarctica. Tucked under his arm was a large, green bike helmet.

"You look cold," Miranda said. "Can I get you something warm to drink? Some hot chocolate?"

"No, no, I'm fine." But his teeth were chattering slightly. "It's just that my mom and dad both took the cars to work today, so I had to come here on my bike. And it's kind of a long ride. But I'm fine now."

To prove it, he placed the helmet on the table and slipped off his mittens.

"I'm really sorry," Miranda said. "Maybe I could give you a ride home later, if I have enough time before the next interview."

Ernest nodded eagerly and muttered his thanks. Then he sat at the table and looked around the room. He frowned at the lens of the video camera, flushed and grimacing, though both might have been the result of his cold bike ride over.

"Oh, that?" Miranda said, sweetly, following his look. "Nothing to worry about. That's left on all the time."

She waited a few seconds. "Tell you what, Ernest, we don't need it for this interview."

She came up to the camera lens and reached to the side of it. "Let me find the switch. There it is."

Hey, Chug thought, don't do that. But nothing changed on the monitor in front of Chug except perhaps Ernest, who allowed his shoulders to relax. There would have been a red light indicating that the camera was on. Miranda must have shut it off. But she also must have had the camera rigged with a switch that did nothing but turn that red light off. She winked at the lens, knowing Chug was at the monitor, probably even knowing his mouth was still open, before she turned around to the boy. Chug decided that maybe he shouldn't have been so concerned about her after all.

She began by putting Ernest at ease, thanking him for coming in. Then she repeated what she'd told him on the phone, that the police were talking to all of Lacey's classmates again in the hopes that someone might remember something that would connect Lacey to Mr. Traynor. And, of course, since Ernest's last name was Abbott, he was one of the first.

He nodded agreement to everything, gulped a lot, looked uncomfortable. But with Ernest, Chug knew it was always a hard call.

Miranda then said she was sorry if she'd be going over ground that the other officer . . . hmm . . . she looked through a sheaf of papers . . . Ah, yes, Officer Robidoux . . . had covered during the last interview with him, explaining that sometimes it was hard to keep track of everything during a complicated investigation. Chug wondered if Ernest thought she sounded a bit slow, but he also was sure that was just the impression she wanted to give the boy.

Ernest eased up a little more, either because she seemed dim or because of her reassuring touches to his arm as she smiled encouragement. She asked about him, his interests, his grades, even his SAT scores. Though Chug had told her about Ernest's early acceptance at Harvard, she gave him a chance to show off a little by asking him if he'd decided on a college yet. He was visibly loosening, the blush fading, the smile spreading more into a less defensive posture.

She asked about a sophomore English teacher they'd both had and whether she still was such a stickler for never writing *alot* for *a lot* and *alright* for *all right.* Then she shared a couple of me-and-you war stories about her time at the school with teachers who were still there. Carefully avoiding Walter Traynor, Chug noticed. Also avoiding any mention of Carstairs.

For a while there, Ernest seemed to be enjoying himself so much that Chug thought the boy was going to ask her to the prom. Even when she segued seamlessly to discussing the murders, Ernest still seemed agreeable and relaxed.

No, he didn't really know Donald Parkhurst well at all. They'd been in one class together last year, and Donald stayed alone a lot.

"I can understand that," he said. "He was new here. And I like being by myself sometimes. But he didn't seem comfortable on his own, if you know what I mean."

Miranda nodded eagerly, her smile still encouraging and warm. When the subject switched to Lacey, Ernest became even more expansive. He'd known Laccy since his family had moved to Prescott when he was in fourth grade. He had liked her. She worked hard for the class. She was a very good actress.

When Miranda carefully approached the subject of Lacey's reputation, the only outward sign that Ernest knew what she was hinting at was the deepening color in his cheeks and the bobbing of his Adam's apple on his long neck.

"We got along well . . . but, well, we weren't really friends. Not after fifth or sixth grade, anyway."

"You had been friends before?"

"Yeah. Kind of. But Lacey got really interested in boys in,

about sixth grade, I think it was."

Miranda was smart enough not to pursue this opening too overtly. She didn't ask Ernest what he meant or how he felt about this since he, obviously, was a boy. But, over the course of the next five minutes, her indirect discussion of the junior-high years had Ernest explaining that he was sorry they'd stopped being friends, but that was okay, since their interests had shifted.

In that objective way of his that had impressed Chug in someone so young, he said, "Lacey was really good at what she did. But I'm not very interested in student politics or drama. So we didn't have much to talk about."

"How about as a girl, then?" Miranda sounded as though the thought had just popped into her head and out of her mouth before she could stop it. "I mean, girl-boy kind of friends? She was very attractive."

He nodded, blushing feverishly.

"Maybe in junior high, seventh grade, I kind of liked her like that. But, uh, she . . . I don't know, it's not important, if you know what I mean. I mean, I don't want to sound snobby, 'cause I liked her a lot. But . . . well, Lacey . . . she just wasn't that . . . *interesting,* if you know what I mean. Not that she was interested in me anyway."

"She wasn't smart."

"Uh, no, it's not about being smart. You don't have to be smart to be interesting."

"And Lacey wasn't interesting?"

He smiled, shrugged.

As for Walter Traynor, when Miranda finally shifted the subject to him, Ernest seemed bothered by his death. No, he'd never had to see Mr. Traynor for discipline, but he thought the assistant principal was an interesting man, with interesting ideas and attitudes.

"He used to talk to me as if I were an adult," he said. "Even when I was a freshman. And I could tell it wasn't because of my IQ testing. You could see he wanted to know what I thought about things, not just how much I knew."

"Ever stop over his house? I know kids were always in and out of there when I was a student. In fact, I was always in and out of there myself."

"No, I never went there, though he told me a couple of times I was welcome to. I didn't . . . I don't know, I guess I just didn't need it."

Chug knew the boy wasn't being cruel, he wasn't even aware of what he was saying to and about Miranda. Even the most objective seventeen-year-old has only had a few years to work on tact.

"How about Mr. Carstairs?" she said after a few moments. "You ever have him as a teacher?"

"Sure, last year. Honors English."

"Did you like him as a teacher?"

"He was okay. A little hyper sometimes, but okay. Why are you asking about him? I mean, what's he got to do with all this?"

"Probably nothing. I was just asking because I saw Mr. Carstairs recently. He showed me something that he got anonymously from one of last year's students. This note . . ."

She slid a sheet of paper in front of him. "I was just wondering, since you were one of his students, whether or not you knew anything about it. Notice these phrases here?"

Ernest frowned as he followed her finger, said, "Why are you showing this to me?"

"Well, I was kind of curious about this sentence in particular, 'I am eager, very eager.' That could be a way of saying the writer is earnest, no? Kind of like a pun on your name? Of course, it's only one little part of the letter." She slid the paper back in front of her. "But apparently Mr. Carstairs got other ones as well. He told me he had them packed away somewhere and he'd look for them."

Ernest kept shaking his head. "I . . . I . . . I d-don't see wha-what this has to do with your murder investigation, that's all."

"I'm not sure myself. It's just something unusual. And I'm trying to see if it fits in somehow, know what I mean? I was talking to Mr. Carstairs, seeing if he had any insights into who might hold a grudge against Mr. Traynor. And while we were talking, Mr. Carstairs mentioned these letters. I thought they were something to look into, that's all. You know? Probably no connection at all."

Ernest was nodding, but he wasn't agreeing.

"That letter . . . that was a threat to Mr. Carstairs? I didn't get to read it all, but that's what it was?"

She looked down at it, then up at him. "More of a prank, I think. It doesn't specifically threaten him."

"And you think I might have sent it?"

"I just wanted to ask you about it, because of that eager part. As I said."

She was looking a little unsure of herself, and this time Chug didn't think it was just to relax Ernest.

"And you think this might be connected somehow to Mr. Traynor's death?"

Chug had warned her the kid was sharp.

"I don't know. As I said before, it's just something unusual, and I was wondering about it."

"I've never seen that letter." He lowered his head and frowned at the tabletop. His blush had turned darker, but his face looked as if he were shutting down, slamming closed some inner gate. For all intents and purposes, the interview was over.

Miranda must have seen that, too. They spoke for a while longer, but it was inconsequential, just chat. On her part. His responses were polite, but monosyllabic. After a few minutes, she thanked him and offered again to drive him home.

"No, no, that's okay."

"No trouble. We can put your bike in the trunk of my car. It's not a police car. And I've got enough time before the next interview."

"I'm not worried about riding in a police car."

He dropped his helmet twice in his haste to pull on his mittens, as he muttered, "I just don't need a ride, that's all."

She was waiting in the corridor at the side door when Chug came up beside her. Ernest was out in the side lot, standing next to a lime-green bike that he must have outgrown years ago. It was much too small for his long and lanky body, and there were action figure decals on the fenders. But his attention was fixed on a pickup truck parked near him, a pickup truck with the Prescott High Faculty Parking sticker in its side window. Visitor parking at the police station was in front, and that's where Chug had assumed Ernest would park. But there was a bike rack out on the side, right near the parking spot Chug had chosen to keep his presence a secret.

"Why do I feel so lousy?" Miranda whispered.

Chug thought Ernest was going to turn around and look at them and backed up a couple of steps into the shadows. But Ernest just strapped his helmet on, drew the parka hood up over it so that he looked like a gangly, frustrated, very cold extraterrestrial, and rode off down the driveway, long grasshopper legs bent awkwardly to compensate for his height. He turned onto Main Road without ever looking back.

"Where'd the letter come from?" Chug asked, as they walked back to her office. "Carstairs told me he hadn't kept any."

"He hadn't. When I went over to talk to him, I brought copies of sections of the letters we got—just a couple of sentences that didn't give away too much. And those 'I am sincere' sentences. He said they looked just like the ones he'd gotten, so

I figured we weren't working on coincidence."

"But the letter that you showed Ernest?"

"Mr. Carstairs and I sort of put it together. From what he could remember about the contents of one of the letters and what I could add, given the style of the ones that've been sent to you and Prosky."

"It wasn't one of the letters Carstairs got?"

She shook her head. "An approximation. I didn't let the boy read too much, and I used your little trick of highlighting the key sentence and pointed it out to him before he could get too far into the letter."

"But if he'd sent them, wouldn't he know the letter wasn't his?"

"I was taking that chance, but I figured it was still worth it. I might've been able to tell just by his reaction—relief, confidence, whatever, that he had written the originals, and that this wasn't one of them."

"And what'd you see?"

"Not what I'd hoped for, that's for sure." She shook her head. "How about you?"

"That blushing and nervous stuttering is kind of normal for Ernest in a stressful situation."

She closed her office door behind them, walked over to her desk and, turning, leaned back against it, watching Chug.

"I thought as much. What else?"

He shrugged. "Inconclusive."

The corner of her mouth flicked up in a small, ironic, and not especially happy wriggle. "That's a kind way of putting it, Matthew. That damned kid got more information than he gave, and he left me feeling like a creep."

"That doesn't mean he didn't do it." He knew his voice sounded a little extra guilty because he was the one who had pointed Ernest out to her.

"Okay," she said after a while. "Tell me what you really think about him."

"I don't know. It's nothing I can put my finger on."

"You don't think he wrote the notes to Carstairs or you?"

"On the face of his behavior? No, I don't think so. On the other hand, there's no way those sentences are coincidental. So he must be connected somehow. I just don't know how. But it's not even that. I just haven't seen him all that good at faking his emotions. And he looked more confused than alarmed that you might suspect him to be connected to the deaths."

"Still, he seems to be very close to the edge, Matthew."

"No argument from me there."

"If he didn't write those notes, do you think he may know who did?"

"Could be. But it's not that either. I . . . I don't know what it is."

It wasn't much help, but it was honest, and Miranda's look seemed to recognize and appreciate that.

"What next?" he said after a minute or so.

"I don't know." She steepled her hands and held them briefly at her lips before adding, "I'll check up on Ernest a little more, see what I can find out about him from people who might know. The school shrink, his guidance counselor. I've already looked into him a little and found out that he doesn't have any close friends. He hangs out with some people in a sci-fi club, and plays one of those 'Dungeons and Dragons' type games with a group he's part of, but even there he doesn't seem to have anyone close to him. Spends a lot of time on the computer alone in his room."

Chug thought her description of the boy was a chilling echo of some of the other kids who had turned American schools into shooting galleries. Of course, he also realized with a sudden hollow feeling, that her description of Ernest was also pretty close to being a perfect match for his son Jason.

"Oh," she said, "I also wanted to ask if you'd consider picking up your mail at the post office in town instead of having it delivered. That letter you got after Walter was killed said he'd mail you the next message. Having your mail set aside by the postmistress might give us a day or so extra."

"That much time?"

"Possibly. Local mail dropped off here gets sent to Boston, where it's cancelled and sent back. But if the postmistress puts anything local to you aside and cancels it here . . . well, it'll be a little edge anyway. Maybe."

"You've already spoken to her?"

"She's an old friend."

"Sure, that's fine with me," he said quickly, sensing by the look in her eyes that she was thinking about another old friend of hers, a friend who wasn't around anymore.

"You'll settle this." He put his arms around her hoping he sounded a lot more confident than he felt.

Chug and Miranda spent a blue Christmas, trying to cheer each other up. She missed Traynor and worried about the investigation. He worried about his book and missed his kids, who were spending the school vacation week in Newport. Ortho-David's parents lived on Ocean Drive, which meant the house must be huge, but the family was also huge, and it was David's year to rough it, Chug guessed, in a harborside four-bedroom condo. Connie wanted them to be at his parents' home for a party on Christmas Eve, so Chug only got to see Sarah and Jason the afternoon they were leaving. When he stopped to pick them up, they brought Amigo along, and Connie, who saw them off, looked alarmed when Chug told the kids he had a gift for the dog too, something he could really use. It was only a *Figa,* a Portuguese good-luck charm to hang from his collar, but Connie didn't wait to hear that.

"You better not have a . . . a female dog companion for him," she whispered to Chug just before he closed the driver's side door. Nice woman like her, he thought, couldn't say bitch even if she was being bitten by one.

"No," he said, grinning. "Wouldn't matter anyway. Don't you remember, I told you the animal-shelter people had him fixed? Down Fall River way we call it 'Doing a David' on a dog."

He closed the truck door quickly and whispered "Bad Dog" in Amigo's ear so, though he could see Connie's mouth working overtime, all they could hear in the cab of the truck was Amigo agreeably barking his fool head off as they backed down the driveway.

# Chapter Nineteen

The week after Christmas moved slowly with Miranda investigating and Chug writing, running, and driving into town for his mail during the one week when he would have preferred the government deliver it to him.

On the Saturday of Traynor's memorial service, Chug was up early and into his run along the lake road before seven. He'd become a lot better about exercising since he had met Miranda. It was a crisp winter morning and a good run: no guilty voices whispering in his ear, no replaying all the mistakes he had ever made in his life. Just him and the road, the thump of his feet, the sound of his breathing. He was, as a runner friend called it, zoned and ozoned.

He was also showered, drinking his first cup of coffee, and ready to work on the book by eight. He was supposed to meet Miranda in town for lunch, then they were going to the memorial service together at one.

The book was now about just the killings. Alice, his editor, had given the go-ahead to develop it that way and, according to Chug's agent, Jeremy, she was very excited about the prospect.

As he roughed out the description of the doctor's house on Sunset Island, Chug was a little surprised to find it going in a more brooding direction than he had planned. But he had finally found a good rhythm and had become so absorbed in re-creating the scene that he suddenly realized he didn't have much time to get ready for the service. He had only one good suit, charcoal with a thin blue stripe, suitable for all occasions. But he had to hunt around in some still-unpacked boxes for his dress Florsheims. Thank god they held their shine since he hadn't done anything in—or with—them in years. A quick swipe with one of his still-damp running socks, and he thought they looked more presentable than the rest of him. He was overdue for a trip to the Laundromat, and the one shirt that looked okay was iffy, at best. The tie was an easy choice, one of three, all gifts from his kids. He had left all the rest that Connie had bought for him, along with his suits and the life she'd wanted for him, back in Bradford.

He hurried out to the truck. He had run it through a car wash on the way back from the post office yesterday. Like its driver, it had a few extra miles on the odometer and more than its share of dings, but it also cleaned up spiffy enough if you didn't look too carefully.

He had decided not to stop at the post office for his mail. He was running late, and it was already nearly noon, the post office's Saturday closing time, but as he glanced over at the small gray clapboard-sided building, he saw Miranda's car parked near the door.

He could hear their laughter as soon as he entered the outer, postal box area, the bass wobbly booming of Mrs. Beckworth, the postmistress, blended with Miranda's light, clear bell. He could see them through the double glass doors, leaning toward each other over the counter. Mrs. Beckworth, an older woman whose face was a Rorschach of wrinkles and liver spots, looked lit by the pleasure of her company.

"Hi, Matthew," Miranda said, her dark eyes shiny. "Am I late? I'm sorry, but we were talking about old times."

"No, I just stopped when I saw your car."

"Got your mail right here, Mr. O'Malley." Mrs. Beckworth slapped a small stack on the counter with a self-satisfied grin, as if she'd pulled it like a quarter from his ear.

"Thanks," he said, but her attention had already returned to Miranda.

He had moved toward a writing counter running below the front windows of the long and narrow room, leaving them to reminisce. He could hear Mrs. Beckworth describing an episode that somehow involved Miranda and a large UPS truck when, in mid-shuffle of his stack of credit card offers and catalogs, Chug suddenly felt as if the UPS truck from their story had slammed into him. There, trembling slightly in his hand, was an envelope just like the one he had gotten about Traynor's death. Plain, white, with no return address front or back, and his name and address in the now-familiar font:

*Chug O'Malley*
*38 Loganberry Lane*
*Prescott, MA*

"Miranda." He held up the envelope.

"What? . . . Oh!"

She knew right away, and came over to the counter where Chug held the envelope carefully in the C formed by his thumb and index finger. His right hand held a small penknife poised. They looked at each other for a heartbeat before she nodded and he slit the envelope. Miranda had already pulled on her black dress gloves, and, as he slid the letter out with his penknife, she carefully folded it open on the counter and they read:

*Hey, Chug-Chug, how you been?*

*Were you waitin' for one more big wet red splash?*

*Well, this time, I gave 'em somethin' they'd really remember, didn't I?*

*Really went out with a bang, huh?*

*'Course I had to go too.*

*I can't be zealous anymore.*

*But that's the way it goes sometimes, doesn't it?*

*No regrets.*

*Try remembering me.*

*Do me the service of making me look good, will ya Chug-Chug?*

"My god," Miranda whispered. "What are we looking at here? A 'big wet red splash' and going 'out with a bang'." She shook her head. "You think that 'I had to go too' is a suicide?"

"Sounds like it. But he's not going alone," Chug said. He checked the postmark on the envelope. It had been mailed in Prescott and . . . "This envelope's got today's date on it. He might have mailed it this morning!"

They hurried over to the counter, where Miranda called Mrs. Beckworth away from a conversation she was having with a young couple.

"This letter, do you know if it came in today?" she said quietly, showing her the envelope.

"Sure did. We empty the box out front at eleven on Saturdays. Not much in it today. About eight letters including that one. The others I sent on to Boston like I always do, but this one I did what you asked. Cancelled it myself not a half hour ago."

"Thanks," Miranda said, then added to Chug as he followed her out the door, "We may have gotten our break here. I don't think our guy expected you to get the letter today. Probably figures you won't get it until Monday."

They both got into her car and sat looking at the letter again.

" 'I can't be zealous anymore,' " Chug read. "Reinforces the idea that he won't be alive. And, of course, there's the 'zealous' with the Ernest connection again."

"But the part about doing something people would really remember. My god, what's he talking about?"

Chug shook his head, said, "He tells me to remember him, too. Do him the service of making him look good . . . the service . . ."

"What?"

"Well, I don't know. He mentions remembering twice here, and he uses a kind of formal phrase about doing him the service."

"Oh my god! *Walter's memorial* service? You think?"

Chug drew in a sharp breath. "I don't know. It might be a leap, but it's a strong possibility. After all, he wouldn't be too cryptic if he thought I wouldn't get this letter until Monday. Hell, even if the post office sent it today, mail doesn't get delivered out to the lake until late afternoon, long after the service'd be over."

"It's noon already," she said. "If he's planning this to happen at the service, then he'd want to get there first. He might be at the church already. Hiding somewhere."

She called the station from her radio in the car and asked for Sergeant Cassidy.

After a slight delay, the dispatcher came back on. "Cassidy's out in Springfield, Sarge. Some kind of CPAC thing, I think."

"Okay, I'm going to call into the station on my cell. Find someone from the task force to talk to me."

She flicked off the radio, took her cell phone from her pocketbook, muttering, "Too damn many people listen in on the police frequency."

She spoke to someone named James, told him to contact Cassidy immediately and make sure the state policeman had her cell phone number. Then she said, "We need to contact all the men on the task force and tell them about this. Also, we should contact the minister . . . what's his name . . . Right, Patterson. Contact him and tell him not to go to the church. We'll have to postpone the service until another day. You know the inside of that church? . . . Me neither. Ask the reverend if there are any hiding places in there . . . No, don't tell him just yet why we want to know. And, who's on patrol up in that end of town? Okay, tell them to meet me at Durgin Crossroads . . . that's right, about a half mile east of the church. Silent approach, no lights, no siren . . . Yes, I'm on my way now, I'll meet them at the crossroads. I'll tell you the rest on the way. Stay on . . ."

She hit the mute button, looked at Chug. "You can't come."

He stared back at her, not saying anything.

"You can't, Matthew. You know I can't let you."

"What's your plan, then? How will you stop this maniac without someone dying?"

"I . . . I don't know yet. Cassidy's not available, and I haven't had time to think about how we can take the killer. I just know I have to make sure no one goes near that church."

She looked quickly at her watch, switched back to the phone.

"I want cruisers on Route 108," she said to the dispatcher. "Let's see, Durgin Crossroads would be one approach. And . . . the Lee's Road intersection west of the church. That'd do it. A couple of cruisers at each of those spots, setting up detours . . . I don't care what you tell them. Maybe I'll come up with something by the time I get to Durgin. If people are going to the service, tell them it's been postponed. Something wrong with the furnace in the church, broken water pipe, or something. No, no, make it a power loss at the church, a downed wire in the road. That'll cover the church and give us an excuse for the detour. And tell them to get the names of anyone they stop. Right. I don't know . . . uh, tell them it's so they can be contacted when the service is rescheduled. But be sure you warn the men that one of those cars could have our killer in it. Oh, and make sure you tell the men silent approach all the way. I don't want any lights or sirens on their way there. We don't want our guy getting suspicious. Hold on a minute."

She hit the mute again, turned to Chug, aimed a thumb at the door.

"I think I've got an idea," he said. "Just take me down to Durgin Crossroads with you, while I try to work it out."

One brow lifted dubiously, but she looked at her watch and started the car, gunning out of the post office parking lot and down the highway toward Route 108.

"Anything else?" she said over the phone. "It's what? Why? Oh, Christ. What about hiding locations? Hmm, okay. Well, have you got those men heading out? Silent approach? Good. Stay on the line."

She hit the mute again.

"He got in touch with Reverend Patterson. Seems his church is wide open. Had a custodian go in there this morning to clean and polish for the service and, since they were expecting some flowers delivered and set up, they just left the door unlocked. If our guy wanted to break in there, from ten o'clock on all he had to do was turn the doorknob."

"What about hiding places?"

"Reverend said there's a room behind the altar and there's the choir loft over the entrance. The loft's been closed the past couple of months for repairs, but somebody could still get up there."

"How about around the outside?" Chug said. He could picture the small white building, set back from the road. If his memory was right, there was open land all around it.

"I think there are some trees out behind the church," she said, swinging the Accord sharply left onto 108. "But they're behind the parking lot, back a good ways. Otherwise, no decent shelter . . . So, what's your plan?"

"If I walked up to that church with you, he wouldn't be suspicious. Whoever it is, he knows we're seeing each other, probably expects us to be there together. We're both dressed for the service. Since the door's unlocked, we could just walk in, see if we can spot where he's hiding. You could stay under the choir loft—where someone up top couldn't see you."

"Then what?"

"Then I speak to him."

"That's it? That's your plan?"

"Well, at least this way, no one gets killed."

"No one? What about you? And on the way in, he could kill both of us. Matthew, this guy's already killed three people. And you saw what he did to Walter. How can you predict how he'll act?"

"I'm the one person he wants alive. This last letter assumes I'll write about him, make him famous. He can't get that if he kills me."

"We don't know any of that, Matthew. We just think it's what he wants. Dealing with a mind this deranged, we can't know anything, not for sure. And what if he was the guy who already shot at you?"

"It wasn't the same guy, Miranda. I'm sure of it. We both know whoever shot at me could have hit me if he'd wanted to."

But she was already shaking her head.

"What's the alternative, then?" he said. "Cordon off the place and send in a SWAT team?"

"We will definitely isolate that church, make sure no one else gets hurt. Then find out if he's there. Then we decide what to do. As long as there's no one else there, we can wait as long as we need to."

"We both think this note says he's planning to kill himself."

"And we both think he's planning to kill a lot of other people first. Preventing that has got to be my primary concern, Matthew. Not saving the life of the killer."

A killer who had horribly butchered a man she had considered a father. Not Ernest, Chug thought. Please, not Ernest.

A cruiser with Harrington standing next to it was waiting at Durgin Crossroads and a second pulled up just as they arrived. Miranda was out and talking to the two policemen, explaining the situation, halting long enough for one of them to flag down a pickup that had come north on Durgin and was turning on Route 108 toward the church. It was an older couple, who looked confused when told they'd have to detour, but accepted the downed line excuse.

Miranda was checking to be sure backup had arrived for the officer at the other end of 108, and a third cruiser soon came speeding down to join them.

"It's twelve twenty-two," she said. "Not only do we have to find out if our guy's in the church, we also have to make sure no one else is there, some innocent early arrivals."

"He probably won't guess anything's up for another ten, fifteen minutes, Sarge," Harrington said. "We could go in there, check it out as if we were just attending."

"Not in that uniform, you can't," she said. "It might set him off before you even got in the door. And if he's as armed as we think, that could trigger a disaster."

"What, then?" Harrington asked.

"I'm dressed for the service," she said. "And I'm a woman. It might be enough."

"He'd also know you're part of the task force trying to capture him," Chug said. "And if it's Ernest, after the interview at the station, he knows you already suspect him."

"Better idea?" She eyed him narrowly.

"I still think I should go in there. Despite his derangement, I'm the only person he won't try to kill. He must be expecting to see me at the service. I pose no real threat to him. I could walk right into the church like an early arrival. I could stop under the choir loft, as I said, and if anyone's there, people who got there earlier, I'll find some excuse to get them out."

"What excuse?" she said, though Chug could see she wasn't buying anyway.

"I don't know yet. I've got a couple of minutes to think of one. But we've only got a couple of minutes before he starts getting suspicious about no one showing up. Then, anyone already in the church is in very real danger. And you might be facing a hostage situation."

He had noticed her looking down at her watch.

"I can't do that, Matthew. I can't let you take that chance. It's not your job. It's . . ."

"It's the only chance you've got to get potential victims out of a very dangerous situation with the possibility of no one being hurt. And you don't want a hostage situation, not with someone who's already killed three people."

"He's right, Sarge," Harrington said. "My family belongs to that church. I know the building and the grounds around it. There's a stone wall running along this side of it so I can get close enough to cover Mr. O'Malley on his way in and out the front." Harrington bent and with a twig drew a quick sketch of a box-like building in the road dust and a row of x's along the left to indicate the wall. "There's only this one small window in the front of the choir loft, and if I'm here at the wall, I can cover that, the front door and this side door."

He drew a circle in the appropriate place and made a scratch along the left of the building to indicate a side door.

"The window's round, stained glass," he said. "But it opens. If it's closed, no problem. No one's looking out. Once Mr. O'Malley's in the church, as long as he stays under the loft as he said, then the guy up top won't be able to see him, and it'll be easy enough for him to make sure no civilians are in the building. If anyone's there, he can call them to him, under the loft, and get them out this door on the left."

"And what about our guy in the loft?" Miranda said.

"That's the best part, Sarge. He won't even know about them leaving."

Using the twig as a pointer, he continued, "That one window faces the front. Even if it's open, he won't be able to see what's happening on the side, especially if Mr. O'Malley and anyone he has with him run this way."

He used the twig to triumphantly hurry Chug and all the people he had rescued from the side door at an angle away from the front of the church to the safety of the wall series of x's.

"Unless he starts shooting when Matthew goes in."

"Why should he?" Chug said, buying eagerly into Harrington's scenario. "We agree that it'll still be early enough so he won't be suspicious. He wants to see me show up for the service. If I'm under here"—he pointed to the sketch—"then he can't shoot at me once I'm in. If there's no one in the main part of the building, believe me, I'll be out of there fast and quiet."

Still she shook her head. Still she glanced at her watch.

"If it's him being a civilian that you're worried about," Harrington said, nodding toward Chug, "then as far as I'm concerned, we never got that letter, never suspected there'd be anybody in the choir loft, and never had this conversation with Mr. O'Malley."

Meaning, Chug thought, that if I'm shot, he won't rat out Miranda, and, of course, I won't be around to blame anyone else.

"That's not it," she said, but she wasn't looking at Harrington. She was looking up at Chug, and he thought he could see something in her eyes, an extra something for him, that he hadn't seen there before.

She looked at her watch again, sighed, shook her head impatiently.

"What if the killer's not in the loft?" she said. "What if he's sitting downstairs in the church? Or in the room behind the altar? What then? No, I'll tell you what we'll do."

Turning to Harrington and pointing to the diagram, she said, "You drive there, park before you get to the church, out of the line of sight from the loft window and get to your spot along the wall here. You have a rifle in your unit, right?"

Harrington nodded as she said, "Then, Matthew, you and I drive up, you at the wheel. You park out here, at the fence in front, with the engine running. The building's a good hundred, hundred and fifty feet back from the road, but I want you to lift the car's hood as if you're checking the radiator, and that's why you didn't go into the parking lot in back. I'll walk toward the church. Wait until I'm almost in the church before you lower the hood. As soon as I'm in the church, you get in the car and drive down the road to the police roadblock."

"And you?" Chug said.

"I'll be doing what Officer Harrington just suggested you should do. But it's my job. And I'll be armed." She patted her purse. "I never leave home without it."

Then she glanced down at her watch again, and said to Harrington, "You go now. Set up with your rifle. I'll be in touch. But remember, this guy is a killer, and he may not even be in the church. For all we know, he could be near the wall or in those woods out behind the back parking lot. Or maybe not there at all."

"Just give me a couple of minutes head start, Sarge."

Miranda was on the radio for the next few minutes, checking the roadblocks for results, warning the men at them to be ready to move at a moment's notice. Then they were in her car with Chug behind the wheel.

"Cutting it close," she said.

"It's only twelve thirty-five. He won't figure it out."

"He'd better not. I don't know if I want to see that damned

stained-glass window opened or closed. Damn, should've thought of that, should've checked with the reverend about whether the window would likely be open at all. No time now."

They were pulling up in front of the church, and Harrington was calling in on his shoulder mike, tersely saying "All set" as Chug backed the car in against the rail fence in front the way they had decided.

"The window's open," Harrington said.

They had already seen that for themselves.

"I can't see any cars in that parking lot in back," Chug said. "There's probably nobody there, except up in that loft."

"I've got to know for sure, Matthew. We go ahead as planned."

He nodded as he popped the hood release, and they both got out of the car.

She came around to the front of the car as he propped up the hood, both of them consciously trying to not look at that damned window.

Her hand was on Chug's shoulder as he stared at the engine.

"Make it look as if you've found the problem," she said. "But be sure I'm just about in the church before you close it, walk slowly toward the car door and drive back the way we came. Fast."

He nodded. The driver's side would be away from the church as he left, an almost impossible target. But he planned to stop as soon as he was out of view of the church and bolt back to see if Miranda was all right. He had no weapon, but he couldn't just drive away from her.

"And Matthew," she said, as she turned away toward the church. "I . . . take care."

"You take care," he said, wanting to hold her, talk her into getting in the car so he could drive the two of them the hell out of this craziness. He also wanted to say more to her, but this wasn't the time to add anything to an already emotionally overloaded situation.

He heard her heels on the walk, clicking confidently toward the church. As he went around to the side of the car and pretended to still be looking at the engine, he kept an eye on her firm steps. He was about to move to the front of the car to lower the hood, when peripherally, which was where his vision was fixed, he saw movement at the front door of the church. He turned that way and saw a lanky figure in camouflage fatigues—floppy hat, jacket, pants—push open the door and come lurching out, squawking something unintelligible, his right hand waving what looked like a rifle. Suddenly there was a burst of gunfire, and Miranda fell.

Then Chug was running to her, his heart in his mouth, his whole being tensed, his mind refusing to accept what he'd just seen. It couldn't be! Jesus, it couldn't! Maybe she wasn't hurt bad. The rifle had been pointed up, hadn't it? She couldn't be hurt! Chug had almost reached her when he heard her call out toward the church, "Police officer! Put down your weapon!" He realized she had dropped to the ground on purpose, and the automatic was out of her purse and fixed on the tall, reeling, camouflage-dressed figure who was stumbling toward them. Chug, on the other hand, suddenly realized he was a very stand-up target and was tensed to dive to the ground himself when, from over behind the stone wall, he saw someone stand. Harrington called out a warning. The camouflage-dressed figure, who Chug now saw was definitely Ernest, turned in that direction and fired another quick burst into the air. Harrington's rifle cracked once, and Ernest lurched crazily two drunken steps forward before slumping to the ground, the automatic rifle still clutched in his outstretched hand.

Chug ran forward, past Miranda, vaguely aware that she was calling some warning behind him, and that Harrington's voice over to the left was yelling out something else he couldn't understand.

Ernest lay sprawled on the ground, arms and legs twisted awkwardly. His fatigue hat had fallen off, and Chug could see the spreading red splotch of blood just above his left temple. His face, streaked with camo-paint, looked oddly calm, composed and relaxed, although Chug could see his chest laboring to maintain his thready breathing, a raspy sound that almost drowned out the ticking sound coming from—Jesus Christ! The boy had a small bundle, about the size of a half pound of cheese wrapped in plastic and strapped to the webbed belt at his waist! And there was a small clock face attached to the bundle.

Chug wanted to run, had even reared back on his heels to get the hell away from there, but he couldn't just leave the boy like that. He reached for the boy's belt. Goddamn, it was buckled in the back and Ernest was lying on the buckle! Chug didn't dare move him, not knowing what it'd do to that bundle. But there was a knife in a scabbard attached to the webbed belt.

"Matthew, are you all right?" Miranda called, coming up behind him.

"Stay back! Stay back!" he screamed at her. "There's some kind of explosive here!"

The knife, thank god, was razor edged and sliced easily through the webbing on either side of the bundle, and Chug lifted the ticking length of belt, yelling, "Stay back! Stay back!" as he raced with it toward the side of the building, the surprisingly heavy throbbing weight of it alive and as deadly in his hand as some deeply angry and venomous snake. He had a frenzied idea of putting it down on the other side of the church, but his nerve ran out as he reached the corner of the building, and he just tossed it around the side and dove back in the direction of Miranda, scrambling to bring his arms over his head, tuck his legs in, suck in his breath. Wait. Wait.

Nothing happened.

“What was that?” Harrington said, running up to Miranda, his eyes fixed unblinking, unbelieving on the boy she was now leaning over.

Chug crawled forward a few yards, then got up, began dusting off.

“I think he had explosives on . . .”

Just then a heavy whump boomed from around the side of the church, followed by a spray of gravel. So much for how much time they’d had left.

“Jesus Christ!” Harrington yelled.

Miranda looked over at Chug, her face a blend of fear and anger, oddly similar to a look he’d seen often on his mother’s face, right after he’d done something really stupid but had managed not to hurt himself too badly.

“Why the hell did you *do* that?” Her voice quavered.

He shrugged, wiped at the dirt on his knees.

After a few seconds to regain her composure, she said, “What do you think it was?”

“I dunno,” Chug said. “Some kind of explosive. There was a timer on it. I figured that since he hadn’t set if off when he came out or when he fell, then maybe it wouldn’t be activated by movement.”

Chug didn’t know why he sounded, even to himself, so calm. And he sensed his logic about setting the explosive off was inconsistent because he had been afraid to move the boy. Maybe he was still in a little shock about how fast everything had happened.

“My suit’s dirty.” He wiped again at his knees and at the jacket elbows.

“Shit.” Harrington looked more closely at the boy. “I don’t believe this.”

[illegible]eed paramedics.” Miranda held a handkerchief to [illegible]leeding head.

"Yeah," Harrington said. "I . . . I called in the backup and said there was at least one injury." It sounded more like a question, a question he didn't want to hear the answer to.

"I didn't want to do that, Sarge." A gurgle of distress bubbled in his voice. "If he hadn't fired that second burst . . ."

"No, no," Miranda said. "You were right. I . . . I don't know why I didn't fire too. You probably saved both of our lives."

Chug knew she meant him and her and she was right. The rifle, lying next to Ernest's outstretched hand, looked like an AK-47. Chug would have run right into a burst of its deadly automatic fire. Or, if they'd tried to disarm him, they'd have been blown up along with Ernest.

He knelt down next to her and Ernest and, while he held the handkerchief to the boy's temple, she gently dabbed with a Kleenex at the camouflage makeup under his eyes.

"How bad is he?" Harrington said, kneeling next to them and pushing aside the knife that, Chug now realized, looked exactly like the one that had killed Lacey.

"Hard to tell." She shook her head. "Maybe not good," she added softly.

Chug held the boy's hand, whispering, "It'll be all right, Ernest. It'll be all right." The sirens of the police cruisers from the roadblocks drew nearer, and Harrington walked back and forth stamping his feet and trying to fight back the tears as he muttered, "Damn! Damn! Damn! Damn! Damn!"

# Chapter Twenty

Chief Everly conducted the press conference held at the police station late Saturday afternoon. He introduced Cassidy and Miranda and, when asked about Officer Harrington, explained that Harrington couldn't be there because of departmental obligations. Chug suspected the departmental obligation was a combination of clearing the shooting as justified and settling Harrington's shaken emotional state.

Sergeant Cassidy briefly mentioned his role but then gave all the credit both for initially identifying the alleged serial killer and for arranging his capture to Miranda Cusack and Matthew O'Malley. He then suggested that the media might want to get details from her.

Miranda, reluctant to star in the press conference, gave a thumbnail sketch of what had gone on, including the note sent that day to Matthew O'Malley and the explosives attached to Ernest. Although the assembled reporters begged for more, she deferred back to the chief, who seemed very happy to take up as much time as the press would give him.

And Chug? He watched the eleven o'clock tape of the conference from the living room of Connie and David's waterfront condo at Newport. He had called first and explained to Connie why he wanted to see the kids, and she was pretty good about it, especially when she discovered he was back on the news again. When he got there, after getting filled in on the details, she and David were even nice enough to go to a party one of

David's brothers was throwing, leaving Chug with Sarah and Jason, which was exactly what he wanted.

Miranda had understood why he wanted to leave for Newport, his need to speak to his children about what had been going on in his life and why he had kept it from them. They shouldn't find out about it first on television, the phone was much too impersonal, and Newport was only about ninety minutes away.

He had briefed Miranda on what she might expect from the press conference. He was tempted to give her a few pointers, but then decided she really didn't need any; she'd be just fine. And she was, of course, even though the press kept ignoring the chief and directing their questions to her. She was cool, sharp, professional.

"She's really apple," Sarah said, sitting draped under one of Chug's arms on the thick condo wall-to-wall. From her tone, he assumed that *apple* was a very good thing to be. Jason, draped under the other arm, nodded but kept stuffing popcorn into his mouth, while slipping a little of each handful to Amigo stretched out beside him.

"What's the deal with you two, Dad?" she said.

At first, he pretended he didn't understand what she was asking, then faked a slow discovery as he said, "You know what the deal is, kid. You've spent enough time with us. Miranda and I are . . . a couple."

What could he say? *"We're going steady"?*

"You know what I mean, Dad. Is it more than that?"

"What makes you think that?"

"I dunno. The way she looks at you when you're not looking. The way she says your name during the press conference, I guess. I mean, look, she insists on calling you Matthew when everybody else is asking her about Chug."

"Noticed that, did ya? I thought Matthew was my name."

"No, not just saying Matthew. It's the *way* she says it. Somehow, it sounds different than the way she used to say it."

Sarah waited, then said again, "So? What's the deal?"

"Dunno, kid. We'll have to see."

She leaned back, looking up at her father. He scratched the top of her head, smiled, and shrugged the shoulder she was leaning against.

She understood. He could see it in her eyes, the surprise and then the hint of pain. She was still young enough to think Chug's loving someone else might somehow diminish his love for her. She took a deep breath, looked back at Miranda on the screen, then back up at Chug.

"I'm glad she feels that way, Dad." She dug her head into his shoulder, her arm squeezing him, her eyes down, where he couldn't see whether or not there were any tears.

"Nothing'll ever change me and you, kid," he whispered and felt her head nodding once, twice, into his ribs and, yes, he could feel a small, warm damp spot there.

Jason, reaching for more popcorn, looked over, puzzled, at his sister, then his father. Chug gave him their familiar *everything's okay* wink and nod, and he accepted that and turned his attention back to the screen, saying, "This is so cool," just before he stuffed the fresh fistful of popcorn into his mouth.

Chug sent them to bed, with Amigo for company, right after the news, explaining that, No, he wasn't planning to spend the night, though he would be hanging around until Mom and David got back. Neither protested that they didn't need a sitter. They knew it wouldn't have done them any good anyway.

Connie and David came back a little after 1:30. David was quiet, shaking Chug's hand twice and mumbling to himself as he made his way unsteadily up the stairs. Connie, on the other hand, was lit up and glowing and smelling of brandy. David must've had a lot of drinks, but Chug knew exactly how many

Connie had had. One brandy never caused any change in her; two and she'd become smiley and attentive, four and she'd be tired and just want to sleep. But if she had three, she'd be ready for the party. She'd had three. And apparently she had decided that for tonight anyway, her ex-husband was the party.

"You're staying the night, aren't you?" Her hand was on his shoulder as they watched David walk slowly into the master bedroom and close the door behind him.

"No, I have to get back."

"But, Chug, it's so late. You'll fall asleep at the wheel of that stupid old truck of yours and kill yourself. There's an extra bedroom and bathroom right over there in the lock-out apartment."

She nodded toward a short hallway near the kitchen. Her hand had begun its old friendly habit of rubbing one of his triceps. He took a half step back, trying to avoid turning this into anything they'd both have to acknowledge and untangle.

"I'll stop on the way for coffee. Besides, I'm wide awake anyway."

Her fingers tightened into a grip so he couldn't get away now without it being obvious.

"Stay here, Chug." She was whispering though there was no one else to hear her anyway. "David'll be asleep already. Since you're wide awake, we can . . . talk about old times. In the kitchen. Or, over . . . in the lock-out." Again, the head nod toward the hallway.

"You can lock yourself in there, in the lock-out. If you want." Her eyes reflected the taunting tone. "So no one'll go in an' try to molest you. Or, you could lock yourself in with someone and lock out everybody else. From the ol' lock-out. Huh? How 'bout that?"

Her voice had dropped into the ultraviolet end of her spectrum that Chug remembered so well. He also remembered that there were some interesting colors all across her range.

But he shook his head. "I've gotta be goin'."

He took another step back as she moved closer, in a strange, improvised dance they'd begun.

"Y'know," she said, taking another step, the fingernails firmer on his arm. "You were the hit of the party tonight, and you weren't even there. I . . . I had forgotten about that."

He smiled, stepped back, bumped against a table.

"I've been remembering some other things about us too, Chug. Lots of good things. One especially."

And she moved in from the waist down. He did a half turn and waved his free hand like a conjurer, still smiling at her, trying to turn this into a joke because it was the only way to slip out of the situation without her feeling angry when she sobered up. And, ironically, he was getting mad because, here she was, the mother of his children, trying to cheat on her husband. Strange. But she was as beautiful as ever. And he could remember a few times when, if they hadn't exactly made the earth move, they sure as hell had nudged it a little.

"I've gotta go, Con. And, you know I didn't want any of the hoopla connected with these murders. I'm still not planning to get back on that publicity merry-go-round."

It took a little while for that to sink in, but he could see when it did by the sudden hardening of the look in her eyes, the visible stiffening of her body.

"That wasn't what I meant, Chug. That's not what I meant at all."

"Well, it's what I meant, Connie," he said, taking advantage of her confusion at his deliberate non sequitur to move out of her orbit and toward the door. He snatched his parka from the open hallway closet.

"See ya later, Con." But he didn't look back, knowing that

there were too many possible expressions he might see on her face. And not one of them would give him any pleasure at all.

He didn't get to his cabin until after three in the morning, and his answering machine was blinking, but he didn't bother to check any calls. He just turned off the telephone ringer, turned off his cell phone, and fell on the bed.

The knocking on his door woke him, confused and foggy-minded, a little after nine. He stumbled to the bedroom door, looked out toward the sound. There was something disturbing about the blonde hair and the dark trench coat that were visible through the curtains over the front door window. That hair . . . that trench coat . . . ? Of course! Tesha Dunbar! Shit!

The door's window rattled beneath the rap of her knuckles, a cocky, insistent beat that was more a demand than a request.

Even when he heard her lilting call of "Chug? Chug O'Malley? It's Tesha" he knew what a cold steel blade she had hidden behind it.

Then she was talking, probably to her crew, saying something about Chug's truck. Must've been debating why the truck would be here and he wouldn't.

Eventually, she gave up, but not before he heard the doorknob rattling. Morty Deacon, the executive producer back at 23, who was a jazz buff, used to say about Tesha in a tone that evenly blended admiration with disdain, "That whore's got chops."

She did indeed.

After they'd given up and gone, Chug dragged himself into the kitchen for a glass of grapefruit juice and, feeling a little sharper now, listened to his voice mail. Jeremy, his agent, was first. Way to go, Jeremy. Nice to see he was on the ball. He was congratulating Chug and telling him how this would likely mean a bump on their advance from the publisher. He also suggested that, now that the case was solved, Chug should get the book out as fast as possible.

More money would be good news, and Chug understood the new deadline pressure, but Jeremy sounded a little too much like Connie, enthusiastically cheering on ol' Chug to get back on the big horse that he hated riding, dangling all the sexual and financial rewards that mounting that sucker again could bring the lucky and resourceful caballero.

Earlier last night his daughter had told him that Channel 23 had run an old ad for the *Action 23* news show. It was a shot of Tesha, Chug, and Harvey Banks, the "anchor you can bank on," walking down the south steps of the state house, talking. Actually, it was Chug who was doing the talking. It was the only time Chug had ever been on those granite steps and the three were shown in slow motion, somebody's idea that this would be more dramatic.

Unfortunately, that only made it easier for lip-readers to figure out that Chug was actually reciting a Dylan Thomas poem, "Lament," lamenting the passing of a man's sexual potency. That may have been what put the smile on Tesha and the concentrated confusion on Harvey's handsome furrowed brow. When the word got out, the story only enhanced Chug's reputation, but Channel 23 had quickly pulled the ad anyway.

Now Chug figured all must finally be forgiven as he listened to the rest of his voice mail and the messages on his landline. Nothing but more people wanting a piece of his new notoriety. He deleted the messages and turned the ringer back on just in time for a new caller, and he waited until the machine kicked on. Someone gave his name, said he was a reporter from *Time* and he wanted to . . . Chug turned the volume all the way down so the voice was a tiny, tinny whisper, a distant cricket on a summer night. He walked over to the cabinet near the fridge only to discover he didn't have any goddamned coffee left in the cabin.

Fortunately, the breakfast crowd had long since cleared out of Cap'n Bill's when he stopped in for the last of the morning glory muffins and the much-needed cup of coffee and, though he hated himself for doing it, he couldn't resist the lure of the Sunday paper. "The Prescott Shoot-out" was front page of the *Boston Globe* accompanied by a picture of Miranda and Harrington watching Ernest on the gurney being lifted into the ambulance. He read the article in the cab of his truck, engine running for the warmth, muffin crumbs all over the seat for the O'Malley ambiance.

Just about the whole story had come out. The notes from Ernest, the fact that Chug was the one who'd discovered Lacey's body, the mayhem at the church. The note to Prosky had been omitted, and any hint of the principal's partial responsibility in Lacey's death. Chug was featured in a sidebar, along with a file picture from his Channel 23 days, and a reference to his first book. There was also an interview with Prosky, which was pretty much administrative boilerplate, and another piece full of quotes from students at the high school, which he skipped because those kinds of quotes were bound to be as predictable as a weather report in the Atacama Desert.

There were four new telephone messages, none of them important, when he got back.

He called Paul Graves to find out if the school would be following a regular schedule the next day and to ask him to call if there were any changes planned. Paul sounded different as soon as he realized who was calling. As he said, "Just a sec," Chug was pretty sure Paul was mouthing to someone, probably his wife, that fame was on the other end of his phone line. Jesus, Chug liked him better as the guy who kept his elbow out as he drove the lane in a basketball game or whined that he'd been fouled every time he missed a shot.

They talked a little about what had happened, about Ernest,

and how, no, neither of them ever thought the kid was the one who had been the murderer, but thank God it was over. And Paul promised to call if he got word about any special meetings at school, but then added, "You know, you'll probably be the first person they call." Chug figured this was meant to make him feel good.

Miranda stopped by in the late afternoon, on her way back from Brigham and Women's Hospital. She had spent the last hour speaking to Ernest's neurologist, who was going to give a press conference later to discuss the boy's condition. He'd told Miranda that he planned to announce an uncertain prognosis, that Ernest might recover from his coma in a day, a month, or maybe later. Privately, he told her that if there were an office pool on his recovery, she should put her money on later rather than sooner.

# Chapter Twenty-One

There was no emergency meeting the next day, but Chug showed up at school early enough to beat the two police cars that pulled up to the gates to keep out the media. Someone in authority had finally smartened up. The grief counselors were back, in even greater numbers than when Lacey had been killed. They'd also been available at the school over the vacation, but since there had been a killer still at large, and he'd last struck in the school itself, Chug figured that not too many students had stopped in for help. Now, though, the killer was both comatose and under around-the-clock police watch at Brigham and Women's. When Prosky called Chug down to his office fifteen minutes before homeroom, Gail, the grief counselor, was a few doors down, smiling benignly and hauling a desk out of a classroom. The familiar shopping bag of tissue boxes was at her side.

Dr. Mackey, the superintendent, was with Prosky in his office, as were the school's three guidance counselors. Prosky looked Chug in the eyes and held the stare. Mr. Frost himself. Ice cubes for balls. Well, if Chug could manage it, there'd be a big thaw coming Prosky's way before this was all over.

"I'm holding a press conference at ten o'clock, Mr. O'Malley," he said. "And I'd like you to be there."

"I've got a class."

"I'll have someone cover it."

"No."

"What?" This, from Dr. Mackey who, until that moment, Chug had thought just might be mute.

"No," he repeated. "I've got a class to teach."

One of the guidance counselors was looking down at her hands. Art Davis was smirking as he nudged her, but she looked away, not willing to be involved even as an onlooker.

Dr. Mackey cleared his throat. When everyone was looking at him, he said to Chug, "Don't you think it's more important to clear up some matters with the press than to miss one class?"

"No, I don't."

"But, but, your connection to all of this, the letters from that boy, finding the girl's body. Don't you think you need to straighten it out, explain how it all happened?"

"The media's already done that. Anything I say now will just pour gasoline on the blaze. If you want to put the fire out, I'd suggest you just don't speak to them. You don't have to, you know. In a day or two they'll go somewhere else, move on to the next story."

Mackey looked confused. Then he looked at Prosky.

"That's not exactly our plan, Chug," the principal said. "But we can understand and appreciate your approach also. And, in fact, I applaud you for your convictions." He nodded, lifted a hand in blessing toward his door. Chug was dismissed.

"You planning to tell the media everything you know about the murders?" Chug said to Prosky from the doorway. "Everything?"

"Yes, of course we do," Mackey said, frowning and following Chug's stare to Prosky, who had suddenly become fascinated by some papers on his desk.

It was good to be out of that office, even though the halls had begun to fill with students talking excitedly. He heard Ernest's name over and over but, as they saw him approaching, students parted. Some looked up and some looked away and probably for the same reasons. They now knew he'd been close to the deaths, too close for some of them to feel comfortable around him.

Still, Chug's picture had been on television, his name in the papers, and it wasn't long before a couple of freshmen in his homeroom asked him about Channel 23. Apparently, the station had run some old *Action 23 I-Squad* footage of Chug to go along with the story they carried, and these kids were acting as if a rock star had suddenly been beamed down into the room. Maybe they hadn't bothered reading about Ernest's twisted motives for killing three people.

Chug downplayed his past as much as possible, but he could see them developing that same suspicious look adults always got when he told them he didn't like the work. Nobody in their right mind walked away from that. Nobody.

At least the experience prepared him for the AP class, which was made even more difficult by Brandon and his buddies standing to give him a round of applause. The rest of the class joined in, though many of them looked a little confused. Chug waved them down, but Brandon maintained the applause a few extra seconds, just for good measure, while Chug fought back the temptation to smack him upside the head.

When they'd settled, he reminded them that if anyone wanted to see a counselor, he or she was free to leave. Then he explained that while he wasn't ashamed of his part in the proceedings, he wasn't proud of it either. He'd been caught up in a series of circumstances beyond his control and had just muddled through as best he could. He also said they should all remember how many victims there were in this tragedy, including too many family members of both the victims and the boy held responsible. What they needed to do now was try to move on.

That done, he asked them to open their copies of *Twelfth Night* to Act 3, which was where they had left off on the last class before Traynor had been murdered. In a way, he was relieved that it wasn't something heavier, like *Hamlet,* fraught with extra meaning for every line. But the events of the past couple of months were so big that, when the boy reading Feste's part read his "O Mistress Mine" song, and ended with "Youth's a stuff will not endure" there was audible sniffling, likely prompted by the awareness that the class that had begun with sixteen members was now down to fourteen.

# Chapter Twenty-Two

January passed with slow and frozen steps. Not much snow, which would have been a kind of relief from the dead chill afternoons when Chug, while running along the dirt roads now frozen and unyielding underfoot, sometimes found it hard to trust the recuperative powers of nature. The mind said the world would recover, but the ground was so cold, so solid, that the heart tended to doubt it. He always felt that during some New England winters, belief in spring was more an act of faith than a fact of nature.

February eased up the cold, but balanced that by doling out an inch or two of snow every few days, so that nothing was cancelled, just made hard as hell to accomplish. As compensation, Chug found more of his time to work on his book. He didn't need Jeremy's regular e-mails to remind him how important time was, especially with a topic as topical as this one. But years of newspaper deadlines had taught him speed. He was still uncertain about how he'd treat Ernest in the writing. The boy remained in a coma, no changes at all. The medical report said he'd taken PCP, which could account for his bizarre behavior that day, but Chug had written the scene at that church at least five different ways, and was dissatisfied with each of them. None of the versions quite conveyed the feeling of unreality he had had when Ernest came reeling out that door, or his surprise when the boy had unleashed that burst of gunfire.

The police, searching Ernest's home, had found the ax that had killed Traynor. He'd hidden it in some bushes behind the house. No fingerprints, but the blood turned out to be Walter Traynor's. The scene describing what that ax had done to Traynor was wrenching to write but, oddly, he was satisfied with his first description of it.

Then there was the question of how he would present Miranda in the book. They had discussed it, especially their relationship, and he was relieved when she asked him to keep it just what it was, personal and private. It would have been hard to pin down in words anyway. They had become closer after what they'd left unspoken at the church, although they still had not spoken about it. And they were still in the relationship discovery stage, with some surprises almost every time they got together. Whenever Chug thought he had her whole photo album, she'd toss a few new snapshots on the table.

During the week before February vacation, for instance, she asked if she could come along to one of the family Wednesday night basketball games.

"Sure."

"Any special way I should dress?"

"Dress?"

"Yes. You say it's in a church hall, right? Is it heated? Do you play in sweats?"

"Play? You want to play?"

"You'd rather I went as a cheerleader?"

"Hmm. Short skirt, pom-poms. Yeah, that sounds great—oof, okay, okay," he added after he caught her elbow in the ribs. "The gym's usually heated. We're pretty flexible with what we wear. I didn't know you shot hoop."

"You never asked, but, yes, I played some. Haven't in a while, but those games sound like fun, and I like all the people I've met in your family. Women do play in these games, don't they?"

"Sure. Well, sometimes. Janice, my cousin Manny's daughter—you met her at my mom's at Christmas? She plays high-school ball and, when she can, she shows up. Her sister Jen is pretty good, too."

But that was about it for women on the court. The Rapoza side of his family was liberated, but it was also Portuguese and only a couple of generations removed from the Azores. Chug had never seen one of the women of his generation even pick up a basketball, and the women around his mother's age would probably think the ball was a funny size and color for soccer.

When Miranda came by for him that Wednesday, she took off her ski jacket to display a set of sweats in a shade of pink that Chug figured you had to be French to pronounce. She even had a matching Scrunchie holding back her dark hair.

She had run with him a couple of times, so he knew she had endurance. And, in what he considered an indisputable proof of God's existence, Chug had also discovered on many occasions what incredible and flexible shape she was in. But he knew basketball was more than stamina and agility, so he deliberately arranged for them to arrive early to get some sense of how the night would go.

With the first shot she took, a jumper from the left corner, he knew he'd been worrying for nothing. Quick and smooth, she was all wrist release with a perfect hand-extended follow-through. Hitting the shot could have been a fluke, but her form was no accident and, when he bounced the ball back out to her, she glided over to the foul line and dropped in another jump shot, just as clean as the first. Then, when she came in for a layup, and he fed her the ball a step too late, she adjusted easily to it, coming under the basket, switching hands and hooking it in left-handed. Maybe it was time to start worrying about how *he'd* look tonight.

"Played *some*?" he said, dribbling the ball out to the top of the key behind the foul line.

"Well, maybe a lot. In high school. And in college. But it's been a while so I practiced a little the past few days."

"You played in college?" he said, clanking his first shot off the front of the rim.

She nodded, snapped the ball back out to him.

"For U Mass?"

"Uh-huh," she said, chasing down his second shot that had banged off the right side of the rim this time.

He managed to make his layup but then, as they shot around, he missed his next half dozen attempts. He felt heavy and slow, maybe because she was so slim and quick and pink. But she didn't seem bothered, just feeding him the ball on his turns, her face businesslike, noncommittal. And she kept making almost every shot she took while the few she missed rattled in and out of the cylinder. Chug knew better than to make lame jokes or even lamer excuses about his own lousy performance and, after a few minutes, his shooting touch finally began to come back. When the ball at last began dropping regularly through the net, it was as welcome as the first crocus of Spring.

Just in time for Tiago to arrive.

"Should be a rule about spotting the other team points if you start practicing early," he said.

Ti had met Miranda at Thanksgiving, and even then Chug could sense how impressed his cousin was from the quiet way he had acted around her. The next day he'd sent an e-mail, "Some guys have all the luck" knowing Chug wouldn't need any explanation. Now he shook hands with her so politely you'd think he was one of the church's ministers. Then, when he saw her drop in a couple of shots, he became even more polite, almost courtly although, knowing Ti so well, Chug could tell he wasn't courting, not even to be polite.

No, he was intimidated by her combination of beauty and

ability, so much so that later, when they had enough players for their first game, Ti didn't even pick her for his team, although there was an unwritten rule that if anyone brought a new player, the other team captain had first dibs. And Ti must have known from watching her that not picking Miranda would be a mistake. Which it was.

Chug got his share of points and rebounds during the three games they played, but Miranda in action was a sheer pleasure to watch. She could no-look pass, slip like mercury through picks, set her own picks with a fearlessness that was scary. Once she even braced Chug's two-twenty cousin, Paul Rapoza, her pick stopping him dead in his tracks and freeing her teammate, Paul's son, Abel, for an easy layup.

Paul just looked at her, then at Chug, muttered "Sonuvabitch" under his breath and grinned as he walked under the basket to inbound the ball.

And, of course, Miranda could shoot from anywhere on the court. She could move without the ball, play in-your-shirt defense, mix it up for rebounds, start a fast break or mess up a fast break begun by Ti's team. Yet she never seemed to be forcing anything, wrenching the game her way. She was in the zone from the first bounce of the ball, flowing with the game, a smooth, pink blur of motion and response, her long pink-Scrunchied hair fluttering behind her.

"That was a lot of fun," she said as she drove them back toward Prescott. Chug had warned her there were no showers at the old church hall but, even after more than two hours of very sweaty basketball, cramped together in her Accord, she smelled good. He didn't want to think what kind of aromas she was picking up from the passenger seat.

"Yep. Always is. You made quite an impression."

She shrugged, but looked pleased.

"Ti's the private detective, right?" she said.

"Yep."

"Former policeman?"

"Yep."

"Is there a lot of work for a private detective down here?"

"If you're bilingual, there is. Especially if you're Ti."

"He's a good player."

"That he is."

"But he can't go to his left."

"That he can't," Chug said.

After her display tonight, he wasn't surprised that she'd picked out that weakness so quickly even though Ti did a good job of camouflaging it with quickness and flashy ballhandling.

"He hasn't figured out how much you overplay him to his right," she said.

"No, he hasn't. It's an advantage I've had over him for years. If he ever figures it out, these games might get a lot tougher."

"They sure would. Or if he ever figures out that you can't go to your left either."

Chug looked to his left, gauging her intent. She was focused on the road. He didn't think she meant anything more than a statement of fact. And it was certainly a statement of fact. Still, he liked her basketball insights better when they were about other people.

He forced himself to spend the entire next week, February vacation, working on his book. He would have liked some distraction, but Miranda was on duty all day, and there seemed to be no one else around. The media had moved on, Sarah and Jason were with Connie and David in the Bahamas, and even Amigo was spending the week in a kennel where, David insisted, the dog would get the discipline he needed.

Although he missed the kids, by the end of the week Chug

felt pretty good about how much of the book he had completed. He still wanted to interview Traynor's mahogany-haired lady friend, who had been unavailable the past two weeks. And there were a couple of others he wanted to speak to about Basic, but the book was nearly there. On Saturday, he finished the chapter about Ernest at the church. That night he and Miranda ate at a Boston restaurant and ended up at her cottage, where he spent the night.

He was up first the next morning and left her a note explaining that he was going to get them some breakfast at Cap'n Bill's. He was driving there with his radio ablast, his voice aholler with the sheer joy of being alive when the song ended and the news came on. The lead-in to the first item declared that some good news had come at last to Prescott High School. The news report was brief, but riveting.

Apparently Arthur Davis, Prescott High School guidance counselor, had just discovered that for nearly a year, he'd been holding a Powerball Lottery ticket worth a little over fifty-two million dollars.

# Chapter Twenty-Three

He bought both Boston Sunday papers at Cap'n Bill's and read them in the truck. The *Globe* said it was a tale worthy of O. Henry. The *Herald*'s headline read "Counselor from Stricken School Hits Big Bucks."

Both highlighted the irony that the same school that had faced all the tragedy now, two months later, had this great stroke of luck in its midst. An added twist was the fact that Davis had come so close to being too late to cash in his ticket.

He had bought the ticket last March, when he'd gassed up at a small New Hampshire convenience store during a ski trip. Then he'd put it in his car's glove compartment but, since some Powerball jackpots had escalated into the hundreds of millions, the unclaimed winning ticket wasn't as big a story as it would have been otherwise. By the time he got back home, Davis had forgotten about it.

During this February vacation he had gone skiing again and, while stopping for gas at the same convenience store, he'd noticed the sign about the unclaimed ticket sold there. He had joked with the owner at the register that he'd bought a ticket there sometime last year and maybe it was the winner. The owner said he'd be crazy not to check it, so Art went back to his car, looked in the glove compartment, and there, amid a few other odd lottery tickets, was the Powerball ticket from last year. With the date of the winning lottery. Some of the numbers even looked a little like the ones he'd seen on the sign in the store.

He explained how his hand had begun to tremble when he went back in and realized that this, in fact, was it. This was the one. This little piece of paper that had cost him two dollars almost a year ago was now worth fifty-two million.

"The worst thing is, I nearly missed it," he'd been quoted as saying. "If I hadn't gone skiing, or if I hadn't stopped at the same place for gas as I did last year, I never would have even thought to check. And in two weeks the ticket wouldn't have been worth the paper it was printed on."

Chug glanced through the sidebars on the school-related killings and Ernest's still-comatose condition before driving back to Miranda's.

"I see you heard about Mr. Davis, too," she said, after kissing him at the door and noticing the newspapers under his arm.

He nodded and handed her the bag of croissants. The coffee was already brewing and there was a bottle of grapefruit juice, which he knew she never drank, open on the table.

"It was all over the local TV news this morning," she said, reaching a fingertip to the corner of his mouth and capturing a treacherous croissant flake to hold up accusingly. "Pretty incredible, huh?"

"Sure is."

Something in his tone must have nudged her because a brow lifted tentatively as she said, "I meant that rhetorically."

He shrugged, smiled. "Guess I'm just jealous."

Still, Chug had to keep reminding myself that Ernest had announced himself in those notes. He was clearly an emotional time bomb. If they hadn't gotten to him first, who knows what carnage he would have blasted through that little church with his automatic rifle and his explosive waistband. And he had fired those bursts of bullets.

It's over, he kept reminding himself, and all the results are positives. Miranda gets to keep the job she loves and is good at. I've got my book just about finished with most of the elements well-meshed. My agent's happy and, more importantly, so is my editor. My kids are proud of me and, for the small nasty pleasure it gives the imperfect yahoo part of me, my ex-wife thinks she re-hitched her wagon to the wrong star. And as if that isn't enough, I have this wonderful, intelligent, loving woman in my life. Everything is tied up, everything good, everything solved. Everything.

Except Ernest.

"What?" he said, suddenly aware that Miranda had called something from the kitchen.

"I just asked what you were thinking about."

"Uh, nothing, nothing. My book. I still have to interview some people about . . . Walter. That woman he dated. And some people at school. Paul Graves, I guess. Maybe a few others."

"How about Mr. Davis?"

"Yeah, 'course him too. I don't see how his winning the lottery would belong in a book about the murders, but he was Lacey's counselor."

"Ernest's, too."

"No kidding? I didn't realize that."

"Sure. And he and Walter were good friends." She brought out the coffee carafe, and Chug wanted to kick himself for being pleased with his life when Miranda was still trying to get over the loss of someone so close to her.

Chug recorded the six and eleven o'clock news broadcasts from different channels, but both ran essentially the same versions of the story, the same clips of Art. He was cautiously cheerful in answering the questions they always ask lottery winners about plans for the future and keeping his job. When the subject shifted, inevitably, to the murders, and he was asked if he knew any of the victims or the alleged killer, his face grew somber.

"Prescott's a small school," he said. "I was guidance counselor to one of the student victims and to the boy accused of the crimes. As for Mr. Traynor, he was a good friend, a very close and good friend. For almost twenty years."

Chug read two additional newspaper accounts about Art's lottery win, but they carried the same information as the Boston papers' articles. When asked about the numbers, Art had explained that they represented various events in his life, with the six the month of his wife's birthday, the thirty-four the number he wore as a college running back, those kinds of connections. The Powerball eight, the last number picked from a separate set of numbers, represented August, the month he first met his wife and the month, a year later, when they married.

As for Chug, he decided to put off interviewing Art until later, when the lucky winner had had a little breathing time away from the media. He thought he'd begin his interviews instead with Dorothy Bramwell, the woman Miranda referred to as Traynor's *lady friend.* When Chug had laughed at the expression, Miranda had flushed, saying, "My God, Matthew, I feel wrong even calling her that! She's a librarian in Bradford, and I never imagined them doing anything beyond talking about books or something. Dull books, at that."

Chug had been briefly introduced to Dorothy at Lacey's wake and had offered his condolences at Traynor's rescheduled memorial service. She was taller than she had looked sitting down, an imposing woman as tough as her mahogany hair, and she had looked him right in the eye. Wouldn't try to slip a book out past her.

But her voice over the phone was surprisingly gentle as Chug explained his book and asked if he could talk to her about Traynor.

"Of course, of course, Mr. O'Malley. I work at the main branch of the Bradford Library and finish at five."

They agreed to meet there on Wednesday and, just before he hung up, she asked, "One question. Are you planning to call Walter 'Basic' in your book, Mr. O'Malley?"

"I hadn't really thought about it," he said. "Fact is, the more I discover about Mr. Traynor, the more I feel that nickname's a little like calling a giant 'Tiny.' "

Her laugh was brief and appreciative, which he thought was nice because he hadn't actually admitted that of course he was going to use Traynor's nickname. Just not exclusively.

She still seemed inclined to give him the benefit of the doubt when they shared coffee in her office at the library, his small recorder on the table between them.

"What is it you'd like to know about Walter?" she asked, sipping at her mug of black, no sugar. No nonsense either.

He started off by asking her some general questions about her relationship with Walter. How long they'd known each other, how they'd met, icebreaker kinds of easy lobs. But, of course, what he really wanted to know about was Traynor and Ernest, and he eventually asked her as gently as he could if she knew anything about Traynor's relationship with the person who had killed him.

"I don't think I ever heard Walter mention the boy," she said, holding her coffee mug as if trying to warm her fingers with it. "No, never. And I have tried. I've discussed this at length with a Sergeant Cassidy and Miranda, of course. But I simply can't remember that boy's name ever being mentioned by Walter—and he did tend to ramble on about the students."

Chug smiled, nodded, understanding her fondness for the man as well as that sense of lingering "if only" guilt. He had been wondering himself if there had been anything he could have done to prevent the murders, if he'd missed a warning that he should have caught right away.

"Do you think it was personal, Mr. O'Malley? I've been bothered by that thought. Did those notes that I understand the boy wrote to you . . . are you free to tell me if the notes from the boy indicated a personal animosity toward Walter?"

"No, they didn't. I think the boy saw the assault more as a symbolic gesture than a personal one, as strange as that may sound."

She nodded, her eyes glistening, her knuckles whitening now on her coffee mug.

"It had to be," she said. "It had to."

After a few minutes, he brought up the subject of Traynor's friends at school and, since Art Davis was so much in the news lately and had been a close friend, he was the logical staff member to start with.

"Yes, yes." She smiled warmly. "Walter and Art had been friends for quite a while. We used to play bridge with the Davises, with Walter and Art partnered. In fact, I remember Walter once joking to us that the only reason he'd even consider burial over cremation was the secret pleasure he'd get from knowing Art Davis would have to be a pallbearer and carry him, since during our card games he'd been carrying Art for all these years."

She blinked her eyes a few times rapidly as she smiled at the memory. Chug had never been sure if this exhuming of memories was good or bad for people he interviewed when he was a reporter. He told himself it helped them, but he still had always felt as if he were poking at a layer of ice that might be a lot thinner than it looked.

"And, of course, they both loved skiing," she said with a smile. "Not something I ever cared to take up."

"That's right. In fact, I read that Art was skiing when he bought the lottery ticket."

"I heard that, too. He was probably on one of the school trips with Walter and the club."

Chug nodded, though from the media reports he had gotten the distinct impression that Davis had been on his own. Still, Carstairs had mentioned him as one of the regular chaperones.

"Mr. Davis usually went with the ski club?"

"Oh, all the time," she said. "Free lift tickets and accommodations, you know. Left him with more money to spend on lottery tickets . . . I'm sorry . . . I don't know why I said that."

She frowned at the recorder.

"That's okay. I edit the interviews." He could see why she was bitter. The man she loved was dead and his friend was now worth fifty-two million dollars. "Did Art buy a lot of tickets?"

"Oh yes, yes. All the time."

"He did?"

In the interviews Davis had made it sound like an impulse buy at the register, but Chug knew a lot of gamblers who downplayed the money they lost before they finally won a jackpot. Of course, in this case it was a lot more than hitting a trifecta.

"Oh yes, all those mega-games and instant scratch-something tickets, you know those long, colorful loops the convenience stores have? Like something you'd be selling to children. Anyway, Art was always making us wait while he got two of these and three of those. And sometimes dozens of the others. Why, I've seen him spend forty, fifty dollars on tickets and not even bat an eyelash."

"Did they all end up in his glove compartment?"

Again, the original picture Chug had of Art's win—reaching into the glove compartment for the ticket in there with a few others—now had ballooned into a glove compartment almost aburst with tickets.

"No," Dorothy said, popping that thought balloon. "The instant ones he always checked right away. The others, well, if we were playing bridge, and it was time for the television to announce the winners, we had to stop, wait until he'd written all the numbers down and then checked them against his tickets."

"Yet he didn't check that Powerball number for almost a year."

"Well, he had so many, I suppose he just forgot about it."

"And he left this ticket in his glove compartment."

Her eyes were shiny as she nodded and said, "That must've been Walter's bad influence rubbing off. If Walter had bought that ticket, he would almost surely have put it in the glove box in his Jeep. But, in Walter's case, he would have forgotten about it until he sold the Jeep. And at that time, he probably would have tossed the lottery ticket into the trash without even looking at it."

"Did Walter buy many?"

"Lottery tickets? No. Sometimes he'd get one, you know, just because he was with Art. But when he did, they ended up just like everything else—in that glove box." She laughed. "He must have had a dozen parking tickets in there, all of which he sincerely intended to pay. And he kept all kinds of receipts, bills, coupons, money, even paychecks he'd forgotten to cash. Once, one of the secretaries in the superintendent's office had to remind him three times, and then the poor woman finally had to walk with him to his Jeep and wait while he fished out the check. I think it was another two weeks before he actually got around to cashing it."

When Chug left her, he went home and listened to the recording, taking notes as he did. He stared at the notes for almost two hours, ignoring the three stacks of essays just waiting for his attention. He didn't even call Miranda, though he wanted to. He felt as if he were balancing some ideas very carefully, trying to build a delicate structure one idea card on the other, and anything might jog him enough to have all the cards fall at once. But first he had to speak to Paul Graves, check out a theory he had allowed to grow for a couple of days.

They met in Paul's classroom after school the next day. Paul was wearing a dark-brown sweater and, with his tonsured bald spot, looked more than ever like a monk. And he seemed to be worrying about this particular inquisition, frowning nervously at Chug's recorder for a while before finally reinforcing what everyone had said about Traynor. Basic had a genuine concern for kids, an incredible generosity with his time and money, and a complete willingness to help anyone. Nope, no connection that he knew of between Traynor and Ernest. Ernest choosing Basic as victim had shocked Paul as much as it had everyone else.

Then Chug asked him about Traynor and Art.

Oh, sure, good friends, got along well together, all of that.

"How about the ski trips?" Chug hadn't really thought the question would go anywhere. He had been planning to set Paul up for probing a little later, but as a reporter he had always thought of every question as a baited line. He'd toss it out there and could never be sure what kind of answer he'd snag. And the answer here was a sudden change that came over Paul, a serious bout of caution, the quick shutdown look as familiar to a reporter as the sound of a quick disconnect to a telemarketer.

"I didn't go on those trips the last couple of years. Y'know, getting a little too old for that stuff."

"No kidding?" The look of someone lying to Chug was even more familiar than the face of someone clamming up. "I thought I saw your name on the chaperone list for some of the club trips," he said, creating on the fly. What the hell, Prosky was the kind of guy who'd insist there were lists like that around.

"Well, sure," Paul said, not realizing how dangerous it was to lie to someone who had considered himself a professional liar for years, "but that was just day trips. That's what I meant. Never cared too much for the overnights."

"No kiddin'? Hell, you'd think those would be better. I understand the accommodations were usually first rate. And free."

"Yeah, well, being around the kids too much can get to you. And Basic's rules meant I couldn't even have a beer with my pizza."

Chug nodded. Sure, he could understand better than most how that could be frustrating. It was just that, in this particular case, he didn't believe that was Paul's real reason. And his instinct had always been: follow the lie and you find the story. So why was Paul lying?

"Well, how 'bout on the day trips, then? What was Basic like?"

That must have been safer ground because Paul became expansive, talking about the earliest days of the club, when the kids went up to New Hampshire and Vermont on the uncomfortable school buses. Basic would attach himself to the new kid, the one he'd probably talked into going on the ski trip in the first place. The kid maybe couldn't afford it, but had been convinced that the school had something called "Beginner Coupons" at the ski area, which meant the rentals, lifts, and lunch were free. Which sometimes meant that Basic had squeezed a couple of freebies out of the ski areas and sometimes meant he had paid for them himself. Then, after they got to the mountain, he'd give the new kid a one-on-one lesson. By lunch, he'd have the kid out on the novice slopes, wedging, and turning, and smiling from ear to ear. By the trip home, the student would be sitting with some new friends, having the time of his life, and Basic would be sprawled across the bus's backseat, snoring up a storm. Only privilege he ever insisted on—the right to spread out and sleep back there. "And God, could that guy snore."

"Day trips any different recently?"

"Huh?"

"Well, you sounded as if they used to be better, somehow."

"Oh? No, no. Not better. But different, sure. These last few years, wealthier families have moved into town. Lots of the new club members were kids with money."

"I've noticed the cars a lot of them drive."

"Yeah. And the buses now are the fancy coaches, with plush seats and mounted video players. Fewer new poor kids willing to join. Too many rich kids in the club. Lots of snowboarders, too. And the snowboarders don't talk much to the skiers and vice versa. Or they rag on each other all the time. Still, Basic slept on the backseat, both trips I went on last year. 'Course, we haven't had any this year. The first ones would've been in January."

"What about the overnights, Paul?"

"I told you, I don't go on overnights."

Yep, that was it all right.

"But you used to."

"Not for a couple of years."

"And Basic was in charge of those too?"

He nodded, his eyes narrowed.

"Something about the way he ran them you didn't agree with?"

"No, nothing like that. Hey, it's not a good idea to speak ill of the dead, Chug. So I'd rather just shut up."

That was the first time anyone had even approached a negative with Traynor. Except sartorially, of course.

"I'm going to write the book anyway, Paul. And I'll be speaking to a lot of people. Maybe it'd be better if I heard something first from someone who really cared about the guy."

"Guy? You mean, Basic? Shit, Chug, he wasn't the one I meant."

"He wasn't?"

"No, of course not. Christ, he was the greatest guy I ever knew," he said, reaching over to shut off the recorder. "It was Lacey McGovern I meant. Lacey and Art Davis."

Paul said he wouldn't have mentioned it at all if Davis hadn't won the lottery. He even prefaced his explanation by saying, "A guy like that, behaves that way and then wins fifty-two million fuckin' dollars. That's just not fair, man."

"Behaves like what?"

"This can't go in the book, Chug. I mean, what I'm telling you has to be off the record," he said, nodding at the recorder he'd just shut off.

"I can promise you that nobody ever got a source from me."

Paul thought about that for a while, understanding what Chug had and had not promised. Of course, since he had committed himself so far, it might have been easier to turn around in midair and vault back onto a diving board he'd just leaped off than not go on with what Chug knew he so much wanted to tell.

"It began when Lacey was a freshman, for crissakes, just a kid. The first ski club overnight of the year, I think it was. Or one of the first ones."

"Davis and Lacey?" Chug said, trying to nudge him along.

"Yeah. We were staying at this motel that we used to reserve near Lake Sunapee. It was cheap, but clean, and not too far from a couple of ski areas. Anyway, Basic and Art usually bunked together on those trips, unless Art's wife came along. But she wasn't on this trip. I don't even know if Art had started anything with Lacey earlier. He was her counselor, so he may have seen her once or twice already that year, though lots of times the counselors don't get to the freshmen until spring. But, whatever, Lacey had been shadowing Art all day. She wasn't in his lap or anything, but never too far away. Like on the bus. She was sitting across the aisle and one seat up ahead of him, where she'd be the person he'd see most of the time, you know what I mean? Hell, even as a freshman, Lacey knew how to work the angles." Then he snorted and added, "I guess in this case, she was literally working an angle, huh?"

"You were sitting with Art?" Chug said, wondering how Paul would have noticed this.

"Yeah. Basic, Art and I were the only faculty on that trip, and Lacey kept looking around toward us, and when I asked Art about it, he just smiled. Now Basic, he was sitting with a bunch of kids. He liked to do that on the way up."

"And you say Lacey shadowed Art?" Chug said, urging him back to the details.

"Huh? Oh, sure. Art and I were skiing together that day, so I'm positive. On most of those trips, you might see a kid once or twice, but they don't exactly go out of their way to hang out with you. Lacey, though, was with three other girls, and all morning they took the same lifts, skied the same runs as we did. Near us. Behind us sometimes, ahead for part of a run. But near the bottom they'd always be behind and, whatever lift we went to, they went there too. All morning long."

"How did he react?"

"He sort of didn't, not really. It's not unusual for a kid to get a crush on a teacher, and I was kidding Art about it. You know, pulling his chain. But he didn't react one way or the other. Just shrugged it off. Then we went over to a triple chair, and it was still early enough in the season that there was no line at all. Well, just as we skied up to it, Lacey came up alongside, on Art's side, and said something like, 'We've got four, okay if I go up with you guys?' There was hardly anybody in that lift line, so of course she and her buddies could've gone up two and two, the way Art and I were going to. I'll tell you, I wanted to laugh. I mean, the kid had so much nerve. But there was something about her, even then. It was like you weren't really dealing with a kid, know what I mean?"

"Yep."

"So she snugged in there, next to Art. That was kind of funny, too. I mean, two men sitting next to each other, and neither of us all that small, and this girl at the end. You'd think she'd be in the middle. But that was Lacey. She knew what she wanted. And what she wanted was Art.

"I don't know what she did on that lift. I mean, we were all sitting right next to each other, and her buddies were in the chair behind us giggling their heads off. And nobody said anything. All the way up. And it was a long lift, too. Not a word from her or Art or me. But by the time we reached the top, Art had changed. When I tried to joke about it after we got off the lift and it was just the two of us, he still brushed it off. Another funny thing, the four girls took off ahead of us down one trail. I pointed to a different one, but Art still just shrugged and said he didn't care. And you know what? We didn't see those girls again that day. Whatever Lacey had wanted to communicate, she'd already gotten across to him. I could sense that he'd made a decision, something he wasn't too proud of but was going to do anyway. Honest, Chug, even then, before it happened, I could sense it. I remember telling him something like, 'Hey, she's only a kid, Art.' And you know what? He didn't even try to deny it. He just shrugged and shoved off down the mountain."

Paul stared out his window.

"Sometimes, something like that can just blindside you," Chug said, feeling like a hypocrite, but hoping to find out more by pretending to be sympathetic to Davis.

"No. If it'd been that, if it had been passion or something like that, I could have . . . well, not respected Art, but I could've understood him. It was more cold-blooded than that, more calculated. It wasn't something he had to do, it was something he figured he could get away with."

He continued, "Anyway, we used to double up on rooms, but on this trip, since there were just the three of us guys, we were going to let Basic have a room to himself. But later in the day Art told Basic he didn't feel so hot, maybe had a touch of flu. And Basic, of course, said why don't you take the single? I'll take the double with Paul. I didn't say anything. Guess I still didn't want to admit what I thought was going on. The room he took was at the other end of the motel from ours, Basic's idea being that separating the chaperones made it easier to keep an eye on the kids."

"And?"

"Well, one of the problems with sharing a room with Basic was that snoring thing I mentioned. That's why we generally let him have a room to himself. He also had no problem falling asleep. Me? I tried everything, but that noise still got through. It felt like you were sleeping in a factory. Finally, I got up a little after five. And I snuck outside for a cup of coffee from a machine they had in the lobby. And I went back out and had a cigarette. And there was Lacey, leaving Art's room. I remember thinking, 'Shit, she saw me smoking.' Like that was what mattered. As for her, she just looked me straight in the eye and slipped into the room where she was staying. I don't know what she told her friends. I doubt that they knew about her visit to Art's room. I don't think anybody knew. But I did."

"Did you say anything?"

"Well, I wasn't really positive, y'know?"

Right, Chug knew. Knew when someone suddenly realized what he was admitting about himself.

"I mean, she might've just knocked on his door, y'know. To

check about something." Paul frowned, squinted toward the door as if someone had left the truth nailed to it.

"Do you know if this . . . if Art kept seeing Lacey after that night?"

"Do I know for sure? No. But I think he did. *If* he'd been with her that night. It was just something in the way he acted around me, y'know?"

"You think Traynor knew?"

"No, definitely not. He would've done something about it."

"Even though the whole thing began on one of his trips?"

"That wouldn't have stopped him."

"Who would he have reported it to, then? Prosky?"

Paul could see where this was going.

"Legally, yes. As assistant principal, Basic's responsibility would have been to report it to the principal. And as a mandated reporter, that was all he was legally required to do. But he never would've left it at that. He would've made sure that Prosky did something about it."

Chug didn't see any point in reminding Paul that he was also a mandated reporter.

"Well?" Paul said, impatiently.

"Well, what?"

"We done?"

Chug could see Paul didn't feel too good about what he'd just told, especially since he'd probably been talking now out of nothing more moral than envy. The one thing he didn't know, and right now Chug was only guessing himself, was what this information might really mean. It was like a connect-the-dots puzzle where, suddenly, the numbers had changed, and Chug still couldn't be sure what the final picture would look like.

Paul had so readily bought the lie about his name being on ski trip chaperone lists that Chug knew they must actually exist and, if they did, then he knew who could tell him where to find them.

Irma, fortunately, was still at her desk, sighing at something on her computer screen. The poorly kept rumor about Chug's real purpose for being in the building had apparently reached her because, when he said he needed some information for something he was putting together, her first response was, "For your book?"

He shrugged, said he could use a little more background on Walter, maybe something about his involvement with the ski club.

"Oh, that was Walter's baby, all right," she said.

"Did he keep lists of the people going on the trips?"

"Oh, of course, we have to publish lists for all school trips."

"Are any of those lists still around?"

"Sure. I keep everything, for four years anyway. The ski club lists may go even further back, since I don't remember clearing those files."

She had begun moving through screens as she spoke, muttered, "Ah, here it is!" and lifted an open palm to him as if offering the lists.

"Could I have copies of, well, last year's would be the most recent."

She nodded, highlighting a number of files.

"You can pick them up over there." She pointed toward a large printer near the front windows where the first papers were already sliding into the tray.

He thanked Irma for the help as he left the office with the . . . hmm, seven lists. The one he moved to the top was for a trip last year, the beginning of March.

Yep, Loon Mountain. A weekend trip, it must have been an overnighter at those parent-owned lodges Carstairs had told him about. Lacey's name was on the list. Walter Traynor's. And, well whattaya know—the weekend Art Davis had bought his Powerball ticket, the weekend he'd given the impression that he had been skiing alone at Bretton Woods, he'd actually been about thirty miles away at Loon. And two of the people he'd been skiing with that weekend had been murdered.

"Okay, so two of the people he'd been skiing with have been murdered," Miranda said as she placed her coffee cup on the small table between them.

Chug had called her cell phone and Miranda had said she'd meet him at Cap'n Bill's.

"Coincidence happens, you know," she said. "That's why they have a word for it."

"You been saving that one up all this time?"

She shrugged, smiled, looked around. Too late for lunch, too early for after-supper coffee, there was only the woman behind the counter, and she was busy arranging the muffin trays.

"Seriously, Matthew, there were—how many?—forty other people on that ski trip?"

Miranda held up the list he'd given her. "I mean, in addition to Mr. Davis, Lacey, and Walter?"

"Sure, but only one of them, as far as we know, had been carrying on an affair with one of the victims, a victim who was very underage when the affair began," Chug said. They both spoke in hushed tones and, since they'd arrived in separate cars, Chug felt a little like they also were having an illicit affair. "And only one of the people on that trip is now worth fifty-two million dollars," he added. "From a ticket he bought on that trip. Yet I checked the recording I made of his press conference, and he gave the distinct impression that, like this year, he'd been at a different mountain when he bought it."

He reached for his coffee and sipped it before continuing, "And this year, if he'd been driving back from Bretton Woods, he'd have to go out of his way to get to that store near Loon. If he just wanted gas, as he said, then there were closer stops off the highway."

"Okay, as for the Lacey thing—Jesus, I'm beginning to wonder just how many men that girl slept with. That's something we can pursue. But what exactly are you getting at? I'm still not completely following you here. Are you saying he didn't buy the ticket on that trip? And what difference would that make?"

Chug thought she was closer than she let on, probably a lot closer than she wanted to be.

"No. What I'm saying—and it's still hypothetical so far—is that maybe Davis didn't buy the ticket at all. It was dated, so somebody had to buy it while the ski club was at Loon."

"But then, who did? Walter? Is that what you're saying, Matthew? That Walter bought the ticket?"

"Did you know Davis well when you were a student?"

"Sort of. He was around Walter's a lot. And I was, too. But he wasn't my counselor. Do you actually think he killed Walter for the ticket?"

"How about this: which one, Davis or Walter, would have been more likely to leave a lottery ticket in his car's glove compartment and then forget about it?"

"I'm not sure about Mr. Davis, but, yes, that would have been Walter to a T. But, that's stretching things very thin."

"According to Dorothy Bramwell, Davis was very tuned in to every lottery drawing. You connect that to his fairly deliberate attempt to *not* mention that he'd been on a school ski trip when he first bought the ticket. And you add to that the deaths of two others on the trip, one of them a girl he'd been sleeping with, and I'm not sure we're looking at coincidences anymore."

She lowered her voice to a whisper as an older woman came in and frowned at them as she passed. "But you're suggesting that a guidance counselor at Prescott High School might have killed two students and his best friend for a lottery ticket."

"For a lottery ticket that was worth fifty-two million dollars, Miranda."

She sat back, her shoulders slumped.

He drank more of his coffee, but didn't feel especially triumphant.

"But, then, what about the boy?" she said, still nearly whispering though the woman at the counter was talking to the woman behind it. "Ernest. The letters? The gun? I mean, you saw him, Matthew. You read the letters."

Right. And he had been the first one to suggest that the letters were Ernest's declaration that he was the killer. And she was the one he had suggested it to.

"I don't know about Ernest, Miranda. I have no idea anymore where he fits in here."

"Well, he was either an accomplice or he wasn't. Do you think they were in it together?"

"I don't know. I don't know how they could be. And if they weren't, then . . . I don't know. I just . . . you know, back when I started out as a reporter, I got used to the fact that just about everybody I spoke to had some kind of agenda, everybody was trying to sell me a slant on a story. And I just never bought into this one, into Ernest being this nutcase serial killer. There was something about it I just never believed, right from the beginning."

"I'm kind of used to being lied to myself, Matthew. But you believe this other theory?"

"I'm not one hundred percent convinced. But it's something I feel I have to look into."

"How are you planning to do that?"

"I'm not sure. If I were writing about this for a newspaper, I'd need a second source to confirm Davis's affair with Lacey.

But for now, Paul's story, combined with what I know about Lacey and Prosky, is more than enough for me to follow up on it. I was going to check the lottery numbers, see if they connected in any way to Walter. Maybe his birthday, that kind of thing."

"What were they?" she said, taking a notebook from her purse.

"Six, twelve, thirty-four, forty-four, forty-nine, eight," he read, as she wrote them down.

"Hmm."

"What?"

"Oh, maybe nothing. I don't know. It's just that last number, the eight. That's my birthday, actually it's August eighth, so it'd be eight and eight. Still . . . I don't know. I don't think so."

"You don't think Walter would have chosen your birthday?"

She shrugged, lowered her eyes.

"Did he usually remember your birthday?"

She nodded, whispered, "Always."

"How 'bout the other numbers?"

She looked at the numbers again, shaking her head. "None of them fit his birthday," she said. "He was born March nineteenth. The age is wrong too. The forty-nine's close, but he was fifty."

"How 'bout when the ticket was bought? It was early last March, March third."

"That's right. He would have been forty-nine then."

She looked at the numbers in her notebook for a while longer, but finally shook her head.

"Nothing else here that I can see," she said. "No address, telephone number, nothing like that. Of course, I don't know all the dates that would have been special to him. Even the eight seems like a stretch."

"I don't think it would've been a stretch—and not because I want it to be about the lottery ticket."

She flipped the notebook closed.

"Anything in there on the investigation?"

"No, that was a different one, the murder book. I filed that one away with my other case notes after we got Ernest."

"How 'bout during the investigation? Anything stick out about Davis?"

"Nothing I can think of off the top of my head. He was interviewed, just like everyone else, though I didn't handle that one. And any alibis he gave for the times of the murders were checked, but I don't know how carefully. I'll go look at my case notes."

The older woman turned from the counter and stared at them all the way to the door. Chug wasn't sure if she was thinking *fame* because of the reporting on their capture of Ernest or *shame* because they looked like clandestine lovers. She did, however, shut the door firmly behind her.

"The case is closed, right?" he asked.

"Technically," she said. "We still haven't charged Ernest with the murder, since he's in a coma. But we've got the charge pending, if he comes out of it. And Sergeant Cassidy's back at the DA's office. Still, I know the chief sure as hell won't want to see anybody looking any further into this. But that doesn't mean I can't poke around on my own time, tie up some loose ends."

"Is this too much?" Chug said. "Too far out? Too paranoid?"

She shook her head.

"I know what this means to you," he said. "I know how much easier life would be if I was wrong, if I could just let this go."

"But you aren't able to let this go," she said, tilting her chin up toward him. "And now that you've shown me another way to look at this, neither can I. So what we have to do now is try to find out if you're right. And if you are, then Walter's killer is still free. That, I can't live with."

★ ★ ★ ★ ★

Miranda left for the station and Chug drove to his cabin. They had agreed to meet at her place later. She'd have the pertinent information from her murder book on the case. Chug spent the next couple of hours working on his own book about the case and wondering which of the murder books held more truth.

"These are the pages on Davis," she said later as she sat next to Chug on the couch.

There were logs in the fireplace, but she hadn't lit them. Chug already knew this wasn't likely to be a cozy evening for the two of them, but he did notice that she had dropped the *Mister* from Davis's name. Must be a reaction to his affair with Lacey.

"There's nothing much there," she said. "Davis has solid alibis for the times of Donald Parkhurst's death and for Walter's. When the boy died, he was at a committee meeting at the school with five other people. Three of them were also checked out as part of the investigation, and they all listed Davis as one of the people who had been there for the whole meeting. His alibi's weaker for the time of Lacey's death. His credit card was used to buy gas in Boston, but you don't need a signature for that. And, let's see, at the time of Walter's death, Davis, his wife, and another couple were at a seafood restaurant on the waterfront, confirmed by his wife and the other couple."

She shook her head. "As I said, there's no real alibi for Lacey's death, but that's not unusual. The murders all took place sometime between five and nine, with Lacey's right around five thirty, and a lot of people we interviewed had no good alibis for any of the killings. Single people, who ate at home and stayed in for the night."

"Y'know," Chug said, "Lacey's death is the one I've never really believed Ernest could do. Donald Parkhurst—maybe Ernest could have walked away from the car. And Walter

Traynor, as strange as it may sound, could be at the other end of the same spectrum. That kind of fury might be unleashed if he'd been holding it in long enough. But that's too different from the way Lacey was killed. Much too different."

"Because he's young or because he's Ernest?"

"Mostly, not if he's the same person who killed Walter Traynor."

Miranda was nice enough to not quote her ex-boyfriend, the shrink, on that subject. "So, you think Davis somehow got the boy to kill the other two, but he's the one who killed Lacey?"

"Maybe something like that."

"To make it look like a serial killing. And if Graves is right about the affair, then Davis might have a motive to kill Lacey. And he'd be able to get her out to that island as part of a plan to entrap you."

"Right. And, if he was having an affair with Lacey, then he might know that she was having sex with Prosky."

"Okay." She spoke slowly, but Chug could see from her eyes that she'd already considered that possibility. "Then he would have written that second letter knowing Prosky wouldn't say anything and knowing he could snare him later with another letter."

"If it's Davis, then all of it would fit."

"And then what?" she said. "After Walter's death, he set up Ernest to kill himself to keep him quiet?"

"Would it make sense?"

"I guess . . . But Davis couldn't have known that you'd be picking up your mail at the post office. And that last letter seemed to assume you'd read it later, after Ernest had killed people at the memorial service and then killed himself. How could Davis be sure Ernest would kill people?"

"He didn't have to kill anyone but himself to make the letter work. Blowing himself up could be interpreted as the 'big wet red splash'. And if Davis gave Ernest the PCP they found in him, then the kid might not even realize he was wearing a time bomb around his waist. Ernest's death would look like his own choice."

"No, I mean, how could Davis arrange it time wise? I'm assuming you figure he was in the choir loft with the boy. Otherwise, there's no predicting what Ernest might do with those drugs in him. But Davis couldn't know we would be there early. And it would take a little while for the drugs to kick in. So . . . well, okay, I suppose he could've given him the drug around twelve fifteen—then just sent him out when he saw us show up, guessing that somehow we had figured out Ernest was there."

"But he would've had to think quickly," Chug said. "And if he'd planned to set Ernest loose later, once the service had begun, Davis might have to explain why he wasn't at the service."

"Wait a minute." She began flipping through the pages. "I thought I saw something else . . . yep."

She looked up at Chug, her face hard to read.

"Remember, I had the men at the roadblocks take the names of everyone they stopped on their way to the church?"

He nodded, knowing what had to be coming next.

"Arthur and Louise Davis." She turned the page toward him. And now Chug could recognize the look—reluctant relief. Couldn't blame her.

"The Davises were stopped at twelve forty-five, Matthew. By then, the ambulance was already on its way to pick the boy up."

He stared for a while at the dead fireplace. "Okay. How about someone else, then?"

She cocked her head, one brow raised, as if she thought he might be joking.

"Do you mean you think that someone *other* than Mr. Davis is responsible for all this?"

"No, I still think it's about the lottery money. But it could be someone else *with* Davis, couldn't it? Someone other than Ernest but with the boy in that choir loft."

"I don't know, Matthew. Would that make Ernest in or out?"

He shrugged. "Does it matter? I mean, if Ernest hadn't done any of this, if he were set up, an innocent fall guy, it wouldn't matter to Davis. Davis was his counselor. He could know about his job, could know the kid wouldn't have an alibi for the times when the murders were committed."

"Right."

"And it was Davis who told me to speak to Carstairs. Come to think of it, he also suggested I discuss my classes with Carstairs, which is what led to our talking about the messages Carstairs got last year."

"But wouldn't that mean he was planning all of this last year, when Mr. Carstairs was still at the high school? He couldn't have guessed you'd be at the school this year."

Oh, right. He couldn't have, could he? Chug stared at the cold fireplace for a while, but couldn't find any answer there. He knew they couldn't find a way to change gears, and he still had a lot of student papers to look at, so after a few minutes he got up to leave.

They kissed warmly at the door, but he still drove home thinking the night would have gone a lot better if he could just drop this damned thing. And, when he got back to the cabin, he tried. But after an hour, he gave up and called Carstairs.

Ten minutes later, he called Miranda.

"I asked him about the messages," he said, after telling her he'd just spoken to Carstairs. "I remembered he had told me he'd gotten them later in the year. He said it might have been around Easter. That was late March last year, not long after the lottery ticket had been bought."

"And the tone of the notes?" she said.

"I asked him about the fame thing, and he said no, he didn't think they had any of that in them. They were more like a paranoid psycho, somebody very dangerous, but not looking for acknowledgment."

"You think it still might be Davis, laying the groundwork for a killing spree?"

"Yep. And changed the tone of the letters when Carstairs took a leave of absence."

"Okay," she said, "but that still leaves us with someone else in the choir loft with Ernest. Any thoughts on who this might be?"

"No clue."

"If we follow your scenario, we know the accomplice couldn't have been his wife or the couple he went to dinner with the night Walter was killed. Other than that, it could be just about anyone . . . wait a second . . . If the accomplice was in the choir loft and was supposed to send Ernest down once the service had begun, how would he get away without being seen?"

"I've been back to the church," Chug said. "Took notes on it for that part of my book. And I went back again this afternoon before meeting you, when I thought it must have been Davis up there."

"And?"

"Well, there's that gallery that runs along the whole right side, from the choir loft to the front of the church?"

"Right. I was up in the loft after the ambulance took Ernest. And I went down the stairs at the end of the gallery. They go to a room behind the altar, near a back door. Which you've obviously also considered."

"Yep. And you know that railing running along the front of the gallery is waist-high and solid. No one down below would notice someone sneaking along there, crouched over. Not to mention all hell would be breaking loose if Ernest had started firing in the crowded church, so I doubt anyone would've been looking up there anyway."

"Makes sense."

"So an accomplice could've gotten out very easily during the service. Or, right after he sent Ernest out after us. And the plastique on Ernest was pretty small. Didn't the Boston PD bomb guys say, strapped the way it was to him, it might not have killed anyone *but* him?"

"So you're saying that if Ernest were serious about making a name for himself, all he had to do was create a larger bomb. And apparently, that's not hard to do, especially if he'd already made the small one."

He thought she still sounded dubious, but that didn't stop her from trying to help work it out.

"I have to know for sure before I can do anything about this, Matthew."

"I know. And I don't think you should do anything just yet. How about if I just look around a little more? My book's a good excuse to ask a lot of questions. Explain that I'm thinking of including a section on Davis and his winning the lottery. It wouldn't really belong in the book, not without undermining everything that came before. But most people I'd be speaking to probably wouldn't think of it that way. Or they wouldn't think about it at all. I want to find out more about that ticket. Whattaya think?"

"If you're right, I think you'll be putting yourself in danger. Especially if two people are involved in this. You've met Davis, so you've probably noticed he's a formidable guy."

"He's big and strong, no doubt about that," he said. He barely resisted adding an adolescent, jealousy inspired "But I can take him."

"And if your theory's right, he's very clever and he's ruthless. And he must be partnered with the person who did that to Walter with the ax."

True. All that did slow Chug down. And he cautioned himself that every skunk who ever crossed a highway figured the cars would be too afraid to drive near him.

"I just plan to try to get more information," he said. "Maybe only find a way to prove the ticket was Walter's in the first place."

"If you find out anything, anything else that supports your theory, let me know right away. Or if there's anything I can do to help now."

"Let me just poke around for a while first." He reminded himself that it wasn't just his own happy little bubble of a book he was set on bursting. In fact, this could help the book in the long run. But, if he were right, then the worst-case scenario would be that they had been duped into a showdown with a drugged seventeen-year-old. And, even though she hadn't done the actual shooting, Miranda had stationed Harrington with his rifle precisely so he could do what he did. Shake that tree and all the apples would fall on her. Chug? Hell, no matter what he wrote, he knew he was still just an ex-talking-head minor celebrity, now a long-term substitute teacher. He couldn't wrap himself in the responsibility no matter how hard he tried. And what if they proved Ernest innocent? There was always that crazy possibility. And if he then died, what then? Though shooting Ernest had actually prolonged his life, Harrington was bound to feel guilty for killing an innocent kid, and there'd always be that dark cloud following Miranda's career and life.

Not for the first time, Chug thought that whoever preaches that truth shall set you free may not be facing a tough enough truth.

# Chapter Twenty-Four

Chug hadn't told Miranda that part of his plan had been to talk to Davis. It made sense, since he had been such a close friend of Traynor's. And showing up with that monster winning lottery ticket must have given Davis a strong taste of media attention.

Davis agreed to meet in his office, after school again. Though Chug tried not to overthink it, he kept remembering the last time when they had sat in there, discussing what he was going to do about the problem of Lacey in his AP class while, if his gucss was right, Davis had already arranged a very permanent solution to that problem.

"I heard about the book you're writing," Davis said, his hand firmly gripping Chug's as he nodded toward a chair. He was wearing jeans, a corduroy shirt and, with his dark hair still in that ponytail, he looked more like a trail guide than either a guidance counselor or a multimillionaire.

"The book sounds like a good idea, Chug. Big market out there for sensationalism."

"It's not going to be sensational."

"Oh, hey, I didn't mean that the way it sounded." Big smile. Big teeth. Big guy. Right now, he was worth big bucks. "All the craziness around me about the money, I guess, has got my thinking a little twisted."

Chug congratulated him on winning, and they talked a little about how Davis was still trying to get used to the whole thing.

"I gave the school six weeks to find a replacement," he said as the final word on the subject.

Chug had heard he was quitting but pretended it was news. "Can't say I blame you. You must be in one of those situations where any money you earn here just gets eaten up in taxes."

"Yeah, something like that. And people driving me crazy looking for handouts. Uh, you're not here to borrow any money, are you?"

"No." Chug smiled. "Just looking for a little information."

Davis nodded, leaned back, taking a sip from a can of Coke he had on his desk as Chug began asking him some questions about his background, his connection to the school.

Davis was cautious, sipping at the soda between questions and often before answering. Still, the questions were deliberately innocuous and so were his answers. He had eased up noticeably by the time they got around to talking about Traynor. Before long he became expansive and anecdotal, though most of the stories seemed to illustrate how Traynor went out of his way to make extra work for himself. Some of the material was kind of funny, although a whole different Traynor personality presented itself through Davis's description. He still came across as well-intentioned Basic, but a little more foolish, maybe even self-centered, a man who wanted the world to acknowledge his qualities more than he wanted to help people. Chug figured that if he was right about Davis's involvement in Traynor's death, then this was the way he was managing to live with it.

"How about his death?" Chug was tired of this approach and wanted to at least break Davis's rhythm. "How'd you hear about that?"

"Oh, I guess like most everyone else—except you and Sparks, of course. When I came to school that morning. The police were already here. I think it was one of the secretaries who told me what had happened."

"And Ernest—did you ever suspect him?"

He had begun shaking his head, so Chug added, "I know what you told the press, but just between us—and not for attribution in any book—did you ever suspect him? I mean, the kid was a little strange."

"I suppose, if someone asked me which of the kids I counseled—and that's a couple hundred a year—might do something like that, his name would be on the list. But not at the top."

"How about Lacey?"

"What about her?" He frowned. "I don't follow you."

"What was she like? I mean, really?"

"You need to know about her for your book?"

"Sure. Even if I don't use it all, the more I know, the more accurately I can describe the background, the setting, of the killings. You always need more information than you're going to actually use in a book like this. But even the stuff that doesn't get in helps infuse everything you write. Gives the book its subtext. Hell, you taught English, you know what I mean."

Davis thought a little, then began, "Well, she was a nice-enough kid, but maybe not as bright as she thought she was. Same as I told you the last time you were in here."

"What about her reputation? Just between us, she came on to me in my classroom after school, and she seemed to know pretty much what she was doing. And I think she wanted me out on the island to try to get some video of us together, with her in lingerie and me looking compromised. Hell, I could've been wearing a suit of armor, and it still would've looked pretty bad."

"Is that right?" Davis looked a little puzzled. "I didn't know about Lacey being like that. To tell you the truth, kids the way they are these days, not too much surprises me anymore. And Lacey always looked as if she knew her way around a bedroom. But I never heard anything special about her."

"Not even on the ski trips?"

"Ski trips?"

"Sure. As I said, I've been talking to a lot of people and mostly I've been asking about Lacey and Basic and Ernest. And a couple of people have suggested that Lacey didn't limit the overnight ski trips to the novice runs. If you know what I mean."

Chug thought it was a painfully stupid metaphor, although he also thought it was about right for Davis, who nodded knowingly, but then began shaking his head again.

"Never heard a thing about that. Let me tell you, Basic would've had a fit if he found out anything like that was going on among the kids on the trips."

Okay, time to push it a little further. "Tell you the truth, Art, some of the people I've talked to have suggested that Lacey might not have been limiting her playmates to her fellow students."

He was good, had to give him that. Davis's face held a trace of confusion for a couple of beats before it turned red, and he narrowed his eyes.

"You better not be meaning me, friend. That's not what you're suggesting, is it?"

"No, 'course not, Art. All I'm doing is looking for information. And right now I don't know what's true and what's just rumor, what's important and what isn't. So what I do is just gather it all together and then later see if I can sort it out. But right now I'm just gathering."

"Well, you'd better watch what you gather, buddy." He leaned in. "Because I don't like your implications."

He bent closer for emphasis, so that Chug was sprayed with a little Coke spittle as Davis added, "You understand?"

He could see that Davis had thought he'd intimidate him, maybe expecting to see a puddle of pee appear at Chug's feet, so the counselor seemed taken aback when Chug calmly asked, "What's that aftershave you're wearing, Art?"

He was going to tell Davis that he thought it smelled a little wussy, just because he didn't like being threatened. But then another thought cut right through the first and, as he stared at Davis's temporarily confused face, Chug suddenly realized there was another direction he might want to go with this.

"The what?"

"The aftershave," he said seriously. "That smell. I remember it from somewhere. Somewhere . . . I smelled it before, y'know? Like somewhere unusual. And I just don't remember where, but . . . I dunno, I'd just like to know what it's called."

"It's *Rodeo Leather.*" Davis nervously squinched the soda can in his fingers. But Chug could see he had had the effect he wanted because the counselor was inadvertently backing away. "Lots of guys wear it."

"Oh, is that what that is? Damn, I wish I could remember where I smelled it before. Not too strong, y'know, but there. Like a name that's just on the tip of your tongue."

A name like Sunset Island, maybe? Chug had his attention. He could see it. The killer had worn gloves, the police already knew that. And he'd been careful enough to not leave any other trace behind. But would he have thought about the trace of a scent? In a house that had been closed up for a month or so? Might just linger. It hadn't, of course, or not enough for Chug to notice it. But it might have.

"Look, I don't want to talk to you anymore, Chug." Davis's face took on the aggrieved look of a kid who was being punished on a technicality, like knowing that even though he'd hit the home run, he hadn't really touched second on his way around the bases. "I just don't appreciate the line you've been taking with this interview."

He'd gradually rolled his chair behind his desk, and now it was all the way to the wall. As far from Chug's nose as he could get in the small office without opening the window and leaping out.

"I'm sorry you feel that way, Art. I certainly didn't mean to imply anything."

He picked up the recorder, clicked it off.

"*Rodeo Leather,* you say that is?" He wrote it down on the pad, though the recorder would have picked up the name. "Have to check that out. Maybe it'll jog my memory. Maybe we can talk again sometime."

Davis didn't respond. He also didn't get up from his chair against the wall. Afraid Chug might pick up his spoor again? But it didn't matter. He already had the ponytailed son of a bitch right where he wanted him: afraid of Chug and wondering what he should do about it. Now all Chug had to do was turn up the heat a little. And in the process find some way to avoid getting himself burned.

# Chapter Twenty-Five

Miranda looked a little drained, disappointed in some deep and quiet way as they sat in the little North End Italian restaurant.

"Any luck?"

"That depends on your definition of luck." She took a small sip of her wine. "I found possible connections to most of the lottery numbers in addition to the eight. Walter's mother's birthday was June twelfth, which would cover the six and twelve."

"And you checked his father's birthday?"

"The other winning numbers are all over thirty-one," she said, leveling Chug with a stare over the top of her wine glass.

Oh, right, birth dates didn't go higher than that.

"I've also checked Dorothy's age, which is a possible since she would have been forty-four at the time he bought the ticket. Then I got a little obsessive and looked up all the addresses he'd ever lived at, his year of graduation from high school and college, the size of his collar and sleeves, waist and pants leg length. The trouble with that approach was I was bound to hit most of the numbers in one way or another. The forty-four, for instance, was not only Dorothy's age, it was also the size of those plaid jackets Walter loved so much, and the twelve, in addition to being his mother's birthday, was his shoe size. So I've been able to connect Walter to all of them except the thirty-four. I couldn't find a single connection to that number. But I don't think it really matters."

"What else have you got?" Chug said.

"No, you go now. I just want to sit here for a while and watch your mouth move. You have a very nice mouth."

She leaned back, sipped her wine, and stared at him, her dark eyes glinting with the wine's reflected dark light.

A little distracted by the thought that she was watching nothing but his mouth, Chug described his meeting with Davis, which drew her gaze immediately up to his eyes. He ended with an explanation of how Davis had responded to the questions about his aftershave.

"There wasn't any aftershave smell at the crime scene, was there?" she said. "There's nothing about it in the report."

Chug shook his head.

"And you never mentioned anything to me about your planning to actually talk to Davis again."

He shrugged, tried to move his very nice mouth into a very nice conciliatory smile.

"Regardless," she said, nodding her approval of his small victory. "I'm not sure just what we've succeeded in doing, beyond letting Davis know you suspect him. Even if you'd been telling the truth, smelling an aftershave at a murder scene is hardly grounds for an arrest."

"I know. I just wanted to shake him up a little."

"What if you're right and you shake him up enough to come after you, Matthew?"

"I'm not enough of a threat for him to do that."

"Not yet."

Any response he might have concocted was derailed by the waiter arriving with Miranda's chicken cacciatore and Chug's manicotti.

"Okay, and now for the rest of your news," he said, reaching for his fork.

"I think I've found an alibi for Ernest," she said. "For Walter's murder."

"What?!"

She nodded slowly. "I was checking the outgoing calls from Baines Computer, the shop where he worked. There weren't any for the nights we were interested in. But I also checked his work record, and on the night Walter died, Ernest had begun by working on someone's motherboard, but then had written *cust. called—will call tomorrow* and apparently switched to another job. I found the phone number for the owner of that computer and called him. He lives in Milton, and he said he remembered calling the place because Baines was supposed to give him a repair estimate but hadn't. He said he'd talked to a kid, who was working on his computer at the time and told him the repair wasn't too complicated. But he didn't know what the charge would be. Baines handled that. So the customer said he didn't want the repairs completed until he had an estimate, and that he'd call again to speak to the owner in the morning."

"And Ernest stopped working on that job."

"Apparently. The key is the time. The man from Milton wasn't sure. 'Sometime after supper' is the way he put it. But he had used a cell phone with limited minutes, and I asked to look at the bill for that month. There was one call to the number at Baines Computer. It was nine minutes long, from eight forty-one to eight fifty p.m."

"That's bad?" Chug said, reacting to the unhappy look on her face.

"Well, we know Walter was alive at eight fifteen because a neighbor of his saw him drive away. It would have taken him at least fifteen minutes to drive to the school and walk into the locker room so we know he couldn't have been killed before eight thirty. According to Ernest's parents, the boy got home before nine thirty that night. And, in fact, his computer has him logging into a role-playing game chat room at nine thirty-two."

"So," Chug said, "if he was at the shop in Braintree at eight forty-one, there was no way he could've killed Walter before he received the call. And if he was still there at eight fifty, there was no way he could have driven to the high school, killed Walter, cleaned up, and still been home on time."

"That's the math," she said.

"Which means Ernest didn't kill Walter."

"Right."

"And Davis's solid alibi means he didn't kill him either."

"Right."

They both thought about that for a while. It only confirmed what he had guessed earlier, but knowing was a lot different from guessing. Knowing meant there were now two people to worry about and not one. And the one they couldn't identify was the one who had butchered Traynor.

Miranda began moving her food a little more as if it were pieces to a jigsaw puzzle, and she was looking for the corners.

"So what are you going to do?" she said after staring unhappily at her plate for a while.

"Stay at it. What else?"

What else indeed? And pray that what he dug up wouldn't be something that would leap out and go for his throat.

# CHAPTER TWENTY-SIX

It took Chug over a week to figure out what his next step should be. When he finally did come up with an idea that he thought would work, it was something he had borrowed from Miranda's bag of tricks. He began one afternoon after school, digging through his desk until he found an in-class essay test Lacey had taken a couple of days before their after-school discussion that had triggered her refusal to work. The police had collected all her other writing, including her journal with the beginnings of her novel.

Miranda said it hadn't been much help. This essay test wouldn't have been any help either, except to prove that Lacey's awareness of *Hamlet* had come almost entirely from the Mel Gibson movie. But it would help Chug in other ways. Her handwriting was large, rounded, with extended bars on her t's and little circles over the i's, and Chug practiced a couple of hours each of the next few days before he felt he had come up with a fairly good imitation. It would never fool an expert, but it should work on Davis. Then he bought a green Flair and a two-pocket folder with a cover that featured a unicorn strolling along a moonlit shore, and began writing a series of notes for Lacey's *roman à clef,* notes that were a stark contrast to the folder's idyllic cover. Mostly they were about scenes of sex between the auburn-haired heroine named Stacey and a high-school principal named Porter, followed by more sex with a guidance counselor named Davidson. He included descriptions of each character that he thought were deadly accurate. Given Lacey's style, he also thought the characters were deadly dull.

Next he added a half page of apparent notes, in which she planned to add a section on an affair with an English teacher named O'Hara, then crossed that out and jotted down: "Davisson says to go to Sunrise? Island and trick O'Hara into seeing things Stacey's way. Good plan. Davison always thinking ahead."

He liked the touch of twice mispelling the character Davidson's name, each time coming closer to the original.

A week after his first visit, Chug stopped into the guidance suite at the beginning of his planning period. There were a few students sitting at the tables, and one counselor's door was closed, but the other's was open. And so was Davis's. Chug leaned in, tapped at the frame, and the counselor's look, as he raised his eyes, was both guarded and hostile.

"What can I do for you?"

"Y'know, it finally dawned on me where I smelled that aftershave you wear, *Rodeo Leather.* Strangest thing, y'know, how a smell will trigger a memory?"

Davis sat back, waiting, while Chug closed the door behind him.

"It was out on Sunset Island, the place where Lacey was killed."

"There was nothing about that in the report, Chug."

"Hey, I never said I reported it, just that I smelled it. I didn't even know what the smell was called until you told me. The thing that made me think of it was the other thing I never mentioned to the police."

And with that, he dropped the unicorn-fairyland folder on the desk.

Davis frowned as he opened it to the title page:

*Love's Awakening*
*A Novel*
*by Lacey McGovern*

"What the hell is this?" he said.

"Something I found yesterday."

Davis frowned, took out the sheaf of papers written in green Flair and began reading.

"I have my students work on creative writing a couple of times a week," Chug said. "We don't share it. And I don't read it. I just make sure they're writing. Two pages. Dated."

He waited, while Davis read on, his breathing sounding shallower with each page he turned. When he came to the last page, with the notes for the next section, a section that would apparently deal with going to an island to convince a very mean English teacher to change his mind about a very clever auburn-haired beauty, Chug said, "You may notice by the date that Lacey wrote those notes on the day she died."

"How come the police didn't see this, Chug?" Davis's eyes were focused to the side, as if most of his attention was fixed on mentally completing some complex mathematical equation.

"Students have writing folders in the classroom," Chug said. "In a file cabinet. I gave all the stuff in Lacey's file to the police, but she must've put this in the wrong file. Another student found it yesterday, when we were putting some new writing in the files. He didn't even read it, just took out the folder and said, 'Hey, Mr. O'Malley. This isn't mine.' "

"So?" Davis's computation was apparently continuing behind those narrowed blue eyes.

"Well, what should I do with it, Art?"

"Why don't you shove it up your ass?"

Ah, the computation was complete.

"Or I could give it to the proper authorities," Chug said. "There are a couple more original pages written in green that I didn't include. And, of course, I've photocopied the ones you have there. You can keep 'em if you like, check for accuracy of content."

He was sure the first thing Davis would do would be to check for the accuracy of the forgery. A guidance counselor would have easy access to samples of his students' handwriting. And the one good thing about Davis being guilty was that Chug was sure he wouldn't go looking for an expert who could easily prove the forgery.

"You know, this is starting to sound a lot like blackmail, Chug. Is that what we're talking about here? Do you want a piece of my winnings based on some half-baked idea you've got?"

"Your winnings. Interesting way of putting it, Art. Let's just say we need to talk again. Just the two of us, in some place private. You've got until a week from this Saturday to think about it. Then I'll just have to do my civic duty."

He opened the door and left. Now that he had Davis's unwavering attention, Chug needed to be very sure about the next step.

He didn't know who looked sadder at the parting, Jason or Amigo. Jason did a better job of hiding it. Amigo, with whom Chug had scrambled through dry leaves and deep snow on most of the weekends since he'd given the dog to his son, was happy to see him arrive midweek in Bradford. And he was eager to leap into the cab of Chug's truck, tail awag, head bobbing around, wondering what wonderful and exciting thing the pack was going to do next. He just wasn't happy to realize the rest of the pack, especially Amigo's pack leader, Jason, wasn't coming along. The dog pressed his head against the truck window, wet nose smushing the glass, all the way down the street and around the corner and nearly halfway to Fall River. For the second half of the ride, he stretched beside Chug on the wide bench seat, his head on his paws, and sighed as he stared up, huge brown eyes patiently waiting for Chug to change his mind.

He was a little more resigned by the time they reached Tiago's house, perking up enough to pee on the shrubbery out front, though he did eye Chug a little suspiciously, in that nervous looking-back-over-the-shoulder way dogs get and, once inside, positioned himself close to the kitchen door just so there'd be no doubt about his intentions of leaving.

"You sure you want to do it this way?" Ti said, handing Chug his holstered Colt before going back into the gun safe.

"If you can think of some other way to nail the bastard, I'm open to suggestions."

He had already told Ti his plan over the phone before heading down, so his cousin had had over an hour to think about it, but still shook his head as he came back out with some of the other guns Chug had told him he'd need.

"I've made out a bill of sale for each of the four guns," Ti said, putting the paper down on the table. "Sign them. You get caught with 'em, I'll put in that day's date. Otherwise, treat them carefully and get 'em back to me."

Tiago was shaking his head as he spoke, still uncertain of the wisdom of Chug's plan.

"I'll be fine," Chug said, realizing what a role reversal this was for the two of them. He didn't know how many times over the years, especially when they were younger, he had grabbed the sleeve of Ti's jacket to keep him from launching himself into sending-someone-to-the-emergency-room mode.

"If anything happens to you, you know I'll get him." Ti placed the other equipment Chug had asked for on the kitchen table.

Chug guessed he meant one way or the other. With Ti, it would probably be the other.

"If it came to that, it wouldn't matter to me," Chug said.

Hell, he'd be beyond caring about revenge.

"No, it'd be for me, Chug. It'd be for me."

Ti helped him carry the stuff out to his truck, while Amigo bounded ahead of them and waited at the passenger door with a "C'mon, c'mon, already" look of impatience and a nervous side-glance at Chug's cousin.

"And you can't just let this go?" Ti said one more time as they let the dog scurry onto the seat. This from a guy with a grip as tight as a torque wrench.

"No. I'm way past that now."

Ti put a hand on Chug's shoulder. "Take care. And contact me right away. Anytime."

Chug nodded, got in behind the wheel and closed his door and, as Amigo sighed with relief, drove back to Prescott.

It was late by the time they got to the cabin, but Amigo was already familiar with the area and, when taken out for last call, was quick about it. When he came back, Chug carefully stowed the handguns and the shotgun he had got at Ti's, set the time on the carriage clock he'd placed on a living-room shelf, and put Ti's cookbook on a shelf out in the kitchen. Then he and Amigo settled in for the night, the dog next to Chug's bed as if he'd always slept there. It probably helped that Chug had left one of Jason's old sweatshirts on the floor for Amigo to rest his head on.

Running in March was usually better than in January or February. The ground had warmed a little, so had the air. Sometimes late March could trick you into thinking that spring had shown up early for once. But not the day after Chug brought Amigo to his cabin. The late-afternoon sky was slate-gray and, though the ground was reassuring Chug that it would warm soon to a spring rebirth, the nasty wind whistling in his ears seemed to be whispering that nothing good would come of it anyway. And the lake, to his right and about fifty yards down an incline from the poorly paved road, was a duller, darker gray than the sky. Hell, he thought, all he needed was a choir of ravens perched up in the naked trees he was running past, croaking a chorus of "Nevermore" to the weak and watery four o'clock sun.

He would've felt better if the dog had been with him, for company if nothing else. But Amigo could only help if he remained a secret. He had, however, brought along one of the Colt automatics he'd picked up at Ti's, even though it made for uncomfortable running, pressed beneath his sweatshirt like a holstered steel fist into the small of his back.

He was hoping the run would clear his head, help him figure out what to do if Art didn't take the bait. He had heard in school today that Davis was planning to travel, though nobody quite knew where. Far away, anyway.

Jeremy, Chug's agent, had left a couple of voice mails and a lengthy e-mail about the book, wondering what had happened to it, since Chug had told him it was just about completed almost a month ago.

*I'm tryin'. I'm tryin'.* It was a stubborn mantra that bonked through Chug's head as inflexibly as the steel pressed against the small of his back, though he didn't know whom he was telling it to. He couldn't work on the book, not when he knew the ending he'd given it was all wrong. None of the events needed changing, just what they all meant. And, what was worse, he still had no idea who had killed Donald Parkhurst or Walter Traynor and set up Ernest to be destroyed.

Though Chug knew he'd made the counselor nervous about Lacey's autobiographical novel, all Davis really had to do was wait him out for a little over a week, call his bluff.

Damn! Almost turned an ankle on a small stone he hadn't noticed in the road. Gotta be careful, O'Malley, he reminded himself. Look where the hell you're going, or you'll be limping all the way back to the cabin.

Which was why he looked at the road ahead, all the way to where it banked left about sixty yards away. Which was why he hesitated a half step, more curious than alarmed, when he saw something peripherally move up there on the left, near a copse of evergreens. Which was why the bullet whizzed in front of him, missing his nose by inches, instead of slamming into the side of his head as it would have if Chug had taken that one full step.

He was already leaping to his right into the underbrush as he heard the echo of the shot. Then he was tumbling down the slight incline and through some brambles toward the lake. Then the brambles behind Chug snapped with one sharp crack, and he knew damned well what had snapped them. But he was up and scrambling low now, to the left, to the right. Another shot snapped near him, an angry spitting sound. No reverberating boom, just nasty, spit, spit, and then he was in among some sturdier cover, a mix of birch and oak bordering the lake. Thunk. The other side of the oak trunk.

He had the Colt out, the slide springing the first cartridge into the chamber. Kneeling so his head would be lower than the shooter expected, he peeked around the side of the oak with the gun up but not showing. If the shooter came down here after him without knowing about the Colt, it might be the mistake Chug needed.

Just then he heard the familiar sound of a neighbor's truck. It was an old yellow Ford that belched and farted its unheeded demand for a tune-up, owned by a retired white-haired guy who favored plaid flannel shirts and spent a lot of time chopping his own firewood. Chug didn't even know his name; he was just a guy he waved to when he ran past the man's cottage.

The truck slowed, then stopped at about the place where Chug had plunged off the road. The driver must have seen something, heard something, though he couldn't have seen someone shooting at Chug, or he wouldn't be stopping there in the middle of the road. Chug was going to yell at him to get the hell away from there, but then the old guy got out of his truck and was staring off toward the area where the shots had been fired. He had his hands on his hips, was calling out something about ". . . out of season, damn it!"

Chug wondered, briefly, just when he might be in season, but then as the old man's voice got louder, calling out, he realized that the person his neighbor was yelling at was heading away, taking off.

He decided it might be a good thing if he did the same thing. First he had to slow his breathing. Then he reluctantly slipped the safety on but kept the gun in his hand as he crouched over and scuttled crablike along the shore.

After Chug's call to the station, Robidoux, the Prescott PD badass fireplug, was the first one to his cabin, pulling up with lights and sirens. Chug had commanded Amigo to silence and stepped outside, and had just begun explaining what had happened when Miranda blew down the lane, Accord springs bouncing and the whole car lurching forward as she hit the brakes.

"You all right?" she said, rushing to Chug. She had herself under control, for Robidoux's sake if nothing else, but Chug thought it was still a close thing.

He told her he was fine, but she was slow to buy it. Robidoux suggested Chug could tell the tale while they drove down to the scene of the shooting, so after they all got into his cruiser, and Robidoux radioed the other cars where to meet them, Chug began again, explaining what had happened. He sort of omitted the part about being armed with his Colt from both versions.

"It sounded like the same kind of rifle as the last time, that night back in September at my cabin. But this time the shooter was trying to hit me. No doubt about that."

Miranda was turned around, looking at him, her hand against the chain link screening that isolated the backseat. Sitting in the police car's cage, behind doors that only opened from the outside, Chug placed his hand up opposite hers, felt her hand's pulsing warmth. If Robidoux hadn't been driving, he'd have found a way into the front seat just to wrap his arms around her reassuring aliveness.

"That old guy who came by in the truck," Robidoux said. "You say he lives around here?"

"About a half mile ahead. White cottage on the lake. Think it's got green shutters. Drives a yellow Ford truck."

"Yeah, thought so. That's a guy named Kasinski," Robidoux said. "Cal Kasinski. Old pain in the ass."

"Place it happened is right up there."

They pulled over and got out as a second police cruiser came racing down the road to meet them.

"The shots came from over there." Chug pointed with his left hand to the small stand of pines on a nearby hill. Then he pointed with his right hand. "I went down there."

Couldn't miss the spread-brambles, crushed-branch path he'd cleared in his scramble toward the lake.

"First shot came by me right about here," he said. "Slug must be in there somewhere. Maybe hit one of those birches. There were at least two more shots at me when I was rolling down the hill there. Another one hit a tree I was hiding behind closer to the lake. It was an oak. I'm pretty sure I can find it again."

Two more cruisers arrived, and Miranda left with one of the policemen to speak to Cal Kasinski. Robidoux and another cop cautiously inspected the shooter's spot. Chug went down the hill with the last cop to look for the oak tree the final bullet had hit because it seemed the most likely place to find a slug.

Since his trail was so easy to follow, and there were only a couple of oaks to choose from, it didn't take them long to find the tree, or the nasty gray chunk of lead still imbedded in it. As the cop pried it out and dropped it in a plastic baggie, Chug was reminded of why they call it a slug. It looked like the one that had been fired at him in his cabin. But he was sure they hadn't been fired from the same weapon.

Four other policemen had arrived by the time they got back to the road, and two helped search the underbrush and among the birch trees for the other slugs, while the rest helped ribbon off the shooter's area and hunt carefully for anything that might help identify him. Chug, meanwhile, leaned against a police car and tried to look as if he hadn't done anything wrong when the infrequent car drove slowly past, faces staring out at it all. Surprisingly, no one actually stopped to find out what the hell was going on. Chug wasn't sure whether that was a very good or a very bad sign of local attitudes.

Miranda was back in a half hour and came over to the car where Chug had begun pacing back and forth, trying to stay warm.

"He says he didn't get a good look at the shooter," she said. "He thought someone was hunting deer out of season, and it's illegal to fire that close to homes. Anyway, he was no help. What's been happening here?"

"Found one of the slugs. Might be the same kind as were fired at me last time. But it wasn't the same shooter."

"You sure?"

"This guy was out to kill me, I know that. Last time, it was those kids from school just trying to scare me. I'm sure it was."

Robidoux was making his way out of the crime-scene-cordoned-off woods holding up a small baggie.

"Would you look at what we got here," he said.

There, glinting in the last of the afternoon gloom, was a most familiar tiny pin in the form of a silver key.

"I don't care if they show me a video of Brandon and his buddies aiming their rifles," Chug said. "They weren't the ones shooting at me."

They were back in Robidoux's unit, the heater on full blast, heading back to Chug's cabin. It had gotten too dark to look around the crime scene anymore. The police had found a second undamaged slug which everyone agreed looked like a .30 caliber. Nothing else to speak of.

"You know these boys better than I do," Miranda said from the front. "But are you positive? Maybe the other killings set them off, they decided to keep up the excitement level. Copycats are always a possibility when there are serial killings."

"And left the silver key there as a calling card? No way. This shooter was trying to kill me. That much I'm sure of. In the first place, I don't think Brandon or his buddies would do that. If for no other reason than it's too self-destructive. But, even if one of them decided to, just for the thrill of it, he sure as hell wouldn't wear the key and run the risk of losing it. And I don't think he'd deliberately leave it behind either, not at the site of an attempted murder."

Robidoux stopped at the top of the driveway, and Miranda got out to open the back door and let Chug out of the cage.

"I'll be back at the station in a while to go over all the reports," she said to Robidoux, who nodded glumly and drove off.

"You think it was Davis, then," she said, as they started down the driveway to her car.

"Or his accomplice. You going to check Davis?"

"Yes. Then Brandon Wainwright and his friends."

"Davis won't be happy to see you."

She shrugged.

"He'll have an alibi," Chug said.

"I'm sure he will."

"Wonder how he'd know about the caliber, though."

"Huh?"

"Of the bullets fired at me that night."

"The local weekly carries a police-log column. I wouldn't be surprised if the article included the caliber of the bullets. The reporter who does that column's a nitpicker. And .30 calibers aren't exactly rare."

"And the silver key?" he said. "Would that have been in the police log too?"

"No." She frowned as she looked at him in the gathering darkness. "But a couple of people on the force are related to teachers or have kids at the school. Something about the key could have gotten into the pipeline there. Davis could've picked up the information that way."

He nodded.

"Is there something else here, Matthew? Something you haven't said?"

"No, no. 'Course not." But he was wondering how Davis thought he could get hold of the copies of the fake Lacey novel once Chug had been shot. Well, maybe he'd have a little while to ransack the cabin. Still, that was a big chance he was taking.

"Do you have someplace else to stay?" Miranda said as they stopped at her car.

"No."

"How about staying with me? You know I have room. And the bed's big enough for two, as you also know."

"That's gotta be the best offer anybody ever made me. But I didn't mean I had no place to stay, Miranda. I meant I wasn't going to stay anywhere else but here."

"And if the shooter comes back?"

"My gun license is still valid, and now I've bought some guns from Tiago."

Of course, since there'd been no money exchanged, technically he hadn't bought anything. But only technically.

"And today?" she said, her meaning obvious.

"Yeah, I had a Colt automatic with me. I didn't get a chance to use it, but I was sure as hell glad I had it."

"Matthew, I saw how you reacted when Ernest started firing, and I saw how you handled that bomb, so I know you can act fast in an emergency. But I wish you'd consider a different approach to this."

Amigo must have heard their voices and decided the command was long past its limits, so he greeted them from inside the cabin.

"Is Jason here?" she asked, puzzled.

"Nope, just Amigo. I'm borrowing him for a while. Part of a plan I've been working on that might settle this once and for all."

"And are you planning to tell me what your plan is?"

"I think it will only work if I don't tell you. There might be some legal angles that'd get muddied if you knew about it beforehand."

"Are you sure about all this?" From her look Chug was a little uncertain just how much *all this* covered.

He nodded and watched her gradually, reluctantly accept it. They were still okay, but he sensed that, at some subtle level, he and Miranda weren't quite as okay as they had been just a little while ago. And he wasn't sure why.

# Chapter Twenty-Seven

Miranda called him later, explaining that Art Davis had been at a late parent conference when Chug was being shot at, the meeting confirmed by both parents.

"He was upset that I even asked him about it," she said. "Claimed that you've been harassing him."

"Did he say he wanted to take out a restraining order against me?"

"No, Matthew." He could imagine her small smile spreading. "But please, please be careful."

Chug and Amigo got along well in the days that followed, their only disagreements coming over a chair. Upholstered and thick-cushioned, the chair was one that Jason had kept in his room, and that's where Amigo used to sleep. Chug had taken it for the dog to use but discovered the bedroom was too small for it and, damn, he needed to keep the dog near him at night. Then, when he left the chair in his small living room, he realized it was the most comfortable spot in the house. Now, Amigo slept on Jason's sweatshirt next to the bed, but he also climbed up and settled in the chair whenever Chug got up from it, even for a fridge run. And the dog was tough to dislodge when Chug came back, obviously feeling his loyalty to Jason was questioned by his leaving that damned chair. Other than that, he was a remarkably patient and cooperative companion. Of course, by the time Chug got back from school each afternoon, Amigo was relieved to be let out, although Chug didn't want him spending too much time outside the cabin.

To keep him a secret, and to avoid a repeat of the gunshot-interrupted afternoon run, as soon as it got dark, Chug would slip the dog into the truck, and they'd drive over to the high school. There Chug would run around the track in the darkness, the Colt firmly holstered at his waist, though he was fairly sure the dog would alert him to anyone too close. What Amigo did most of the time, however, was run circles around Chug in between dashes across the football, baseball, and soccer fields, the tennis courts, the basketball courts, and then a couple of times back around him just for good measure.

Chug tried to do his schoolwork before supper so his nights, after the run with Amigo, could be spent fine-tuning the book that he had no idea how to complete. He had a meal at Miranda's one night, but most of the time was dedicated to the book with occasional breaks spent fighting Amigo for the comfortable chair.

By the second week of his ultimatum to Davis, Chug was getting impatient. Working on the book had become just putting in time, and the next day he would rewrite almost everything he had written the day before. He felt the same way about the pages of Lacey's book that he'd faked. They were no good. Except for the one attempt to shoot him, by the person he still thought of as simply Davis's partner, the killers seemed to have stopped worrying about Chug or bothering to go for the bait. Maybe he had included some seemingly insignificant detail in Lacey's notes that had alerted Davis to the forgery. Chug had tried to be vague in the writing and, though he couldn't find anything obvious when he read and reread the pages, he couldn't be certain. He had given Davis until the upcoming Saturday to contact him. If he didn't react by then, there was nothing Chug could do. Nothing. A second possibility was that Davis might react, but not exactly when or where Chug wanted him to, which could mess up his plans completely. He tried not to linger on the third option, that Davis's partner would strike again, and this time Chug could easily end up dead.

The attempt finally came very early on Thursday morning. Three twenty-one by the clock radio. That's when Amigo began growling. Chug hadn't been sleeping well recently anyway, hearing many of the early-morning hours bonged off on Ti's carriage clock out in the living room. The dog hadn't helped matters either by reacting to more than a few cats and owls passing through their night neighborhood. But this was different. Amigo was up, alert, ears back and his growl deeper than Chug had ever heard it before. As Chug slipped out of bed, Amigo looked up at him eagerly, looked back toward the window. There had been a spring snow the day before and the three-quarter moon reflecting off the thin white cover helped light the room even with the shade drawn.

"Quiet," Chug whispered into his ear, grateful for the dog's eager, breathing company.

Amigo obeyed, but reluctantly, his eyes dancing impatiently.

Way to go, Jase, Chug thought. You trained him well. Even though Amigo obviously thought Chug was being a jerk about this, and he was shaking his head to let Chug know that this wasn't a cat or some other animal out there, he was quiet.

Chug quickly pulled on jeans and a sweatshirt and scuffed into his slippers. Then he reached over to the far side of the bed, felt the Remington shotgun's cold barrel and lifted it quickly, the heaviness a reassuring weight in his hands. He picked up the cell phone from the night table, and crept on all fours out into the living room. Amigo, alert to the new game, nudged against his shoulder. Front door, back door? As if in answer, the dog moved toward the back door, but remained silent, his near eye looking back impatiently. Good boy, Amigo.

Chug moved quietly into the kitchen area and over to the shelf above the stove where the large cookbook rested between a couple of canisters.

He couldn't be positive. Amigo might just be reacting to a raccoon or a skunk, or some other animal that had happened to hit his olfactories harder than normal. Whatever the hell it was, it was awful quiet out there.

Then he saw the doorknob shiver. Just a fraction of a movement, a testing to see if he'd been careless enough to leave the door unlocked. But the knob had definitely moved. Amigo had seen it too, his look now a clear series of questions: *See that, Chug? Can't you smell him? Can I growl now? How 'bout a bark? How 'bout that, huh, Chug? How 'bout I just pad my way up to that door and let out a roar that'll scare the shit outta this guy?*

But Chug had to finish pressing a couple of numbers on the cell phone before he could lean closer to Amigo and whisper "Quiet." He leveled the shotgun. The doorknob moved again. There was a faint scratching of metal, as if someone were trying a key. But Chug knew it wasn't a key.

Still, might just be some random thief breaking in, even though, with Chug's truck parked out front, this obviously wasn't one of the places closed for the winter.

Then again, it might be Brandon and his idiot buddies, up to some new stunt.

But all the guessing stopped when the cheap lock on the door clicked and the door swung slowly open, and there was a large—a very large—presence sliding like a thick, dark shadow into the kitchen, not fifteen feet away from where the dog and Chug now stood at alert.

Chug pumped a shell into the chamber, the sound singular, riveting and demanding of attention, especially at three in the morning when someone's just broken into a house where he thinks his victim's fast asleep. The thick dark shadow froze.

"You know what that sound means," Chug said quietly. "I've got this aimed at your belly and it's loaded with double-aught buck. So whatever that thing is you're holding, you'd better place it very carefully on the floor and put your hands up, or at this range, you'll be splattered all over that wall behind you."

The shadow believed him. His hand reached out, slowly lowering something long and metallic onto the linoleum.

Chug reached over and switched on the lights. The man standing in front of him was Arthur Davis, although he looked a little different with his ponytail tucked up beneath a black watch cap. He was wearing gloves, too, and on his feet were—what the hell? His shoes seemed to be covered with plastic grocery bags, elastics binding them at his ankles. In front of the bags, at his feet was a rifle.

"So, what's up, Art? A coupla months late for trick-or-treating, no?"

"What the fuck you think is up, Chug?"

Chug had surprised him all right, but Davis sure as hell didn't look as intimidated as he might have, standing at the scary end of a twenty-eight-inch barrel.

"You weren't plannin' to use that rifle on me now, were you, Art?"

"I just wanted to scare you, that's all. Just enough to get the rest of Lacey's writing. How about you, Chug? Are you planning to use that on me? I'm not armed anymore. Have you got the balls to use that shotgun on an unarmed man?"

"Sure do." He meant it, too. He could see Art's understanding of this register slowly in his eyes, as they lost the glint of confidence they'd held for that second, and his body eased from its coiled readiness. Good thing, too, because, if Art had made that move toward him, Chug knew he would've fired. Maybe a little low, but at this range, the way that double-aught shot would spread, even low would've more than done the job.

"What the fuck is this?" Art said, forcing a laugh as he noticed Amigo for the first time. The dog remained at alert and didn't seem at all embarrassed by Art's laughter.

"Sit, Amigo," Chug said, and the dog sat, calmly, confidently. Of course, Amigo hadn't seen what had happened to Lacey or Traynor.

"Once again, why're you here, Art?"

He sighed, shrugged, and leaned back against the wall. If Davis was only acting calm, he was doing a hell of a job at it. And that, of course, had Chug second-guessing his plans.

"I suppose I'm here to play 'Let's Make a Deal.' Right, Chug? And you get to find out what's behind door number two."

"So, instead of getting shot in my sleep, I get . . . ?"

"I told you, I wasn't planning to shoot you, for crissake. But anyway, how about half a million dollars? Cold cash. From me to you. How does that sound?"

Chug thought it sounded like something that, if he'd been stupid enough to agree to, he'd never get to spend.

"So, instead of using that gun to force me to give you those journal pages, you're going to pay me a half million dollars for them?"

"Sometimes you have to be practical, Chug," Davis said with a shrug and a smile that managed to be both so relaxed and so menacing that Chug found himself glancing down just to be sure he was the one holding the shotgun.

"And this was all about the lottery ticket?"

"Fifty-two million fucking dollars, Chug. That's what it's all about."

"Walter Traynor did buy the ticket, then?"

He shook his head a little, side to side, took a deep breath and let it out slowly. "Sure, he bought it. Of course he bought the fucking thing. But it was my idea to go to the store, and it was my idea for us to buy a couple of Powerball tickets in the first place. And I had to practically twist the stupid bastard's arm before he'd go ahead and spend the goddamn two dollars."

"And what about Lacey? Did she know about it?"

"She was there when we bought them. I had my own car that trip and I needed gas. So we were going on a food run for the kids, me and Basic. But Lacey insisted on coming with us. I'd warned her about that, about dropping hints there was—well, you already know, don't you?—something going on between us. But I think she wanted the other kids to wonder about it. She thought it would make her look cool."

"And the winning ticket numbers were ones Traynor chose?"

"What's the difference, Chug? I'll give you the half million dollars, you'll give me your copy of that stupid bitch's stupid novel, and we'll never see each other again. How does that sound?"

"Y'know, there was just one number I couldn't figure out," Chug said. "The thirty-four. The others were all connected to Basic or people he knew, but I couldn't figure why he picked that one."

"It doesn't matter." He frowned, slouching a little for the first time.

"C'mon, Art, humor me. I'm the kind of guy loves to figure out things. And this has been bothering the hell out of me for weeks."

"The thirty-four was for me." His arms were crossed, his face turned toward the living room. "Same as I told the press, it was the number I wore when I played football in college. He knew I used to play that lottery number all the time. Thirty-four."

"Sounds like he thought of you as a good friend, Art."

"He wouldn't have even *played* the fucking numbers if I hadn't told him to. And he never would have won without using my favorite number. Then the stupid bastard didn't even check to see how he'd done. If he ever found it, he probably would have tossed the fucking ticket in the trash."

"But you knew? You remembered?"

"Kind of," he said slowly. "Most of the Powerball numbers sounded familiar, when I checked. The thirty-four I remembered, of course, and a couple of others."

"So you stole the ticket?"

"When I found out the ticket had been sold in that store we'd stopped in, sure, of course I took the ticket. It was still in the pocket of his ski jacket, all crumpled and damp like a goddamn used Kleenex."

"But you couldn't cash it in because then he'd realize all those numbers were his."

Davis frowned a little deeper, staring at the floor. His boots, wrapped in the plastic bags, looked ludicrous, the snow from the bottoms melting on the linoleum. But they'd leave no distinct footprints, and his cap kept him from leaving a stray hair at the scene of the crime. Then there were the gloves, which he now slowly removed and put in his jacket pocket.

"And Lacey had been with you and Basic, so if he challenged you on the ticket, she'd have been a witness."

Still silent.

"Why didn't you just convince her to back up your story? That you'd bought the ticket," Chug said. "She'd do that in a heartbeat, wouldn't she?"

"Maybe . . . I thought about it, but . . . she was becoming a problem. And if I got her to go along with this, I'd never get rid of her. She'd always have that to use against me. And she was the kind of bitch who always wanted to have a little leverage against you, know what I mean?"

He was right about that. No question. No telling how Lacey would use that power over him.

"So she had to die too?"

"Hey, you should thank me for that, Chug. She was out to

get you. I just had to suggest she try blackmailing you, and she was all over the idea. Even the island was her suggestion. And she wanted me to take some pictures of the two of you together out there, her in that lingerie. I said why not video, but she said no. If the video had your voice on it, you might not sound guilty. With the pictures, even if you weren't doing anything, they'd be incriminating enough to get you fired. Prosky would see to that. Especially if she also threatened him that she'd throw in a video she took secretly with one of those little nanny-cams of her screwing the good principal. As I said, she liked leverage. How's that for a manipulating, conniving bitch?"

"But you had a surprise for her."

"Yes, I did. I kind of hated to do it, too. Even though she was getting to be a problem, she was one sweet little piece of ass. Believe me, Chug, you don't know what you passed up."

"And after you killed her, how'd you get back to the mainland? A hidden canoe?"

"I own a kayak. I hid it on the far side of the island. Told Lacey it was so you wouldn't see it when you arrived."

"And it couldn't be seen from the house?"

Davis nodded, his arms crossed, his expression bored, but Chug could tell he was a little proud of himself. In fact, Chug had counted on it.

"Okay, Art. You killed Lacey, but who killed the other two? I know it wasn't you. And Ernest never hurt anybody. He was just set up to be the scapegoat. So who's your partner in all of this?"

A small smile, a poker player letting you know that maybe he had better cards than he'd led you to believe when you'd bumped him. Then a shake of the head.

"I gotta know that, Art. If I make a deal with you, I'm also making a deal with your partner. He's the one who killed the Parkhurst boy and took the ax to Basic. And he must be the one who shot at me after I gave you the journal, so I really need to know who it is. Or we can't make any deals at all."

Davis shook his head a little more emphatically. "No way, Chug. No way."

It was hard to tell if he was being a loyal partner or was maybe just a little fearful.

"If I don't know who he is, how do I protect myself from him?"

"Look, Chug, if you don't know who the hell it is, and the money you get is coming from me, why should my partner care about you? In fact, my partner told me you had nothing on me, but I didn't want to believe it. So here I am, and how do you want the money? Hundreds okay? Damn, half a million is going to be one helluva stack of bills."

"I don't want the money, Art." Chug wasn't entirely sure what he'd just been told but felt as if the floor had begun to shift a little beneath his feet.

"Huh? What are you talking about, Chug? I thought we were making a deal."

"In this deal you get what's behind door number three. That would be the prison cell, Art. For life, unless I'm mistaken."

The man's confused look turned angry, and Chug could see him measuring the distance between them.

"Don't even think about it, Art. Just don't." And right now, even a shift forward by him might have been enough to push Chug's trigger finger.

"You've got nothing on me anyway. Nothing but that stupid story, and I'm still not sure the DA's office would be able to use it."

Chug didn't want to tell Davis yet just how wrong he was about what he had on him, so they spent at least another ten minutes with Chug trying to find out who Davis's partner was and him not telling. Mostly, Chug was buying time. Mostly, Davis was trying to convince Chug to lower the shotgun. He even upped his offer to eight hundred thousand, then to a million. But he could just as easily have offered eight million, since Chug knew he'd never see any of it anyway. If Davis had only come here to threaten, why the precautions against leaving hairs or footprints?

Finally Chug heard what he'd been waiting for, the sound of a car coming fast off Lakefront and onto Loganberry. He didn't think Art heard, but Davis couldn't miss the brakes screeching to a halt out front and the car door quickly thunking shut. Still, though he frowned, Davis didn't seem as concerned as Chug would have preferred.

Miranda must have had her key out because the front door flew open almost immediately, and she was standing in the living room, face flushed, eyes alert, Glock automatic sweeping the room.

Amigo leaped up and went over to greet her, wagging his tail enthusiastically.

"What the fuck is this?" Art said.

Miranda swung the automatic past Chug's shotgun and on to Art, and said, "What's going on, Matthew?" at almost the same instant.

"I paged Sergeant Cusack when I heard you breaking in, Art. My guess is that she's going to arrest you. For breaking and entering and for murdering Lacey McGovern and being an accomplice to the murders of Donald Parkhurst and Walter Traynor."

"No way, Chug. No way," he repeated, looking to Miranda, his hands held out in front of him as if they could ward off the bad news rolling his way. "I don't know what he's talking about."

"Quiet," Miranda said, her gun trained on him. "Matthew?"

Chug turned and lifted the cookbook.

"It's all here, Art. A recipe for your arrest, trial, and conviction. What was it you told me Lacey used to film Prosky, a nanny-cam? You really should've considered the possibility."

And Chug was sure Davis would have, too, except he thought breaking in here in the middle of the night was his own idea, so a setup like this was the last thing on his mind. But, then, Davis hadn't considered how he'd been placed in a situation where this was the only thing he could do to get Lacey's writings back. If he went for the bait, he had to come here to Chug, and he had to come in the middle of the night. Amigo, the early-warning system brought here for just this eventuality, yawned.

"You can't do that," Art said, after he'd had about a half minute to absorb the news and consider how much of a confession Chug had been taping. "You were holding a shotgun on me. I was under duress. Nothing I said would ever show up in a court."

"Not exactly. What happened here had nothing to do with the police. This cookbook was my idea, a surveillance camera set up to protect me since my life's been threatened more than once. It's hidden in the cookbook in case someone broke in while I was away."

He took down the cookbook, opened it and turned off the camera.

"Sergeant Cusack didn't know anything about the recorder, didn't participate in any part of what's just gone on between us. The only reason she's here right now is that I told her I'd send a coded message to her cell phone if I thought my life was being threatened again. As for duress, I've had the shotgun trained on you because, as the video will clearly support, you broke into my home while carrying a rifle, an obvious threat to my life. At no point did I use this shotgun to coerce you into confessing anything."

Miranda had caught on quickly. Chug could see that she was still evaluating the chances of getting away with this legally.

"Mr. O'Malley never told me a thing about this," she said to Davis. "I came here as a friend of his, but I'm arresting you as a police officer. I've got cuffs out in my car, Matthew. In the glove compartment. Would you get them, please?"

As he left, the shotgun still in his hand, he heard her begin to say, "You have the right to remain silent . . ."

Even in the moonlight, the late March snow looked played out and dirty, though cold enough under Chug's slippered feet. No sign of Davis's car. Must have parked it up on Lakefront and hiked down in the moonlight. Chug found the cuffs and was closing the passenger door when he heard a car turning onto Loganberry.

When he realized it was a police car, he held the shotgun against his leg, alongside Miranda's Accord. It was Robidoux. Since Chug had almost been shot for holding up a cell phone a few months ago, he had no idea what would happen if a policeman saw him with this Remington.

Robidoux pulled up behind Miranda's car, opened his door, and stretched one leg out to the ground, though he kept the headlights on Chug and the engine running.

"You . . . uh, okay? I pulled a double shift and the guy I'm filling in for said I'm supposed to keep an eye on you because of that shooting. But I don't want to . . . interrupt anything." He jutted his chin toward Miranda's car.

"No, that's okay, she'll be glad to see you. Uh, I've got a shotgun here and I'm gonna hold it up," Chug said, slowly lifting the shotgun stock forward and holding it up for him to see. "I used this to get the guy really responsible for those three deaths. He's inside."

"What? Who?"

"The killer. It's Davis, Art Davis, the guidance counselor from the high school. The guy who claimed he won the big lottery."

"But . . . that kid, Ernest, at the church. The one that got shot? Wasn't he our guy?"

"No, just another victim. I'll tell you about it later. We should go in."

"Huh? Oh, sure, sure." He hurried ahead of Chug into the cabin.

What with Amigo, and Miranda, and Art already there, the kitchen was starting to feel crowded. Robidoux took his handcuffs off his belt and, after asking Miranda, "This the guy?"—though he only had Art and Amigo to choose from—drew Art's arms behind him and snapped the cuffs onto his wrists.

"I've already read him his rights," she said. "You want to call this in?"

"Sure, sure. But what's the deal?"

Chug pulled out one of the kitchen chairs and sat near the far wall, across the small room from the three of them. Amigo sighed and settled at his side. Robidoux, for the first time, seemed impressed by something Chug had done. At least he nodded his head at all the right points as Miranda went into the details.

Throughout the retelling Art glowered unhappily at all of them. Amigo sighed again, loudly, perhaps in protest over his extended bout of silence, and Chug whispered "Quiet" again to him as the dog lay his head on Chug's slippered feet.

"That's incredible," Robidoux said, after all the explanations and modifications. "So all this time, it was this guy? And he did it so he could cash in Traynor's lottery ticket?"

"Yep," Chug said. "Him and his accomplice."

"But that kid at the church had a gun! He even fired it at you two and at Harrington."

"He actually fired up into the air," Miranda said. "And he was out of his head on PCP, which could make him very receptive to suggestion. If someone convinced him he was taking part in one of the fantasy role-playing games he loved, and told him to race out firing a burst at us, he wouldn't have been able to tell the difference between fantasy and reality. And, of course, he was carrying his own death wrapped around his waist."

"Any ideas who this accomplice is?" Robidoux said, putting his cap on the table and running a hand over his shaved scalp.

"We don't have that from Mr. Davis, yet," Miranda said. "But I'm pretty sure he'll see the wisdom in telling us before long."

"We do know it's somebody connected with the police, though," Chug said, leaning back in the chair but keeping his grip firmly on the shotgun across his lap.

"What?!" Miranda said.

"The police," Chug said. "The accomplice has to have a police connection."

Robidoux looked puzzled. Miranda looked confused. Art looked like he was holding his breath.

"Why?" Robidoux said.

"Something Art told me in his office. It didn't completely register at first, but I just remembered it when I was talking to him earlier. I saw him twice in his office in the last couple of weeks. First time, I told him I thought his aftershave smelled familiar, that I'd smelled it somewhere before and couldn't quite place it. I was lying, but I wanted him to think I was on to him as Lacey's killer. Then, the second time I spoke to him, when I told him about finding Lacey's writings, he said that I hadn't told the police anything about a strange smell at that house. If he knew that, he must've somehow had access to the police report and the case notes sometime between our first and second meetings."

Miranda had been listening to him very attentively, her dark eyes glinting.

"And when did you figure this out?" she said, moving slightly away from Davis and Robidoux.

Chug sighed, kept the fingers of his left hand lightly on the barrel of the shotgun, his right hand resting near the trigger guard.

"As I said, just a little while ago. Just before you got here. And isn't it time for somebody to call this in to the station?"

Miranda could use Chug's phone, or the one in her car, but Robidoux just had to click on his shoulder mike.

"Sure," he said, reaching up toward it, while Chug watched the long fingers of Miranda's right hand reach over slowly, absently, to scratch at her elbow, just below the shoulder holster.

Chug knew what she was doing, though, and he took a deep breath, let it out slowly. Twenty feet away, out in the living-room area, the carriage clock bonged four times.

But Chug must have missed some secret signal between Davis and Robidoux because the sudden move, when it came, caught him off guard. Art shoved himself sideways, slamming into Miranda just as her hand moved toward that holster, pushing her into Robidoux, who wrapped his right arm around her as his left hand suddenly appeared at the side of her head, his automatic pistol pressed just above her ear.

"One fuckin' move with that shotgun, O'Malley, and she gets blown away!" Robidoux screamed.

Goddamn, he was fast for a muscle-bound guy! And Miranda's fall, combined with Robidoux's sudden lunge behind her, had left Chug aiming the barrel of that shotgun right at her belly.

Amigo had leapt up, alarmed and growling, his head bobbing up.

"That goes for the fuckin' dog, too, O'Malley. He moves, she dies."

"Quiet, Amigo," Chug said. "Sit. Sit. Good dog. Quiet."

"Yeah, good fuckin' dog," Robidoux said. "Now you break open that shotgun and put it very slowly on the floor . . . Okay, now kick it over toward Davis."

Next he drew Miranda's gun from her holster and stuffed it in his back pocket. "Okay, Davis, over here."

Art, who had struggled to his feet, turned. Robidoux released his grip on Miranda, but kept his gun at her head while he unlocked the cuffs.

"What now?" Davis said, rubbing his wrists. "Want me to put these on him?" He nudged his square jaw toward Chug.

"Yeah, sure . . . uh, no," Robidoux said. Then quickly added, "No need." But Chug had already guessed what he was thinking. Cuffs leave imprints on your wrists. Hard to get rid of the marks after that person's been shot. The medical examiner might want to know why a policeman had to shoot a guy who'd already been cuffed.

Davis picked up his rifle again. There were a few seconds of silence while the four people and one dog froze in a strange tableau: one man in a chair against the wall, a dog resting uneasily by his feet, a second man casually holding a rifle, staring impatiently at the third, the man in the police uniform, his pistol still held to the head of the lovely woman he seemed to be once again embracing from behind. Chug listened eagerly for any noise from outside the cabin, but there was nothing. Inside, all he could hear was Amigo's steady breathing and the ticking of the clock on the mantle out in the living room.

"So, what's it gonna be?" Davis said.

If there was one thing Chug didn't want, it was anybody hurrying Robidoux along. Chug looked at Miranda. Her lips drew back in a sad smile, her brows up in a "Sorry 'bout that" shrug. And she knew exactly what Robidoux and Davis were deciding, knew they were only thinking about how they were going to do it.

Chug noticed her glancing quickly up toward that pistol at the side of her head, then back at him, the question clear. She wanted to know if he thought they should try to jump the two men.

He shook his head fractionally. Robidoux's finger already seemed to be pressing a little too firmly on the trigger.

As if reading her mind, Robidoux pushed Miranda away, toward Chug. "Put your hands on your heads. Both of you. And, uh . . ."

Chug stood slowly. "You mind if we sit out there? At least there's enough chairs."

Robidoux looked at the three kitchen chairs, shrugged, but there was a spark of amusement in his eyes, and Chug thought he knew why. Why not, make 'em comfortable, make 'em think they may be able to walk away from this. That way they won't force us into killing 'em fast and sloppy.

"Sure, what the hell," he said. "But keep your hands on your heads."

Chug went first, settling quickly into the easy chair. Miranda sat in the old wooden rocker. Robidoux and Davis sat on the couch facing them, conversing in whispers, both with guns trained on their captives. Amigo came slowly from the kitchen, looked balefully up at Chug, turned a couple of circles and settled on the hooked rug beside the chair.

Chug was guessing they'd go for murder-suicide, using Miranda's gun. Robidoux would know about powder burns, stippling, all the precautions they'd have to take. There was the problem of motive, of course. Maybe that's what was taking them so long. Maybe they'd finally just opt for a break-in, Chug and Miranda murdered in bed. They'd never get away with it. But right now the thought of their getting caught for his murder didn't cheer Chug up at all.

The hands of the carriage clock were nearing ten after four.

This had all begun almost forty minutes ago. Chug figured they had about five minutes left to live. Not enough time. It'd be close, but no damned cigar. So if he was going to do something, it had better be soon.

He stood, slowly.

"What the fuck you think you're doin'?" Robidoux said. "Siddown."

"Look," Chug said, hands held out open and empty, "I gotta take a leak real bad. You think it'd be all right? I mean, he can come with me if he wants, with the rifle. It's just . . . y'know, I really gotta go."

He took a tentative step toward them, away from the chair and toward the rifle. Still at least twelve, fifteen feet away, so they didn't feel threatened, though Chug did notice a look of disbelief flicker quickly across Robidoux's face like the shadow of a hawk gliding over a field mouse. He knew the policeman's thoughts now too: *This asshole O'Malley still doesn't realize we have to kill both him and his girlfriend.*

"Won't be long," Davis said with more determination than regret in his voice, and he waved the rifle barrel at him.

Ah, finally Chug heard Amigo's claws scratch on the floor just off the hook rug as he stood, heard the dog's deep sigh as he crept onto the warm spot in the chair they always fought over.

"Oh, for Chrissakes, Amigo!" Chug turned around and took the two steps back to the chair. "C'mon, now."

And he reached for Amigo, pulling at his haunches with his left hand, while with his right he reached behind the dog, back behind the thick seat cushion. He'd gotten three automatics as well as the shotgun from Ti. One was still holstered in the bedroom, but the other two he'd hidden like lethal Easter eggs in the little cabin: one beneath some towels stacked near the bathroom sink, and this one, behind the cushion in his favorite chair just in case Amigo hadn't warned him about an intruder. Robidoux was the more dangerous, Chug was sure of that. Art had the rifle. Thank God he hadn't picked up the shotgun. With the rifle, at least, Chug thought he had a chance. And in the chaos, Miranda might be able to make it out the door.

Amigo was standing next to him as Chug said over his shoulder, "Damn dog acts like he owns the house sometimes." He slapped at the chair with his left hand as if trying to get rid of dog hairs, hoping he was covering the sound of the safety he was slipping. Now, raising his voice just a fraction, in apparent exasperation, Chug added, "Bad dog, Amigo! Bad dog!"

Chug's back was still turned to both of the men and the dog. Amigo, given his release finally from his chains of silence, let out a howl, then a torrent of yelping, a spasm of bad temper from his barrel chest that echoed in the small cabin, and all his unleashed frustration was directed at Robidoux and Davis. And just as the dog began his fierce barking, Chug spun around with the automatic, dove to his left so he'd be away from Miranda, and squeezed off three or four shots at Robidoux. He fired until he saw Robidoux's startled look, saw him frown and fire before he fell. Chug felt a bullet from a different direction zing past his ear before he heard the crack of the shot, and he was trying to lift the automatic to fire at Davis, but his hand was empty, his shoulder stung hot and hard and his goddamn automatic was skittering across the floor, bumping into the dog, who—aw shit!—was lying there, bleeding. And Chug looked up at Davis, who was lifting his rifle to take careful aim. His face was set, his eyes eager, as if arriving finally at some long-awaited destination and, as the barrel rose to a level with Chug's eyes, the thought "I'm sorry! I'm sorry!" flashed through Chug's mind, but he wasn't sure to whom he was apologizing or what he was asking forgiveness for. It felt like it was maybe the whole goddamn universe. For everything.

But then something crashed off the side of Davis's head. He stumbled sideways, startled, but still on his feet, still holding the rifle though it was now pointing at the floor. Somewhere bells were chiming. Chug saw Davis turn to aim the gun now at Miranda, who was coming at him low. Chug leaped at Davis's gun arm from the other side, grabbing the barrel with his left hand and lifting it. The rifle shot boomed toward the ceiling just as Miranda's head collided with Davis's solar plexus. He gasped out a tremendous "Oof" before doubling over between the two of them. Davis's fingers opened, and Chug fell to the floor so he could knock the rifle away with his left arm. At the same time, Miranda was crushing her knee into Davis's groin. His gasp of pain bellowed in Chug's ear. Davis jackknifed into a fetal position. The side of his head, where Miranda had bashed him with the clock, was bleeding heavily.

While Davis flopped there like a very big fish in the bottom of a rowboat, Miranda retrieved Chug's Colt and held it at the back of Davis's head. Chug crawled over to Robidoux. Jesus, he didn't look too good. There was blood on his chest, but even more from a wound in his thick bull's neck. His troubled breathing was more serious than Davis's, the gurgling of blood mixed in with the air, his perpetually angry eyes tinged with fear now, gradually becoming aware of what was happening to him.

But then Chug remembered the dog and turned to him. Amigo's eyes were opened, and he was whimpering and struggling to get to his feet.

"No, no, Amigo. It's okay." Chug crawled to him and cradled his head. "Don't move. It'll be okay. It'll be okay." Amigo had been wounded just above his left front leg, and Chug found himself wondering where the hell a dog's heart was anyway while he stroked Amigo with his left hand. The dog's large and trusting brown eyes stared up that long nose into Chug's. What was he gonna tell Jason? Aw, Jesus, what the hell was he gonna tell Jason?

He heard Miranda speaking into Robidoux's shoulder mike, something about emergency and ambulances, but she was starting to sound very far away and a little out of focus, almost as if he were hearing her from the other end of that mike. And, for some reason, he wanted to tell her to be careful with the clock she'd thrown at Davis. It might not be broken. But that made no sense even to him. He felt real weak, real tired, real eager for someone to carry him upstairs to bed. Oh, no, there was no upstairs here, and no one to carry him anyway. Oops, as if in answer, his cousin Tiago was at the door, flanked by two guys Chug didn't recognize.

" 'Bout fuckin' time, Ti!" he squawked. "We started without ya!"

And, for some reason, despite everything that had happened, Chug thought that was hilarious, that crack about time, and he meant to begin laughing but, instead, he heard myself muttering "Time out." And then, when he couldn't bring his useless right hand up to bounce it off his palm in the basketball time-out signal, he gave up and just let himself give in to the darkness as he slumped forward over Amigo.

# Chapter Twenty-Eight

The voice was low, sultry, whispering, "You'll be okay, Chug. You'll be okay," while gentle fingers stroked his forehead. It was a pleasant sensation, even a somewhat familiar one, but somehow it was wrong. Wrong voice. Wrong name. *Should be calling me Matthew, not Chug.*

Suddenly, he knew who it was, knew why the voice and manner had been so familiar, and with a jolt he realized he'd been awake for a while, just listening to the sounds around him. If he'd been dreaming, he couldn't remember it. Or thought he couldn't because he wasn't sure that the memories of Miranda, Art, Robidoux gradually filling his waking consciousness hadn't been the dream. If he opened his eyes, would Miranda cease to exist? Would the drawn-out and painful breakup with Connie never have happened? Would he be back in that big house in Bradford, late for a conference at *Action 23 I-Squad*? Oh shit, please not that. Please?

"You think he's awake? I think he might be awake."

"I dunno. He could be faking."

Jason and Sarah. Well, at least he'd be lucky to have them in either reality.

But something about Jason . . . something Chug was forgetting there . . . the dog! That's right, Amigo! If everything hadn't been a dream, then he'd gone and gotten his son's dog shot, maybe even killed.

"You think he's faking right now, Mom?" Sarah's voice said,

close at his left.

"He sure is," her mother's voice said from the other side. "That's the same look he used to have when you guys were little and one of you woke up crying in the middle of the night."

"Not so," Chug said, his throat sore and raw and his voice raspy, as if it were being scraped over glass. "A veritable bald-faced lie."

He opened his eyes to a blindingly well-lit hospital room. Sarah was leaning over to hug him, her eyes glistening with tears. Jason, behind her, was beaming. Connie was on his right, and when she leaned over to kiss his cheek, Chug felt pain shoot through his shoulder but tried to not show it.

Good sign, though. Because he'd also remembered being shot. Now he knew at least his arm was still over there, swathed though it was in bandages.

"Where . . . ?"

"Saint Mary's," Connie said. "And it's almost eleven on Friday morning. You've been out for over thirty hours."

Wow. All that rest, you'd think a guy'd feel a helluva lot better than he did right now.

"Amigo?" he said, looking at Jason.

"He's okay, Dad. He'll be fine."

"The dog rebounded a lot faster than you did," Connie said, though for once the warmth in her voice didn't seem to have been produced by some form of friction. "I guess some Fall River mongrels are tougher than others."

"The vet said he'd be limping for a while, Dad," Sarah said. "But he'll be all right."

"Robidoux?" he said.

Connie shook her head, looking at him carefully as if to gauge his reaction.

Strange. Until he'd seen her confirm it, Chug thought he'd feel worse. Maybe part of him was triumphant, simply because he'd cheated Robidoux out of the last two deaths he wanted.

"I couldn't help it." His kids needed to understand. "It wasn't supposed to happen that way, but he gave me no choice. I didn't want that to happen."

"We know, Chug," Connie said. "Miranda explained everything to the press, about Robidoux killing that Parkhurst boy and the assistant principal."

"Yeah," Jason said, "And how he worked with that guy Davis to try to kill your student, the one they framed, at the church."

"And how it was Davis who killed the girl, Lacey," Connie said.

"For a stupid lottery ticket," Jason chipped in.

"Worth fifty-two million," his mother finished.

"It's been all over the papers and television, Dad," Sarah said.

"Right," Connie said. "If you thought there was a lot of hoopla after Ernest was caught, you're in for a big surprise."

"No, I don't think there's much they can do that'd surprise me. Just make sure none of them get in here to see me."

"No way we'll let 'em, Dad." Jason drew himself up to his full height. Chug would have to tell him later how the training he had given the dog had saved Chug's life and Miranda's.

"Your agent's been calling every hour or so," Connie said. "He keeps asking if you're awake, but I think he really wants to discuss that book you're writing. He says there've been requests from all of the network news shows for interviews with you."

"Network?"

"Yes! And all the local stations, of course."

Chug shook his head. He didn't want to think about that right now, any more than he wanted to talk about what had happened in the cabin. All he really wanted to talk about was how Sarah and Jason were doing and, for every question they asked him, he got in at least two about them. But then, he was a trained professional.

They were interrupted by nurses and a cranky older doctor who came in to check his vital signs, but everyone agreed that Chug was very fortunate, very healthy for someone who'd recently been shot, and that he should be up and about in a few days which he interpreted to mean he could leave tomorrow.

Connie and the kids left after a couple of hours, though after sending Sarah and Jason off toward the elevators, Connie came back in to tell Chug privately that Miranda had spent hours sitting up with him, that in fact she'd been in the room when they'd arrived.

"Thanks for telling me." But it hadn't been something he really needed to hear. He knew Miranda would do whatever she could for him, for as long as she could.

"She's even prettier in real life than she is on the news broadcasts," Connie said.

Chug smiled, knowing that, for Connie, this was a huge concession.

"Take care," she said, leaning over to kiss him on the cheek.

Chug had just started on the turkey stuff on the plate of food that had been brought in when Ti came in.

"See Connie?" Chug said.

"As I was getting off the elevator. She told me you couldn't play basketball. I told her I knew that a long time ago."

"You wish." Chug tried the mashed potatoes. Yep, hospital food. "Sorry 'bout the carriage clock. Did it break?"

"No. Well, if you mean the clock, yes, of course the clock broke, you goddamn idiot. But if you mean the camera, no, the video's fine."

"Nobody saw the camera? I mean, after I passed out?"

"Nah. Miranda was only interested in you. Once I checked and made sure you weren't on your way to being permanently cancelled, and I knew the Prescott cops were on their way over,

I figured I'd better take out that micro-cam. Get the video out before they confiscated the clock as evidence. Had to sneak it into the bathroom, take out the damned micro-cam, and put the clock back just as the whole Prescott police force was stormin' through your front door."

"Thanks, Ti."

"You could name your own price for that video, y'know." Ti handed him the tiny camera. "Even without any sound."

"I know, but there's no way I'm selling it."

"You should. Miranda'd be a star."

"Yeah, ain't she a pistol?"

"Damned straight," Miranda said from the doorway.

Chug figured she'd been in the lobby, waiting for his family to leave. Her suit looked as if she'd been sleeping in it, and her face was drawn, her eyes tired, but Chug wanted to leap out of bed to hold her. She hugged Ti then leaned over Chug. Her lips were warm and tasted of coffee. Then she sat on the edge of the bed and held his hand.

"Catch ya later," Ti said. "Got a couple of sales slips to fill out."

Ah, his guns, Chug thought.

Miranda filled him in on a few particulars of the case garnered from the interrogation of Davis. Robidoux, using his uniform and police car, had coerced both the Parkhurst boy and Ernest to take what he had called a field sobriety test. He had actually given them the drugs that were later found in their systems.

"Oh, and Davis told us that Robidoux was trying to work out some way to get into the hospital to kill Ernest. You probably saved that boy's life again."

"No change in his condition?"

"Not yet, but his brain's still active and his neurologist said he was hopeful."

Then she told him that the town police had found the video of Lacey and Prosky that Davis had mentioned while Chug's mini-camera in the recipe book had been recording him at the cabin.

"It was hidden at the McGovern home," she said. "We're bringing charges against the principal. And with Lacey's video, he won't be hard to nail."

It looked like Dr. Prosky was about to take a sharp detour off the education highway, Chug thought. Served the bastard right.

It was another half hour or so before she got around to asking Chug why he hadn't told her that he thought there was a police connection to the murders.

He had been waiting for the question ever since he saw the confused look in her eyes at his cabin, so he was sort of prepared.

"I hadn't really thought of it before Robidoux showed up." He squinted as he looked out toward the window. "It seemed too much of a coincidence, his coming right then, when we'd just caught Davis. Like he was expecting something to be going on at my place. That's when I remembered what Davis had told me and realized someone must have given him information only the police would know."

She nodded, but slowly, tentatively.

"And you kept that shotgun leveled between Robidoux and me because . . . ?"

"I was waiting for him to make his move. If I pointed it more directly at him, he might not go for the bait. And I still wasn't sure he was the police connection."

"I see. And you didn't tell me about the gun you had hidden in that chair because you didn't want me compromised." Her voice was level but her dark eyes probing.

"Yep. Same as the hidden Minicam in the kitchen."

"Uh, I never got the chance to tell you, but in this state it's illegal to tape someone without their knowledge if there's sound with the video. So that video could never be used in court."

"I know. Ti told me that. I figured Davis wouldn't know that. And I guess he didn't."

"Very slick, Matthew. Speaking of Tiago, he told me you'd paged him when you paged me."

It was a quick move on her part, a kind of crossover dribble, but he'd been expecting it.

"Yep. Ti and the guys who work for him were backup."

"But they had to come all the way from Fall River."

"Right. But I wasn't sure I'd just be dealing with Davis."

"Couldn't our town officers get there a lot faster than your cousin? Even after you'd gotten Davis to confess?"

Ah, there was that.

"Unless, of course, you already suspected a Prescott police connection when you made your plans," she said.

She didn't add, *And never told me about your suspicions.* She didn't have to.

He shrugged, thought about faking a sudden attack of pain in his wounded shoulder. "I was never sure about a connection."

She nodded, accepting it more than believing it.

"Why didn't you wait for Tiago, then, before getting out that hidden gun?"

"Robidoux and Davis both had their guns out. If they heard Tiago driving up, he'd be walking into an ambush. And Robidoux seemed to be making up his mind about what to do with us. I didn't think I had much time to act."

"Well, it was a little reckless, but I'm glad you did."

She reached her hand to the back of his neck, her cool fingers caressing it.

"You saved my life, Matthew," she said. "I'm not completely sure how I feel about that."

"Well, if it helps, I figure I'm also the one whose stupid plan almost got you killed in the first place. So it only seems to balance out."

"No, no," she said, her words breathed on his cheek as she massaged the back of his neck. "It was the way you did it that really matters. You're right-handed. Everything you do is right-handed. As I told you when we played basketball, you can't go to your left worth a damn."

"And your point is?" His brow was raised though she was too close to him to notice.

Her lips moved to his ear, her breath warm as she whispered, "When you turned to fire at those two bastards, I was on your right. You dove to your left. It was much more dangerous for you to move that way. And you must've known that, if you shot Robidoux, Davis would fire his first round at you and not me. I'll . . ." He could hear the sob bubbling up even as her lips pressed against his ear until she regained control. "I'll never forget that, Matthew. Never."

Chug smiled. He thought about mentioning his other concern at that moment, in addition to wanting to protect her. If he dove to his right, his gun hand would be under him when he landed. He thought about telling her.

Miranda's warm lips pressed softly against his.

He thought a little more about explaining that extra concern.

She leaned in, gently against him.

Maybe it wasn't worth mentioning after all.

# ABOUT THE AUTHOR

**James T. Shannon** is a college English teacher, but spent much of his career teaching high-school English in a school similar to this novel's setting. He has had a number of informal essays published in the Sunday supplements to the *Providence Journal* and the *Boston Herald.* He has been published in magazines as varied as *Mad* and *TV Guide* and had several mystery stories published in *Alfred Hitchcock Mystery Magazine* and *Ellery Queen Mystery Magazine.* He has had mystery stories in the anthologies *Seasmoke* and *Still Waters* and won the New England Mystery Writers *Al Blanchard Award* for best mystery short story. He is also a coauthor of *A Miscellany of Murder.*